ACKNOWLEDGMENTS

I would like to acknowledge my editors, Susanne Holland and Jennifer Lamont Leo for all their help and insights while editing this book. I would especially like to thank the Coeur d' Alene Chapter of the Idaho Writers' League Thursday Critique Group for their valuable evaluations and support. All of you have made this book possible.

CHAPTER ONE

op. Pop. Pop-pop-pop.
Firecrackers?
Beth Ann Raines lost her train of thought mid-sentence when she heard the noise in the hallway outside of her high-school classroom. Some jokers always caused trouble on the Friday before a holiday. She imagined teenage boys throwing down those *Pop-it* things, the kind of noise-maker that, when it hit the ground, exploded with a loud crack. She sighed. She really needed spring break as much as her students.

Suddenly, the fire alarm shrieked to life. Beth scrambled away from her whiteboard and grabbed hold of her desk, losing her right shoe in the process. To the giggles of her students, she wriggled her foot back into the loafer and laughed. A blush raced into her cheeks. Her grandmother promised she'd grow out of her chubby, awkward phase, but she never did.

What the heck is going on? Beth couldn't imagine that those tiny poppers would start a fire, would they? No matter, she had to get her students out of the building and to their meeting spot on the football field, even if it was just another drill. But, they'd had a training drill earlier this morning during first period. It seemed silly to have another so soon.

Something wasn't right.

Her stomach rolled with anxiety. The kids wouldn't learn a darn thing today if the school administrators kept this up.

"All right. Put your pencils down and get lined up in order," Beth fused both calm and urgency into her voice. The sooner this was over, the better. The kids were high-schoolers and knew the drill. By now, they'd practiced fire drills about a hundred times.

Beth forced her breathing to slow. Her heart raced, and her body vibrated with adrenaline. Why had her fight-or-flight response kicked in? Her hands visibly trembled, and she slipped them into the pockets of her tan wool slacks to hide them. Fire drills were ordinary, but two in one morning—creepy.

The teens casually gathered their belongings, stood from their desks, and chatted happily. Getting out of English Class was no hardship for them. Readily, the boys lined up behind Sandy Atherton. The girls dawdled. Katy Walberg stopped to refresh her lipstick.

Beth needed to control her class, and grabbed her roll book, hugging it to her chest. A scowl wrinkled her brow. If this wasn't a practice, they could get out better and faster if they organized.

"Stop talking and hurry!" She wiped a wayward dark brown curl away from her cheek. "Hustle it up, ladies!"

At the beginning of the school year, she'd chosen Sandy Atherton to lead the third-period drills. Sandy was handsome, smart, and a beefy football star. He quickly controlled the boys. Most of the boys admired and respected him. If this were a real fire, he would be able to clear any debris that might hamper their progress down the stairs to the main building door and out to their assigned position in the field. She'd assigned Teddy Marshall to sweep position. He and Beth would go last helping anyone lagging behind if they stumbled on their way to safety.

The mysterious popping noise rang in her ears, louder this time, Beth spun toward the door. A secondary echo reverberated between the fire alarm blasts and off the walls of the empty hallway outside. Now, real fear clawed at her throat. A tiny inkling of thought tried to surface—a notion she couldn't allow. She cleared it with a quick swallow. But it didn't work, not all the way.

Beth felt annoyance flushing up from her belly. Why hadn't Mr. Radcliff collared the culprit with the fireworks? Radcliff was the only other teacher on the second floor and one big sissy. The skinny, four-eyed weasel occupied the classroom across the hall. She was more of a man than he, and she was as feminine as they came. She rolled her eyes. As usual, he waited for her to take charge of all the second-floor students.

Again the popping sound—even louder.

A sickening dread gushed into her mind like a flash flood after a thunderstorm. *Gunfire? A shooter? A school shooter?* She wanted to refute it. No one could get past the police security guard at the front entrance. How'd anyone get through the metal detectors with a gun? Where were the text messages? There should be text messages from the principal, or at least an administrator, if this was true. She looked at the face of her iPhone on the edge of her desk. Dark. Blank. Nothing.

"Miss Raines! Miss Raines—that's—that's gunfire!" Sandy gasped, his eyes bugging wide with shock. *Was it?* "I go hunting with my father all the time. I know that sound—like the shooting range."

Is he right? But, that would confirm the very thing she wanted to deny.

What should she do now? Her heart fluttered, as if it had flopped over in her chest. At last, her training kicked in.

"Get to the back closet! Get down, lower the desktops in the last row like we practiced, and stay quiet," she commanded, motioning toward the back of the room with her hands. The school board had spent the money on the new desks after being harassed by two very loud and persistent mothers. Built like a shield, the desk's writing surface lowered on its front hinge. The top was wood, but underneath, a solid sheet of steel offered some bullet protection. That would buy them time if the shooter breached the doorway. *The doorway!* She had to secure the door.

Follow procedure; get the kids down on the floor behind the desk shields, lock the classroom door, turn out the lights, wait for help. Her mind regurgitated the list of instructions to follow if she couldn't get them all safely out of the buiding. She watched helplessly as the kids noisily stampeded to take cover, all except Sandy, who crouched down beside her.

"Miss Raines?" Sandy's face was desperate. He didn't want to die; neither did she—not today.

"Stay calm. Call 9-1-1." She grabbed hold of his hand and squeezed it. "Stay down. I'll go check."

Beth stood, gulped back her terror, and carefully removed her shoes. On tiptoe, in stocking feet, she crossed the room. Quietly, she placed her shoes on top of her desk. When she reached the wall abutting the hallway, she pressed her back against it. Cold from the concrete block oozed through the pink silk fabric of her blouse, making her shudder. She felt the rough surface of the blocks snag at the fibers as she crept along. *Crap!* Small beads of sweat formed at her temples, under her arms, and on her upper lip.

Just as she reached the steel doorway to the hall, she glanced back at her students. All twenty huddled together and sat on the floor against the closet wall behind the last row of desks. There was a pause in the fire alarm, the familiar five seconds between cycles. She heard faint sobs and smartphone notification dings as the students texted messages to family and friends.

Sandy whispered to the 9-1-1 operator. At least the police were on the way.

Beth shuddered as the alarm resumed. She locked the door and flipped the light switch, killing the overhead lights. That plunged the classroom into an eerie semi-darkness. The pale sunlight streaming through the windows on the west side of the room shimmered on dust floating weightlessly in the air, creating a strange wavering curtain. It blurred the student's silhouettes, and they shapeshifted to look almost like another row of desks. She breathed out a trembling sigh. If the shooter glanced in briefly, he might not see them.

The popping noise started again. Beth clenched her fists in fear and frustration. *Stop being such a ninny! You're the adult.* Still confused by disbelief, she scolded herself. She had to do her part.

The sound had changed. It was closer. *These children had their whole lives ahead of them. Keep them safe!*

Beth ducked under the rectangular window in the door. She paused, then cautiously straightened and peeked through. She couldn't see anything or anyone in the hallway. *Damn it!*

The fire alarm abruptly stopped, replaced by a steady *tick-tick-tick*. The schoolhouse clock on the wall above the front whiteboard monumented the passing seconds.

Waiting seemed interminable. *How long had it been?* She hadn't heard gunfire for a while and decided to look. If the hall was clear, she could get her students out of the building.

In her imagination, she hustled them quickly down the two gray brick-lined flights to the lobby on the first floor and out to their designated place on the lawn.

Slowly, she walked her fingers along the right side of the steel door, reaching for the knob. Unlocked it. Little by little, she pressed the lever handle down. Her senses revved to high alert as she pressed her weight against the door, intending only to open it an inch. But the heavy door swung to the left, dragging her out into the hallway with it.

"Damn it!"

The corridor was chaotic with shadow and light. Bundles littered the escape path—not bundles exactly. Beth couldn't make sense of the shapes. An odd scent lingered in the draft swirling up through the ventilation grates. Hot gunpowder and metal—copper and blood! Goosebumps erupted on her skin. Her mind refused to accept it—think it—but she had to. They were not bundles. They were bodies.

The bodies of Mr. Radcliff's students cluttered the passageway. In their haste to respond to the fire drill, they'd stumbled into a trap. She clapped her right hand over her mouth to stifle her scream, and tears pooled in her eyes. In that moment of agony, she realized she heard moaning.

Still alive! Someone is still alive! Before she could move toward the sound, she froze. Her gaze settled on the dark figure backlit by the daylight spilling through the long rectangular window at the end of the corridor. A specter, dressed all in black, chest and legs bulked up by some sort of padding, like an outer-space visitor, turned to face her. He wore a helmet with an orange-tinged mirrored faceplate, and it reflected the surreal carnage between them.

Beth couldn't breathe.

Finally, grabbing a gasp of air, she tried to reason with herself. Sandy had called the police. *Is this man a police officer from a SWAT team like I've seen on television? Is he our rescue?*

"Oh, thank God!" Beth relaxed a little. Still unsure, she moved toward an injured student on the hallway floor. They needed her help. She stopped and stiffened as the Shadowman lifted the black tactical rifle and aimed it right at her.

"Wait! I'm a teacher here," she cried. Before she could react, she saw the white-hot muzzle flash. Instantly, the bullet seared through the flesh in her left shoulder and slammed her back into the door. Shocked, Beth dove into her classroom, yanking the door closed with all her might. She fumbled with the lock. Finally, the deadbolt clicked into place. Panting, she searched for Sandy. He scurried on all fours to her side.

"Oh God! Oh God! He knows we're in here! He knows we're here!" She reached out for Sandy. He took hold of her hand. Her pulse drubbed a staccato in her ears.

A bullet plinked into the steel door, deforming the metal next to her bleeding shoulder. Gasping, she lunged away. The shooter fired two more rounds, each instantly denting but not penetrating the steel. With Sandy leading, she crawled along the wall, leaving a streak of blood each time her shoulder touched the cold surface. They reached the closet where her other students hid. She inched up the wall to stand.

The terrifying rhythm of the gunfire broke the silence again.

Beth convulsed as each shot pinged into the door. Trembling with fear, she felt tears trickle down to the corner of her mouth and could taste the salt. She heard the Shadowman rattle the door handle. He was trying to get in. *Hold, please God, make the lock hold . . . .*

Now, all at once, pain throbbed in her shoulder with every heartbeat. *Have to be strong! Have to save the kids!* He hadn't broken through—yet. She looked around the closet for something, anything, that would keep them safe—anything they could use to fight back.

Nothing.

Defeated, she let a sob shudder through her whole body. *Tired. Why am I so tired?* She hung her head and stared at a dark red stain seeping through the pink silk sleeve of her blouse and down her arm. Her legs went weak and rubbery. Confused, she slumped back against the wall and sank to the floor. She could hear Sandy's faint and faraway voice.

"Stay with me, Miss Raines, stay with me. Please, please, police are on the way." He gripped her hand. Beth could hear the distant wail of police sirens.

"Damn it!"

She'd bought the silk blouse to impress Sam Moore, the new football coach, and her after-school date. Her new blouse would be ruined. He'd be astounded if he saw her now! *I paid over a hundred dollars for this blouse!*

Weird! At this particular moment, she thought, *The dry cleaning bill for this blouse is going to be a fortune!* She closed her eyes.

CHAPTER TWO

Tim McAndrews leaned back in the swivel chair behind his assigned desk. The Behavioral Analysis Unit at the FBI's training headquarters in Quantico didn't provide the quiet he'd enjoyed when employed at the King County District Attorney's Office in Seattle. His new space didn't offer any privacy from his team members. It wasn't meant to. The open floor plan was designed to encourage them to share their thoughts on pending cases.

Cheery and bright, the main floor was well lit. The art on the walls, though abstract, announced joy in bold, bright reds, yellows, and blues. Tim assumed the higher-ups decorated this way to counter the darkness of the evil they hunted down. Serial killers, murderers, child traffickers, pedophiles, and other miscreants were their prey.

Though the workspace was on a level below ground, the building designers had created a glass-roofed arboretum with trees, flowers, and ferns just outside the window beside Tim's desk. No matter the weather, team members could safely take a few moments in the serene garden to regain perspective.

Solving crimes against children was one of his unit's specialties. Tim's team worked hand-in-hand with the National Center for Missing and Exploited Children, exposing predators' crimes and then bringing them to justice. Only weeks ago, he stumbled upon a trafficking ring. His contribution closed the trap on a sting operation that his team members painstakingly built for months. The FBI and Bonner County Sheriff's Office rescued all fifty children they'd found just minutes before they were to be flown to an offshore island to be transported, sold, and enslaved who knows where.

Tim scrubbed his left hand through his hair, thoughts rolling behind his eyes. He contemplated the coincidences. If he hadn't been on a forced leave of absence from the DA's office, if he hadn't been skiing at Schweitzer Mountain, if he hadn't gone to Senator Shearer's party, what would have been the children's fate? He groaned.

Even though he'd worked in the criminal justice system since he'd graduated from law school, he'd never been on the front lines or prosecuted anything like this. He recalled the saddened faces of the SWAT team members as they carried the kids to safety. Tough, well-trained, and battle-hardened men so shaken by what they found that night had openly wept.

At the time, Tim had been too angry to let any other emotion surface. Crimes against children were unconscionable. But later in the stillness of the early morning, in the tenderness of his wife's arms, he'd been swamped by such overwhelming compassion for the children, it made tears well in his eyes. This empathy was followed by an icy resolve to stop predators whenever and where ever he found them. That morning, he morphed from naivety to manhood. Without looking back, he accepted Elias Cain's offer to join the FBI permanently.

On the left-hand corner of his desk, a large stack of dogeared case files awaited his attention. He glanced at his watch. It was 1:05 p.m., only two minutes later than the last time he looked.

He studied one of the framed photographs he'd placed on the right side of his computer monitor. Next to one of his wife, Dani, and his daughters' beautiful faces, he'd put a shot of himself and his two older brothers. They'd snapped this photo last year as a gift for Mom at Christmas, and he made a copy. Looking at the picture, he smiled to himself. He heard it many times from others, but it was indisputable just how much he looked like his two older brothers. They had the same strong jawline, straight nose, sandy blond hair, and intense blue eyes. The genetic roulette gave Tim at least two inches in height over his siblings' six feet, but the family resemblance was unmistakable.

It was going to be an adjustment to be this far away from family. They'd been his support system before he married. His brothers had practically lived Tim's college days vicariously since neither went to college, but instead, both joined their father's business right out of high school. The two older boys turned their father's small mom-and-pop cabinet shop into a multi-million-dollar enterprise, supplying their beautifully designed custom cabinets to the West Coast construction industry.

While still in law school, Tim contributed to the budding business by designing all McAndrews and Sons legal contracts. After graduation, and while with the DA's office, Tim and his brothers bought and refurbished foreclosure properties. Tim's share of the profit was enough to pay off his student debt, buy a nice condo, and build a good savings account. He established himself in the community in just three years. Tim hoped that the famous McAndrews' work ethic, which helped him get through his first years of adult life, could help him settle in, away from his brothers. Instead of being jealous or resentful, the older boys had become Tim's mentors and protectors, even though they'd been twelve and ten when he was born.

Tim was excited and anxious to see Dani. Married for only six short months, she was his family now. It had been sixteen weeks since he'd started his training with the FBI and the Behavioral Analysis Unit, and two since they'd seen each other. Warming at the memory of her, he felt the flush of satisfaction that always seemed to surface when she crossed his mind. She would be at the hotel in DC by now, waiting for him. Best friend, confidant, and lover, Dani, completed his life. He couldn't imagine being without her.

He thought of Lettie and Chloe, the two little girls he and Dani took in and intended to adopt from the children he'd helped rescue around Christmas. Bold little Chloe immediately adapted to her new life and seemed to flourish in their family. Lettie was a worry. She appeared withdrawn as if waiting for the monsters to return and take her away. Lettie often woke in the night, screaming in terror. Tim and Dani vowed they would do everything in their power to get her through this, no matter what it took.

With fondness, he remembered the girls' tea party send-off before he left for FBI training. He'd be glad to have his family settled here, and he'd have affection and warmth to go home to instead of an impersonal hotel room.

With four weeks of FBI training ahead, he'd kissed his family good-bye two weeks ago. He hoped his training time would speed by. It had, but even with all the study he'd completed so far, he still didn't feel like a profiler. He swiped his left hand over his lips and down his chin. His boss and mentor, Elias Cain, had high hopes for him, and Tim wasn't sure he could fulfill them. He looked around the room, glancing at each team member for a second.

Tim twisted in his chair and gazed out of the window to the outside. A steady rain beaded on the arboretum's glass roof and streaked down the greenhouse's above-ground dome. Tears from heaven, he thought. But in the mix, he noticed a couple of white snowflakes. Briefly, he wondered why rain's metaphor was tears and sadness. When the rain turned to snow, it became magical. For a few seconds, he watched before returning his attention to the files in front of him. After adjusting the necktie he longed to shed, he pulled the next folder from the stack.

Tim split his days. Mornings were devoted to the regular special agent training at Quantico. The second half of the day, he spent with his Behavioral Analysis Unit (BAU) team. Elias arranged for special clearances for Tim since he had a law degree and served four years with the King County DA's office. Elias told his superiors he needed Tim now, and they agreed, especially after he helped break up the child-trafficking ring they pursued for years.

Today, he reviewed old case files and wrote the perpetrators' profiles based on the evidence gathered at the crime scenes. All the actual suspects and police theories were stripped out, so his thoughts wouldn't be prejudiced. It was one of Elias's fast-track tests. *Get inside their heads, Elias had instructed. Try to imagine who committed the murder and why.*

Tim took this week's assignment very seriously. How he performed made a difference. The sooner profiling became second nature, the sooner he'd be allowed in the field.

Sometimes though, the cruelty and crazy he encountered in the files baffled him. He was no angel, but intentionally doing evil to another living being wasn't in his make-up. Elias had explained that here in the profiling unit, they dealt with the worst of the worst. Some of the crimes were unfathomable. Demonic. Elias said the team was often the line between civil society and chaos, good versus evil; sanity and reason against the reprobate mind.

Next week, Elias planned to add Tim as an actual working member of the team to finish his training. He wanted to be a valuable contribution, not a fumbling novice, and he wasn't sure he could live up to expectations. He opened the folder and started to read.

Tim found it difficult to concentrate and watched Roxie Stauffer remove her reading glasses from their perch on the bridge of her nose and twirl them by the temple piece as she walked to his desk. She bit at her bottom lip and lowered her chin, so her glare became a challenge.

Tim had always thought Roxie was an attractive woman. She was exceptionally fit, as expected for an FBI Special Agent. Her shiny brown hair curled around her chin, and her big brown eyes sparkled with intelligence. When just out of law school, twenty-four, and a newbie with the King County District Attorney's Office, he'd been assigned by the DA's office to work with the FBI on the Fynn Creek Serial Killer Task Force. At the time, Roxie was a special agent with the Seattle field office, six years his senior, and impressive as hell. He acknowledged there had been a spark back then. But, he was at the bottom of a long list of admirers and no candidate for anyone's boyfriend. Romance wasn't in his plans.

One morning, after their case was closed and the killer caught, Roxie came to see him in his office with a specialty coffee in each hand. She closed the door, gave him one of the beverages, and plopped into the chair in front of his desk. They weren't working on anything together at the time; still, he assumed she had a case that needed help from the DA's office.

She stared at him and said, "I've been offered a position with the BAU. They want me to move to Virginia."

Roxie talked incessantly about becoming a profiler, and he was happy that she'd landed the position of her dreams. He admitted they were friends. They'd compared notes and brainstormed about the case when it was active, but he never let it go further than that.

"Wow, that's cool. Congratulations." He took a sip from the too-sweet drink and discreetly set it aside.

She stood from the chair and walked to the small window overlooking the city park below. She spun to face him. "Yes, it's cool. What I always thought I wanted."

Flummoxed, he couldn't imagine she wanted a position with the King County DA when she could be a profiler, but he assumed that's what she was after. "I don't have anything to do with hiring, Roxie. I'll put in a good word for you. But wouldn't working here be a demotion?"

"If I wanted a job, Tim. Why would I come to you? I'd just go to Goddard."

He sat back in his chair. She had to see the confusion on his face. She sat down, put her elbow on the desk, and rested her chin on her knuckles.

"Okay. What's up?" He asked.

"Tim, give me a reason to stay in Seattle."

Tim was young, but when it came to women, he was no rube. It was clearly a come-on. His current flirtation with celibacy was self-imposed, but he wasn't in any position to be a boyfriend or lover to anyone, no matter how attracted he might be. He devoted over sixty hours a week to the DA's office, and any leftover evenings and weekends he spent with his brothers, working at the family businesses.

The complications a woman would add to his life—he couldn't afford. His carefree college days were behind him, and he had too much respect for Roxie to take advantage of her. He remembered thinking it was out of character for him, but maybe this was his new, more grown-up character. Roxie deserved more than a meaningless one-nighter. He played it safe. Four years ago, he needed to get his career off to a solid start before he gave any thought to including a woman in his life.

"Ask me to stay," Roxie said, a seductive, sultry tone in her voice.

How was he going to handle this? Afraid a woman might take him up on it, he'd always refrained from flirtatious banter with co-workers. He at least wanted to preserve his friendship with Roxie. They were both in law enforcement; it was likely they'd work together again. He looked down at the surface of his desk, trying to formulate his words carefully.

"Roxie, you're just scared. You don't know anyone in DC. But, you'll be great and make new friends. If I asked you to stay, you'd hate me for it later. You don't want to pass up this chance." An awkward blush raced into his cheeks as he waited for her to break the silence.

"I'm just kidding you. You should see your face!" Embarrassed, she giggled, but he suspected it was only cover.

So, he congratulated her on her new job and wished her well. After she left, he never reflected on what could have been. Without regrets, he had chosen his vocation over a fling.

That all changed three years later when he met Daniella St. Clair. Dani took him by surprise. He had to have her, marry her, everything else, including the profession he'd worked so hard for, be damned.

Roxie called and expressed her congratulations when she heard he'd married, but her voice rang with resentment. He knew she wasn't at all thrilled about working with him now. He could see the hurt she tried to hide lingering in her smile. Didn't she understand she was lucky? He could've used her and chose not to.

"We're all going for drinks at The Taphouse after work. You in, McAndrews?"

Tim knew she expected him to decline. She waited for a beat and then asked, "Are you scared of me, McAndrews?"

"Everyone's scared of you, Roxie," Miguel Gonzales answered for him and laughed.

Tim noticed her smirk and the flirty tip to her head after Miguel's tease. Quickly he decided to give his meager profiling skills a try. Was it a crush? Roxie and Miguel. That could work. The best cure for unrequited love was to love someone else.

He could understand why she'd be infatuated. Miguel had been a member of an elite SEAL Team before he retired from the navy. Tall, dark, handsome, and smart, Miguel was any woman's Mr. Right. But Miguel's closeness to Dani and her family made them like brothers, and he confided a secret to Tim. Miguel still held on to a dream of his own. Dani's older sister Rachel had captured his heart when they were teens. Rachel married another while he was away serving his country. Miguel hadn't been able to let go. Maybe a flirtation with Roxie would be just the ticket.

Tim noticed the rest of his team stopped their work and directed their attention to the conversation. They all moved in the direction of his desk. So far, he'd refused their invitations to socialize. He knew it made him look snobbish. Passing his proficiency tests were on the top of his to-do list, not comradery. Once he made the cut, there'd be plenty of time for getting to know one another.

Mostly though, the truth was he couldn't wait to get back to the hotel each evening so he wouldn't miss the Skype calls with Dani and the girls. Despite thinking he would never be a dad, he was turning into a family guy like his father and brothers before him. He grinned to himself as he remembered teaching the girls to ski at Schweitzer Mountain, reading to them before bedtime, and even allowing them to wake him by jumping on his bed in the morning when he tried to sleep in.

"I have an appointment. But thanks, anyway. Maybe next time." Tim answered her, returning his attention to the case in front of him. Roxie sat on the edge of his desk. The other female team member, Melissa Grant, did too. Melissa had joined the FBI right out of college. According to stories, the blue-eyed blonde had skipped several grades early in her education and now had a master's in criminal psychology at twenty-two.

Roxie reached down and closed the file he worked on. Confused, Tim looked up at her.

"You always have *an appointment* when we invite you," Melissa argued. "You go out with Miguel all the time. We don't bite, you know," she continued in an accusatory sing-song.

"We're bros." Miguel chuckled and patted Tim's shoulder as he joined in the teasing.

"All right." No way out, Tim realized he had to explain, though he didn't want to.

"You'll go, then?" Melissa asked, glancing at Roxie like she'd won some sort of victory.

"No. Dani is flying in this afternoon, and I haven't seen her for two weeks. No offense, but I want to spend alone time with my lady."

"Are your daughters coming, too?" Roxie asked, glancing over at Melissa with a sly smile on her lips.

"Not this week. Dani's setting up the new house. Then the whole family arrives. Right now, I'm still at the hotel, and I'm ready to have a home." Leaning back into his chair, he hoped that would be the end of it.

"Daughters? You have daughters?" The corners of Melissa's mouth turned down in surprise. Then she reached behind her and lifted the framed photo to look. He hadn't meant to make her feel snubbed. Reluctant to share his personal life with his co-workers, Tim understood to establish trust, he'd have to.

"Haven't you heard?" Roxie started dismissively. "Tim and his wife are adopting two of the little girls we rescued from that trafficking ring we busted right before Christmas." Her tone set him back. She challenged him with her glare, as if she thought they adopted the girls as an attention-grabbing stunt. Tim could thank his media nemesis, Beebe Knoll, for that. She'd written an obnoxious story about the adoption for her station SBC-23 Seattle. He always shied away from media attention. But these days, no matter what he did or where he was, Beebe was there to 'get the story.' At least his move to Virginia had put the damper on her pursuit; Beebe was stuck in Seattle. Tim grinned to himself.

Still, he had to do something to get Roxie on his side. She acted like the woman scorned and disputed everything he did or said when Elias asked for his input on profiles in progress. Twice so far, she'd embarrassed him by openly mocking his ideas as 'utter rubbish' in front of the whole team. The second time Elias stepped in and dressed her down. No. Tim wasn't sorry he hadn't gotten involved with Roxie. As resentful as she was now, he imagined the dumpster fire he would have set agreeing to a cheap tryst. Confronting her would make her dislike him all the more. But if they were to work together, he needed to and soon.

Tim could see Melissa had questions for him circling like carrion birds in her mind. She started to speak, but his phone intercom buzzed. He pressed the button, engaging the speaker function, when he saw Elias's extension number on the other end of the call.

"McAndrews," Tim answered quickly, wanting to escape the grilling by his co-workers.

"Tim, we've been invited to consult on a case." Tim looked up at the mezzanine where Elias's stood looking down on them from his office window. "All of you come to my office . . . that is if I can tear you away from your social gathering."

CHAPTER THREE

"What's it like to be married to a woman who looks like a movie star?" Miguel asked. Tim followed his gaze to Dani's picture on his desk.

"Sweet," Tim answered as a smile spread across his face. He took one more look at the picture. Dani had always left him breathless. From the first day he saw her at the traffic light at James Street, he'd been fascinated. He loved how her soft fawn-colored curls caught the morning sun, and her blue eyes sparkled when she smiled at him. "Do you think we'll be overnight?"

"Yep," Miguel picked up his go-bag and pointed his index finger in the direction of Elias's office.

"I'd better call her." Tim opened a bottom desk drawer, retrieved his overnight gear, and set his kit on the floor next to his chair. He dialed Dani and broke the disappointing news. Dani showed her usual grace and accepted it. But Tim knew she shared his frustration.

Once he understood what was expected, and how long they'd be needed, he'd update her. Still, he didn't relish the delay in seeing his wife. Two weeks without her was long enough. The tone in Dani's voice confirmed she longed to see him just as much as he did her. She reminded him she'd send her pilot, Mitch Brady, to fly him back and forth if need be. He chuckled to himself.

Why didn't I think of that? Still, after these months of being married, Tim wasn't used to Dani's wealth. Her solutions to problems were always simple, just more expensive than he could even imagine. Tim hadn't been poor growing up, but penthouses, ski resort cabins, ranches, jets, and vineyards hadn't even crossed his mind when he'd dreamed of what his life would be.

When he'd decided to accept the job with Elias and the FBI, Dani took up the task of finding them a new home as he finished the paperwork from his last case. They'd still been on vacation at Schweitzer when she'd hired a realtor and chosen three homes that met her criteria. After viewing the virtual showings, Dani sent the head of her real estate acquisition department to arrange the necessary inspections. She made a cash offer within days. Escrow closing was scheduled for this coming Monday.

While he finished his training and started the job, she planned to decorate and furnish the house. He loved her take-charge attitude and had watched it in action on more than one occasion. She snapped her fingers, and everyone around her stampeded to get things done.

Now, his phone call finished, Tim and Miguel made their way to the mezzanine, taking the stairs two at a time. Excitement raced through Tim. Was this a chance to prove himself a valuable team member ahead of schedule? He hoped so.

Miguel knocked on Elias's open office door. Tim stacked his go-bag next to Miguel's along the outer wall when his boss motioned for them to come inside.

From one of the leather chairs in front of Elias's desk, Section Chief Markus Watts uncrossed his legs and stood as the team took their places at the conference table. He didn't wait for them to sit.

"We've been called to assist on an active shooter situation at the James Madison High School just outside of Culpeper on Old Schoolhouse Road. An FBI SWAT team is already at the scene." Watts paused to breathe.

Tim's jaw tightened. "Damn," he whispered. He closed the door on the compartment that held his thoughts of Dani and focused. Already trepidation's crooked fingers squeezed at his stomach. This was going to be bad.

"'Damn' is right. Last count: four dead, twenty-three injured," Elias said, efficiently handing each team member a folder as they took their seats. When everyone had a case file, he glanced at his watch. "No suspects. They need us to profile the unsub." He breathed out a heavy sigh.

"According to SWAT, the shooter is in the wind," Watts added, his voice grim.

"Tim, Miguel, Roxie—the school is about seventy miles from here. I've ordered a helicopter. You should arrive on-site in about thirty-five or forty minutes. Meet up with Sheriff LaCrosse in front of the high-school building. She's cleared the building, and I want you in there when the Crime Scene Investigation team starts its work," Watts commanded. "Melissa, Kandar, and Elias will connect with deputies to help take witness statements. They'll be right behind you with vehicles and your gear."

"Sheriff LaCrosse says it will take them another half hour or so to attend to the victims before CSI can go in. There isn't much in your case files: pictures of the school, a building layout, and a town map. You can look at them in flight." Elias frowned.

Accentuating the dread, Tim knew Elias's daughters attended high school. He shared every parent's worry. What if it had been his daughters' school? There were twenty-five school-grounds shootings last year, and even just one could inspire copycats.

"Get going. We'll bring your stuff."

Tim caught Miguel's stare, and they both stood from the table and turned to head up to the helicopter pad. Roxie seemed frozen in place. Her lips quivered as if she wanted to protest. It was clear to Tim she wished she had landed the witness-interview part of the assignment.

Elias lifted both hands in the air. "Well? Get out of here," he demanded.

Miguel tapped Roxie on the shoulder. "Let's go, Rox," he said and tipped his head in the direction of the elevator. She rose.

"I can't believe I'm stuck babysitting Junior on an active shooter case," she complained to Miguel, loudly enough for Tim to hear.

"I've got to learn sometime." He grinned at her, then let it collapse to seriousness.

"Yeah, Roxie, Tim's got to learn sometime." Miguel laughed. No one spoke on the elevator ride to the rooftop, but animosity saturated the air like Houston humidity.

When they opened the rooftop door, rain-soaked rotor wash splattered in their faces. Tim was glad he'd grabbed an umbrella. Living in Seattle had taught him you never knew when you'd need one. Tim gently placed his hand on Roxie's back to move her quickly under the spinning blades. She stared hard at him, her lips in a tight smirk as he opened the right front door of the helicopter. Finally, she climbed in.

"We need to talk," Tim shouted over the noise of the spinning blades. Putting this unfriendliness behind them would be best for both of them. She didn't answer, but wrenched the door closed.

"Women," Tim said. He climbed into the seat behind her, buckled up, and pulled the earphones out of the seat pocket in front of him. At least his disparaging thoughts didn't apply to Dani. She was the one woman who didn't give him grief.

———

The helicopter landed in the freshly mowed grass on the high school's football field, whipping a spiral of clumped, wet, green clippings into the air. Beyond the chain-link fence encircling the area, a figure dressed in a sheriff's uniform waited, half in and half out of the open door of a patrol car. An afternoon storm spit raindrops at them as Tim disembarked. He held the helicopter door for Roxie as she emerged, receiving a harsh glare for his trouble. Miguel laughed, clearly getting a kick out of the enmity between them.

After they ducked under the slowly spinning blades of the JetRanger, Tim snapped open his umbrella as the rain intensified. At first, he considered letting Roxie get drenched. She hadn't prepared for the downpour. But he wasn't raised to be a jerk. He could almost hear his mother's words. *Always treat a woman like she's a lady. Open doors for her, pull out chairs for her at the table, even when she acts like she doesn't want it, because in truth, she really does.* With a sigh, he handed her his umbrella. For a moment, he thought he saw a twinkle of thanks in her eyes.

A uniformed woman approached them.

"Sheriff LaCrosse?" Tim asked.

The woman nodded. "Yes. FBI, right? Let's get out of this deluge." They dashed for the brick school building. Sheltered under the white Southern-style entry portico, Tim waited for one of the senior agents to make introductions. He raked his fingers through his wet hair, keeping rainwater from running down his face. He glared first at Roxie and then Miguel. Was Roxie testing him, trying to trip him up? When no one else stepped up, he took charge.

"I'm Tim McAndrews. This is Special Agent Roxie Stauffer, and this is Special Agent Miguel Gonzales. We're from the Behavioral Analysis Unit. We're here to help profile your shooter."

"Thanks for coming." They shook hands all around. The sheriff was beautiful, the epitome of an Amazon warrior princess: flawless black skin, expressive brown eyes, almost as tall as he was, athletically built, and yet as lithe as a ballerina.

"At first, we thought the shooter committed suicide. Most of these end that way. But none of the victims had any injuries that are common to self-inflicted gunshots," she said, her brow pinched with worry. "I'm afraid in the pandemonium, the shooter escaped."

"We're here to help," Roxie offered, shaking the water from the umbrella, closing it, and balancing it against the wall in the first foyer. Her whole demeanor softened. Tim watched with relief as her focus changed from her dislike of him to the investigation, like a magnifying glass concentrating sunlight.

"Let's get to work," Miguel said.

Sheriff LaCrosse escorted them through the double glass doors and the metal detector to the main lobby of James Madison High School. The main hallway was a beehive of activity. In white protective gear, surgical gloves, and masks, crime scene technicians looking like personnel from a hospital isolation ward, were busy gathering evidence. Tim stepped into the automatic shoe cover dispenser one foot at a time as he slipped his hands into the pair of new latex gloves he'd brought with him. His mind shifted immediately to prosecutor mode. What evidence would he want and need for court?

The historic mixed red and tan brick schoolhouse was retrofitted with the newest safety equipment. As Tim walked through to the lobby, dark emotions of loss and sadness filled his senses. He wasn't alone. Other law enforcement friends had described this unnerving experience to him. It was as though the dead begged for justice. Whispers of *Find our killer* seemed to come from every corner. He took in a deep breath and let it out.

"We lost four: the safety officer, two girls, and one boy were killed. Twenty-three others are wounded," the sheriff said.

Tim glanced over at Miguel and watched a shudder run along the top of his shoulders. Even now, a faint scent of expended gun powder and blood hung in the air. Roxie's jaw tightened as water pooled in her eyes. That's why they were here, wasn't it? Life and death, right and wrong, mattered.

To his left, the administration-office door lurched precariously on the remaining lower hinge. An unexpected bullet pattern—two single shots, followed by a tight grouping of three— scarred the center of the wood surface. To the right, the double doors that led to the cafeteria were closed, but small uneven squares of safety glass sparkled on both sides of the empty aluminum frame.

Brass bullet casings—dozens of them—littered the floor. Tim took a ballpoint out of his suit jacket's inside pocket, bent down, and retrieved one by slipping the pen into the hollow opening where the bullet used to be. From the information stamped on the rim, Tim discovered the shooter used a Federal 5.56x45mm 62-grain NATO round. Typically, this ammunition was for an AR-15 type rifle and as common as dirt. The concrete block walls would deform the bullets on impact, making ballistic comparisons difficult. He turned and studied the administration-office door. There might be better samples in the wood.

The ArmaLite-15 was one of the most accurate and reliable, light-weight tactical rifles on the market. According to public perception, the much-maligned AR-15 was a favorite of school shooters. But that was media hype. According to the FBI's very own statistics, semi-automatic pistols comprised the most-used weapon in school shootings, with AR-15 type rifles accounting for six out of the 517 incidents since records were kept.

"Five point five-six NATO?" Miguel asked as he pulled a small plastic evidence bag out of his pocket and opened it. Tim nodded and tilted his ballpoint, and the casing dropped into the container. Tim collected several more. As a *cover-your-ass* backup, they would send these and duplicates of other evidence to the FBI Forensics Lab. The FBI had taken a big hit in their credibility when the press disclosed they'd had advance information on the Parkland, Florida, Marjory Stoneman Douglas High School shooter and had failed to act.

Sheriff LaCrosse had already marked where each child killed had fallen. Tim groaned under his breath. This kind of senseless violence broke his heart, and his mind raced to find a reason, a motive for it. *Why? Why would anyone shoot up the school? Why did these kids and their families have to go through this?*

"I understand about ten kids saved themselves by playing possum," LaCrosse said. He guessed she meant to give him the bright side. There wasn't one.

"At least there are survivors," he answered. It could've been worse, much worse.

Next to one of the evidence markers, Tim saw a distinct footprint in blood. It started boldly, each square of the waffle-patterned sole clearly defined as if painted on the floor on purpose. Then they faded in diminishing shades until they were gone at the base of the stairway leading to the second floor.

"Have your CSI team luminol the stairs. See if the prints continue up," Tim said.

LaCrosse acknowledged him with a tip of her chin.

These particular prints stood out to him in the middle of all the patterns, scuff marks, and smears on the floor. The direction of travel opposed every other in the chaos as if illuminated by neon. In two instances, someone had stepped on the original, but the unique sole pattern was intact, leaving Tim to speculate that the blood had dried before being overstepped.

Discreetly, Tim compared the size of his own shoe by standing parallel to a print. He wore a size eleven; this print was at least a size larger. The length of stride between the steps indicated the shooter was in no hurry. The unsub took his time without fear of the police, arrest, or death.

Tim turned and faced the main entry door. How did this go down? The sheriff said the perpetrator passed through the metal detector without challenge and shot the school safety officer. He looked up toward the ceiling and noticed the black globe of a surveillance camera. Tim faced Sheriff LaCrosse, lifting his chin in the direction of the device.

"Did you pull the surveillance video?"

"Not yet. Waiting for you." Her posture was slightly defensive, but he wasn't accusing her, just gathering information. Immediately, she directed one of her deputies to get the video up on a school computer. They'd take a look-see when he'd scrolled to the correct time frame.

"When you arrived, the school safety officer was already down, right?"

"Yes. He was shot right here, just inside the front entry, " she answered, lifting her brows as if expecting him to elaborate on why that was important.

"Had he drawn his weapon?" Tim asked, studying her reaction. The autopsy would reveal the bullet's trajectory.

"No. His service revolver was still in the holster. It hadn't been fired. He must not have had time . . . ." She dodged his glare, and her cheeks flushed with color. Tim had too much experience reading would-be jurors during voir dire to miss; she didn't believe what she told him. He wiped his hand over his lips and down his chin, forcing away any appearance of disbelief. *No time?* Tim tried to imagine it. He couldn't make a direct assault at the main door work. Did the unsub stroll up from the parking lot with a fully loaded, scary-looking, tactical rifle in hand, pass through the bulletproof main entry and the metal detector? Then shoot the deputy point-blank? A competent safety officer would've called for back-up and confronted the shooter long before they stepped on the bottom concrete stair from the asphalt. No sale. Tim didn't buy it.

"Is there another way into the building?" He asked.

LaCrosse pointed down the long corridor. Tim walked it, noting the banks of brown metal lockers on the walls as he passed by. At the end of the hallway, he found a set of glass double doors in a right dogleg. Unlike the ones in the cafeteria, the glass was intact. He tested them. They were locked, but different from the front entry, this access point was not protected. He opened the doors and studied them. A simple key secured this entrance, and there were no tool marks or signs of tampering. The doors released from the inside, in case of emergency, and locked automatically when closed. If the shooter used this as his way in, he'd have to have a key or help.

Tim's thoughts went for a spin. The sheriff seemed defensive, as if she were hiding something. What were the possible reasons for a cover-up? Was her hire for school safety officer a mistake? Was he complicit? Did she have a theory she wasn't ready to share? Was she afraid of being held accountable or fearful of someone higher up? Did she know the shooter, and was she protecting him? All these questions raced through his mind. On the other hand, Elias had nothing but the highest praise for the sheriff. What was he missing?

Tim returned to the front of the corridor and joined the sheriff and his colleagues.

"We believe the unsub started his rampage here and then headed upstairs," LaCrosse said. She tried to smile, but the horror didn't allow for it. Instead of rampage, Tim saw cool, calm, methodical, well-planned . . . .

"I think we should mark these footprints. We'll need to eliminate everyone who has legitimate business here at the school, unlike our shooter. But you'll do that anyway." Tim knew he was thinking like a prosecutor again. He shrugged. It was his nature, his fall-back position to ready each case as if for trial. Sheriff LaCrosse motioned for one of the CSI investigators to help. Tim pointed out the specific prints he wanted preserved and explained that they should gather shoe impressions from everyone as they left the crime scene. Later, they would collect the information from EMTs who had already gone to transport patients to the hospital.

Tim remembered, too, that if he measured the length of the stride between the footprints, he could estimate the unsub's height with a simple formula. That would help when they delivered their profile.

LaCrosse caught up to Tim, readjusted her forest-green baseball cap, and pulled the mass of dark brown spiral curls through the opening in the back to make a ponytail. She stared at him, and he let a small smile tick across his lips for less than a second. Suddenly, she seemed intimidated by the fact that the FBI had swooped in and taken control of her investigation. What had she expected when she called and invited them?

"We're here to help," he reminded her.

"I know," she said in a whisper. She swallowed, almost as if she wanted to say something more. He waited, but she shook her head and mumbled, "No."

Miguel brushed past them, heading for the second floor. Tim intentionally broke off from his team and walked with the sheriff. If she had something to say, he wanted to be there to hear it.

"He pulled this fire alarm," LaCrosse said. Tim could see the black residue of fingerprint powder on the handle. They continued up to the second floor, walking on the edges of the steps at Tim's urging. CSI hadn't performed the luminol test yet.

They entered the upstairs corridor. An abundance of natural light flooded in from the large single-pane windows at either end of the hallway.

"Here's where most of the carnage took place. The shooter blocked one of the two escape routes," the sheriff said.

In his mind's eye, Tim imagined the scene. When the fire alarm sounded, the students poured out of the classrooms. As they headed for the main entrance on the first floor, it was too late. Helpless and defenseless, when they turned to run, he shot them, some in the back. Anger began to roil in Tim's stomach.

Along the left wall, there were pockmarks where the bullets had missed their human targets and exploded into the concrete block. Tim studied the pattern—two singles followed by three in a tight grouping. Roxie walked up next to him as he ran his fingers over the bullet holes.

"What do you think? AR-15 with an echo trigger?" she asked, leaning forward and inspecting the wall.

"Not sure. An echo would fire one round on the trigger pull and one on release. This is a burst. A three-round burst. This is automatic weapon fire, not semi." Tim answered her. "An M16, maybe." He looked to Miguel and received a nod of agreement.

"Definitely," Miguel said.

"This is our first real lead. Without a special permit, it's illegal for a private citizen to own a fully automatic weapon," Roxie said softly, looking Tim square in the eyes.

"Roxie, shooting people is illegal, no matter what gun you use." Miguel grinned at her. "Criminals don't care about the details of what is or isn't legal."

She replied by flipping him a middle finger. Miguel laughed harder.

Tim lifted his arms and linked his fingers together on the top of his head as if it would enhance his thoughts. "I'm calling this in. We need to see who has an M16 permit and a kid enrolled in this school."

CHAPTER FOUR

"Just like that, our young hero solves the case and saves the day," Roxie teased, crinkling her nose as if Tim's idea stunk to high heaven. "That's too easy."

"Eliminate the easy stuff first, Rox. Then it's out of the way, and we're on to the next theory." Miguel came to Tim's defense. Briefly, Tim wondered if he'd misjudged Roxie. Maybe her put-downs and sarcastic remarks were just a way to cope in a predominately male arena. It made her feel good to make him feel stupid. Anyway, that was his current profile of Roxie Stauffer.

"You don't think Sheriff LaCrosse hasn't thought of this? She wouldn't have called us to help with the profile, if that's all there is to it." Roxie tipped her head in a so-there gesture. Tim didn't think LaCrosse would've had time to think, period. She had to be operating off her training and pure adrenaline. When the shooter wasn't found among the victims, and it became obvious he'd slipped through their perimeter, she would realize she was going to need help. FBI had already sent a SWAT team. Why not add profilers? The more resources, the better because the vultures in the press were waiting just outside the school's main doors to savage her. Tim remembered seeing news vans pulling up as their helicopter landed.

"Ask her. She's right over there," Tim challenged. He already called Research and Support for information on who might have an automatic firearm permit in a fifty-mile radius around the school. If any of the names matched a kid registered here or shared the same address, they'd hit the jackpot. The gun owner would win an interview with the FBI, at the very least.

Roxie glowered at Tim for a moment, then chuckled and made a beeline for the sheriff, taking him up on his dare. Tim smiled at Miguel and shook his head.

"That's just Roxie," Miguel mused, watching as she got the sheriff's attention.

"We think our shooter may have used an automatic weapon. We need a list of the students and their addresses. Do you know if any of the students' parents might have a special permit?" Though Roxie addressed the sheriff with the respect that she hadn't given to Tim, it could easily be misconstrued as an affront to the sheriff's professionalism.

"Automatic?" Sheriff LaCrosse's mouth fell open. "I guessed an AR-15, but not a full auto. I'll do that now." Her gaze darted to the bullet patterns on the block wall. "In answer to your question, no. I was too busy directing traffic. I had to secure the perimeter, coordinate with SWAT so we could catch the shooter, and get EMTs safely in and out to take care of the wounded. This is a small town—twenty-three injured—we were overwhelmed. We only had five medic units close enough to be of service. Some came from an hour away."

For a fleeting moment, Tim thought he saw fear, the same fear he'd seen downstairs, flash from her eyes. No matter what she did, she would need to prepare for the media second-guessers, who would scrutinize every move with the benefit of hindsight. She turned from Roxie and walked a few steps down the hall to speak quietly with one of her deputies. Tim scolded Roxie with an icy stare as he walked to join the sheriff. His team certainly didn't need to alienate her.

"We already have Support working on that. Special Agent Stauffer was just making sure we didn't duplicate work," he quickly explained to the sheriff. Her smile froze, and worry flashed briefly across her lips. "Need to talk?" Tim asked.

She stopped and looked up to the ceiling as if damming up emotion. "This is my fault. The state legislature attempted to pass a gun confiscation bill last year. I was one of the sheriffs who threw down the gauntlet. I announced on national TV that it was unconstitutional, and I would not participate in any attempts to disarm citizens. Now, look at what's happened. These kids didn't deserve this." She took in a trembling breath and rubbed her right hand back and forth across her brow.

To Tim's surprise, Roxie showed her most human reaction of the day. She slipped her arm along the sheriff's shoulder and gave her a quick squeeze. "The only person responsible for this is the shooter. He chose this, not you. Remember that," she said.

"Quite honestly, disarming law-abiding citizens is unconstitutional," Miguel added, raking his fingers through his short black hair. He had plenty of reasons to say it. Tim remembered Miguel's harrowing story of his family's escape from Venezuela, just as Chavez went full socialist. First, they were disarmed, then their businesses were seized and nationalized. If it hadn't been for Simon St. Clair, Dani's father, they would be in one of the dissident prisons or dead.

In college, Tim minored in history. Miguel's wasn't the only tale of flight from tyranny. Tim thought of the Vietnam Boat People, braving the Pacific Ocean to get free after the fall of South Vietnam; and the Cubans, who to this day try to raft to Miami and freedom, even through hurricanes. His mind raced through some of Earth's populations since the turn of the 20th century and their fate when disarmed and defenseless: the Jews in Nazi Germany, the Ukrainians under Stalin, Mao's murdered millions, the killing fields of Pol Pot and the Khmer Rouge, the thousands tortured and eliminated by Che Guevara in Cuba, the ethnic cleansings in Rwanda and Bosnia. Who could forget the peaceful protestors run down in Tiananmen Square? And more recently, the thousands murdered at the hands of

ISIS. The list was endless. He believed the sheriff was right to stand up for the Constitution, but he didn't weigh in. He couldn't. Though he didn't regret it, Tim was here, now, and not an attorney in the King County DA's office because he'd shot and killed a man who had broken into his home. Big reason or small, the right to self-defense was fundamental. He believed in the second amendment not only in theory but in practice.

Tim returned his attention to gathering evidence.

"This is the door to the last classroom on this floor," Sheriff LaCrosse stated, as a frown robbed the sparkle from her eyes. "The teacher, Beth Ann Raines, saved her whole class. She was shot, but not one of her students was harmed. She's in surgery as we speak. The hospital is supposed to call me when she's in recovery and awakens. You'll want to come along when we interview her."

Absently, Tim dipped his head. He was amazed by the steel door in front of him. It had held despite being riddled with bullets. It appeared the shooter changed to fully automatic mode and sprayed it with a zig-zag motion, top to bottom. It maintained its tenuous integrity only because the unsub shot at the center of the door, not at the hinges or knob as he had at the administration office on the lower level.

"At least he didn't use an armor-piercing round," Miguel commented as he strolled further down the hall. "This door would be Swiss cheese."

"Yikes! Can you imagine if he had?" Roxie blew out a breath.

A picture of the unsub started to coalesce in Tim's mind, but not one of a troubled sixteen to seventeen-year-old high-school kid. His inexperience gave him pause. Though Elias had always encouraged him to trust his instincts, he wasn't sure he could. He envisioned an older man, thirty to forty, someone with military or paramilitary experience. Maybe someone in law enforcement—one of their own.

Standing before the mutilated door, he briefly closed his eyes. His imagination reeled through the possibilities like a film in slow motion. He would wait to hear from all his team members before he jumped into the deep end with some wild hypothesis. He was the new guy; what did he know?

It was time to look at the victimology. If what his instincts told him were true, he'd have to find a motive. According to the sheriff, the safety officer, one boy, and two girls died. He needed to see the medical examiner's notes to learn the exact cause of each death. Intuitively, he knew precise kill shots would point in a different direction from an indiscriminate hail of bullets.

"The shots fired into the walls, and these in the door might have been out of frustration at not being able to get to the last classroom, but also could've been meant to terrorize, not necessarily to kill," Tim said out loud to no one in particular. Both Roxie and Miguel nodded their agreement.

"I had the same thought," LaCrosse replied.

"Let's go take a look at that surveillance video," Miguel suggested, wresting Tim from his thoughts.

Sheriff LaCrosse used her wireless shoulder mike. "Jimmy? Are you ready for us?" She asked, impatiently rubbing the tip of her right index finger against her thumb.

"Ma'am, there is no video," the answer came back.

"What do you mean? What are you talking about?" She asked, pulling at her shirt collar as if it had suddenly become too tight. "There has to be video."

Wide-eyed, Roxie looked over at Tim. This was a significant setback. He forced himself to show no reaction or emotion as he used to do in court when a defense attorney presented an absurd theory of a client's innocence. He didn't want to put more pressure on LaCrosse.

"It's blank, nothing but static. Timestamp says since seven this morning," Jimmy reported.

How did that happen? No doubt someone on the inside helped the shooter. Tim watched as Miguel sucked in his cheeks. Without saying a word, he knew Miguel held the same suspicion.

"That's that's—well, isn't that convenient—for the shooter." LaCrosse stammered.

———

Tim called Dani before heading to the sheriff's office to meet Elias and the other half of the team. Not sure it was a good idea, or if Elias would approve, he and Dani decided that she should fly here to Culpeper. Mitch, her pilot, could land the Cessna P340 at the small airport located about fifteen minutes northeast of the hotel. Dani would make all the arrangements and arrive just about the time they finished for the day. He couldn't wait to see her.

Now though, he set up the laptop he brought with him in the dimly lit alcove the sheriff offered them as a workspace. The only desk was scarred and battered by overuse. While they waited for Elias, he had to concentrate, but his thoughts whipped around in his mind like a tattered flag in a stiff breeze.

The last three EMT crews to leave the scene still needed to drop by the station to provide their shoe prints. They had rushed in to save the gunshot victims' lives without a thought for preserving evidence. What the hell? They never thought of it, not their job.

Miguel and Roxie leaned side by side on the desk's leading edge, discussing their theories about the shooter. Tim listened, but just barely. His mind was elsewhere. After a few minutes, Miguel hauled a couple of chairs over and sat down in one.

"This was well organized. I'd bet the unsub planned it for weeks," Miguel commented.

"Yep, I agree," Tim said as he scrolled through images on his computer.

"What are you doing, McAndrews, shopping?" Roxie stretched across the desk, tugging at the laptop.

"Shoes," Tim said absently, turning the device so she could see.

"You're shopping for shoes? Right now?" Incredulity creased her brow.

Tim chuckled. "Yeah, I thought I needed a new pair." He shook his head. "No. Roxie, there were footprints at the school that seemed different—like someone stood over one of the victims and then headed for the stairs. I wanted to see if we could match the prints to a brand."

"With all the people marching around in that place—good luck." She moved around the desk and supported her weight on her elbows to get a better look at the computer screen.

"I know. It's a long shot, but a couple of prints were overstepped, and yet the sole pattern held." He retrieved his cell phone from the edge of the desk and showed her the pictures he'd taken. "I sent these and a copy of the CSI prints off to Forensics."

"They can tell us the brand of shoes in a few hours. You'll have a report by morning," Roxie said.

"I didn't want to wait."

"Aren't you the eager beaver?" She studied the image on his phone. "Wow, the blood was dry. You are right; these just might be the perp's prints. Hey, you might make an investigator after all," she winked at him. She took the phone from his hand and flicked back through the pictures. She began comparing them to the shoes on the computer screen. "You're looking at men's military boots. Why? Have you ruled out a woman?" She didn't glance his way but concentrated on the digital store catalog. It was a test. Before accepting him, Tim guessed she'd give him a whole series. Roxie would want to know he had a sharp, logical mind and had her back before trusting him.

"I'm a size eleven. This shoe was bigger, maybe by a full size," he answered. "I don't know any women that wear a men's twelve."

"Umm," Roxie stood and looked down at her own feet.

Tim followed her gaze. "Nice try, but my guess—you're closer to a women's seven." It was a bluff. Dani wore a seven, and they were about the same size, so he guessed.

"Ha-ha. You're right." Roxie again bent over the desk and continued her search. "Holy crap! Look at this." She turned the screen so both Tim and Miguel could see and set the phone down beside it. She clicked on the picture of the sole pattern. In addition to the waffle squares, at the ball of the foot, a large triangular shape distinguished this brand from all others. "The unsub wore Nike SFB Gen 2 tactical boots." Roxie ran her tongue across her teeth under her smile. "You get a gold star, McAndrews!"

"Rein it in, Roxie. We have to eliminate everyone else that was marching—your word, not mine—through the crime scene." Miguel laughed. "Print the picture, and we'll have it. If no one with a legit reason for being there *marched* through the crime scene, then we can attribute it to the unsub." Miguel hiked to the small wireless printer on the bookcase against the wall across the room.

The cute young deputy who staffed the reception desk appeared in the open doorway.

"Did you need something?" Tim asked.

"CSI and the EMT crews are ready for you, sir," she said as a flush of color raced into her cheeks.

CHAPTER FIVE

"**D**amn it! The fricking press is already blaming us for this."
Tim looked up from shuffling through the copies of
the pages of footprints he'd collected when Elias's deep
voice reverberated off the blue-green alcove walls. Elias ducked his
six-foot-six-inch frame through the archway into the dimly lit work
space the sheriff had given them.

"And it's raining like Noah's flood out there," Elias said, looking
around and scowling at the accommodations. Tim, Miguel, and Roxie
had done their best to round up a big corkboard and added two spare
chairs from the main sheriff's office.

Usually, Elias didn't let much get to him, so the media must have
been particularly egregious today. When Tim went to get the remaining
print evidence, he'd seen them through the window, setting up on the
courthouse steps across the parking lot.

Melissa and Kandar followed the boss timidly into the room and took
seats in chairs against the wall. Tim guessed the witness interviews this
afternoon didn't go as well as they hoped, adding to Elias's foul mood.

Wiping the back of his large black hand across his forehead, Elias
cleared away the remaining raindrops. He peeled off his tan overcoat
and tossed it angrily across the edge of the desk.

"That stupid jerkwad congressman from California, Aaron Patterson, is standing out front, giving interviews. He has set himself up as the go-to authority on school shootings. He is promising to "nuke" all citizens that refuse to surrender their weapons on national TV. Can't these braying jerks stop politizing and let us do our job before they start spouting off?" Elias glared first at Tim, then Roxie, and finally at Miguel. "Did the shooter really use an AR-15 like he's spewing?"

Who said that? Tim shrugged. It wasn't anyone from their team. He shook his head.

"Don't think so. We're pretty sure it was an M16. The burst pattern on the walls at the school indicated the shooter used a fully automatic select-fire rifle," Miguel answered.

"Well, Patterson wouldn't know an AR-15 if it was a snake and bit him on the butt. How on God's green earth did a schoolkid get his hands on an M16?" Elias roared. Tim assumed the question was rhetorical, asked in frustration. Elias knew they didn't know, but they could guess. Close to seventy percent of school shooters acquired the weapon from their own home or that of a relative. But they didn't have a profile yet, let alone a suspect.

"We have asked Support to find who might have a special permit and a kid in this school," Roxie answered as if that would calm the storm flashing from Elias's eyes.

Elias talked over her, and his shoulders sagged. "Not one. Not one kid we interviewed had any idea who would do this. No one engaged in behavior that gave them concern. The shooter told no one." According to the class he'd just finished, Tim learned in most school shootings, other students not only knew the attack was going to go down, but failed to notify an adult. The 'no one knew' story set him on edge, and he caught himself thrumming his fingers on the desk. He'd studied the statistics; he saw where his team members were headed, and yet, like the incessant three-year-old, he kept asking why. The puzzle pieces didn't fit, and he had to keep turning them until they did.

"Talking or not, I think the shooter had help inside the school. Someone opened the back door and let him in, right after they'd disabled the security cameras at the computer source. The school's computers have been turned over for a forensic exam," Tim reported. Elias stared as if weighing his input. Tim looked back almost without blinking.

"Then we think he walked up to the safety officer, surprised him, and shot him," Miguel added.

"Sheriff is checking on students with prior arrests for violent behavior and computer expertise." Roxie tipped her head to one side as if admitting she didn't know what else to do.

"Are you all in agreement?" Elias asked.

"Not the sheriff, she thinks the unsub walked up the front steps from the parking lot." This didn't work for Tim. "The school safety officer would've called for backup the second he saw the threat. The first call to dispatch came from a student. The school safety officer was already incapacitated or dead."

"So, guess what this dude looks like?" Kandar interrupted, scooting his chair forward to the front edge of the desk. "Darth Vader sans the cape." A grin crept across his face and he ran his thin fingers through his black hair. Kandar was a twenty-nine-year-old from India and a big kid. He had a master's degree in computer technology, loved the research he was assigned, but also loved fantasy video games. "We asked all the kids we interviewed if they knew anyone who was a big Star Wars fan." On their last case together, Kandar had been the one who'd suggested that the culprits were vampires. As it turned out, he was close to the target. They'd used the blood of children for a questionable medical treatment. When Kandar had a theory, Tim listened. Then he converted Kandar's imaginative pictures to real-world possibilities.

"The witnesses said he was dressed all in black," Melissa finally joined in, shoving her short blonde curls away from her face.

Tim set his elbows on the desk and linked his fingers together under his chin. "Motocross," he said, just above a whisper. The helmets for that sport had some pretty unique shapes for the rider's protection. Quickly, he cued up a motorcycle site on his laptop.

"Like this?" He asked, turning the computer for everyone to see. "Fox Racing makes their V3 Motocross helmet in solid black. It would definitely be Darth Vader-ish. We should check to see if the sheriff or any deputies noticed anyone riding a dirt bike or a motorcycle away from the school just as they arrived."

Miguel looked at Tim as if he'd just remembered the elusive word that completed this morning's crossword puzzle. He picked up the file they'd been given to read in the helicopter. "A guy on a dirt bike with a rifle slung over his back would stand out, but not if he disappeared into the woods." He pinned the satellite map to their case board and pointed to the copse of trees abutting the football field at the edge of several hundred acres of forest.

"Good one. Another gold star," Roxie teased. Tim sat deep in the chair. For the second time today, Roxie didn't trash him. Was she finally considering him a contributing member of the team? *Too soon to take that to the bank.*

"Print a pic of the helmet," Miguel said. "A copy for us, and one for the sheriff."

"If he's a school kid, someone is going to know this dude," Tim said.

"Roxie, go find out if the sheriff or any of her deputies saw someone riding a motorcycle. Oh, and take this to give to her sketch artist; she's working on a drawing now." Elias handed her the freshly-printed photo of the helmet and looked out to the central part of the office. "He could've easily ditched the rifle in the trees." He picked up his phone to call the SWAT Commander and ask them to look for it.

Elias moved behind the desk and motioned for Tim to give up his seat.

"Age before beauty," Elias grinned. Tim smiled back and stood. "Good work, Tim." He patted him on the shoulder as they passed each other.

"Thanks."

"The unsub is a real drama queen—or king, as the case may be," Melissa said.

"Witness descriptions sounded like he had on full body armor: legs, arms, the works." Elias sat and studied the computer screen. Once again, Tim thought of motocross. The riders wore protective attire that looked like a combination of football and ballistic gear.

"That narrows the chances that he wanted to commit suicide," Tim commented.

"Is wearing all-black a statement? His disguise was perfect. All his features were masked." Elias sighed. "This kid is smart."

Tim realized he was the outsider in his thinking. Ninety-five percent of school shooters were current students. But, he kept seeing someone from the five percent—older, with tactical experience.

Roxie returned and stood next to Tim. "No one noted a dirt bike or motorcycle, not even our own SWAT team."

"All right. Tomorrow is going to be a busy day. I understand from Sheriff LaCrosse, the teacher who saved her whole class will be cleared by her doctors to talk to us in the morning. Melissa, you and Roxie will interview her. Tim and Miguel, I want you to attend the autopsies. The pathologist starts tomorrow morning at nine o'clock sharp. We will meet in the hotel coffee shop at seven a.m." Elias nodded his head in Kandar's and Melissa's direction. "Let's get our 302's from the interviews in order and filed as fast as we can. And you three," he pointed to Miguel, Roxie, and Tim one at a time. "I want you to give me a written report on everything you noticed today at the scene. Kandar and I will start compiling the information while you are out on your assignments. We must get a profile together as soon as possible. The more information we have, the better." Elias was finished. Everyone knew it.

"I'll write the report and text it to you for approval," Roxie volunteered.

"Great," Miguel gave Tim a thumbs-up behind her back. He didn't want to do the report either. Dani was joining him tonight. The thought of seeing her made a small smile cross his lips.

The team members started to pack up the things they'd need for their overnight assignments and drifted toward the main door.

"Oh, Tim, hold up a second," Elias said. Tim pivoted. "Come with me. LaCrosse asked that we be there for her official press conference." Tim noticed Roxie had turned and narrowed her eyes at him, confirming any hope that they'd made progress was just an illusion. Elias hadn't spotted or intentionally ignored the inter-team rivalry. Tim knew he wouldn't tolerate it.

"Goddard said you were his brick wall when it came to the media. He said you could pull off "no comment" better than anyone else in the office." A big grin tickled the corners of Elias's mouth, neatly tucked beneath his signature handlebar.

Tim disliked media interviews. He got it; they were a necessary part of a free society, but they often twisted words and intentionally took things out of context, just to add sensationalism. He didn't complain, but felt sure the expression on his face betrayed him. "Is that what you want me to say? No comment?"

"The sheriff has to do all the talking. For now, we'll be there as props to show solidarity between the locals and the Feds. But I'll need you to step in if the press gets too pushy. And, if this jerk is playing Darth Vader dress-up, I don't want him getting any press for it."

The men joined the sheriff on the front steps of the red-brick court-house, waiting for the media to finish setting up under the shelter of a porch held up by white Southern-style columns. Elias took the sheriff aside to help her decide what she should or should not say.

Tim stood at the edge of the portico, watching the storm that had plagued them all afternoon move off to the east. Transfixed for a moment, he breathed in the scent of rain-washed air. As the sun descended below the horizon, raindrops caught the remaining rays of light and shimmered like liquid gold as they fell and splashed onto the pavement.

Tim thought about all the history enshrined in Virginia. He couldn't wait to go sight-seeing with Dani and his girls, though he wondered if the kids might be a little too young to understand it all.

Across the parking lot, the media set up a white tent to keep their equipment dry and interview witnesses willing to talk to them. When Elias rejoined him, he asked, "What's in there?"

"Media," Tim answered.

"And, I suppose Congressman Putz-erson, I mean Patterson, is there too?" Elias grumbled under his breath. "How that mo-fo got through law school is lost on me. Can you believe that idiot used to be a prosecutor?" Elias rolled his eyes. He obviously wasn't a fan. Tim chuckled, but immediately sobered as he watched the congressman head in their direction. The purposeful stride made it clear he was going to confront them. Patterson's media entourage trailed behind. A woman, half-hidden under her large black umbrella, dodged puddles in black spike heels. Once she was out of the rain, she motioned to her cameraman where she'd like to set up, shook the water off the umbrella, and snapped it closed. Tim groaned.

"Isn't that...?" Elias asked, surprised and raising both eyebrows.

"Fuck me! Did you know she was here?" Tim wiped his right hand over his eyes and down his jaw, giving himself a few seconds to reestablish composure.

Elias slowly shook his head.

The petite blonde climbed to the step just below Tim, looked up, and recognition flared in her eyes like a squirt of lighter fluid on hot barbeque coals. Without any concern for who else might hear, she blurted out, "Jackass! Fancy meeting you here."

Tim sucked in a deep breath and delivered her a smile as bogus as a forged check. "Beebe Knoll, who let you out of Seattle? What brings you to Virginia?"

"Didn't you hear? After I broke my child-trafficking story—it's up for a Pulitzer, by the way—SBC News promoted me. I'm now their top correspondent at large."

CHAPTER SIX

Since she had time on her hands, Dani decided to use these few free hours to explore the DC area for a location for a new wine shop. Anne Hawks of Hawks and Brighthall Realty jumped at the chance to show her properties. Dani knew she would. In a few days, Anne stood to earn a million-plus dollar commission when the farm Dani selected as their new home closed escrow. Earlier today, she'd transferred the necessary funds by wire so that the house would be theirs on Monday.

Dani couldn't believe her luck. The first property on the list was in the Quantico Center Mall, just four blocks away from the base and the FBI Training Center. As she waited for Anne to meet her and unlock the door, she wished she'd worn something a little warmer. The brown tweed pencil skirt overlapped her leather tall boots, but still, a cold wind whipped around her legs. The chocolate-colored cashmere sweater under the taupe puff jacket should've been enough, but the rain was cold, only a few degrees above freezing. She shivered as she huddled under her umbrella.

To forget her discomfort, Dani thought about her new wine shop. It was time for Easterners to experience some of her Delight Valley wines from her Columbia Gorge and Walla Walla vineyards. She'd add new tasting flights to the menu to complement her company's already popular Napa Valley and Clarksburg varieties.

When Tim accepted the job offer from Cain, she'd instructed her attorneys to prepare the necessary paperwork for a new wine shop. She just needed a suitable location to complete the project. *Could this be the one?* And, to have a place this close to Tim's work—she'd pay extra.

When she made up her mind, she knew she could be a real pain. She'd set a schedule for opening that everyone would brand impossible. Her father had always told her a business executive solved problems and made things happen. Corporation by committee was a recipe for failure.

She couldn't imagine a better spot than this one. Though it was smaller than she would've liked, it was across from the Louis Vuitton Shop and next door to Sweet Stuff Bakery and Deli, and had room for outdoor seating when the weather allowed. Already she could picture customers enjoying wine on balmy evenings in the wrought-iron fenced patio.

Anne hustled up behind her, and Dani caught her reflection in the storefront window. Always dressed stylishly, Anne was the image of a very successful real estate agent. Her black hair was fashioned in a neat French roll and flattered her symmetrical dark features.

Dani loved her professionalism; the woman knew the market. When she'd called, within minutes, Anne had a list of properties to show her.

"Mrs. McAndrews? It's lovely to actually meet you." Anne studied her. "You're so much younger than I expected."

Dani didn't know what to say and just smiled. She knew she looked younger than twenty-eight, but that was just genetics. "Shall we have a look?"

Anne unlocked the door and, once inside, flipped on the lights. The interior felt warm, and for that, Dani was grateful.

The large rectangular space had a lovely walnut plank floor. The walls were stripped bare and painted with a bright white primer, so the new tenant could decorate with any colors they chose. Dani explored. There were two restrooms (both needed updating), space for an office, and extra storage in the rear. All along the north wall, she'd install a long bar and elegant wooden wine racks so customers could buy bottles of wines they'd tasted. The shop was like a blank canvas on an artist's easel, just waiting for colored brush strokes to come alive.

Though she wouldn't actually work at the shop, only visit to make sure things were going right, she started to plan. Dani considered designing this shop after her Seattle tasting room, with its hardwood wainscoting and ornate crown moldings, and add features to match DC's historical legacy. Betsy Ross flags and replica muskets for the walls filled her imagination. Standing in the spot that would become the office, she turned in a slow circle, thinking about where the new interior walls would go. To keep the ambient light, she'd put in two large plate glass windows, one in the front and one on the side, in the walls. She could easily run the family empire from here.

She stopped and stood quietly for a moment. Before the move to Virginia, she and Tim had always found time to meet for lunch a couple of times a week. The girls would be in school, and she hoped they'd be able to keep up their tradition. *Their tradition.* Warmth flashed throughout her insides. In spite of her proper upbringing, Tim brought out a lusty playfulness she hadn't thought she was capable of.

She remembered one morning, back in Seattle. She'd slipped a lacy pair of red bikini panties in the pocket of the suitcoat Tim planned to wear that day. At lunchtime, he'd appeared in her office doorway; closed it, locked it, and shut the blinds covering the window. When he turned to her, the look on his face left no question as to why he'd come. His stare could've burned through her clothes. Her heart took off like a rocket. Casually he strolled over, removed the panties from his pocket, and dropped them on her desk.

"I got your invitation," he said, his gaze not straying from her lips. He wanted to kiss her, and she wanted him to. He pulled her from her chair to her feet and swept all the papers from the desk. As she watched, the last few pages fluttered lazily to the floor. She recalled laughing inside and thinking, "Well, dummy, when you played this prank, what did you expect to happen?"

When his lips met hers, she could not resist. Unintended consequences? No. She'd wanted this to happen and reached out and loosened his tie. Even now, the memory evoked delicious feelings that sent a shudder through her body.

After they'd made love, they sat on the desk in her office and held each other in the afterglow.

Tim whispered against her hair, "Probably better not do that again; I'd hate to think what would've happened had I been in court," he joked. "Ah, your honor, may we have a recess, like NOW?" They both laughed.

She'd never told him all her thoughts out loud. She knew men didn't like to be called beautiful, but he was. She roughed up his sandy blond hair and traced the back of her fingers along his cheek and jaw. His ice-blue eyes radiated warmth and love.

They were a mess, clothes half on and half off, wrinkled beyond repair. Lifting both sides of his open shirt, he shook his head and laughed. "I have to go back to work. Think anyone will guess what I did for lunch?"

"Sorry. You said you didn't have court today."

"I don't. But when I discovered your—message, I was getting a search warrant signed in a meeting with Goddard and Judge Mattison. I thought they'd never shut up and leave." He chuckled and brushed his lips against hers, soft and dreamy. And then they were lost in longer, deeper kisses bringing waves of aching desire. "God, woman, I love you." All she could do was cuddle against his shoulder and purr like a satiated kitten.

"Mrs. McAndrews?" Anne placed a hand on Dani's shoulder, and BOOM! She was back from her daydream.

"I love it. I'll take it. Write it up," Dani faced Anne, delighted she'd have a shop close to Tim's work. They'd make new memories. She couldn't keep from smiling.

"Where were you just now?" Anne asked. "You seemed so far away."

"Oh, just imagining where things would go. Decorating." Dani smiled.

"I'll present your offer to the landlord and get back to you," Anne explained but lifted one eyebrow with an unspoken question that Dani would not answer. "He'll want your business plan and a financial statement."

"Of course. You remember Randy Cantwell, my real estate manager?" She shuffled through her purse, found his card, and handed it to the older woman. "He'll be in touch with you later this afternoon and finish up the negotiations. I'd like to move on this right away. I'll pay all cash." Dani glanced at her watch. "Oh, I have a flight to catch. Off to my next appointment." She shrugged her shoulders. Mitch would be waiting at the airport for her, ready to fly her to Culpeper and Tim. "Will you excuse me?"

—

As the limo wound through traffic toward the airport, Dani quickly put together a business plan. She'd e-mail Randy with her instructions when they were in the air. She had to get all her business distractions out of the way. Then she planned to devote herself to Tim. She'd missed him terribly, and she had so much to tell him.

At last, the initial adoption papers for their little girls had been filed with the family court. They were one day closer to becoming a mom and dad. Everything was going her way. Even Lettie, so frightened at first, had a breakthrough. Dani's heart was so full of happiness, it was ready to explode! She pulled out her iPhone and contacted her wine distributor who also supplied the White House. She ordered several cases of Schramsberg's Blanc de Blanc Champagne. Two bottles were to be delivered by private messenger to the airport—the other cases would go to the new house after closing on Monday.

—

"Tim, slow down!" Beebe called out. He knew his stride made her trot alongside him to keep up, in spike heels, no less. He didn't really care. The sheriff's press conference was over, and he had nothing more to say to the media. He ignored her.

"Can't we forgive and forget?" She tried and reached for his arm. When he slowed and turned, her momentum caused her to slam into his side. He caught her by both of her upper arms before she lost her balance completely and fell into a muddy puddle in the parking lot. Once stable, he released her, stepped back, lifting both palms in the air to stop her from coming any closer. *Forgive and forget, after what she pulled? He'd forgive her when she could sneak sunrise past a free-range rooster.*

His jaw tightened. He narrowed his eyes, and asked: "Did you follow me here—to Virginia?"

She shook her head, making her short blonde curls dance sassily around her face. "No. Tim." There was a whine to her voice that said the exact opposite.

"Nothing's changed. Don't even start—"

"Was I really that bad at Schweitzer?" She replaced her hand on his arm. He brushed it away, tipping his head in warning.

"Yep." He stared hard. She'd bordered on crazy at the ski resort. She could've caused irreparable damage to his marriage and his child-trafficking case had he not seen her for what she was—a sneaky, conniving nutcase.

Beebe looked down at the ground and back up. "Would it help if I told you I'm dating someone?" She kicked at the puddle in front of her, spattering drops of muddy water on his wool flannel trousers and leather shoes. "Oops."

He squinted at her. Beebe was a walking, talking disaster and completely untrustworthy. He growled, "What do you want from me?"

"An exclusive?" She hunched down into her shoulders and then peeked up at him, brown eyes veiled by dark lashes. "You know a lot more than you're letting on. You're the cops. I'm the press. We work together."

Tim snorted a laugh. "Okay, here's your exclusive. No comment." A semicircle of other reporters had started to join them, and camera operators lifted their equipment to their shoulders to get a shot. He rolled his eyes and said louder. "No comment. When we know more, we will tell you more." He shook his head at Beebe.

"Jackass," she muttered. He glared at her.

The soft splash of the SUV tires pulling up next to him gave him his out. He quickly grabbed the door handle, opened the passenger side, jumped in, and slammed the door behind him.

"Go. That woman makes me crazy!" Tim complained. "If I murdered her, would I be arrested, or would I get a medal?"

Elias laughed and eased the SUV forward, scattering reporters like pigeons in the park. "Is she still stalking you?"

"She says she just wants an exclusive."

"Do you believe her?"

Tim reached behind him and grabbed his seatbelt. "No—yes—I don't know. She's such a big sack of trouble."

Elias guffawed. "But you wouldn't be on my team if she hadn't caused you so much trouble in Seattle, so I kinda like her," he said as he flipped the signal to indicate his right turn onto the main drag.

Tim sucked in a deep breath and stared at Elias as seconds ticked by and then chuckled. "You might not like having me on your team after I tell you this. I'm not fully on board with the rest of the team's theory of the shooter. I don't think it's a kid. Older guy with millitary experience. Maybe one of ours."

Elias didn't take his eyes off the road, but Tim could see the muscles along his jaw flex tight.

"We are only halfway there, Tim. Assumptions can and do change. I received a call from Support while you were beating back the reporters. No private citizen has an automatic weapon permit within a hundred-mile radius of the school. So, no, the shooter *didn't* get a permitted gun from his dad's gun safe or his uncle Joe's basement."

Tim sighed. "Rules out the legal guns. Who thought this was going to be easy? Did you think it was going to be easy?"

"I will inform the rest of the team when we get inside." Elias pulled up to the hotel's main entrance and turned off the engine. "Don't discount any ideas just yet."

Tim smiled and nodded.

"You want to meet for dinner?" Elias asked.

"Dani—I forgot to tell you—Dani's flying in."

Elias's eyes lit up. "Well, give her my best. See you in the morning. Seven. Don't forget. Seven."

In the hotel lobby, creamy white marble floors gave way to dark oiled hardwood counters on the left side of the room. Carved doors with signs announcing the various conference rooms and ballrooms were to Tim's right. In between, several groupings of sofas and chairs in shades of brown provided guests with places to sit and chat. Tim made his way to the counter to check in, only to find that Dani had already secured their suite. The clerk gave him a magnetic keycard and offered to have the concierge take care of his one small suitcase.

Tim sent Dani a text: Hi Baby. At hotel. Where R U?

Within seconds the reply dinged on his phone.

He arranged for the bellman to bring his overnight case to the room in about a half hour.

"Sportsman's Lounge?" he asked the lanky receptionist.

She pointed to an open door beyond which seemed to be only darkness.

Tim smoothed his hands down the lapels of his dark gray wool flannel suit and stood in the entryway to the bar off the hotel lobby, letting his eyes adjust to the change in light. Being away from his wife for the last two weeks had been more challenging than the early hours and late nights he'd spent in his FBI training.

Scanning the darkened room, he located her on a stool at the far end of the bar, just as it curved back to the wall away from the rest of the patrons.

She happened to him all over again. The helpless feeling of being swept away by a sneaker wave he hadn't seen coming left him breathless. He never expected to love a woman this much. For a moment, he waited and enjoyed the body rush before making his way across the room to her. Maybe he was crazy, but he relished these secret moments of just looking at her. Like every guy he knew as a boy, the thought of marrying a pretty girl had crossed his mind. He never believed he actually would, but here he was. He loved the way her long, honey-brown curls shimmered under the pale lights. He anticipated seeing her face light up, like sunrise, when she did finally see him standing there.

This time he'd waited too long to make his move. A young man who'd been sitting at the end of the bar, watching Dani, rose as if to approach her.

Oh, no, you don't, buddy. Tim chuckled to himself. He needed to reassert his claim. Loosening his dark blue and gray tie and unbuttoning the collar of the white shirt underneath, he strolled across the bar and placed his hand on the back rail of Dani's stool.

"May I buy you a drink, miss?" he asked. The man who'd wanted to flirt with her bristled. To defuse a brewing fight, Tim lifted his left hand showing his wedding ring. When Dani turned and smiled at him, everything and everyone became nothing but background noise. She slid off the barstool to her feet. Tim pulled her into his arms, breathing in the scent of her perfume, his favorite. For a moment, they stood inches apart, and the chemistry sparked between them like electricity. He studied the inviting contours of her face. His lips found hers, and they were soft, like the velvety petals of a rose.

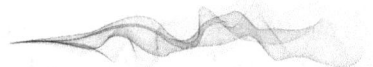

CHAPTER SEVEN

To avoid any whispers of impropriety, Dani had canceled Tim's room, saving him the trouble of completing an expense report and saving the government a couple hundred bucks. She'd booked this suite at her expense to replace it. She also had to house her pilot and his wife, and even though the FBI might be responsible for Tim's accommodations, they weren't paying for hers, and certainly not for Mitch and Shannon's. Tim struggled with her wealth at first, but decided he should worry about things he could change. He fell for a rich girl. He needed to accept all that went with it.

Before they made love, Tim noticed very little about the place. The room Dani claimed as theirs had a king-sized bed. That was all he'd cared about at that particular moment.

But now, Tim enjoyed this part of being married, holding Dani in the bliss that followed lovemaking, talking about life and their dreams. With all work compartmentalized and cleared from his mind, every cell in his body relaxed and satisfied, he helped Dani settle against his left shoulder. He pulled the crisp hotel sheets and blankets up over them as she cuddled against his side.

After the home invasion back in Seattle, he always mapped out a defense strategy, including an escape route should it be necessary. This bedroom was one of the two bracketing the suite's great room. Dani's pilot and his wife occupied the one on the other side.

Pleasantly decorated with modern walnut furniture, calming green walls, and meant to give a home-away-from-home feel, it still looked like a hotel room. A covered deck ran the whole length of the suite, accessible by sliding glass doors. The bedroom's luxurious bathroom was down a small corridor across from the closets. He'd secured all the doors when they first arrived.

Entry to the bedroom from below would be near impossible since the suite was on the top floor. An assault from above would require a risky rappel down from the roof, and over a decorative cornice. He didn't like feeling paranoid. No one had a reason to attack him, but Dani's wealth made her vulnerable. Lately, he'd tried to talk her into hiring private security when he was away.

Tim had placed his FBI-issued Glock 19M in the bedside table drawer. The rest of his clothes were left where they had fallen, mixed with Dani's in random piles on the floor. He thought about at least hanging his suit in the closet, but that would require getting up and ending this delicious moment. He didn't want to and closed his eyes, drifting.

"I found a place for my new tasting room today," she said and pressed her lips against his shoulder.

Teetering on the edge where the cliff of contentment dropped off into the abyss of sleep, Tim forced himself back to consciousness. He wanted to talk to her and hear everything she had to share with him. Lifting his right hand, he rubbed his brow and opened his eyes. He smiled at her. "Where?"

"In the Quantico Center Mall. About four blocks north of the base."

"Oh, that's good," he chuckled. He remembered all the times back in Seattle they'd had trysts during the workday after she'd agreed to marry him. He hoped it wasn't true, but he'd read many articles that doomed this kind of fiery relationship. Though he didn't really try, he couldn't keep his hands off her. But his parent's love affair still burned hot after years of marriage and three kids. They were best friends. Dani was already his best friend. He expected a similar outcome.

"Also, Brad filed the adoption papers with the court today. We're almost a mom and dad."

Adoptions usually took months. It amazed him some of the things Dani's money could buy. "Did you bribe the judge?"

"Of course." She pushed her luscious lips into a pout. "If I did, would you care?"

Would he? The girls would be on solid ground. Safe and stable. So, would he?

"I'm trying to be one of the good guys. I can't have my wife bribing judges." He chuckled.

She traced the back of her hand along his cheek and jaw. "I didn't."

Tim turned his face just enough to kiss her fingertips and found himself, once again, submerged in waves of desire.

"I love you, baby." Advice from his father had been: Every time you think it, say it. That's the key, son. *Women just want to know you love them.* "I can hardly wait to see the girls. Funny, I never thought I would be a dad, let alone like it, but I really miss them," he said.

"They miss you, too. But next week, if everything goes right and the house is ready, Mitch will fly them in." She paused. He could see she had more to say. It wasn't like her to hesitate.

"What? What else, baby?" *Please don't admit you really did bribe the judge.* He adjusted himself to a more comfortable position and enveloped her in his arms. Her skin was wonderful to touch, as soft and fine as expensive silk. The intoxicating scent of her perfume lingered in the air—the scent of roses.

"I told you I was taking the girls to the ranch . . . remember?" She held his right hand and took one finger at a time and kissed each tip. Her lips were so lush and warm; he grabbed a breath to slow the need pressing him to make love to her again. She was a drug, and he, the junkie on the corner, desperate for a high.

"I remember."

"I gave them each a horse." She said it quickly.

Tim gasped and sat up, bringing her to a sitting position with him. They'd already had this discussion, and he thought it was settled. No horses until they were at least seven or eight. Desire was cut off as if he had jumped into an icy lake created by snowmelt. "Dani, they're too young…"

"I had my first horse at four. I was showing at six." Dani laughed at him and playfully shoved him back into the pillows.

He frowned. Horses were so big, and the girls were too little. "What about ponies? They're smaller." He offered the compromise.

"Ponies can be very mean. There's no horse sweeter than an Arabian mare." She continued to snicker at him.

"Yeah, but both your parents were into horses." He squirmed. He didn't know anything about horses and wasn't fond of the whole horse thing in the first place. He only tolerated it because he had no choice and Dani loved them so much.

"My father wasn't. He was into making money. Wine and beef were just one of his many investments and a means to an end. He knew in order to keep his family captive in the country, he'd have to give in to my mother's dream of raising horses. It was only after I started to bring home blue ribbons that he showed any interest."

Tim tried to become stone-faced like he did in court when he didn't like the direction the defense case was going. But Dani was on to that maneuver.

"You're just afraid you'll have to learn how to ride," she joked, but then turned serious. "Remember how we could barely get Lettie to talk? She was so scared and shy?" Dani reached across his chest and caressed the muscles in his right arm. Tim knew she was trying to bring him over to her side, and she'd even use sex to get there. Not that he minded that.

"She opened up a little when we taught her to ski." Resisting, he lifted both arms and linked his fingers above his head. Dani countered by stretching across his body, resting her forearms on his chest, and then set her chin on her hands. She felt incredible there, and he hungrily anticipated the kisses that would soon follow.

"This is a bad idea. They could get hurt," he said. He lost focus when she started one kiss at a time, inching down his chest toward his belly. The tease was exquisite. She watched his eyes for a reaction. He blew out a breath, trying to tamp down arousal. He wasn't going to take her until it was impossible not to.

"Tim, Lettie talks to me now. She tells me everything that happens between her and her horse. It's almost like I'm her mom. The therapist says she's having a breakthrough," Dani insisted, persuading him with reason this time.

Tim narrowed his eyes at her. Sure, he'd read about successful therapy with animals. It didn't ease the worry that much. But if scared little Lettie was having a breakthrough…

"No stallions," he finally said, making sure his voice was firm. "They are dangerous and unpredictable." But then he remembered Dani's gray following her around the pasture like a puppy, side-stepping up to the fence when she sat on the top rail and offering her his back. And then there were all the tricks he'd do for her in exchange for treats. He shrugged. He'd just lost this argument. For Lettie's sake that was probably a good thing.

Dani pressed her lips tight, blocking a smile. She knew she'd won. He was glad she didn't gloat. "I let the girls choose from the six-year-old mares. They're broke to ride and even ready to show. Lettie chose Dark Angel and Chloe, Flame's Sunrise. Ryan and Phil handle those mares all the time."

Tim recalled both mares from the ranch and had watched her foreman's boys manage them with ease. Ryan and Phil weren't that much older than Lettie and Chloe. But if he said out loud that he thought the situation was different because they were bigger, stronger, and boys, Dani would laugh him off the planet. And he would deserve it. He didn't really believe in male superiority. He knew women were plenty capable.

Good examples were Dani and the female special agents on his team. He didn't fully understand the drive to protect his family. It just was. He needed to keep Dani and the girls safe, not to *feel* like a man, as the feminists suggested, but because he *was* a man.

"I wish you'd talked to me first." His tone was all wrong. He knew that the second the words left his mouth because she stopped kissing him.

Her mouth fell open, and all lightheartedness left her eyes. She sat up and looked at him as if he'd slapped her.

"I did it again, didn't I?" She raked her fingers through her hair, holding it up and away from her face. He loved it when she let the curls fall back down around her shoulders and how the soft light accentuated the wonderful curves of her body. Beautiful and bewitching.

"No. baby, I left you on your own to do my FBI training. I wasn't there to help with anything."

"I could've called you . . . ."

"Well, we did talk every night." He chided her, but not with any force.

"I'm so used to being in charge, making all the decisions for the businesses—I just take over and railroad right through. Are you sure you can stand me?"

"Yes, I can stand you. You are the only woman for me. Bossy— but still the only one." He laughed and then pulled her down into an embrace. "Besides, if Lettie is doing better because of a horse, that's all I care about."

They held each other for a few seconds.

"Tim! We just had our first fight." She startled him.

He laughed. "That wasn't exactly a fight. Was it? More a discussion."

"I like that: a discussion. You were mad at me, though, weren't you?" She kissed him on the edge of his chin, restarting the lusty surges through his body.

"I'm never mad at you," he whispered. Dani wriggled against him like she did when she was ready for sleep. But the way he responded to her touch, sleep wasn't in their immediate future.

CHAPTER EIGHT

Tim plugged his iPhone into the integrated tablet holder on the elliptical trainer in the hotel's gym. It was early, and he was the first to exercise this morning. The scent of disinfectant still hung in the air from the overnight cleaning crew. He could feel the cool draft from the air conditioner brushing against his skin.

Tim hadn't looked over the crime scene notes Roxie had sent him last night. He had to do it now. Elias expected them later this morning. He opened her email on his iPhone, placing it on the book stand.

Setting the trainer to a steady climb, he planned his cardio workout. His thoughts strayed to Dani. Maybe he was all good in the cardio department after last night. He smiled to himself. *God, I love that woman.*

When he'd asked her if she wanted to join him in the hotel gym, she'd glanced at the clock, pulled a pillow over her head, and asked if he was crazy. Slightly disappointed, he went on his own. But, she was from the Pacific time zone, where it would only be two a.m. Adjusting to Eastern would take her several more days.

He appreciated that he was the gym's only occupant. There would be no distractions, and he would be able to think. He pressed a set of earbuds into his ears and turned on the music on his phone. He climbed onto the machine, set the digital timer, put his phone on the bookrest and began both his morning workout and Roxie's report. He found himself walking to the sexy Latin beat of Shawn Mendes and Camila Cabello's duet, *Señorita*.

When the timer buzzed, Tim had finished his second time through Roxie's notes. He grabbed a towel from a stack on a small table and wiped away the sweat. From the log he'd typed on his phone yesterday at the scene, he merged several of his observations into the text. If they were going to catch this guy, they needed to consider everything, even the tiniest detail. When with the DA's office, he had a reputation for uncovering minutiae that led to convictions. Though his co-workers had meant it to be disparaging, he liked and wanted to keep that reputation and enhance it. He read the report once more, making sure he hadn't missed anything essential, and added some pictures he'd taken as exhibits. He emailed it to her and a copy to Miguel. *Better in the nick of time than never.*

Deciding there was time for a brief lifting session, he turned his attention to the long rack of weights behind a bench in front of a wall of mirrors. He slipped the phone into the front pocket of his shorts and scrubbed the towel over his hair. Since his high-school football days, Tim had practiced a stringent fitness routine. Elias and the FBI required that he be in shape, both mentally and physically. As he headed for the weights, Roxie and Miguel came through the gym's door. He grinned at them.

"Hey, McAndrews, where's your review of my crime scene report?" Roxie challenged him without saying hello. She glared at him, looking him up and down judgmentally. "If you don't have anything to add, it goes to Cain as is. You look like crap."

"Thanks. Report's in your inbox." He glanced down at himself. The blue workout shorts were old, discolored with some bleach spots from the time he'd messed up his laundry, and the oversized tank-style t-shirt was sloppy, but this was a workout, not a photo shoot for *GQ*. It irked him that Rottweiler Roxie intentionally tried to make him feel self-conscious.

"I needed it last night," she said, walking by and leaning in to get in his face. "Apparently, you were too busy picking up hot women in the bar."

"Me? Picking up women?" Tim slowly shook his head and pointed to himself. He never considered meeting Dani in the bar as 'picking up women,' but it could've looked like that to someone on the outside.

Miguel laughed. "I didn't see any hot women in the bar." The barb was meant for Roxie.

She threw Miguel a dismissive glance. "You wouldn't have missed this one. It was before you got there. Melissa and I saw you, Tim. So, don't try to deny it."

"Okay, I won't." Tim licked his lips. "She is hot. I agree."

"Did I say hot? I meant expensive. Usually don't see the classy type this far from DC."

Her comment hit a nerve and he sucked in a breath. He knew what she meant. Washington, DC, was notorious for beautiful, pricey call girls. He felt a touch of anger flash up into his cheeks. "That's enough, Roxie. The woman you are so casually insulting is my wife."

She cringed a little and then straightened up. "Oh, I didn't mean to insult her. I intended to insult you." She moved to exclude Miguel from hearing the conversation. "You said we needed to talk. Did you forget?" She turned her side to him and flicked her fingers under his chin as she passed by. He stepped back. The exaggerated flirt was Roxie's MO. In the old days, before Dani, four years ago, she had half the King County Sheriff's Deputies panting after her. He was on to her back then, just as he was now. She was a tease.

"I didn't forget," Tim said. "It's not going to be that kind of talk."

She looked around the room and then tipped her head toward a bench at the other side. He followed her and sat down, leaving space between them.

"Okay. So talk."

"Can we call a time-out? Roxie, we have to work together. You challenge everything I do and say. Whatever I've done . . . ."

"You don't know? Oh, please don't tell me you don't know." She laughed, then paused, leaving him in suspense.

"I don't know."

She sighed. "I joke around with everyone. I have to keep you on your game. Challenging you makes you think. Don't take it personally." She sat back against the wall, holding onto the edge of the bench with both hands.

Tim didn't answer. As far as he could tell, he'd been her only target.

"You should see your face. For the first time, Goddard's pet and the silver-tongued young prosecutor is at a loss for words." She elbowed him as if trying to confirm she kidded everyone. "Let's see what you've got." She motioned for Miguel to join them, took reading glasses from her shirt pocket, found the report with his additions on her phone, and cruised through it.

"You think you know how tall he is?" Roxie removed her reading glasses and lifted the left corner of her mouth and eyebrow in disbelief. Miguel slid onto the bench on the other side of Roxie. She handed him her phone so that he could read the report.

"Aren't we supposed to help out by providing a profile? Wouldn't a physical description be part of that?" Tim asked.

Roxie nodded. "But you can't possibly know how tall—just how'd you come up with that?"

"I had CSI measure the length of stride between the bloody footprints, just in case. Yesterday afternoon, we all agreed that the footprints were likely the perp's, right? We eliminated everyone else. Anyway, I divided the length of stride by the average body ratio of 0.41. He's probably 6 feet give or take an inch," Tim explained.

It took her a few seconds of a flat stare before she closed her mouth.

"You amaze me, that's all," Roxie said, and fooled with the clasp that held her dark-chocolate-colored ponytail in place.

"Don't be amazed." Tim laughed. *Amazed* could be good or bad. He decided to go with the idea it was a compliment. "I didn't know that shit —I Googled it."

"Good job, Tim," Miguel said. "We rely too much on the geeks in Support."

Roxie glared at Miguel. "What? Now we have our own geek on the team? That's harsh!"

Tim laughed. He'd been called a lot of things. What was one more? Better than Beebe's 'Jackass.'

"Well, Rox, did you think of it? Or the boots, or the helmet? No. You didn't. You were waiting for Support. Tim may have just saved us hours." Miguel took up for him, and Tim was grateful.

"You keep assuming it's a man. What if it's a woman?" Roxie threw down a new gauntlet. Tim shook his head.

Miguel glanced up at Roxie as she scooted back against the wall, exhaled, and crossed her arms over her chest.

"I've got it," Miguel said. He held up an index finger, and an amused smile flooded over his face. "Our shooter is a five-foot-two, fifteen-year-old girl. She weighs about a hundred pounds, dripping wet. She's clomping along in a pair of men's size twelve military boots—like clown shoes. She disguises her height, specifically to fool the cops, by jumping from one foot to the other, changing her natural stride." Miguel stood and demonstrated the jumping part making the visual in Tim's mind all that much funnier. "All while she's wearing a motocross helmet, body armor that weighs as much as she does, *and* she's wielding an M16 that's more than half her height. Is that what you want us to believe, Rox?" Miguel asked. Tim tried his best to hold back, but little bursts of laughter kept escaping each time he imagined the scene.

"Come on, Rox, let's agree the shooter is a guy," Miguel was emphatic.

"I said woman, I didn't say she was short," Roxie argued, but her whole body started to shake, and finally, she doubled over, cracking up. "See McAndrews, you aren't the only one who gets teased around here." She wiped tears from the corners of her eyes and sniffed. "I suppose you think it was a guy, too?" She asked it directly to Tim.

"Right now? Yeah. But I don't know enough to dismiss your woman theory. Let's talk after you interview the teacher in the hospital, and we get back from the autopsies." Tim stood and glanced at his watch. "Gotta go. We have just enough time to get cleaned up and down to breakfast."

Tim laughed each time he thought about Miguel's exaggerated description of the teen girl shooter he'd made up to rib Roxie. Luckily, he rode the elevator to the top floor on his own. When the elevator stopped, he disembarked, only to notice he was on the wrong floor. A man in a tan trench coat brushed past him and entered the car. Tim followed him back inside.

"Morning. Got off on the wrong floor. Are you going up?" Tim asked.

"No, down." The doors closed, and the elevator bumped as it started to ascend.

"This one is going up. Sorry." Tim said, glancing at the dude's shoes. Since he'd found the bloody footprints at the crime scene yesterday, he'd been doing that to everyone. The man's pant legs were too long to tell the type of shoes he wore other than black.

For some unknown reason, Tim felt his danger alert do an icy crawl down his spine. The guy held something tight to his body under the trench coat. Warily he stepped back and looked him over. He noticed a canvas-colored, woven nylon band by his white shirt collar. *Rifle strap.* Tim automatically thought, and then just as quickly disregarded it. It could be something else. A suitcase. A computer case. Almost as if the subject knew he was under scrutiny, he quickly adjusted the strap so it was no longer visible and smiled nervously.

Tim aced his FBI training class in micro-expressions, and when recognition flashed for a fraction of a second in the guy's eyes, he caught it. After that, his façade became closed off, and any smiles or glances seemed posed. Tim was at a disadvantage. Mr. Trenchcoat knew him— but from where? Did he also know Tim was FBI?

"Do you mind if I get off on the next floor?" The man asked as he pushed the button for the next floor. Tim's stomach squeezed tight. If he were hiding from the cops, he'd want to get off on the next floor to get away. To make things worse, Tim realized he'd seen Trenchcoat before. But where? His mind raced through likely places. In the hotel lobby? The bar last night? On a prior elevator ride?

Tim had broken the cardinal rule: don't go anywhere without your credentials and your Glock. *Not even to the hotel gym.* If this guy cloaked a rifle and decided to draw down on him, he might be in big trouble.

The man disembarked at the next stop. As he walked away, Tim noticed the white Nike checkmark on the side of his boots. But the elevator doors were beyond the point where he could stop them from closing. He jerked his hand back. Tim was on his way up.

Suddenly, he remembered *exactly where* he'd seen Trenchcoat before. The subject had been in the crowd at the sheriff's news briefing last night. He'd stood in the back at the edge of the gaggle of reporters. Tim noticed him because he asked no questions. Would a guy who just finished a school shooting come back to a press briefing to hear about the carnage? Would he be curious to know what evidence the sheriff had? There was the old adage about a killer returning to the scene of the crime. Trenchcoat just became a person of interest. Tim called Elias Cain, but there was no cell service in the elevator. Tim decided to follow to see where this led. If he was wrong about him, no one needed to know.

As soon as the doors rolled open, Tim dashed full speed for the emergency stairway. He body-slammed the door's touch bar and clambered down the steps two at a time. *Too slow!* When he was close to the last switchback in the staircase, he vaulted over the rail to the bottom level.

Panting and out of breath, he made it to the lobby and shoved the door open just in time to watch the suspect pass through the main entrance to the outside. Quickly, he slipped through the foyer, slowing just enough when necessary so that Trenchcoat wouldn't see him.

Tim pulled the earbuds out of his pocket and quickly pressed them in place. He knew he was being obvious. He'd just been on the elevator with the guy. The bleach-damaged shorts and too-big t-shirt were a giveaway. His mind struggled for a ruse. Outside the reception doors, Tim noticed two newspaper dispensers side by side under the hotel's portico. Fumbling in his front pockets, he realized he had no change. For a moment, he froze, deciding what to do. He strolled outside, pretending to read the headlines of the paper. Out of the corner of his eye, he watched.

Trenchcoat's car was parked about three spaces away from the far side of the hotel's exit driveway that paralleled the portico. Morning still slept under the blanket of dark clouds. Beneath the dim orange glow of the sodium lights, the man opened his trunk and, after looking around him, unbuttoned the trench coat.

Tim moved from behind a pillar to get a better view and shifted his phone's camera to video mode. To his dismay, the suspect turned his back. He seemed to fumble for a second, unclasped the strap, and pulled a tactical rifle from under his coat. He slipped it seamlessly into the trunk and closed it.

Tim pressed his body tight against the post when the subject started a slow three-sixty to make sure no one had seen him. That eliminated the other possibilities. It was a rifle and appeared to be an M16. When Tim dared to look again, Trenchcoat walked briskly toward the driver's side door.

Tim tried Elias again and took two steps to his left and pressed his index finger against the earbud to get better sound. He memorized the Virginia plate. *Now what? No gun—no badge, dressed like a jogger.* He couldn't attempt a stop. With the shooting so fresh, the circumstantial evidence adding up, he knew he had probable cause. *Elias, pick up, damn it!* Tim needed backup. Sequentially, he tried Miguel, then Roxie. No answer. Not from anyone.

The man backed out of his space, and Tim took a picture of his plate with his phone's camera. The silver Chevy continued out of the parking lot.

Here we go! Tim couldn't let him just get away and trailed after, watching the direction of his turn.

Tim slowed long enough to dial the special number Sheriff LaCrosse had given each of them. Vibrating with adrenaline, he jogged in place to ease the anxiety. He needed to do something—anything—even if it was stupid. He had to control that urge. Trenchcoat had a rifle, and he could have any number of handguns stashed within reach.

"Sheriff LaCrosse's office."

"Special Agent Tim McAndrews here . . . ." There were several clicks. *Did you just hang up on me?* He heard another round of clicks and breathed out.

"Sheriff LaCrosse."

"Leanne, Tim. Tim McAndrews, FBI." Tim shadowed the car as best he could, staying out of the subject's sight and weaving through the cars parked on the side of Main Street.

"I know who you are." She broke his train of thought.

"Good. Listen. I just watched a guy load a long rifle—looked like an M16—into the trunk of his car. I'm tracking him from the Culpeper Best Western. He's headed north on Main. Silver Chevy Impala or Malibu, License MXC856."

"You are in pursuit?"

"On foot. Damn! The unsub just ran the traffic light. The first left out of the hotel parking. He's made me."

"Slow down, McAndrews, how did you connect ..."

"He was at your press conference last night. Six-foot, white male, 220 pounds, receding dark brown or black hair, M16 rifle in the trunk, Nike military boots. He's worth a look."

"You said he ran the traffic light?"

"Yes, ma'am." In the background, he could hear her drumming her fingernails on a desk or table. It was early; he could've even rousted her from bed.

"We'll execute a traffic stop. Maybe he'll give us a reason to search his trunk. You better be right, McAndrews."

"I'm right. He ran a red light and has an M16. You have probable cause. Damn it! He's turning left onto Highway 95!"

"We're on it." LaCrosse disengaged.

Tim kept eyes-on as long as he could, but after Trenchcoat noticed him, he punched it. He ran after, but it was a losing battle. Like a 400-meter sprinter at the end of a race, he bent forward to catch his breath. The car was gone. Tim stood there, staring after for a few seconds as if that would do any good.

It was only then that Tim noticed the red flame glow of sunrise on the underside of the morning clouds. He watched as a lower level mist formed in the air and cloaked the shoulders of the surrounding hills like a lace shawl. The dawn chill felt good on his overheated skin but didn't wash away the foreboding. What was that adage about a red sky in the morning? Whatever it was, Tim knew he'd screwed up.

Slowly gaining back his composure, he strolled back to the hotel lobby. Once inside, he sank into the cushions of one of the gold-and-brown wingbacks. *What a rookie mistake! What a colossal fuck-up!* How could he leave his ID and gun in his room? *If this guy is the shooter and gets away—it's all on you.* Tim filled his lungs with a huge breath and slowly let it out. Time to face the music. He dialed Elias.

CHAPTER NINE

Elias rushed from the elevator and studied Tim as if scanning for injuries. Before sitting down in the chair next to him, he unbuttoned his brown tweed wool jacket. "What happened? Are you hurt?"

"I'm fine. I didn't follow protocol; my ID and weapon were in my room. I wasn't prepared." Exasperated with himself, Tim huffed out a breath.

Elias's stern expression softened a little. "Don't beat yourself up. You've been with us for what—sixteen weeks? So, you weren't expecting a potential suspect to be hanging around our hotel?"

"No." Tim slowly shook his head.

Elias's face broke open in a big grin. "Guess what? Neither did I, nor did the sheriff or any of the rest of our team. We were all getting ready for this morning's breakfast meeting."

"Exactly what I would've been doing had this guy not gotten on the elevator with me." Tim rubbed an index finger on the overnight stubble on his chin. He couldn't calm his mind. Who was Trenchcoat? Was he the shooter? Or was he just some schmuck buying an illegal weapon on the sly? Questions swirled in his mind like fruit in a smoothie blender.

Elias nodded his head. "You did what you could, right? The unsub probably made us in the hotel last night and decided to sneak out unnoticed early this morning. So, today's lesson—always expect the unexpected." Elias reached over and squeezed Tim's shoulder. "Now, for the good news, we have a description of him, his car, and his plate number. Get cleaned up and head down to the sheriff's station. We have work to do."

"Did they get him?" Tim leaned forward, elbows on his knees, and turned to stare at Elias.

"Not so far," Elias answered. "I know you think you failed, but you didn't. Good job, Tim. Quick thinking." Tim stood. Elias tossed him a set of car keys. "See you at the station. Twenty minutes." The tone in Elias's voice left no confusion. Elias twisted the ends of his handlebar, and it was an exclamation mark at the end of a sentence.

—

Tim crossed from the elevator in the hotel hallway to his suite's main door. He slipped the magnetic card into the keyless entry box, and when it clicked, he opened the door.

Rather than scold or fire him as Tim had expected, Elias commended him on a job well done. It was just like Elias to dwell on the positives and dispel the negatives. Tim was relieved.

Tim's older, experienced man theory shot to the top of the list. He would give anything to be there when the sheriff's deputies made the traffic stop. In the worst way, he wanted to see what else they'd find in that car's trunk.

Tim closed the suite's door quietly behind him. He guessed everyone would be asleep. It was only a few minutes after six. Suddenly hit with the delicious mix of freshly brewed coffee and crisp bacon on the air, he realized they were awake.

Dressed in her robe, Dani sat across the dining table from Mitch and Shannon Brady. Mitch stood and greeted Tim. Of Dani's closest employees, Tim had to admit Mitch was his favorite.

Mitch had retired from the navy, where he'd served as a fighter pilot. His experience with takeoffs and landings on a pitching aircraft carrier made him seem fearless. Nothing rattled him. There wasn't a flying machine he couldn't pilot. When the airline job he'd landed after his honorable discharge proved to be too dull, he'd hired on with Dani. Mitch had once told Tim in confidence that Dani paid better and offered more comprehensive benefits.

Dani's travel needs weren't an everyday thing, so Mitch had free time to pursue other hobbies. And since he and Shannon were childless, Dani was happy to let his wife accompany him on trips.

On two occasions, Mitch's cool head and tactical experience had come in handy when Tim needed him most. Now the two men shook hands.

"Can I get you a cup of coffee?" Shannon asked.

"Thanks, but I don't have time." Tim walked over and stood behind Dani, kissing her on top of her head.

"You smell good," he whispered against her clean hair. The scent of her shampoo, her soap, her perfume triggered rushes of desire. He pushed those thoughts aside when he glanced at his watch. "Got to get going." He hugged her shoulders and headed to get cleaned up and ready for work.

Tim stopped cold when he entered the bedroom. With care, Dani had laid out clean clothes. The last person who had done that for him was Mom, and she'd stopped doing it when he hit seven years old. He wasn't sure how he felt about it, but he liked thinking Dani wanted to help him in every way she could. She'd just cut the time he needed to get ready nearly in half.

Tim dialed in the water temperature for his shower, stripped, and stepped in. As he lathered his hair, his thoughts shifted to Mr. Trenchcoat. What motive could a man in his forties have to shoot up a high school? He thought about the victims: two girls, one boy. The safety officer's death was easy to figure; he was law enforcement and in the way. Criminals seemed to think of the police as expendable.

Sheriff LaCrosse speculated at the scene that the boy had tried to shield the other students and had sacrificed himself. Both respect and sadness moved Tim.

The children that died yesterday—what would've they become if they'd been allowed to live? Another Einstein? Concert pianists? Biologists who would find the cure for cancer or Ebola? Tim pushed his forearm on the tiled wall and rested his brow against it. He let the warm water stream over his body, hoping to wash away his sense of grief.

He turned off the water and wrapped the towel around his waist and went to the sink to shave. He noticed Dani standing in the doorway. He watched her watching him and remembered a time he'd stood in the bathroom door as a little kid. His parents looked at each other this way. This was it. This was the backbone that made everything else in life possible. She loved him, and he loved her. They were a family. For a moment, he savored the feeling. But he had to snap out of it. He was pretty sure the twenty minutes Elias had allotted him were up.

Tim dressed in the things Dani set out for him, while she finished getting ready as well. He glanced at his watch. Five minutes behind schedule, he had to hurry. He checked both of his weapons and inserted the magazines. He slid the FBI-issued nine-millimeter Glock into his shoulder holster and the smaller .380 Walther at his ankle. He stashed his credentials in his right pocket. He was never going to be caught without any of them again.

—

Tim took hold of Dani's right hand in his left as they rode the elevator to the lobby level. Just before they arrived, Dani dropped his hand, adjusted his tie, smoothed her hand down the lapels of the charcoal gray, cashmere and wool blend suit she'd brought for him. He strayed from the traditional hedge-fund manager/business tycoon look Dani had intended. The jacket accommodated his concealed weapon. And he had to have the hybrid wingtip shoes with a gripping rubber sole in case he actually had to chase down a bad guy.

"You look so handsome." Her blue eyes softened and took his breath away.

The ding announced they'd arrived at the lobby level. As they waited for the doors to open, Tim grabbed her hand, pressing her fingertips to his lips. "Can you come back tonight?"

"If you want me to," she stared at him, holding his gaze.

"I want you to." They stepped out together into the lobby. Tim could see through the entrance doors Mitch waited for her by the SUV they'd rented at the airport. Outside, the sky was cold, clear, and blue. The morning clouds and mist had dissipated, but the early spring sun was stingy with its warmth.

She glanced at her watch. "I promised the decorator I'd meet her at nine. I have just enough time to make our meeting."

Tim nodded and escorted her to the hotel's main door.

"McAndrews! Tim McAndrews!" Tim turned when he heard his name. Beebe Knoll jostled her way across the lobby from the bank of elevators at a jog. She tugged Congressman Patterson along like a puppy resisting his first time on a leash.

Tim groaned. "I forgot to tell you Beebe's been promoted to correspondent at large. She says she's here to cover the school shooting," he explained as Beebe and the congressman headed in their direction.

Dani tipped her head with suspicion. "Maybe I should cancel my meeting," she snickered, slipping her arm under his and weaving her fingers into his as if she needed to affirm he was hers. The words hadn't been invented yet that described how much he loved her. Dani didn't need to be jealous of Beebe.

"I hate seeing her here. She's so much trouble," he said under his breath, just before they caught up.

"Hello, Beebe, nice to see you. What brings you to Culpeper?" Dani pasted on one of her smiles that revealed her feelings inside as readily as locked safe. Tim nodded his greeting.

"I'm here covering the shooting. Do you know Congressman Patterson?" Beebe turned toward the congressman. "This is Tim and Dani McAndrews." They shook hands.

"Beebe has told me so much about you." Patterson slipped his arm over Beebe's shoulders. "I've been trying to meet you for a long time, Miss St. Clair."

"Mrs. McAndrews," Dani corrected, but Patterson didn't seem to notice or acknowledge it. Tim was insulted. In most politicians' minds, FBI agents and other law enforcement officers occupied a lower rank in society than they did. But just like Patterson, Tim had a law degree and had served in a district attorney's office before his current job. He'd even bet hard money he had a conviction record that Patterson could only dream of. Patterson's elitism and snobbishness were irksome.

"We have some charity and education department issues in common, Miss St. Clair. I'd love to have a moment to talk to you," Patterson continued.

Dani held on to Tim's arm tighter. For some reason, she signaled she needed him to protect her. No doubt, Patterson was going to ask her for money.

"Dani, you have got to go. Sorry to cut this short, but Dani has a meeting in DC. She has a flight to catch." Tim smiled but narrowed his eyes at Patterson.

"There's a flight from here to DC? I had no idea." Patterson raised his eyebrows. Tim shrugged. He wasn't going to give the man a reason to ask to be included as a passenger on Dani's private plane. He wasn't going to let her be trapped in the air and forced to listen to this stale windbag.

"It was nice to meet you. Excuse us." Tim turned Dani toward the door.

"So, McAndrews, are you going back to DC?" Beebe asked. She and Patterson followed along as Tim got Dani out to Mitch and the SUV. He kissed her cheek before closing the door and tapped twice when Dani was secure. He needed to get her out of here before Patterson realized he could beg a ride.

"No." Tim kept his answers to one word.

"Are you going to the sheriff's office?" Patterson asked. "I heard about your little—incident this morning." He flicked his dark eyebrows as if he were an insider in the case.

"Incident?" Tim acted dumb to buy himself time. How in the hell did Patterson know about any incident? Who leaked? He ran his hand over his hair and ground his teeth together.

"I heard that the shooter was here—staying at this hotel. Can you believe it? Right here, right under *our* noses." *Our noses?* Now Patterson had inserted himself into the investigation. They didn't know Trenchcoat was the shooter. He was only a person of interest. Why would Patterson assume he was anything more than that? Tim bristled. Suspicion ran cold through his veins, but outwardly he showed no emotion.

Tim sized him up. He was at least four inches shorter and twelve years Tim's senior. Beebe Knoll was going for an older man. Knowing Beebe, news stories were her ultimate goal. If it took screwing this plastic-smiled troll to get the inside scoop, she'd do it. Tim didn't think there was a woman on Earth he respected less than Beebe.

"You know I can't comment on an open investigation."

"I was hoping, since you and Beebe are friends, that we could make an arrangement. You keep me up to date. You can never have too many friends in DC."

A threat crawled under the surface of his words like earthworms in a garden plot. "Come by the sheriff's office. I'm sure she'll be giving an update later this morning."

"I want to know what you know before anyone else," Patterson spoke in a hushed but slimy tone.

Tim bit the bottom lip of his smile. He let that be his answer.

CHAPTER TEN

Tim walked briskly through the busy sheriff's office. In the background, he could hear phones ringing and conversations buzzing like a hornets' nest. Sheriff LaCrosse talked with Elias in the small alcove she'd donated as their workspace. When he crossed through the institutional green archway, he knew he had to address the leaks.

"Tim, you're here. Leanne has the sketch artist all set up in Interrogation Room 1." Elias's smile peeked out from under his neatly trimmed mustache. "The sooner we get the description out to patrol, the better."

"Who told Congressman Patterson about my encounter this morning?" Tim looked from Elias's face to LaCrosse's and back again.

Elias's eyes widened. Tim knew Elias despised Patterson and wanted to review information to decide what was released to the public to protect the integrity of the case. Tim ruled Elias out immediately as the source of the leak. "I didn't. You didn't, did you, Leanne?" He sounded worried.

"No. Why would I?" Tim noted her eyes were clear and devoid of deception.

"Someone did . . . ." Tim's words dissipated like steam. Suspicion flashed through his mind. Was the congressman involved somehow?

Had the congressman watched the scene unfold from his hotel room? He could've if his window were located on the right side of the hotel. Tim decided he'd check that out this evening when he returned. Right now, he needed to get the sketch artist going on the person of interest's picture.

"I'm headed to the hospital with Melissa to interview the teacher. You work with the artist. I want to give a profile to Leanne and her deputies by this afternoon," Elias said.

———

After working with the sketch artist, Tim stared at the finished product. It was a good likeness. The artist caught perfectly the narrow eyes, the slight hook in the nose, and the V of his receding hairline. Armed with this picture, patrol officers could recognize the man on sight. Tim nodded his approval, and a deputy dispatched the image to all area law enforcement agencies.

Tim returned to the alcove. He watched as Miguel picked up his coffee in a Styrofoam cup, grimaced before swallowing, and returned to work on the computer. Roxie glanced up at him from whatever she was doing on her phone. Tim handed them each a sheet of paper with Trenchcoat's likeness on it.

"Is this elevator guy?" Roxie asked, her gaze coursing over Tim, top to bottom. She snickered. "Your mommy dressed you funny this morning."

Miguel looked up and grinned as if ready for the teasing to begin.

Tim took in an annoyed breath and ignored her. He wasn't in the mood for her crap this morning. He peeled off his jacket and hung it on the chair. He stood in shirtsleeves behind the desk with a computer.

Without sitting, he turned on the computer and began to read through the file they had compiled so far. He sent pages to the printer and collected them. He pulled out a yellow-lined legal pad, sat behind the desk, and started making notes. Writing down his observations seemed to help cement them in his mind.

Within a few seconds, Roxie rose from her chair, walked over, and stood beside him, leaning forward to read his computer screen. "Don't get your little feelies hurt, McAndrews," she chided him. She petted the suit jacket hanging on the back of his chair. "Oooh, that's so soft! I know Daniella St. Clair is rich, but really, cashmere? That's a bit much, isn't it? Even for you."

Roxie made him look at each of them and compare. Roxie wore the ladies' version of a dark-colored suit; Miguel dressed in the men's. The difference between Tim's and theirs was only the fabric. Dani could easily afford cashmere, Roxie and Miguel could not. Tim knew he'd have to talk to Dani about her wardrobe choices for him. Roxie was right, suits costing several thousand dollars and police work were incompatible. But he'd been moved by Dani's desire to help this morning, so he'd just gone with it. His other choices were yesterday's suit (Beebe had kicked muddy water all over that), the sweats he'd brought with him, and this fine suit. The first two were out of the question.

"Like you said, Roxie, my mommy dresses me funny." Tim accentuated his retort with a smile as icy as a polar vortex. "Elias wants a profile by this afternoon. I'm going to sort through the witness interviews. What did the medical examiner have to say?"

"All four victims were killed with two precise shots—one to the chest—the heart actually, and the second to the head. Leanne believes the security officer was first. The ME believes Aiysha Conrow was next, then Marty Schultz, probably as he tried to defend Aiysha. Finally, Julie Anderson, the second girl, was shot." Miguel stood and joined Roxie at Tim's assigned space. Miguel leaned on the forward edge of the desk and crossed his arms over his chest. Tim in turn, set his elbows on the flat wood surface and rested his chin on his hands. Precision kill shots screamed professional assassination. And, so did Trenchcoat, just by his demeanor. But who would call for a hit on fifteen-year-old schoolchildren?

"The three kids killed were all good students, no trouble, good grades," Tim said.

"Not *that* good. Both girls were sexually active within eight to twelve hours before their deaths. Aiysha was even pregnant," Roxie said casually as if this were an everyday occurrence, and maybe it was. But the girls were only fifteen. Tim tried to remember what he was like at that age. He realized that if it hadn't been for his older brothers' guidance, he could've become a dad at fifteen.

Tim knew his mouth was hanging open. He swallowed as his mind raced, exploring the possibilities. "How far along?"

"The ME guessed six to eight weeks," Roxie answered. "Does that matter?"

"If the girl, Aiysha, realized she was expecting, the father could be a suspect. Are six to eight weeks long enough for a girl to know she's pregnant?" Tim asked, furrowing his brow with the question.

"Never been. How would I know?" Roxie's tone was almost accusatory.

"Don't look at me." Miguel laughed, and Roxie responded with an indifferent tip of her head. Tim chuckled to himself.

"Usually, you suspect pregnancy if you miss your monthly—fun. But fifteen-year-olds have to deal with the *it could never happen to me's*. The drugstore tests are ninety-eight percent effective about 4 to 5 days after a skipped period. She could've known." Roxie turned serious.

"Rohypnol metabolites were present in both girls' and the boy's blood and urine. Rohypnol mixed with alcohol equals amnesia. And, the girls had rough sex, very rough sex. Looks suspiciously like date rape to me. ME is doing rape kits on the girls and a DNA test on the fetus." Miguel half sat on the desk with his right side. His left foot still touched the floor.

"So, what if the school shooting was a cover-up? Murder the pregnant girl, delete the problem," Tim thought out loud.

"Good one, Tim. Only these three students and the school safety officer were killed," Roxie said, and Miguel nodded in agreement. "All of the other kids had non-life-threatening injuries and were treated and sent home."

"But why the other two kids? Only Aiysha was pregnant." Tim pondered this question, but no answer came.

"They could rat out the father?" Miguel said, adding to emerging profile.

"Maybe the kids met up with ol' Trenchie. Probably an internet thing. He dosed them with roofies and got Aiysha in a family way. We need to get their computer and cell phone records," Roxie said. The visual that surfaced in Tim's mind made anger seethe in his gut. He thought of his own daughters. If this happened to his family, he'd want blood.

"Let's get the parents in here and find out what they know." Tim scrubbed his hand over his hair. He could feel that rush, the heart-pounding excitement he always experienced when they started to close in on an unsub. Could it be the girls hooked up with an older man on the web and were drugged and raped? "Was he grooming them?"

"We won't know that until we get the DNA back *and* have a suspect in custody to compare it to," Miguel stated.

"I'll go find out if the sheriff has an update on collaring Trenchie. That's what we're calling him, right? We need to find out who he is!" Roxie straightened up. "I'll get the parents rounded up." She headed out of the alcove.

"Here, Miguel, you take half of these interview notes. Let's find out which students were close friends of our victims. They know something. Kids always do, even if they're not talking at first," Tim said. Miguel grabbed up a stack of papers and returned to his desk.

They started reading through the 302s, sorting them into four piles. Group one: kids that saw nothing and didn't know the victims. Two: the students that saw something. Three: the teens that saw something and knew the victims. And the final one: the teachers and administrators.

For a few minutes, the only sound in the alcove was the clatter of the ancient forced-air heater and the rustle of a page as it was placed onto one of the predetermined stacks. When Tim finished skimming the interviews, he stretched and got up to get a cup of coffee.

"Grab me one, cream only," Miguel said, putting the last page in place.

"Do you have the 302 for the principal?" Tim set two cups on the small table that held the coffee fixings. He filled them and added a splash of cream to each.

"Don't you?" Miguel asked, matching Tim's stare, eye to eye.

"This is all of the interviews, right?"

"As far as I know," Miguel replied.

Tim laughed quietly. "Don't tell me no one interviewed the principal. I thought I was the only screw-up around here."

Miguel made a soft clicking noise in his cheek, "Ahhh, nope. We're all capable of messing up."

Tim brought Miguel's coffee over. He turned as he heard footfalls hitting the vinyl floor. He looked up as Roxie crossed the threshold to their confined space.

"Oh, *Special Agent McAndrews*—there's a Susan Bower and her mother here to see you," Roxie announced in a smart-ass sing-song tone. "They saw you on the TV news last night." Roxie put her hand over her heart, fluttered her eyelashes, and faked a big sigh.

"She asked for me? Not Elias?" Tim tipped his chin in surprise. He intentionally ignored Roxie's little drama.

"She asked for you. Says she was Aiysha's best friend and has something important to tell us."

"Let's put her in interview room one." Tim grabbed his cashmere jacket and started to slip his arms into the sleeves. "You coming?"

CHAPTER ELEVEN

"**R**oxie, be ready in case this is too sensitive for the girl to discuss with me, okay?" Tim asked, grabbing up his file and a yellow legal pad for notes. She took too long to answer. It was her job to help him but she hadn't decided if she wanted to. Making him wait was terribly satisfying. The muscles along his jaw tightened.

"Of course. Go. I'm right behind you." She got it. The Bower women may have wanted to talk to McAndrews at first because they recognized him from the TV news conference, and he was pretty. But, when they had to get to the grit, they might change their minds and prefer a female agent.

They walked into the interrogation room and closed the door behind them. The light gray concrete block walls were blank and unadorned, so there would be no distractions. Roxie looked up to make sure the light on the video camera mounted in the north corner glowed red. Next, she pushed the audio button on the intercom that turned on the outer office speakers. Now the sheriff and Miguel could hear the interview. It would be recorded. Miguel and Leanne stood side by side in front of the two-way mirror, each with a cup of coffee in hand.

Susan Bower's and her mother's red swollen eyes betrayed they'd spent some time crying. But their reaction to Tim McAndrews sickened Roxie, and she rolled her eyes, annoyed. She felt jealousy pricking her as if she'd fallen into a bed of barrel cactus. Elias was in love with the guy, showing him off at the press briefing. The sheriff was mesmerized and spent most of her time with him at the crime scene yesterday. And even Miguel, her favorite team member, was overly impressed by Tim's ability to translate Kandar's fantasyland descriptions into normal gear you could find on Amazon.

"Good morning, Mrs. Bower, Susan. I'm Special Agent McAndrews, and this is Special Agent Stauffer. You asked to see me?"

Mrs. Bower's cheeks flushed with color, and she became a flutter-pated fool, unable to complete a sentence, a reaction Roxie knew well. Obviously too young for him, Susan fussed with her dyed magenta curls in a clumsy attempt at flirting.

Tim gestured for the women to be seated across from him and Roxie at the well-worn wooden table. He dropped his file and legal pad down in front of him. For a man as good-looking as Tim, he sure didn't realize how he affected women.

Roxie knew she was just as guilty as the Bowers of being tongue-tied around Tim. It infuriated her that he made her feel that way. Embarrassed that still, even after four years, just looking at him could leave her speechless. Roxie folded her arms across her chest. When Elias said Tim was joining the unit, she couldn't imagine having to work with him every day. Roxie dreaded the mishmash of emotions he'd bring out in her. She was the senior agent, six years older, and far more skilled in fieldwork than Tim. Elias's favoritism really rankled her. Tim was too inexperienced to be giving TV briefings and now in charge of an interview.

Roxie had first met Tim at a serial killer joint task force meeting four years ago in Seattle. It wasn't like she didn't have any other suitors; she had plenty. But with him, she could check off all the boxes on her list of what she wanted in a husband.

Before taking the job with the BAU, she finally screwed up enough courage to confront him about what she believed was a mutual attraction. She'd thrown herself at him, and he'd made no effort to catch her. Even now, she remembered him struggling to make eye contact and grappling for a gentle way to turn her down. Her lips tightened into a thin line, and a rush of heat filled her cheeks, remembering how excruciating and humiliating it had been. She'd tried to pass it off as a joke.

Tim hadn't changed that much in three years. If anything, he was even more striking. His short cut, slightly unruly sun-streaked blond hair gave him an unexpected masculine carelessness that made him utterly irresistible. He was still the clean-cut boy-next-door she'd fallen for back in Seattle.

When he arrived for his first day at the BAU, Roxie hoped she'd outgrown her fascination with young testosterone-fueled males that earlier in life had wowed her. She expected an arrogant, full-of-himself jerk. Most young men were, especially when they had a little success under their belts. His conviction record while with the King County DA was remarkable for a kid.

She felt the sting again. She'd placed her bet, played her cards, and lost. He'd married someone else. Why couldn't it have been her? Daniella St. Clair's money, of course. Who could compete with that? She wanted to hate him, but she couldn't. Her only control was to belittle him relentlessly about anything—everything.

"We have your permission to tape this interview, correct?" Tim asked softly, bringing Roxie back to the present. She shook her head to clear unwanted thoughts from her mind.

"Yes," Both women said in unison.

"Would you like to start at the beginning, Susan?" Tim asked.

"It was Mr. Crenshaw!" She blurted out and burst into tears.

"Mr. Crenshaw? Edmond Crenshaw, the school principal, is the shooter?" Roxie asked, scooting her chair back from the table. Roxie's eyebrows shot up, and she looked over at Tim, stunned. She could hardly believe his calm, unreadable face. Roxie knew they'd be going to the principal's house after this—for a little chat.

Mrs. Bower returned a glare filled with a chill of certainty. She slipped her arm across her daughter's shoulders and touched her forehead to forehead.

Tim produced the composite of Trenchie. "Is this Mr. Crenshaw?"

Roxie learned no one had interviewed Crenshaw, and there was no photo of the man in the file. And the illustrious McAndrews wasn't able to work his Google magic.

Susan stared at the drawing for several seconds. "No," she dismissed it.

"Have you ever seen this man before?"

"No." Susan shook her head, and her eyes filled with unspoken questions.

"Okay. Do you want to tell me why you think Mr. Crenshaw would shoot up the school?" Tim's voice was soothing and steady. Roxie's admiration for him spiked up, but just barely. They were blindsided by shocking information, and he was as composed as if she told him to expect sunny weather.

"Aiysha is . . . was pregnant . . . and it's . . . his baby," the girl said in ragged breaths, causing her accusation to come out all choppy.

There's your motive. As Roxie remembered, Mr. Edmond Crenshaw, school principal, was a married man. If Susan's accusations were true, everything was on the line. Exposure would cost him his job, his marriage, everything.

Susan looked up. "Aiysha and I did her pregnancy test together."

"That proves she was pregnant, not who the father is," Roxie said, looking over at Tim. He was so maddening. His demeanor revealed nothing.

"The Medical Examiner found Rohypnol, the date rape drug, in Aiysha, Julie, and Marty's systems. Can you tell me anything about that?" Tim asked.

Sometimes kids used that drug just to get a loopy high. The dosage was the key. Were they fooling around with a dangerous drug they didn't understand? Roxie wondered.

Susan sniffed and set her hand on the interview table. Her mother covered it in a reassuring gesture. "Go ahead, darling, no one is judging you. You are the victim," Mrs. Bower said, her eyes welling up.

"We belonged to a club. If you got straight As,' you got to be in the club." She shook with a sob.

"How many kids were in the club?" Roxie asked.

"Seven. Me, Aiysha Conrow, Rose Bronson, Marty Schultz, Julie Anderson, Keenyon Smith, and Tina Zachariah." She counted on her fingertips.

Tim scribbled the names on his yellow pad as Susan said them. Though he sat utterly expressionless and still from the waist up, he diffused emotion by bouncing his right leg under the table. Roxie could see he braced for what would come next. So did she.

"Mr. Crenshaw," Mrs. Bower grabbed at her chest, "Mr. Crenshaw said the field trips were a reward for their hard work. He said there were chaperones. We believed him. I even signed permission slips." A new flood ran down Mrs. Bower's cheeks. She had to be feeling guilty. Guilty for trusting a principal? If not him, who could you trust? Roxie wondered.

Tim leaned forward on the desk, set his elbows on the table, and rested his lips on his folded hands and studied the woman. Roxie wondered if he believed her. It was a pretty fantastic story.

Tim dropped his hands to the table. "Tell me about the field trips."

"He would take us to movies, the opera, the ballet, museums, monuments, and we would stay over in a hotel. At the end of the outing, we'd all go to his room to play games and discuss what we'd seen that day. He'd give us refreshments," Susan continued.

"Alcohol?" Tim asked. Roxie watched him scribble the word 'contributing' followed by a question mark on his pad next to the word 'date rape.'

The teen nodded. "And a couple of times, I woke up back in my hotel room and couldn't remember what had happened or how I got there. Then one day, when I got home from a trip, I noticed that my—um . . . um . . . my panties were inside out." Looking at her mother for support, she said the last part as quickly as she could, as if hoping it wouldn't be so embarrassing. Still, her cheeks colored bright red.

Mrs. Bower's dam burst, and she sobbed uncontrollably. Disgust soured Roxie's morning coffee in her stomach. The knuckles of Tim's interlocked fingers turned white as he squeezed his hands tightly together. Now that he had adopted two girls, Roxie imagined detaching himself from crimes against children was impossible. A lot of law enforcement officers struggled to divorce themselves from emotion in these cases. Roxie knew she did. Tim's manner seemed different now. Roxie thought she saw anger doing a slow burn in his eyes.

"Then what happened?" Roxie coaxed her to continue.

"I wasn't sure anything really happened. It could have been my mistake. I could've dressed in a hurry or something." The girl didn't want to admit it, not even to herself.

"When did you notice this?" Roxie asked.

"A month ago, I think," Susan replied. Too late for a rape kit, Roxie thought.

"When Aiysha skipped her period, I got scared. You see, we, Aiysha and I, pledged to wait until we were married to . . . well . . . you know." Susan's hands began to tremble. "The next time the club met, I pretended to drink what he mixed for us. I poured mine into a potted plant. I pretended to fall asleep. Another man I didn't know came into the room. I saw the other man take Aiysha's clothes off and do something to her. Mr. Crenshaw did things to Marty. When I thought they weren't watching, I crawled into the bedroom closet." She let go of the waterworks, and rivulets ran down her cheeks and chin and created a small puddle on the table. "I was so scared they'd come for me. I prayed and prayed. They fell asleep." She sniffed and let out a sad little laugh. "They didn't come looking for me! When I was sure they were asleep, I snuck back to my room."

Clever girl, Roxie thought.

Tim set Trenchie's picture in the middle of the table again. "Was this the other man?"

Susan stared at the image for a few seconds and then shook her head no.

"Did you go to the club meeting on Thursday night?" Roxie asked. She lifted her chin, fighting emotion that tore at her heart. This shit was the very reason she'd joined the FBI.

"No. And I begged Aiysha not to go. I begged her. But she didn't believe me. She didn't remember anything about the parties in Mr. Crenshaw's room. She called me a liar. She thought maybe her boyfriend, Jazz Montgomery, was the father. But we had a pact, we weren't going to . . . until we were married. Jazz was in the pact, too." Susan swept her hand across the table, pausing to toy with one of the deep scratches in the wood by tracing it with her index finger.

"Can you think of anything else?" Roxie asked.

Susan sat quietly for a moment, then shook her head no.

"Do you have any clothing that you wore to one of these meetings that you haven't dry cleaned or washed?" Tim asked.

Mrs. Bower tipped her head as if confused.

"DNA. Mr. Crenshaw or the other man may have left some DNA on Susan's clothes." Roxie filled in the gap.

The young girl looked down at her hands.

"Check for me, okay? If you find something, call us immediately. We'll come to collect it." Tim stared at the girl until her gaze met his, and she nodded in the affirmative. "Mrs. Bower, you may want to take Susan to her doctor for a check-up."

The older woman nodded her agreement.

"You may go. If you think of anything else, call Agent Stauffer or me." Tim's voice was soft and sympathetic. He passed both business cards across the table. "Thank you for your help."

Outside the interrogation room, Tim and Roxie watched them go. Roxie was glad Susan had a supportive mom.

"We need to have the ME check Marty's body for sexual assault." Tim swallowed as if forcing back bile.

Roxie could tell Tim struggled with the horror of it. She took hold of his left hand in hers. "She could be lying, you know." She dropped his hand.

"Yeah, I know." He took in a deep breath. "We're not going to just take her word for it." He smiled. "I didn't detect any deception in her body language, though."

"Neither did I. We can do a lie detector to confirm."

"We need to get the other club members in for interviews before they talk to each other." Tim looked at his list on the yellow pad.

Roxie noticed Elias walking with determination in their direction from the busy main office.

"Good interview." Elias set his large black hand on Tim's shoulder. Love-hate mixed into a strange brew in Roxie's mind. She was there too, and Tim got all the praise.

"Kandar and I will start interviewing the 'club' members. I sent Melissa and Miguel with a deputy to question Crenshaw. We are hoping he will volunteer DNA. I've already started the process for a warrant, just in case," Elias informed them. "And last but not least, deputies found *the car*. The one you chased this morning, Tim. Abandoned. On a dirt backcountry road. It's a rental. Our person of interest used a fake California driver's license with the name John Smith, not his real name, and his address is a vacant lot in Visalia, California. He used one of those prepaid Visa cards to rent the car and the same card at the hotel."

"Huh, that's a surprise," Tim said. His sarcastic tone reflected Roxie's thoughts exactly. "I take it he didn't fill out the form on the card's website. Did Support trace where he purchased the card?"

"Yes. Walmart, Livermore, California, with cash. I've sent agents to see if we can get the video for the date of purchase. Roxie, you and Tim, go work the car. CSI will meet you there."

"But, is Trenchie still a person of interest, now that we have Crenshaw?" Roxie asked.

Elias grinned. "He's still on the top of the list. Now, go work the car."

CHAPTER TWELVE

Congressman Aaron Patterson is a complete idiot, Beebe Knoll thought as she sat across from him at the hotel restaurant. She studied his soft face, which reminded her of a typical grade-school fat boy. He'd grown up, lost weight in adulthood and was better looking than he used to be, making him incredibly vain but still insecure. He had that pasty, sickly, fragile demeanor that screamed consummate momma's boy that was never allowed to play outdoors. Just by looking at him, Patterson's weak, slightly underslung jaw and vacant brown eyes confirmed he was about as intelligent as a Jersey cow. The scruff on his chin, popular with Hollywood stars, was not attractive on him. Instead, it made him look unkempt, dirty even, in his navy-blue Brooks Brothers suit. His medium brown hair was neatly cut to frame his satellite-dish-meets-Dumbo ears.

Before her encounter with him at that hotel bar in DC, she'd done her research on all the presidential candidates. Patterson was married to his second wife after dumping the first for the second. This was the very kind of man Beebe would never get emotionally involved with. If he cheated once, and was hitting on her for twice, he'd be unfaithful the minute she got involved. Infidelity was a serial crime.

Patterson had graduated from a large, but not highly ranked, college with a mediocre law school. He served as an assistant DA in his home county, with an unimpressive conviction record. Yet, he thought of himself as another Mark Geragos. Other than getting elected upon the retirement of a more prominent statesman, he had little to show for his eight years in public office—two bills: one to request charity funds for the Fiji Islands and one to name a post office. *Snore.*

Beebe could hardly believe Patterson demanded that Tim McAndrews keep him up to date on the school shooting before anyone else. She'd picked up on Patterson's subtle threat, and no doubt so had McAndrews. She'd warned him McAndrews was the king of *No Comment*. The man said the two magic words before you formed your question and opened your mouth to speak it. Back in Seattle, he'd had the well-earned reputation of being a brick wall. Everyone in the press complained about McAndrews' sense of justice. He believed everyone was entitled to their day in court and would never taint a jury pool. He didn't try his cases in the media. Every time she tried to extract information from him about a trial when he was an ADA, he blocked her. For that, she gave him the well-earned nickname of Jackass. He was as stubborn as a damned mule. Every once in a while, he could've been a nice guy and given in. He never did.

In the hotel lobby, Patterson also took the opportunity to flirt with McAndrews' wife in front of him. It took Jackass less than half a second to figure out that Patterson would hit her up for money. McAndrews had skirted his wife away to safety as fast as he could. Just once, Beebe would like to have a guy like that to defend and protect her.

Beebe stared out of a large walnut-framed window abutting their booth. A jet-black horse and several brown cows grazed peacefully in an expansive green pasture that sloped upward and ended at a leaf-bare forest covering the top of a gently rolling hill, like a brown straw hat. She was here for one reason and only one. She wanted to be SBC News Team's White House and Capitol Hill correspondent, and eventually their national news anchor.

Patterson paid no attention to her, and she scowled at him as he scrolled through his Twitter feed on his iPhone. The man's fragile ego was on a level she'd never experienced before. He counted his followers on social media daily like a teenaged girl.

"I have a thousand new followers, and my last tweet was retweeted twelve thousand times." He looked up, and Beebe immediately changed her expression to a big smile.

"That's great." But what she really thought was, your last tweet was moronic. If the man spent any time listening to his constituents or had an ounce of common sense, he'd know threatening them with higher taxes wasn't a winner.

The waitress brought them each a mug of coffee and left the table, promising to follow up with their breakfast order in a few minutes. Beebe doctored her coffee with two sugar packets and struggled to open two tiny tubs of cream she found in a bowl in the corner of the table.

This morning, SBC expected her to update the shooting, live, her second report since the incident, to boost their ratings. If only there were a way to grab up some breaking information to supercharge her report. Something the police were reluctant to share, something no other network had. She tickled her long fingernails along the table's Formica top. For now, her plan consisted of hanging around the sheriff's office, and if they didn't notice, she might inadvertently glean some information she could use.

Later on, she had to give an update on Patterson's campaign for president. The man was so dumb, she couldn't imagine him being able to tie his shoes, let alone run the country.

Beebe was embarrassed that she'd gotten involved with him. He was in the middle of his second rocky marriage and headed for an even rockier divorce. She had to remember the prize. Though Patterson was stupid and repulsive, he had the connections to get her where she wanted to go. She'd slept with worse to achieve her goals. After all, her bosses made the rules; they couldn't condemn her for playing by them.

She remembered the night she'd met Patterson. Alone and sitting at the hotel bar when he'd approached her, she perceived his weakness.

He'd had too much booze. Add a dash of flattery, and he was all hers. Beebe knew how pretty and irresistible she was. She'd officially become a news-whore and was ready, willing, and able to do whatever it took to land another prize-winning story.

Patterson's run for office wasn't that story. He was going to flop like a third-rate off-Broadway play. But the school shooting just might be it, especially since Jackass McAndrews was working the case as a profiler, no less. Every time she'd decided to follow where he led, she came up with a blockbuster. Serial killers, pedophiles, corrupt politicians didn't have a chance with Jackass on the case. Ooh, she liked that and typed it in the Word program she'd downloaded to her iPhone, replacing Jackass with his given name, of course.

Sooner rather than later, she wanted to use her liaison with Patterson to land the White House Press Corps position she coveted desperately. Every congressman, even those as ridiculous as Patterson, had strings they could pull.

Rumors around the station suggested that Joe Mangan, their long-time national news anchor, was retiring. Beebe adjusted her short blonde curls in the reflection on her black iPhone screen, letting her mind go with the fantasy of her occupying the anchor chair for a few seconds. She tapped the screen, bringing back the start of her article, and typed a few more words.

The waitress brought their food and set plates before each of them, taking the congressman from his social media and Beebe from her daydreams.

"So, who called you at five this morning?" Beebe asked, staring at Patterson across the table.

For a moment, shock froze Patterson's face, followed by a big guilty grin. He stopped dribbling syrup on his pancakes from the small stainless-steel pitcher. "I'm sorry, did that wake you this morning? It was my wife. She's checking up on me."

Beep! Wrong answer! Who did he think he was kidding? Beebe could read a lie from a mile away. A few minutes after the call, Beebe heard the faint knock on the hotel room door. She pretended to sleep but watched with one eye open as Patterson slipped from under the covers and tiptoed across the room. He retrieved a manila envelope from the inside pocket of yesterday's suit coat hanging in the small closet. She wiggled to Patterson's side of the bed to get a better view of the door but could only see a shadow. He passed the package to the person on the other side. When Patterson started to turn, she hustled back where she belonged and feigned sleep.

The lie only piqued her curiosity. What was he up to? Was he passing top secret info to a foreign spy? He was, after all, on the House Permanent Select Committee on Intelligence. *Patterson—intelligence. Now, that was an oxymoron!*

Was he paying up on blackmail, paying a PI to get dirt on his wife, or engaged in some sort of pay-to-play? She rejected that it was something innocent like paying to get his shoes shined or suit pressed by the concierge. Maybe, just maybe, he wasn't the dull bore she assumed, and there was a story here, after all.

CHAPTER THIRTEEN

Tim stood in front of the corkboard they set up to help visualize their theories of the crime. Kandar posted a topographical map and placed a red circle where the abandoned vehicle was found. On the map, three forest-covered hills occupied the space between the town of Culpeper and the broad valley comprised of farms and the western edge of the famous DC Beltway.

The freeway started its curve to the south around the northernmost peak. Lush pasture land encompassed each knoll, and access roads hugged the woodlands, so every acre of usable ground could be planted. The gravel farm roads connected to freeway onramps to the west, and to a narrow two-lane paved road to the east. The southernmost prominence abutted the high school's football field and had the most forest cover.

"Elias wants us to get going," Roxie said as she positioned herself next to Tim in front of the map. He glanced her way.

"Yeah, okay," Tim answered her but hesitated. "You know Miguel's theory that the shooter used a dirt bike to escape makes sense if you look at this map." Tim pointed to an access road that skirted the backside of the hill closest to the school. "When Susan said another man joined Crenshaw during the assaults, it dawned on me; this could be a team effort to get rid of the pregnant-girl complications."

Roxie pursed her lips. She seemed to be considering it. "What if the unsub parked here. Rode his dirt bike through the forest to the edge of the football field. Then, walked across and entered by the back door to the school?"

"Works for me," Tim said. "He'd have to have a key. Even during school hours, the admin secretary said the back is locked to entry from the outside. Someone on the inside disabled the surveillance cameras and could've let him in. It makes more sense to me than the idea the shooter strolled up to the front door from the parking lot, dressed like Darth Vader and wielding an M16."

"By a key and inside help—you mean Crenshaw." Roxie moved forward for a closer look.

"If Susan's account is true, it fits. I guess we need to hear what Crenshaw has to say." Tim traced a line on the map from the back of the hill along the ridgetop and down to the school. He calculated the scale. "That's about a four-mile trek. Easy on a dirt bike. But none of the witnesses mentioned hearing a motorcycle. If it had a two-stroke engine, they probably would've. They have a distinct sound."

"But would they remember that in the confusion? What about a mountain bike?" Roxie asked.

"Let's take the unmanned aerial system, see if we can find a trail through the woods that could accommodate a dirt bike or a smaller mountain bike. There doesn't seem to be a trail on these aerial maps, but who knows when they were taken." Tim ran his index finger along his lower jawbone.

"The trail could be just under the treetops. We'd kill two birds with one stone. We can work the car, and find how the shooter got to the school." Roxie tipped her head in the direction of the parking lot. "Shall we?" She gestured an after-you motion with her arm.

In the parking lot, Tim loaded the protective case that held the unmanned aerial vehicle (UAV) in the back of the Suburban. Drone technology was relatively new to law enforcement, with the FBI admitting to using it only eight times since 2006. But he could see where it could be valuable for all kinds of surveillance, including some that could easily be construed to violate the Fourth Amendment. The FBI's system was cutting-edge.

Through a cell phone nexus, Tim could send images to the sheriff's office. Kandar, trained in everything technological, could take over the flight from there, should they get in a position where they couldn't fly it, as long as his cell phone was connected. Designed with vertical take-off and landing (VTOL) capability, the quadcopter could be used practically anywhere. Equipped with batteries with fifty-five minutes of flight time, the UAV could be used for more extended surveillance activities, like search and rescue. Tim brought two additional battery packs for a quick change to extend the flight time.

The UAV was equipped with two cameras. One had both a normal and wide-angle view and a zoom feature up to twelve times magnification. The second camera had Forward Looking Infrared (FLIR) capabilities for seeing in the dark, through smoke or fog, or dense forests or vegetation. With the iPhone application, the image could be read in black on white, white on black, and in rainbow variations.

The UAV's onboard computer had other advanced options. It had a tracking mode, where a person or vehicle could be kept under surveillance and their location sent in real-time to officers on the ground.

Since they were looking for a trail, Tim knew he wouldn't need a warrant. He left any permits required by the FAA to Elias. They would be using the device under the four-hundred-foot elevation limitation.

Tim removed his suit coat and placed the cashmere carefully across the back seat. After making sure he'd chosen the ones rated for rifle fire, he put on his bulletproof vest and tossed one to Roxie. He believed the unsub was armed with an M16. An unexpected encounter could be deadly.

"What's this for?" Roxie asked. "We're just meeting CSI."

"Humor me." Tim grinned, tamping down the trepidation that tightened the muscles in his shoulders. He'd first noticed his newfound caution when he'd married Dani and they decided to adopt the girls.

At first, he chalked it up to his inexperience as husband and father. He needed to keep his family safe and was overprotective. But now he realized he, Roxie, and the team played a dangerous part in high-stakes games. The shooter had killed the school safety officer point-blank and murdered fifteen-year-old children to protect himself from exposure and arrest. He'd eliminate them without a second thought.

Roxie slipped into her vest. "I'm driving," she announced.

"Whatever." Tim tossed her the keys, changed direction, and climbed into the passenger's side. Roxie took the driver's seat and just sat there.

"What?" he asked, instantly skeptical. He seat-belted in and then stared at Roxie, waiting for her to turn over the engine. She hesitated.

"You said we needed to talk." Her right hand hovered at the ignition button, but she didn't start the car.

Crap! He'd hoped they were all square after this morning's talk. "So, at the gym, when you said I was overreacting and that you teased everyone—that wasn't the whole story?" Automatically, he flinched slightly further away from her. He'd asked for it. He'd wanted to clear the air. Now, he had to.

Roxie set the GPS feed to the abandoned car's coordinates and started the SUV. She wrinkled her nose, looked him square in the face, and gave him one of those you-caught-me smiles. "Miguel was there. I didn't let you talk. So, if there was something you wanted to say . . . ."

"Did I do something in Seattle to make you lose confidence in my abilities? Elias invited me to join the team, and I want to work out whatever problem you have with me," Tim said, watching for a reaction.

Roxie shifted and backed out of the space. Tim noticed they had a half hour to get to the abandoned car, according to the estimated time of arrival on the GPS screen. This was as good a time as any to resolve his differences with Roxie.

She left him dangling and didn't say a word until they turned onto the freeway and merged into the northbound traffic. Tension settled between them like a spring thunderstorm.

Tim opened his window a crack while waiting for Roxie to speak. The low hills surrounding the small town were nothing like the Cascade Mountains of western Washington he was used to, but like the mountains, brilliant green spring grass carpeted the pastures and meadows. The maple trees started to bud in the last couple of days, and a light yellow-green halo colored the ends of the branches. There was a delightful earthy rain-washed scent on the air that made him want to fill his lungs. Wild tulips, crocus, and daffodils carpeted the base of the trees at the edge of the forest in bright reds, blues, and golds, like harbingers of spring and new life.

"Were you attracted to me? Back in Seattle, I mean?" she asked out of the blue.

She took him by surprise, and Tim took in a deep breath and let it out. "Odd question. Can I plead the fifth?" He laughed, trying to lighten the mood that had suddenly turned weird.

"No. Not if you want to resolve this. It's not funny. So, were you?"

"Come on, Roxie, that was four years ago." Tim realized by her stone-faced expression she was serious. "You were kind of a big flirt, and everyone was attracted—the field agents in your office, half the sheriff's department deputies, two-thirds of the Seattle PD. Everyone was impressed. They followed you around like wolves with their tongues hanging out."

"Were you one of the wolves, Tim?"

He shifted uncomfortably. *Was he?* There were a couple of times back then he'd given Roxie more than a second thought. She'd made it obvious she wanted more than to be just work-related comrades.

"So, were you?" she asked, breaking the silence.

"Yeah, sure, I was one of the wolves. I just wasn't the alpha." Anyone who watched nature shows on TV knew, if you weren't the alpha in a wolf pack, you didn't get the girl. "Is that why you're mad at me?"

"When I came to you in Seattle and asked you to give me a reason to stay, why didn't you?"

"You didn't want a reason to stay. You wanted encouragement to go. Being promoted to the BAU was all you talked about."

Roxie took her eyes off the road and glared at him for a little too long, and had to adjust her position quickly back in the lane.

"Whoa, keep your eyes on the road, or I'm driving," he scolded her, almost reaching for the steering wheel.

"Everyone thought we should be together. Did you know that? All my friends and co-workers, everyone."

Tim cringed inside. He never meant to hurt her. This wasn't the first time a woman cast him as the leading man in her life's drama without him auditioning for the role.

He'd always respected Roxie. He might actually enjoy being on the BAU team with her if they could resolve this. She was smart, tough, and sexy as hell. But back then, what she wanted and what he did were oceans apart. Getting involved would've been a disaster, and he'd had no desire to set that dumpster fire. He chose not to act on the attraction.

"When we met, I was only three months out of law school and had just passed the bar exam. I had to prove I deserved the job at the DA's office before I could be a permanent hire. I owed thousands for my education. I was a DA by day and a carpenter by night. Any spare time I had, I worked at my family's cabinet shop. I wasn't in a position to get involved with anyone. Whether or not I wanted to didn't really matter."

"I told you I didn't care about all that money stuff." Roxie pulled off at the next exit ramp and stopped. She stared hard at him, anger making the muscles in her mouth twitch.

Contrary to the new normal of basement-dwelling soy-boys, looking for and expecting a free ride, Tim had always worked. Even as a youngster, he had weekend and summer jobs in the family business. He would never start a life and family in debt. *I cared.*

"Well, you sure didn't care when Daniella St. Clair came along and rescued you. You married her for her money fast enough."

"Wow! Is that what you think of me? No wonder you don't like me." Tim ran his tongue over his teeth, tamping down frustration. Like so many others, she assumed he'd married Dani for money. It exasperated him. "Have you seen Dani?" He knew Roxie had and let this comment percolate for a few seconds. Beautiful, intelligent, fun, and successful, Dani had it all. So what, if in the beginning, his motives weren't exactly pure? It was never about money. "Well, you should count your blessings, then. You escaped getting hooked up with a money-grubbing prick."

She shoved the car into park. He slowly shook his head.

Roxie crossed her arms over her chest. "What am I supposed to think?"

"Ask me. Hey, McAndrews, why did you marry Daniella St. Clair?"

"Maybe I don't want to know the answer." The expression on her face said both. She did want to know—she didn't. At this point, what he needed was more important. He had to get them to a place where they could work together without all the conflict.

"You'd been in DC for three years, and I wasn't in the same place when I met Dani. Job probation was over. I had a good conviction record and was up for promotion, maybe even to chief deputy. My brothers and I had taken advantage of the housing market. We'd bought and refurbished a truckload of foreclosures. Sold some. I paid off my student debt. Bought my place, a car, and had a pretty good savings account." Resentment flashed from Roxie's eyes. He'd made it worse.

"You never called me."

He hadn't. He hadn't even thought of doing it. "Why would I? Max Murphy kept all of us in your *wolf pack* up to date on the latest news. You were dating a special agent in the Counterintelligence division."

"Max told you that?" She took in a deep breath and narrowed her eyes.

"You aren't being fair. You don't get to be mad at me. You didn't call me, either." When he said it, he heard a hint of a gasp, and Roxie's eyes sparked. She was as much to blame as he was. But saying so wouldn't move this in the right direction.

After a few seconds of awkward silence, she shifted the SUV into drive. Looked both ways and turned right onto the cross street heading east toward the country road.

"Okay, I'm asking." Roxie glanced his way, a defiant, upward tip to her chin. "Why did you marry Daniella St. Clair?"

Now, he'd put himself in a fix. Tim was no love expert. "I'm as clueless about love as the next guy." He paused. He had to choose his path carefully. Hurting Roxie wasn't in his plans, but clearing the air was. Tim couldn't say with any degree of certainty which attributes made Dani stand out above all others.

"I adore her. She's gorgeous, anyone can see that. Over time, our relationship developed into a deep friendship. It's comfortable, easy, a partnership. We talk about everything. I love being around her, even when we are doing nothing at all. And *she* loves *me*," he said with amazement. The sex—beyond fantastic. He decided he better leave that part out. "Dani is just right for me. I fell in love. She feels like home."

Roxie's whole body heaved with a sigh. "That's so sweet."

Tim felt his whole body relax. *Whew!* "Truce?" he asked.

"Okay, truce." She conceded but reluctantly. "But you can't keep being the center of attention. You're not the only one who can do media interviews."

"Wait a minute. That's what this is about? Why do you always assume the worst? Do you know why Elias asked me to do the press conference last night? Do you know what the press called me in King County?"

She slowly shook her head.

"The brick wall. Mr. No Comment. And my personal favorite: Jackass." Tim chuckled. "He used me because we had to give a news conference, and it was too soon. We didn't know squat. My reputation with the press was already in the trash heap. Elias knew I could hold them at bay. He also knew he could use you—nice guys, later on when he needed to."

She snickered. "I love that. Jackass. It fits."

"Careful. I'm a pretty good-natured guy—I have limits," he warned.

Roxie laughed.

For a moment, he found himself wondering if Jackass did fit. Beebe called him that because he refused to give her media stories before all the facts were known. Roxie didn't have a reason he considered valid. No one had the power to force another person love them.

If he and Roxie could get along now, he guessed he could let her call him anything she wanted to. He'd keep that info to himself.

Roxie followed the voice command from the GPS device and turned right onto the dirt road. The narrow road was carved into the hillside and started to climb from a shallow, grass-covered meadow and ended in a rounded top with its steepness disguised by thick maple and oak forests on either side. As they crunched along, gravel pinged against the undercarriage, and a plume of dust roiled behind them like a rocket's contrail. The mineral smell of rock and the sweetness of the sugar maple forest mixed in the air. Tim started to feel uneasy as they rounded the curve that hugged the hill like a boa constrictor.

"Roxie, slow down. Let's launch the UAV while we have a minute. I didn't see the CSI van behind us. They left after we did, and they'll need a few minutes to set up. Maybe we can find that trail while we wait."

She pulled over. Tim was out of the door in seconds and unpacked the quadcopter from its case. He had plenty of experience flying drones. He used to accompany his best friend, Detective Scott Renton, on weekends when he practiced with one belonging to the Seattle PD. He'd also learned to fly the FBI's UAV just two weeks ago. He called Elias and had him hook into the feed at the sheriff's office. That way, Elias and Kandar could take over command if the terrain became too rough for them to follow the trail and fly the machine simultaneously. Tim connected his iPhone to both the video and audio.

"Get hooked up," he told Roxie.

"You're entirely too enamored with this technology, McAndrews." An annoyed smile played at the corners of her mouth as she put an earpiece in her right ear.

"I know. I'm a big kid. But think of the perks. We can have aerial surveillance without the helicopter noise and expense. We aren't going into situations blind. We can even switch to infrared." Tim guided the drone to the west until it got to elevation. The UAV was no bigger than an eagle and was nearly soundless. The image coming back to his phone screen was bright and crystal clear.

"I've got picture and sound. We are adding the feed to a big screen, and the police radio." Elias's voice came through the earpieces.

"Boys and their toys," Roxie said curtly. Tim handed her his phone. Before she tried her hand at flying the drone, she tossed Tim a dismissive glower.

"Just wait, you'll like it."

"Oh. My. God! This is fantastic." Roxie guided the UAV through a couple of circles before handing it back. Immediately, she linked her phone to the system.

"So, girls like toys, too?" He directed the device toward the peak where they suspected the trail would be.

A loud crack suddenly echoed off the surrounding hills, causing Tim to drop instinctively to a squat behind the SUV. He grabbed Roxie by the hand and pulled her down beside him.

"Was that gunfire?" Tim pressed his earpiece tighter. "Elias. I think someone might be shooting at us."

CHAPTER FOURTEEN

From their position, crouching behind the SUV, Tim changed the UAV's direction. He flew it around the curve ahead to where the abandoned Chevy Malibu was supposed to be.

Up ahead, from the drone's eye view, he saw the abandoned car and in front of it a deputy's cruiser with both the driver and passenger side doors wide open. Red and blue flashed from the lightbar on the roof. The CSI team they were supposed to meet wasn't there. His situational awareness turned on like a vehicle's high beams, and his senses alerted.

Once more, gunfire shattered the silence.

Tim pressed his earbud deeper into his ear.

"10-00, 10-00 Officer down." The report blasted over his earpiece.

Roxie leaped to her feet. Tim immediately grabbed her, forcing her back down. The deputies had been ambushed; that much was clear.

"Damn it, Tim!"

"Wait! First, we get a situation report. We don't have to go in blind." Tim set his hand on her arm and stared at her face until she agreed. He steered the UAV for a better view. "Both deputies are on the right side of the cruiser. They have taken cover on the ground. They are both armed," he reported to Elias, just above a whisper. "I'm going to see if I can locate and identify the shooter." With a simple command from his iPhone, he switched to the infrared camera. A body would radiate white-hot against the cool forest. Adjusting the flight path to follow the estimated direction the two deputies pointed their weapons. He guided the drone over the trees.

"Backup is about fifteen minutes out," Roxie reported. "We've got to help them."

"Can you find out how badly the deputy is hurt?" Tim asked Elias.

"Shot, left arm. His partner has controlled the bleeding. Ambulance is on the way," Elias said.

"Stay down, Roxie," Tim said calmly, even though he could feel his heart thundering in his chest and a rush of adrenaline surging in his bloodstream. "Shooter is engaging the deputies. He may not know we are here."

"What's your plan?" she demanded. "We can't just wait for backup."

Tim ignored her. "Got him!" Tim looked at the white image shimmering on his phone screen. He showed her. "The shooter is up the hill about twenty feet from the left side of the road. We'll circle around behind him." Tim's stare locked with Roxie's. He waited until she gave him a nod in the affirmative.

"Elias, we are going in. Tell Kandar to keep the drone circling overhead. Advise the deputies we're here as backup and to keep the shooter distracted. Once we get close, they need to stop firing, so we don't get caught in the crossfire. We will be the images approaching from the west and hopefully above the shooter."

"Kandar and I have your position, the deputies', and his," Elias reported.

"You'll need to guide us. Once we start, we won't be able to look at our phones. Brush is thick," Tim said, reaching into the open back of the SUV and hanging a set of binoculars around his neck. He handed the other pair to Roxie.

"I'm putting my life in the hands of a newbie. You haven't even graduated from training yet. God! I hope you know what you are doing!"

Roxie held her head in both hands for a second. She gawked at Tim as he chambered a round in his Glock.

Tim smiled at her. "Ready? Let's go."

"Do you even know what you are doing?" She pulled back the slide on her pistol, arming her weapon.

"I do." Of course, the last time he did anything like this, Miguel was his guide. He trusted Elias and Kandar completely.

She took in three consecutive breaths, in and out. "Have you ever done this before?"

"I have," he answered, motioning for her to follow him across the road and up the hill. He lowered his profile by ducking and sprinted to the forest on the other side of the road.

The wild kudzu covering the forest floor grabbed at Tim's legs like a monster in a horror film. No wonder it had been dubbed *the vine that ate the South.* It was everywhere, covering whole trees in its path. The vine's big tri-lobal leaves cushioned each step. Moving as soundlessly as possible, making only a soft rustle, they approached the shooter. Roxie was good at this—her stealth far beyond what he had expected. When Roxie went into FBI agent mode, she was formidable. She kept in sight. With a quick sideways glance, he confirmed her position about ten feet downhill from him. He couldn't have asked for a better partner.

He motioned for her to hold up a second. They each stopped and took cover behind the nearest large tree. The tangle of branches above his head played with the shadows and light on the ground. Tim assumed the unsub was wearing camo, or they would've seen him in person by now. He realized he and Roxie were not, but the sporadic exchange of gunfire confirmed the shooter still concentrated on the deputies below him.

Tim leaned back against the tree and took out his phone. "Kandar, switch to infrared," he whispered and studied the new image that appeared there. The shooter's image glowed white behind some branches. "Looks like he's in a blind of branches and forest litter."

"Do you have a shot?" Elias asked.

"I do. Once I announce we're FBI, our advantage is gone."

Tim heard the sounds of tires on gravel and car doors being opened, then slammed shut. He speculated CSI and more deputies had arrived. He couldn't see them, but billows of gray wafted skyward, and he could smell the dust.

"Reinforcements, or are we in trouble?" Roxie quietly asked.

"Reinforcements," Elias answered. "Tim, do you see the path?"

Kandar had switched the camera on the UAV to high definition and zoomed in. Tim studied his phone. From the bird's eye view, about ten to twelve feet in front of him, the kudzu yielded to a narrow path only a little wider than a deer trail. It ran north to the top of the knoll and south to the road. He stuffed the phone in a pocket in his vest and lifted the binoculars to his eyes to get a better look. Near the west side in the shooter's blind, a cleared, level spot in the brush moved in and out of the tree shadows with the breeze. Tim tightened the focus. A knobby front dirt bike tire stood out black against the forest's green.

"I see the trail, and he's got a dirt bike. I can see the tire."

He studied the tepee shape of the blind, coursing over it inch by inch, branch by branch. Tim noticed the vented end of a tactical rifle barrel snaking its way forward through the wall of the blind. The unsub was getting ready to fire on the deputies below on the road.

"He has a rifle," Tim whispered.

The deputies below the shooter weren't ready. They had not taken a defensive position. But Tim wasn't going to let them be sitting ducks. He stood from behind the tree.

He yelled, "FBI! You're surrounded. Drop your weapon and come out with your hands up!" The barrel shifted to the direction of his voice. Tim belly-flopped to the ground, hoping to be below the bullet's trajectory. He really hadn't expected the guy to give up.

The forest erupted with the sound of gunfire, splintering wood, and fleeing birds and wildlife. Tim heard the sound of the deputies rushing forward in the brush. He crawled ahead, positioning himself to take a shot when he heard the dirt bike engine sputter to life.

"Roxie. Where are you? Roxie!"

She didn't answer. He had only let her out of sight for a second. Adrenaline raced through his system. He called out to her once more. He needed to find her. Was she shot? He moved to a crouch in the brambles. The unsub made a run for it. The bike's engine roared as the shooter dashed from behind the blind and onto the trail. Tim stood. To his horror, Roxie blocked the avenue of escape. She stood mid-trail, gun drawn, and ready to shoot.

The unsub clambered forward, balancing the bike on the rough trail with one leg and then the other. He straightened his left arm and fired two rounds from a pistol into Roxie's chest. She crumpled to the ground. The unsub swerved and blew past her body and up the trail.

Tim aimed and fired two shots. The perpetrator dodged but didn't slow and exploded up through the brush. Tim squeezed the trigger again just as the shooter went airborne at the crest of the hill, almost hitting him. He saw the blood blowback. He knew he'd hit him, but the rider barely flinched and kept going over the ridge.

Tim sprinted after, but the vine grabbed him, tripped him, and sent him headlong deep into its tangle. He heard the woody branches rip the sleeve of his shirt and felt them dig into his biceps and scrape across his left cheek.

With all his strength, he kicked free and scrambled to his feet. When he looked up the trail, two deputies were in pursuit on foot. They would never catch him. But the UAV could. He wrestled his phone from his pocket. "Kandar, engage the tracking!" he yelled.

"Roxie!" Tim raced down the trail to where she had fallen. He dropped to his knees, sliding to a stop beside her. She was gasping for breath.

"Are you hit?" He didn't wait for an answer. Ripping open the Velcro holding the vest in place, he inspected her white blouse underneath for blood. None. He picked up the vest and studied it. Two deformed and flattened bullets decorated the front of her vest like lead buttons. It had held. Tim could feel relief flushing hot into his cheeks. She'd be bruised, maybe have a broken rib or two, but she would live.

"Vest . . . caught . . . it." She could barely get the words out. "Hurts . . . hurts!"

He looked her over head to toe, making sure he hadn't missed anything. "No bullet holes. You're going to hurt, but you're going to live." The thought of internal injuries briefly crossed his mind. He blew out a breath, trying to calm his heartbeat. "I've got to get you down to the EMTs. Can you sit?"

She tried. The second time she clutched onto his arm, and he helped her.

One of the deputies, Red Sanger, returned from the ridge. "We lost him. He's long gone. You okay?"

Roxie nodded.

"Kandar, did you get a lock on the suspect?" Tim asked.

"Yes." The report came back. "He's still heading north through the trees."

"We didn't lose him for long. The UAV is tracking him. It sends coordinates in real-time, and it anticipates his direction of travel. We've got about forty minutes of flight time left." Tim said, lifting both eyebrows in a gesture of hope.

"I think you hit the guy. There's blood on some leaves at the top of the hill." The deputy said.

"I did, more than once. He stood to jump the ridge just as I pulled the trigger. Call it in. Hospitals need to contact us if they get an emergency gunshot patient with .9mm bullet in his—right glute."

A big grin swept across the deputy's face.

"Don't . . . it hurts to laugh," Roxie groaned, digging her fingers into Tim's arm.

The deputies agreed they'd muster forces from neighboring counties. And if they could, they'd establish roadblocks. Kandar linked the deputies into the drone feed. They raced back to their vehicles. The chase was on.

"Can you stand?" Tim asked Roxie.

"I think so. Help me."

"I've got you." He let her lean her weight on him. She moaned in pain. "Screw this. Put your arm around my neck." When she did, Tim slipped his right arm under her knees and scooped her up. She laid her head against his chest. With care, he walked down the deer path, knowing each step might be excruciating if she had broken a rib. She let him carry her until they came within a few feet from the edge of the forest.

"Put me down. I can walk," she angrily demanded. "Put me down, now!"

"Yes, ma'am." Tim slowly let her down until both feet were on the ground, stood back from her, and chuckled. She looked up into his face. Pain, defiance, and stubbornness mixed in her eyes. "I'll help you. Put your arm around my waist."

"Stop looking at me like that. I'm not hurt that bad. I can walk. Quit treating me like some delicate flower," she said, annoyed. Tim understood. He remembered toughing out injuries from his high-school football days. He wasn't sure it was the appropriate response here, but he'd let her try. He could easily change things if she started to falter.

"I'm right here if you need me." He walked with her every step, bracing her when she weakened. He only relaxed when she sat in the open doorway of the medic unit and was attended by the EMTs.

A black SUV pulled up in a cloud of dust, and Elias jumped out of the passenger side door. He jogged over to the medic unit. Elias cared deeply about each of his team members.

Tim stepped back and walked a distance away while Elias conversed with Roxie and the EMTs. Miguel came from the SUV and stood beside him.

"Roxie okay?"

"She took two to the vest. I'll bet she's got a broken rib or two. Her blood pressure is holding, so I'm hoping for no internal bleeds."

"I heard the guy is going to have a hard time sitting down. It's all over the police band." Miguel licked his lips, and a huge smile broke across his face.

"He shot at us without hesitation. I reacted. He stood to jump the crest of the hill just as I pulled the trigger. Shoot at the police, shit happens." Tim tried to sound confident, but in reality, anxiety squeezed his stomach.

Elias joined them.

"Tim, Roxie wants to talk to you," he said. A frown furrowed his brow. Elias was disappointed. Tim felt anxiety begin to smolder in the pit of his stomach. He'd failed to protect his partner.

Furthermore, in the new "woke" environment, every move by law enforcement was scrutinized. No one would care that the suspect fired on them with an automatic rifle and fled. He was now the victim of imagined police brutality.

"Go see what she wants to say to you. Miguel and I will start with CSI on the car," Elias said. "Don't worry, we have drone video. It's a justified shooting." He reached out and squeezed Tim's shoulder.

As he walked to the ambulance, Tim replayed this afternoon's adventure over in his mind. He tried to decide where he'd made the wrong move. He'd lost sight of Roxie for only a second.

He was sure he'd get an earful when they got back to the sheriff's office. Maybe, carrying her to safety was too impatient, too macho. He admitted to himself, but wouldn't to her, that he'd been just plain scared—getting her to medical attention was all he could think about.

He stepped up to the back of the ambulance. Inside, Roxie lay on a stretcher. They had started a line and a saline drip.

"Is she that badly hurt?" he asked both EMTs looking first at one then the other, trying to read their faces.

"It's just a precaution," the taller of the two answered. "She could have internal organ injuries. She has a broken or severely bruised rib. She'll need x-rays to confirm."

"You can go inside," the other said. "But make it fast."

Tim climbed in and sat opposite Roxie. She reached for him, and he took hold of her hand. "You're going to be fine," he reassured her.

"I know." Her eyes were soft, and a weak smile crossed her lips. Tim wondered if the EMTs had administered some sort of pain killer. "I need to apologize to you, Tim. I've been a real witch. You didn't deserve it."

Tim shook his head. "Roxie, don't. No need for the deathbed confession. You aren't going to die," he teased her, a big grin on his face.

"Don't make me laugh. It hurts to laugh. I want to start on a new page. Do you think we can be friends?"

"Yes. Of course. Friends." He was so relieved. He let out the breath he didn't realize he'd held.

"And you can treat me like a delicate flower if you want to."

He chuckled. "Okay. But, you can't call me Jackass."

"Don't make me laugh! It hurts!"

CHAPTER FIFTEEN

The CSI team arrived and began processing the abandoned car. It yielded interesting and incriminating results. CSI found a box of Federal American Eagle 5.56 mm 62-grain NATO rounds where it had fallen between the back seats. They would match them to the shell casing and bullet fragments found at the school.

Tim noticed a partial print in mud on the driver's side floormat that looked similar to the bloody footprints they'd found at the school. "Take the whole mat out," he instructed.

"Send it on to the FBI lab," Elias said. Then he returned to watching the screen on his phone. The UAV still tracked the unsub northward. Deputies were converging from all directions. The unsub had to choose: the freeway or a rundown log cabin-type motel on the frontage road. Tim bet on the motel.

"He's going to take a room. By now, his bullet wound will be taking a toll," he said.

Elias smiled and fussed with his mustache in the way he always did when he agreed. "Once he goes inside one of the rooms, he'll be surrounded. Deputies are almost to his location as we speak, and an FBI SWAT team is on the way."

Tim leaned into the open car door. A flash of color caught his eye. He motioned to one of the CSI team members.

"Lisa, grab that for me." He stood back as the woman carefully retrieved a crumpled bright yellow-green soda can from its resting place, tucked up under the seat. More than once in his former career as a prosecutor, DNA or fingerprints recovered from a soda can brought a criminal to justice. No self-respecting assassin would abandon a car with so much incriminating evidence left behind. Tim looked up the hill toward the hunter's blind.

"This guy had no intention of abandoning the car," he announced to Elias. Elias motioned to the sheriff.

"Leanne, do you know who owns this property?" he asked.

"Bozz. Bozz Bozwell."

"We have probable cause. But it would be good to get his OK to take a look at that blind," Tim said.

"It always works better with authorization." Leanne stepped away and made a phone call. On that point, they all agreed.

"Miguel, you and Tim go up and check it out," Elias said.

Tim turned to Miguel and gestured with a flick of his head in the direction of the hideout.

Sheriff LaCrosse approached, and Tim couldn't miss Miguel's response. He stood taller, squared his broad shoulders, and smoothed a hand over his black hair. An engaging smile signaled an openness Tim had not seen in Miguel before. He was a little surprised but realized attraction, sex, and love were almost always there, simmering in the background of human interactions.

"Damn, she's one beautiful woman." Miguel directed his comment to Tim under his breath before the sheriff could hear.

Tim nodded. The sheriff was statuesque and elegant, even in her unattractive olive drab uniform. Tim suspected she enjoyed the effect she had on the men under her command. She was always professional, never flirtatious. She wore a dramatic shade of red on her lips and fingernails that announced she might be a sheriff, but she was also a woman. Her deputies respected her, but they also were a little in love with her. And now, so was Miguel. Tim chuckled.

"We're going to check out the guy's blind. He fired on the deputies with an M16 he didn't take with him. It could be the weapon he used at the school," Miguel said. "Wanna go?"

Tim felt awkward, as if he were the third wheel on a date.

"I do. I just got consent from the farmer that owns this piece." She motioned to a deputy, and he brought over some protective gear. She handed them each a suit, shoe covers, and nitrile gloves. Tim stuffed the gloves and shoe covers in his pockets, hung the suit around his neck. The trek to the hideout was steep, and the kudzu vine was a massive beast in disguise. He'd almost slipped twice as he carried Roxie down to the EMTs, and the vine managed to take a good bite out of his shirt sleeve. No way the heavy paper protective suits supplied by CSI would survive the climb.

He started up the path with Miguel and Sheriff LaCrosse on his heels. As he ducked several branches, he replayed the shooter's escape. *Why hadn't Roxie taken her shot?* She had the guy front on and wasn't the kind of woman to panic or lose her concentration. He remembered the day the team had gone to the FBI firing range. She had aced the pop-up target test, hitting all the bad guys and leaving the 'civilians' untouched. But in the field, she froze? It didn't make sense.

Tim hated it when his mind took these journeys. It was one thing to be at a desk with a yellow legal pad, where he could write down his thoughts in preparation for court. It was another thing entirely when he barely had time to think before something else happened. He slapped a low-hanging branch away from his face and wiped at his left cheek with the back of his hand. He'd forgotten about the gauze bandages the EMTs had placed over his scratches after cleaning the wounds. The adhesive on the tape was starting to itch.

The clearing in front of the entrance of the hunter's blind appeared just ahead. Stopping at the level area where the unsub had stashed the dirt bike, Tim slipped into his protective gear. He wasn't about to be the guy to contaminate the blind. Without waiting for Miguel and LaCrosse, he stepped inside.

Natural light filtered through the tree branches and forest litter and dappled the ground with shadows. Tim turned on the flashlight application on his phone. The blind covered up a small cave, about twelve feet wide by thirty-six feet deep. It was not a natural cave. There were tool marks along the limestone walls and ceilings. But the scrapings were not new. On either side of the entrance, weathered sliding barn doors hung from a long metal track chiseled and bolted to the solid rock. On the right side, a chain and padlock hung from the door handle. On closer inspection, Tim noticed that the padlock had been snipped with bolt cutters.

A cold, dank, musty smell permeated the air. Tim speculated early settlers carved the cave out of the limestone for fruit and vegetable storage during the winter. It was on the north side of the hill and received no direct sunlight.

The shooter's rifle leaned against a cutout in the wall. Tim walked over, making sure he touched nothing. The unsub left a sole pattern in the soft dirt, much like the bloody ones at the school. Countless shell casings gleamed in the diffuse light and littered the floor. He slipped his hand in the pocket of his protective suit and found numbered markers. He dropped them next to the new evidence and took pictures. CSI would use an alternative light source and get better shots, but he wanted to get his own.

Tim turned and studied the cave. Lengthwise and down the center of the ceiling, individual battery-operated lanterns hung at four-foot intervals. Two picnic tables with attached benches were stationed beneath them. Each table could accommodate up to six to eight men.

Close to the back wall, four bunk beds, each with its own rolled sleeping bag at the end, waited for its nighttime guests to return.

Temporary snap-together shelves lined one wall and were filled with various canned goods and plastic storage containers of freeze-dried survival foods. Cases of individual-sized bottles of water still in their cellophane wrappings were stacked floor to ceiling. Occupying the space along the opposite wall stood a wood stove. Somehow its chimney pipe was vented through the rock to the outside. A pallet of firewood was close by. A large wood meat smoker and a propane barbeque grill leaned up against the wall. *Were the property owners preparing to survive a world war?*

Tim turned as Miguel and LaCrosse entered the hideout.

"Wow. This place is set up," Miguel said, turning in a slow circle.

Sheriff LaCrosse used her flashlight to illuminate the inside.

"Do you know if this belongs to a hunting club, or if any survivalist groups or extremist groups are active in this area?" Miguel asked.

"This is Bozz Bozwell's place. He and his sons are avid hunters. If there are any groups, they haven't had any run-ins with the law," LaCrosse answered. "But, I imagine we have some. Everything is going crazy in the world today." Her shoulders slumped forward.

"Guess we better talk to Bozwell," Tim said. "It looks to me like our unsub broke in. Used a bolt cutter."

Tim considered the sheriff's countenance. From their conversations at the school, he knew Leanne blamed herself for the shooting. Tim wondered if that's what the unsub wanted her to do. "Leanne, you aren't responsible for the school shooting. Every person has a choice to act according to their own conscience or lack thereof. If our suspect shot up the school, he chose that, not you."

"Let's nab this creep and bring him to justice," Miguel added. He slipped his arm over her shoulder. She sidestepped, a rebuff but not a rejection. Tim couldn't keep the smile down and turned away. If Miguel could end his obsession with his sister-in-law, Rachel, and find happiness with the pretty sheriff, maybe that would be a good thing.

Carefully, Tim walked forward into the cave and switched on the hanging lanterns one by one. He kept his eyes peeled for booby traps, though the unsub had probably had time enough to disengage any he'd found. He'd had no time to activate any. At the end of the second picnic table, he found a plastic container that looked like a tackle box. He opened it and examined the contents. Inside were two open containers of 5.56 ammo, and underneath, color photographs. Tim took them out and set them side by side on the table.

Shock delivered a dose of adrenaline directly to his bloodstream. Aiysha, Julie, Marty, and Susan's senior pictures smiled up at him. Tim ran his hand over his chin. *My hitman theory is correct? He targeted these kids.*

Sheriff LaCrosse glanced at Tim's face. She made her way to stand next to him and placed her palms flat on the table to get a look. The panic in her eyes mirrored his own. She reached up to her shoulder and spoke into her microphone to her deputies. "James, get out to Susan Bower's place, right now!"

CHAPTER SIXTEEN

"Fifty-five year old men shouldn't be climbing mountains!" Elias grumbled when he reached the hunter's blind. Tim looked up and smiled at him. Elias was exceptionally fit. Tim believed Elias enjoyed portraying the gruff persona.

Laura Cain, Elias's wife, told Tim at dinner one night a couple of weeks ago that Elias had come up through the Army Military Police ranks. His keen mind and puzzle-solving abilities caught the attention of the brass. When he retired in 2003, he left with not only an honorable discharge but with a written recommendation to any law enforcement agency he chose. Elias was immediately recruited by the FBI seventeen years ago. Within five years, he'd completed a bachelor's degree in psychology, and his immediate section chief recommended he be transferred to the BAU. Tenacity made him finally acquire a Ph.D. in criminal psychology. When the BAU's section chief retired, Elias would be the logical choice for the job.

Now Elias looked around the cave and made his way to the end of the picnic table where Tim, Miguel, and the sheriff stood. He stopped and studied the 'Darth Vader' Motorcycle helmet the unsub had left in his hurry to escape. Tim knew CSI might be able to find fingerprints, hair, and sweat inside to produce DNA.

Elias reviewed the pictures of the teens one at a time. Anger flashed in his eyes like lightning at midnight. "God! These kids are the same age as my daughters."

After he stared at the photos for a few seconds, he looked up. "Miguel, you and Tim go to the hospital and pick up Roxie. She's discharged and is mad as a hornet. She thinks we're leaving her out of the investigation. Take her to the hotel. Then stay with her, because she'll insist she's fine and want to be there when we arrest the unsub. I can't allow it."

No explanation was necessary. Roxie was stubborn.

"Do we know who he is yet?" Tim asked.

"No. The UAV tracked him to that roadside motel and got a great face shot. We've sent it on to support to see if we have him in our face recognition software database." He stared at the pictures again. "Waiting for the crime lab to process the evidence is the hardest part."

"We can arrest him for assault with a deadly weapon and attempted murder of a federal officer," Miguel said.

"True. But if he's the school shooter. I want him to pay for the lives of the kids." Elias tipped his head in the direction of the cave opening. "Kandar and Melissa are collecting the UAV. The sheriff has deputies on stake-out, and we have a SWAT team ready to grab this guy the minute he emerges from his room. Go get Roxie."

—

Tim and Miguel started to drive the twenty miles back to town and the hospital.

"Why don't they just bust in and take the guy down?" Miguel asked, breaking the silence.

"You and I would, but maybe that's why we aren't in charge." Tim laughed and pulled the bandage off his cheek. He lowered the visor to see the scratch in the mirror. It was minor. Sometimes EMTs got carried away; removing the tape hurt worse than the actual injury.

"What did you get out of Crenshaw?" Tim asked, eyeing Miguel's profile. He glanced Tim's way and then returned his concentration to the road.

"He said he wasn't at the school because he was at a Department of Education conference in DC. His alibi checked out."

"Of course, it did. But did you believe him?" Tim asked.

"I didn't. His body language said liar. But we don't have enough evidence to prove otherwise—yet."

"It was a hit. Why would the unsub have the kids' pictures? We need to take 'Trenchie' alive. SWAT busts in, he starts shooting, SWAT takes him out, and Crenshaw skates away with an alibi and all his problems solved." Tim absently closed the visor.

"Not if Aiysha's baby has his DNA."

"A pervert serves less time than a murderer," Tim said.

"Sometimes the pricks get away with it." Miguel flipped the signal for a right turn into the hospital parking lot.

"Not if I have anything to say about it."

Miguel parked, grinned, and lifted his hand to slap Tim's in a high-five. "Let's nail this shit." He took in a deep breath. "We need to put Susan and her family in protective custody for now."

"Just in case the 'second man' is someone other than Trenchie?" Tim asked, expecting no answer.

"Before we go too far down the road on the crazy train, we should run it by Roxie. She has a lot of common sense."

Tim frowned. "She doesn't much care for my ideas." He bit at his bottom lip, released his seatbelt, and left the car.

Miguel grinned, "That's just Roxie."

Tim and Miguel opened the door to the hospital corridor to the emergency room. In contrast to the outside, the sharp scent of medical alcohol wafted in the air.

The reception desk was a semi-circle, so the staff could efficiently handle the constant flow of customers. The small hospital was still new, and everything was crisp, clean, and cheery.

Both men strolled up to the receptionist's station.

"May I help you?" the young woman asked.

"Roxie Stauffer?" Tim made sure she saw his FBI Lanyard. He didn't want to argue with her about not being family. He didn't ask about the injured deputy. He'd heard his wounds were not life-threatening, and he'd make a full recovery.

She looked up at him, studied him, and her mouth dropped open.

"She's our partner," he explained before she could ask her question. He could tell she wasn't satisfied. "Oh, I had a wrestling match with some kudzu vine. I lost," he grinned and shrugged. She immediately twittered.

"Trauma bay three." A blush raced into her cheeks. "Miss Stauffer said you'd be coming for her."

"Thank you, Miss—Warren." Tim read her nameplate. He turned toward the bays and found the large black three on the wall above one of them.

He pulled back the curtain encircling the space, knowing she was impatiently waiting for them. Roxie sat on the edge of the bed, fully dressed and ready to go.

"Thank God. Get me out of here," she said, but when she tried to stand, she quickly sat back down as if she was dizzy.

"What did the doctor say?" Miguel asked.

"I'm going to live," she quipped. She slowly got up off the bed, and Miguel moved in to support her. "I'm discharged, so let's go. Now!"

Tim noticed that even though she would briefly look at him, she was on edge. He assumed she wanted back in action and knew Elias would never allow it. Not this afternoon, anyway. "We've been instructed to take you to the hotel and see to it you stay there."

"What?" she spat, locking stares with him. "How are you going to do that?"

"What's going on with you?" Miguel asked. "Did you break a rib or what?"

"Cracked rib. I'm all taped up. Let's go. Don't you say a word, Tim. Not one word."

Tim narrowed his eyes at her. She was giving him signals he didn't understand. No one wanted to be in a hospital. But there was something else in her eyes. Something unexpected. *Fear?* He got it. No one in their right mind wanted to be shot, even with a protective vest.

"All right. Let's go." Miguel took one side and Tim the other. But Roxie refused to be helped, so they walked beside her.

"Quit treating me like a fragile flower!"

"But you just told me I could," Tim laughed.

"Miss Stauffer, Miss Stauffer." The voice was insistent. Tim turned. A nurse with a wheelchair rushed up to them. "I have to give you your medication and discharge papers. And we must help you out. Don't you want your medication?"

Tim glared at Roxie. Anxiety rose from her body like a mirage shimmering off hot pavement.

"I don't need your help, thank you." Roxie's tone was brusque. He took the small prescription bottle and papers the nurse held out. He read the bottle. It was OxyContin. Keeping Roxie at the hotel was going to be easier than he initially thought. One of these, and it would be lights-out for hours.

"Miss Stauffer, I must insist you go in the wheelchair."

"No, thanks." She continued on her way to the door. Tim gave the nurse an apologetic grin.

"She can take one every four hours for pain. After a couple of days, she'll be okay with over-the-counter Tylenol. No NSAIDs for a few days." The nurse nervously adjusted her glasses on the bridge of her nose.

"Thank you," Tim said. "I'll see to it she takes these as prescribed." A small smile ticked across his lips. When he looked over at Miguel, he realized he was baffled by Roxie's behavior, too.

Something had Roxie spooked and wary, like a child who believes a monster is hiding under the bed or in the closet. She clutched Miguel's arm, coaxing him toward the door.

Roxie hustled toward the exit. Tim thought, if she could've, she would run.

"What is wrong with you?" Tim asked as the hospital's sliding doors closed behind them.

"Not here."

"What's that supposed to mean?" Miguel demanded. Roxie didn't stop walking and wouldn't answer until they were in the parking lot, near the SUV.

"Turn off your cell phones. Put them in the car. Close the door."

Tim gestured with both hands asking why.

"You heard me, turn them off," Roxie insisted. She walked a few feet away from the car to a spot under one of the overhead lamp poles.

"Let's humor her," Tim said.

They reluctantly did as she asked and followed.

"Go ahead, Tim, ask me what you're dying to know. Go on. Ask."

"Okay," Tim nodded. "All right. Why didn't you take the shot? You had Trenchie, but you didn't take the shot."

Miguel moved in closer, the same question sparking in his eyes.

"He is one of ours," she said so matter-of-factly, it sent a chill like a Siberian blizzard down Tim's spine. "I've seen him before."

"Of course you have. That's the drugs talking. We all saw the composite," Miguel explained, a puzzled tip to his head. Roxie looked at him as if he'd just bitch-slapped her for no reason.

"No. You don't understand. I didn't make him from the composite. Why do you think he didn't kill me? He could've. He recognized me. I remembered I'd seen him at FBI headquarters, more than once." She looked at the ground and then back up, her gaze steady, assured, truthful.

"Roxie, get real. He tried to kill you. Where have you seen this man before?" Tim asked.

"Counterintelligence. I remember passing him in the hallway. He's not an agent, but he's an asset."

"Did you tell Elias?" Miguel asked.

"Have they arrested Trenchie yet? Have they?" She looked from Tim's face to Miguel's, demanding an answer like a Spanish inquisitor.

Tim shook his head. The implication mystified him. Miguel had to be right; the drugs they'd given her were making her crazy and paranoid. But then, Tim remembered Roxie had once dated a guy in Counterintelligence.

"They haven't arrested him, and they're not going to." She raked her fingers through her dark brown hair.

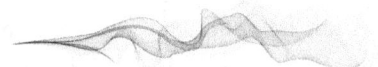

CHAPTER SEVENTEEN

Tim and Miguel were both shocked to silence when Roxie revealed she recognized Trenchie. Every time he tried to come up with a reason she might be wrong, Tim also found the reason she could be right about the arrest. But no matter which way his thoughts turned, he could never believe Elias was involved. He tried to ignore Miguel and Roxie's arguing back and forth about whether or not Trenchie would be arrested.

The streetlamps along Main Street flickered on. Their sodium orange blended with the sun's coppery reflection on the underside of the clouds. Darkness edged in as the day receded.

"Enough!" Tim raised his voice to stop Roxie and Miguel's bickering. "We need to solve the problem." He scrubbed his right hand over his short hair as if it would stimulate thought. "What kind of asset?"

Roxie stopped pacing and stared. "What difference does that make?"

"I don't know. I'm just buying time, so I can think," Tim answered.

"Do you remember his name? Is he an informant or an assassin?" Miguel asked.

"Wait! Does the FBI hire assassins?" Tim interjected. The image of ninjas all in black overran his thoughts. International law regarded assassinations as illegal. But the United States Government argued that their targeted assassinations were in self-defense and part of an armed conflict with defined enemies. He knew the military and CIA used such tactics. The FBI engaged mainly in domestic law enforcement. But then, anything was possible.

"Who knows what Counterintelligence does or doesn't do?" Roxie evaded his question, which he took as a yes. She started pacing again.

"This guy's a hitman. We know that much by the photos we found in that weird cave." Miguel lifted both eyebrows. "If he'd been a participant in the rapes, he'd already know what the kids looked like."

"Good point. Stop pacing, Roxie, you're making me crazy," Tim rubbed his hand over his forehead. "He's not coming after you. He's under surveillance by the sheriff's deputies, and FBI agents are right outside his hotel room door."

"Don't forget, he also has a chunk of lead in his ass." Miguel licked his lips.

"Idiots! They won't send *him* to do clean-up," Roxie growled. "They will send someone else."

"I have a plan," Tim said, ignoring her assessment. Both Miguel and Roxie stopped and turned to him, expectantly. "You and Miguel stay with us in our suite tonight. Dani can get a new room for her pilot. We tell no one what we are doing."

"Not even Elias?" Miguel asked, his eyes dilated with incredulity.

"Of course not, dummy!" Roxie's voice cracked with fear.

Tim analyzed her for a moment. He knew she was scared, but her fear of Elias was unreasonable. However, her fear that another part of a government agency might not have her best interests at heart was not.

"For tonight only. If nothing happens, the arrest goes down, and we all wake up safe and sound, then we tell Elias. I'm giving you the benefit of the doubt, but my offer is for one night and one only," Tim warned her. He clenched his jaw. Elias couldn't be involved in this. He just couldn't. Both Roxie and Miguel grimaced as if his plan was stupid. Tim tossed his hands up. "Do you have any better ideas?"

Miguel and Roxie looked down at the ground and back up as if synchronized. Tim studied their faces, one after the other. They were reluctant but in agreement.

Tim sighed. "Okay, we walk through the hotel lobby. Get on the elevator and push the buttons for our floors. We want the elevator to stop as if we each got off and went to our rooms. Dani reserved our suite under one of her businesses. So, if they are really coming after you, they wouldn't think to look for Dani. She'll be waiting and let us in."

"You can't tell her," Roxie fretted.

Tim rolled his eyes at her. "I've got to tell her something. I'm not going to just descend on her, bark orders for her to give her pilot the boot, and let you stay in his place. If you have a better idea, spill it. I'm the junior guy. Help me out here."

Roxie looked down at her hands and played with her fingernails.

Tim caught himself tapping his right foot to expel the nervous energy building up inside.

"I'm in," Miguel said.

"Oh, me too. I guess," Roxie conceded.

"All right, we're in the Liberty Suite," Tim said. "Now, when you saw Trenchie, you were going to meet up with the agent you were dating, right?"

Roxie screwed up her mouth, shrugged, and finally said, "Yes."

"Call him right now. See if he knows Trenchie's name," Miguel added, with excitement. "We can text him the composite."

Tim agreed. They'd be one step closer to arrest if they knew his real name.

"I can't."

"Roxie! You can, and you will," Miguel demanded.

She replied by looking at the ground and kicking at some small rocks that had come loose from the asphalt.

Tim watched her. Her body language said loud and clear that she was hiding something. He surmised she could call her ex, but she didn't want to. "What did you do to him? Are you the dumper or the dumpee? Tell me his name. I'll do it."

"David Berkstad," she mumbled, never making eye contact with either him or Miguel.

"Oh, crap!" Miguel looked up at the sky and then back at Roxie with a harsh glare. "Section Chief David Berkstad? Is that what you just said? That's the guy you were dating? The Section Chief of Counterintelligence David Berkstad? Jesus, Roxie, brilliant career move! Not only is he one of your bosses, he's fricking married."

"If I needed your sage advice, I would've asked for it," Roxie said, royally annoyed.

Tim groaned and started laughing. "Could this get any worse? And it's my first case in the field." He shook his head. "We're all adults, here. Come on. He'll set his feelings aside and help us."

"You don't know him," Roxie sucked a breath through her teeth. "They don't call him a vindictive prick for nothing. He tried to get me fired when I broke it off. Elias wouldn't have it."

"Like I said, I'll call him. I can come up with some excuse—I can show him the composite, say we are asking everyone for leads," Tim offered, trying to reassure her.

"You better let Miguel." Roxie swallowed.

"Why is that?" Miguel asked, grinding his teeth together.

"He found out Tim and I worked a couple of cases together in Seattle. He assumed Tim *is* the reason I broke up with him."

"I think this just got worse!" Miguel wiped a hand over his lips.

"That's ridiculous; I'm married..." No one had to say anything. Berkstad was too. He was a cheater, and he assumed Tim would be also. Tim locked eyes with Miguel.

"Whoopie! I get the short straw. All right. I'll call him. Let's get back to the hotel." Miguel put his arm around Roxie's shoulders.

"I'm sorry. I really am," she said.

"What the hell. That's what partners are for." He laughed.

When they got back to the SUV, only a whisper of pink light colored the horizon. The hotel bar would be full of patrons and locals enjoying happy hour. Tim hoped no one would notice the ragtag band of FBI agents slinking through the lobby. Tim called Dani and explained some friends were coming by the suite for drinks. He would tell her the rest in person.

They almost made it to the elevators. Almost. Tim groaned when he saw Beebe Knoll and Congressman Patterson sitting in two wingback chairs facing the entry door as if they were looking just for him.

"Tim. We've been waiting for you," Beebe called out and grabbed her purse with Patterson in tow.

"Go," Tim said to Miguel and Roxie. "Go, I'll catch up."

Roxie and Miguel quickly split off and made their way to the elevator.

"Miss Knoll, Congressman." Tim acknowledged them with a nod.

"What happened to you?" Beebe asked, looking him up and down.

For the first time, he decided to check his appearance. The plate glass in front of the hotel's men's shop window gave him a pretty good idea. He should've put his suit coat on, he decided. Though he held the folded jacket to cover the Glock in his shoulder holster, that was all it did. Stains of blood, dirt, and green kudzu plant marred his white shirt. The left sleeve was ripped from his shoulder to the cuff, and a long gauze bandage covered the wound on his arm. The top few buttons of the cotton shirt were undone, exposing the neckline of his t-shirt underneath. His tie hung open around his neck, one side longer than the other. Half of his shirttail was untucked and fell randomly over his belt buckle. Both knees of the cashmere slacks were caked with dried mud from his slide next to Roxie just after she'd been shot. His left cheek sported a red, scabbed-over scratch, and dark brown soil smudged the right.

Tim laughed at the image in the glass. "You should see the other guy."

"Did you make an arrest?" Beebe, never one to leave a good tale untold, perked up and scrambled to pull her phone out of her purse to record the details. Tim put together a mostly true story in his mind.

"No. No arrest. I didn't mean to mislead you. I was up behind the school with some deputies. We were trying to see if we could find anything that would lead us to the shooter. I tripped in some kudzu vine. Nasty stuff." He grinned. It was unlikely she knew the truth. For security reasons and to protect the case's integrity, they had changed to a private channel on the police band radio this morning. Even if Beebe had a scanner, she wouldn't have been able to find out what had transpired this afternoon.

The private channel had sounded like a good idea at the time. But now, Roxie's fears had him second-guessing everything. He would withhold judgment until morning. The drugs could be giving her paranoid delusions.

"So, you have nothing new to report?" Congressman Patterson's eyes turned dark, almost black.

Tim put on his best counterfeit smile. "I wish we did. Sheriff LaCrosse will let us know if there's a break in the case."

That seemed to satisfy Patterson, but not Beebe.

"What's the shooter's profile?" she demanded, studying his eyes. He put on his courtroom poker face like a mask. Beebe had inserted herself in investigations before and wreaked havoc. Tim wasn't about to let her this time.

"We haven't quite got that together yet."

"You mean you won't tell me, don't you, Tim?"

A grin slipped across his face, and he shrugged. "Listen, I'd like to get cleaned up. When I have news, you'll be first to know."

"Promise?" Beebe knew after the years working with Tim in Seattle; he kept his promises. He decided it wouldn't hurt to give her a few tidbits an hour or so before the other newsies, just to get her off his back.

"Promise," he said.

"And remember, we still would like you and Dani to join us for dinner." Congressman Patterson reminded him.

"Yes. As soon as we catch the shooter, we should make that a date." Tim waited a beat, then turned and headed for the elevator.

———

"What a cool liar McAndrews is." Beebe squinted after him as he stepped into the elevator.

"You think he's lying?" Patterson whipped around to watch the elevator doors close.

"He knows more than he's letting on. Didn't you see his team members scatter like cockroaches when the kitchen light turns on? All we wanted was an update. We are entitled to that. The public is entitled to that." Beebe pursed her lips and lifted her chin.

"Come on, Beebe, turn on the charm. I've never seen a man resist you yet." Patterson's voice had a conspiratorial tone to it.

"Charm McAndrews? Been there, tried that, didn't win the t-shirt."

"You said you could get him to talk to me. I need this for my campaign," Patterson reminded her. "It's important for the new legislation I'm presenting next week. We need to get an assault weapons ban through before the session adjourns."

Oh yeah, Beebe remembered. She also knew when she made that promise, she could not deliver. The only thing that mattered was her ultimate goal. She had to keep Patterson on the hook long enough to accomplish that. Twice already, he'd speculated on national TV that the shooter was some gun-toting lunatic, a President Gunderson sycophant. There was no evidence whatsoever to support his theory. The congressman should try his hand at fiction, he lied so often.

Sometimes Beebe worried she wasn't going to be able to keep up her deception. But, every time she wavered, she remembered the prize. Patterson was the fast track. First, she'd become a member of the White House Press Corps. Next stop, the top. SBC's National News Anchor.

"Oh, we'll get him to talk to us. He always comes around," she lied. She had to figure out a way.

CHAPTER EIGHTEEN

Tim slid the keycard through the scanner at the door to the suite. When it clicked, he opened the door. Miguel, Roxie, and Dani sat at the kitchen island, sipping on some beverages. Dani turned to face him. The expression on her face started as joy, but quickly faded to horror. Her mouth fell open as if she wanted to speak, but no words came. He knew he was a mess.

He quickly walked to her and took her into his arms. "I'm okay. I just fell into some brush in the forest." He realized Miguel and Roxie had probably told her the details of the day. He could feel her heart pounding. He moved back from her and tipped her chin with his fingertips, gazing down into her eyes. He took in a deep breath, trying to ease the tightness in his chest. Frightening Dani was never his plan.

She reached up, her fingers hovering above the scratch on his cheek, then withdrew her hand as if afraid she'd hurt him. She stood back from him, inspecting every inch. Tim's glance darted first to Roxie, then Miguel, hoping they would bail him out by confirming he'd only fallen.

Dani fingered the torn sleeve.

"It's nothing. Doesn't even hurt," he tried.

A small laugh, nothing more than a worried lament, escaped her lips.

She moved close and kissed his smudged cheek lightly. "Will you excuse us," she said, looking to Miguel and Roxie for confirmation.

Tim heard mumbles of, "Of course, yes," and then, "Uh-oh." Tim figured his partners expected he was going to get an earful.

Dani took his hand and led him into the bedroom. She closed the door by leaning back against it. For a moment, she stared at him as if deciding what to do. In his prior relationships before Dani, the woman would be yelling, even in front of guests, wailing, and accusing him of being careless and ruining her life. He prepared himself for a tirade and felt like a little boy about to get a whipping from his mother for spoiling his Sunday clothes. But that didn't last. She took his suitcoat from his arm and carefully spread it across the back of the chair. She slowly removed his shoulder holster and hung it over the bedpost the way he usually did. Dreading the fight he expected to explode, he was confused by the sensuality of her movements and touch, and how aroused he'd become.

He knew she hadn't wanted him to take this job. She'd wanted him to join Brad Hollingsrow's firm. It would've been safe. Boring, but safe. She had never said so, but he knew it. Now he'd confirmed her fear. Every time he walked out the door, there was risk. But instead of the tongue-lashing he expected, she was so tender.

"I'll start a bath." Her voice was soft, almost seductive. She kissed his lips lingering there just long enough to send him spinning like she always did. He'd never loved like this before. She owned him and didn't know it.

With her palms pressed gently against his chest, she edged him back against the bed. He liked this direction much better than the one he'd anticipated. She smiled when he sat down, turned, and walked to the bathroom. He heard the water start.

Tim removed his ankle holster, kicked off his shoes, and peeled away the socks. He started to remove his lanyard and tie, but Dani returned and took both from his hands. She set them neatly on the dresser behind her. As if perplexed and not sure where to begin, she stood in front of him. The way she looked at him made desire surge and crest like a breaking wave.

"Are you upset?" he asked, watching for her reaction.

"No. Should I be?" She shook her head. "Did you do something wrong?"

"Wrecked my clothes. I don't think cashmere and police work are compatible."

She laughed. "I thought I was helping. I should've asked you what you wanted me to bring. I made a stupid decision. You shouldn't have to worry about your clothes in the middle of work."

"I'm glad you brought them for me." He tried to lessen her frustration.

"What the heck. I like you better without them on, anyway." She smiled coyly.

He grabbed a breath. "Okay. Help me get them off." This wasn't the first time her openness surprised him. He knew deep in the back of his mind she loved and wanted him. It excited him to hear her express desire out loud.

Dani took his left hand and unbuttoned the shirt cuff, slowly, and then the other. Even that simple act turned up his anticipation to high. His heartbeat quickened.

Standing between his legs, she unfastened the buttons on his shirt, starting at the top and finishing at his belt. He could only watch her, drowning in lust. She pulled his shirt free and brushed it from his shoulders. As it fell away, she kissed his lips like the tickle of a breeze on the surface of a pond. He wanted to strip away the rest of his clothes and race to the inevitable, but he'd learned that Dani's way prolonged pleasure and intensity. She tugged his t-shirt off and took two steps away from him, love radiating from her eyes, fueling his. Color raced into her cheeks, and she traced her lips with an index finger. Her invitation was irresistible. He stood. All he could think about was how much he wanted to be inside her, remembering how it felt, needing to have her now. She stepped toward the bathroom. He followed.

She turned off the water. As he took her in his arms, she rotated to face him. They kissed. He could feel the thrill of her unbuckling his belt and unbuttoning the waistband of his slacks.

"Tim, no. Wait. We shouldn't. We have company. We've got to get back to our guests."

"Guests? They aren't guests. They're my partners. Are you under the illusion they don't know what's going to happen in here? Don't kid yourself. Trust me, they know." He laughed. "They know I can't resist you. And they know where to find the snacks and beer."

"Did you tell them that? That you can't resist me?"

"Baby, I didn't have to. It's written all over me."

With that, Dani yielded. He pulled her blouse free from her jeans and over her head. He smoothed his hands over her curves, feeling the soft lace bra. He felt her nipples harden under his touch. Anticipation like an alcohol rush surged through his body.

"Wait, this is embarrassing. I don't want your friends to think . . . ."

"To think what? I have sex with my wife? They already know it." He grinned at her and drew her to him.

"We need to wait. Tonight. When everyone is asleep." She took his hands, pressed his fingers to her lips, and turned him toward the tub. He looked back at her.

"I don't want to wait. Get in with me," he whispered. "Don't say no." He longed for that moment of connection when she was entirely his, and he was hers. "Please don't say no."

He stepped into the tub of water and relaxed into its warmth. Dani knelt by the tub, took a damp cloth, and lovingly wiped away the dirt from his cheek. She twisted the lid off a jar of sugar scrub. The clean fragrance of sun-dried linen saturated the air. He anticipated the pleasure of feeling the granules caressing his skin. She encouraged him to lean forward so she could massage his back.

"Get in with me," he murmured. Thoughts of her body touching his exploded his need. She didn't answer but stood. Trying to catch his breath, he watched as she slipped out of her jeans, unhooked her bra, and let her clothes fall to the floor. She was so beautiful, every part of her. Her tanned skin was smooth and satiny under the light. He reached for her as she stepped into the water.

CHAPTER NINETEEN

leaned up, comfortable in his sweats, and delighted by the Skype call they'd just finished with his daughters, Tim smiled at Dani. Tomorrow she would sign the papers on their new home, and by the coming weekend, the whole family would settle in together. He looked forward to it and formulated building plans for a treehouse for the girls in his mind.

Every kid should have a treehouse, he thought. He remembered all the happy times he and his best friends had in the one his father built. They'd solved their first mystery there. Maybe that's why the three were all in law enforcement to this day.

Tim slipped his arm over Dani's shoulders and walked with her through the bedroom door to the suite's main living room. Roxie and Miguel were seated at the brown-and-white granite-topped kitchen island, sipping craft beer.

"We should order food. Snacks, dinner or both?" Dani asked, beaming and beautiful. Tim marveled at how contented and how much in love he was with her.

"Both," Miguel chimed in, pouring the last of his dark amber beer into the glass.

Tim wasn't sure Roxie should be drinking with the painkillers the hospital had prescribed. *What the heck!* She was a grown-up, most of the time, anyway.

He couldn't imagine they were really in any danger from rogue FBI Counterintelligence agents, even if Roxie's ex was still pissed-off about being dumped. Tim was well aware, though, that love, especially unrequited love, was one of the top three motives for murder and all sorts of bad behavior.

He poured himself two fingers of Maker's Mark Whiskey in a small glass from the cabinets above the suite's minibar. While the rest of his team conferred with Dani, shouting out orders for chicken wings and lobster pizza, he stared out of the wall of windows looking eastward to the room's deck and beyond.

The clouds had dissipated, and the stars twinkled in the midnight blue sky. He picked out several constellations and found Mars glowing red near the black silhouette of a hilltop on the horizon. He took a sip of his whiskey.

His mind rummaged through the evidence on the shooting like a child through old trunks in the attic. He needed to connect Trenchie with the school principal. Crenshaw had a solid alibi. Bank records might do the trick, but first, they needed to prove that Susan's allegations were true. The DNA evidence was still outstanding. The pictures and bullets found in the cave were strong evidence it was a hit. But, it didn't begin to suggest who'd ordered it. He thought it more likely that an FBI informant would rat out a conspiracist once the money changed hands rather than do the wet-work.

Having the DNA back would give such a better picture. Until then, everything was speculation. He pulled out a leather-topped stool next to Dani and sat down. "Waiting for lab results is pure torture," he said, turning toward the kitchen island.

"I bet it is—for you." Roxie smirked. "You're used to getting everything after all the hard work is done."

"Are you suggesting preparing for trial isn't hard work?" Tim laughed, remembering the hours and hours it took him to mount an effective prosecution in his past life.

His phone vibrated. He wrestled it from his left front pocket and looked at the screen. "It's Elias, so quiet, everyone."

A hush fell like a heavy snowfall over the room. He slid his finger across the answer bar and press speaker mode. "McAndrews."

"Tim, I found you. I've been calling for over an hour."

"Sorry. I didn't hear my phone. I was in the shower, I guess." He looked over at Dani and grinned. She smiled, touching the back of her index finger against her lips as if remembering their kisses.

"I've been trying to get Miguel and Roxie. Can't find them either. There's been a break in our case."

Roxie frantically shook her head no. When Tim looked at Miguel, he just shrugged.

"Have you seen them?" Elias continued.

"Roxie is probably sleeping. The doctor prescribed a heavy pain killer," Tim answered, his frown as fleeting as a nervous tick.

"What about Miguel? His phone is going to voicemail."

"I'll bet he's staying with her. He said he might, just to make sure she's okay. He probably turned off his phone, so it wouldn't disturb her." Tim rolled his eyes and brushed his hand over his hair. *That's the dumbest excuse ever!* Miguel could turn his phone to vibrate and still receive his calls. Tim was the world's worst liar.

"I'm down in the bar. Meet me for a quick drink. My apologies to Dani."

"I'll be right down." Tim disengaged. He stared at Roxie, tapping his fingers on the granite countertop. "How did I ever let you talk me into this? We should just tell Elias."

"You promised me," Roxie said, fear flashing from her eyes.

Dani stood and hugged her shoulders, looking at him as if he were Benedict Arnold. "Tim." It was all she had to say.

"Agghhh! I can't fight you both." He sighed.

"Want me to go with?" Miguel asked.

"If Roxie's right, you'd better stay." Tim slid off his stool, swigged down the rest of the whiskey in his glass, and went to change clothes.

He sat on the bed and placed his backup .380 Walther in his ankle holster under his blue jeans' left leg. He looked up when Dani entered the bedroom. She gently closed the door behind her.

"Roxie told me. Do you think it's true? Will someone really come after her?" She sank to the floor beside him and rested her hand on his knee, looking up into his face.

He petted her hair. "No. I think she's paranoid. But, Miguel and I decided to humor her. So here we are." He could see the worry in her eyes. He wouldn't say so, but if they came after Roxie, he and Miguel were on the list, too.

"I don't want you to go."

"It's just downstairs. Miguel will stay, and I'll only be gone for an hour or so." He helped her to her feet as he stood. "I'll call Mitch. He and Shannon can come to the suite as reinforcements. Would that make you feel safer?"

Dani moved close to him, snuggling up to his chest. "I'll do it. I'll ask Mitch," she said and stood back from him. They'd made the decision together about his career move. Her half-smile was unmistakable; she regretted it. He also knew she wouldn't say so.

"I've got to go. Sooner I leave, the sooner I'll be back." He reached beside him and took his shoulder holster from its place on the bedpost. He slipped it on over his gray t-shirt. For a moment, he embraced her, feeling the warmth radiate from her body. "Are you having second thoughts about this move?"

She wouldn't meet his eyes with hers. "No. I want you to be happy."

He tipped her chin with his fingertips so she'd have to look at him. "There's nothing to worry about. Roxie's just scared, and the painkillers are intensifying it."

"I hope you're right," she said, but the worry didn't leave her brow.

"I'm right," he said but had no reason to. He had no idea if what Roxie feared was imagined or real. They walked out to the living room. Dani handed him a zip-front hooded sweatshirt to cover up his shoulder holster. He put it on and kissed her.

"Miguel, Dani's pilot, Mitch, will be joining you. If I'm not back in an hour, come down to the bar."

—

Tim stepped out of the elevator on the lobby level. He glanced around the space, his gaze landing on each patron and hotel employee, sizing them up like a bunny on an ambush predator's menu. A little gray-haired lady with a rolling suitcase covered in a brightly colored unicorn print stood at the registration counter. A bellman stacked other matching luggage on his cart to follow her to her room. Raymond, the nighttime concierge, stood at the bell station, his face erupting in a big smile when he saw Tim. *Tipping well has its perks.* A man in a swimsuit covered by one of the hotel's signature terrycloth robes headed for the stairway to the pool. Nothing threatening, nothing alarming.

He crossed the lobby to the arched entry to the bar and waited until his eyes adjusted to the dim light. The spicy smell of the Sunday Basketball Buffet reminded him he was hungry. The crowd had dispersed after the game, leaving only two patrons lingering at the bar. Tim studied them. A dark-haired overweight car salesman, in a blue jacket with a Honda emblem on his breast pocket, nursed a whiskey or scotch over ice. The other drinker was a young woman, pleasant-looking, but anxious, as if waiting for a clandestine lover to arrive. At the darkest corner table, he spied Elias and another man he didn't immediately recognize, sitting side by side. Apparently neither of them wanted to sit with their back to the door. Tim headed their way.

"Tim, over here." Elias gestured, inviting Tim to sit. "This is Section Chief David Berkstad. David, this is Tim McAndrews, my newest team member."

Tim paused. His stomach flopped like it did during the first downhill on a rollercoaster ride. The section chief looked exactly like the picture he'd seen on the mezzanine level above his workspace in the BAU. Neatly trimmed silver hair, symmetrical handsome face, but his steel-gray eyes had a hard, unsympathetic edge to them. Berkstad seemed like a man who'd seen too much, lost most of his empathy for the human race, and blocked off any remaining benevolence in self-defense. Did he look like the kind of man who would go after Roxie because she spurned him and compromised one of his informants? Realizing he was taking too long, Tim sat in the only remaining chair, even though it put *his* back to the door.

"David called and came to see me this afternoon because he knows the identity of our shooter," Elias started.

"When I saw the composite you'd sent out, I recognized him as one of my former assets." Berkstad motioned for the waitress to bring another round. "What will you have, Tim?"

"Maker's Mark, rocks," Tim answered. He didn't like the way Berkstad was playing this. Too nonchalant. Too coy. Even after the waitress had returned with the drinks, he still hadn't revealed the name.

"So, who is he?" Tim's words were as direct as his stare.

"Hamish Bounds, former MI-6, retired. Moved to the U.S. five years ago. Currently employed by Blackmark Security. It's a firm that supplies personal security services for some government contracts overseas, but its U.S. operation is mostly private clients. Rock stars, movie stars, high-level financiers, that sort," Berkstad said. Tim thought he sounded too casual. Berkstad took a sip of his drink, not disengaging eye contact. He read Tim while Tim read him.

"You said former. Did you fire him?" Tim swirled the ice in his glass of whiskey. Sensing it would be wise to stay sharp, he decided against drinking it.

"Yes. The man was corrupt. He leaked some highly sensitive information to the press. To the highest bidder, I might add."

"Well, your corrupt leaker guy is holed up in a motel room with a bullet in him. We have enough to arrest him right now. Let's go get him." Tim smiled with his lips, but not his eyes. "The SWAT team is ready, isn't it, Elias?"

Berkstad looked down into his drink. Tim locked eyes with Elias.

"Sheriff is there, waiting on my call," Elias reported.

"The guy shot a deputy and a federal agent. And, we think he shot up the high school." Tim watched Berkstad's face turn deadpan. Tim's danger senses automatically dialed up to maximum. The muscles in his core went rigid, and he shifted in his seat.

"There are other considerations," Berkstad said.

"What other considerations?" Tim asked. He looked from Elias to Berkstad and back again.

"So, Tim, where's Roxie?"

CHAPTER TWENTY

"We checked Roxie's room. She's not there," Berkstad said, narrowing his eyes, and then picking up and sipping his beer as if disinterested. Treacherous and cruel, his smile was like a road glazed with black ice. Was Roxie's fear coming true?

Tim ran his tongue over his front teeth, holding back the sudden rush of anxiety that tiptoed along the top of his shoulders. If the man had gone to Roxie's room, did he also know about Dani's suite? How was Tim going to get them both out of harm's way?

"Why would you go to her room?" Roxie had dumped the guy. Tim knew he would tip his hand if he called or texted Dani to warn her. He glared at Berkstad.

"You dropped Roxie off at her room after you picked her up from the hospital, didn't you?" Elias asked. He silently queried *what's going on here* with a slight sideways drop of his chin.

Tim knew it would be useless to lie, but he needed a moment to figure out his next move. A master at micro-expressions and a flawless interrogator, Elias could size him up in a second. Until he determined whose side Elias was on, the less he said, the less they would know. In the meantime, Tim put on his famous courtroom poker face like a mask.

First he needed to clear away any preconceptions. He realized Roxie's description of Berkstad as a "vindictive prick" could cause him to misjudge the man. What he construed as malice could be jealousy instead. In situations like these, he knew the prudent choice was to wait.

"We just wanted to make sure Roxie is okay," Berkstad said.

"Who's *the we* you're speaking of?" Tim countered Berkstad's coldness with a chill of his own. He considered himself a good-natured guy. Threaten Dani, though, and he became more dangerous than a pissed-off grizzly bear.

"I think you're reading this situation wrong, Tim." Berkstad finished his beer in a quick swallow. ""I understand she took two shots from a .357. Vest or not, that's got to hurt. Are you hungry? I'm starving."

"Last I saw Roxie, she was with Miguel. Maybe they went to dinner." Tim wasn't exactly lying, just omitting some of the facts.

"Tim's right. Who is *we*? And how did you get into Roxie's room?" Elias demanded, squinting at Berkstad, holding back his alarm.

"Did I say we? Sorry. *I* stopped by her room. No answer." Berkstad backtracked.

Tim quickly glanced around the bar. They were the only patrons at the tables. Under the pale lights above the bar, he noticed Lover Girl was still there. So far, her paramour was a no-show. The chubby Honda salesman was gone. In his place, a middle-aged man dressed casually in a red-checked flannel shirt sat quietly, sipping a beer directly from the bottle. *Nice.* Tim figured out the *we*. The two undercover agents in disguise at the bar were Berkstad's.

"I'm going to grab some of the snacks off the buffet before they clear it away." A crooked smile teased at the corners of Berkstad's mouth. He reminded Tim of the type of guy from the movies that would slip you a Mickey Finn, and you'd wake to find yourself strapped to a torture chair. "You guys coming?"

"How about you, Elias?" Tim rose from his seat and joined Berkstad at the buffet table. Elias lagged behind to order another round of drinks.

"So, I'm going to cut to the chase. Are you seeing Roxie?" Berkstad asked Tim while piling some hot wings on his plate.

Tim chuckled in surprise. *Interesting.* Berkstad clearly saw Roxie as a possession. "I see her at work, but if you mean romantically, no. I'm happily married." Tim remembered after he said it that Berkstad was married too. Just because Tim was faithful to and very much in love with his wife didn't mean everyone shared the same experience.

"You know Roxie and I used to see each other. I'm very concerned about her." Berkstad's tone softened. *If at first you don't succeed, try another approach?* Tim thought.

"Did you?" Tim replied, pretending he had no idea. "She'll be fine. Hopefully, she's gone home to rest. She has a broken rib and some bruises . . . ."

"She decided she didn't want to see me anymore when Elias announced you were joining the team at the BAU. Coincidence?"

Tim licked his lips. "I couldn't say. I really don't know Roxie that well." *Berkstad's jealousy was a festering wound.*

Inadvertently, Roxie had embroiled Tim in a mess. Now he had to extricate himself. He had the distinct impression Berkstad didn't give two fucks about his former informant holed up in the seedy roadside motel, but cared a lot about what Roxie was doing.

"Is that why you're here? I thought we were waiting for the go-ahead to arrest the guy that shot up the school." Tim made sure he gave him a look that conveyed his disapproval.

"You worked with her in Seattle, though, didn't you?"

"I was one of the King County ADA's on the Fynn Creek Serial Killer Task Force. Roxie was with the Seattle field office." His plate filled, Tim tipped his head in the direction of the table. Berkstad followed, and both men sat down.

"Did you date?" Berkstad asked.

"No. I was too poor to date anyone." Tim laughed. Berkstad took in a breath as if he understood.

Tim shook out his napkin and placed it on his lap. "So, what's the connection between your guy Bounds and a group of honor students at the high school?" Tim watched Berkstad carefully, observing his response.

"Frankly, I'm puzzled. When I saw the composite drawing and recognized him, I was shocked. Bounds was Counterintelligence. He worked mainly overseas, even with Blackmark. Do you have a theory?" His expression opened up with honest curiosity.

"We do," Elias said, setting his plate in front of his chair and taking a seat. "We believe the school principal, Edmond Crenshaw, may have established a sex-grooming scheme. We have evidence that the children in his honor-student club were drugged and raped. When one of the girls turned up pregnant, he panicked."

"Then, you believe he hired Bounds to assassinate the kids to cover his crime?" Berkstad looked as if he was having a full-blown *aha* moment. For the second time this evening, Tim re-evaluated his initial impressions. Was it possible to be an ethical and straight-shooting FBI agent and a jealous, spurned lover at the same time?

"Yes." Elias took a bite of salad.

"I hate to be the guy to say this, but I found Bounds to be thoroughly amoral. Assassination would be right up his alley," Berkstad informed them.

"Even kids?" Tim grimaced.

A startled Elias pulled his vibrating phone from his pocket and read the screen face. "Ha! Sheriff LaCrosse and SWAT just arrested Bounds. He was trying to climb out of the motel room's bathroom window. We're to meet them at the hospital. Let's go."

Tim dropped his fork onto his plate and stood. He dialed Dani as they hustled through the bar to the lobby. Berkstad followed, coming along for the ride.

When Dani picked up, Tim said, "We are arresting the school shooter. I want you to go to DC. Now." He pressed one of his wireless buds in his ear.

"What about Roxie?" Dani asked.

"All of you. Go. I'll catch up." He disengaged, smiled back at Berkstad, and shrugged. "My wife."

"She's here?"

"Yeah, closing escrow and setting up our new house," Tim answered. "We better get going."

"Going where?" Tim turned behind him to the sound of the familiar voice. Beebe and Congressman Patterson stood there dressed in jeans and hiking boots as if ready for an adventure. Obviously they'd been listening in on a police scanner.

He searched quickly for Elias, who waited impatiently at the hotel entrance. Beebe had him trapped. He had to think of something, anything to keep her at bay.

"Meet me at the sheriff's office—two hours. I'll give you your story. Right now—gotta go." He brushed past her, glancing back to make sure Berkstad was in tow. He caught the look that passed between Berkstad and Patterson. The two men knew each other and very well. Suspicion dropped on Tim like water from a bucket rigged in a doorframe.

CHAPTER TWENTY-ONE

Setting down her phone, Dani stared across the granite kitchen island at Roxie and Miguel. Mitch was about to pour himself a whiskey, but stopped before one drop left the bottle.

"What's wrong?"

Dani realized her expression had set them all on edge. Tim's simple instructions were clear. The tone in his voice, clipped and urgent, left her chilled to the bone.

"Tim said we need to go to DC. *Now*." Adrenaline rushed into her bloodstream and surprised her. She sort of liked the feeling and rolled her shoulders one at a time.

"Did he say why?" Roxie slid from her kitchen stool, alarmed.

Miguel began to pace back and forth along the kitchen side of the island. "I think Berkstad is here. Likely, they've already searched your room," Miguel said to Roxie. "Maybe even mine."

Dani raked a hand through her hair. "I don't understand. Who's *they*, and why would they search your rooms? What are they looking for?" She stood. "We need to go to DC. Now. I have a suite at the Marriot. We can go there. Mitch, go get the SUV and pull around front. We'll take my plane to Dulles. Let's leave everything as if we are coming back tonight."

"Hold on a second. Slow down." Miguel raised both palms. "Did you rent the suite here under McAndrews?"

"No. Under SC Holdings. Is this important?" she asked.

"Very. It will take Berkstad some time to chase that down, connect Tim to you, and you to SC Holdings" Miguel blew out a breath. "We may have a few minutes to think this through."

Dani watched Mitch take a seat across from Miguel and stared at him. More than once, Mitch had helped Tim when he needed it. Now he seemed ready to help Miguel.

"Explain this to me. I deserve that," Dani said, looking from Miguel's face to Roxie's. "How can I decide what to do if I don't know what's going on."

"Repeat what Tim said to you, word for word," Roxie requested, unsettling Dani even more by holding her gaze.

Dani parroted Tim's comments. "He said, 'We are arresting the school shooter. I want you to go to DC. Now.'"

"And you asked, 'What about Roxie?'" Miguel was troubled, only adding to Dani's trepidation. "What did he answer?"

"'All of you go. I'll catch up.'" Anxious, Dani wanted to go, get out of there. She wrung her hands.

Miguel drummed his fingers on the granite counter. "He said 'all of you' and didn't specifically call out Roxie. That means Berkstad is definitely here. And if I know Berkstad, he's not alone."

Dani stuffed her cell phone in her purse and handed the rental car keys to Mitch. Miguel reached for her hand and covered it with his.

"I know it's hard, but try to stay as calm as possible," he said.

"I'm sorry, Dani. You shouldn't be involved in this." Roxie wrinkled her brow.

Dani tried but couldn't stop the questions. "What exactly am I involved in? Then I can decide whether or not I should or shouldn't be."

Roxie took in a deep breath and let it out. "Counterintelligence Section Chief David Berkstad is stalking me. And he's using his rank and power to do it."

Dani groaned. She'd had her own experience with stalking. Many women had. More than the public knew. It was terrifying. "Tim knows this; I take it?" She set her hand on Roxie's forearm in sympathy. "He's protecting you."

"He knows some of it. Not all. I did date David." Roxie swallowed. "Tim and I know each other from Seattle. We worked together on a serial killer task force. David assumed Tim's the reason I broke it off with him." Roxie looked down at the ground and back up to lock on to Dani's stare.

Dani felt a pang of jealousy swirling from deep inside like a midnight mist rising from a forest floor. She hated that emotion. "Did you break it off with him because of Tim?" Her voice was calm, steady, and belied the turmoil she really felt.

"No. I quit him because he forgot to mention one small detail. *He's married!* When I found out and confronted him, he was all weepy and apologetic. Promised to leave her. You know the drill." Roxie rolled her eyes. "I didn't want him back. He wasn't going to leave his wife; he has three kids. He forgot to tell me about them, too. He became possessive and demanding. Tried to get me fired. Tim had nothing to do with it." Roxie pursed her lips into a pout.

"Oh, Lord! We need to make a plan to get you out of here." Dani walked to a small desk close to the entry and against the wall. She took out a pad of stationery and a hotel pen, then came back to the counter. "If I remember the layout correctly, the hotel is in sort of a 'U' shape." She drew a picture on the pad. "We are here." She marked the northeast corner.

"There are emergency stairways at both ends of the corridor," Miguel added, pointing to Dani's map in progress. "The elevators are in the center."

"Our SUV is parked in the front lot here." Mitch pointed to a spot, and Dani marked it with an X. "Here's what I think we should do."

—

Tim thought he'd appeased Beebe and the congressman, but they tagged along after him and Berkstad. Elias had his back turned, talking on his phone, so Tim stopped short, not wanting to intrude on a private conversation.

He looked over the small group. Patterson and Berkstad knew each other, but were pretending not to. It was reasonable for them to know each other. Berkstad was the section chief of the Counterintelligence Division of the FBI, and Patterson was on the House Permanent Select Committee on Intelligence. Why act like they didn't know each other?

Beebe's motives were transparent. She wanted a big, important breaking-news story. She was the most ambitious and brazen reporter he knew.

Patterson was here to get name recognition and face time on TV. He was a politician, after all.

Berkstad's motives were murky. Was he here to help with the investigation? Was he here out of concern for Roxie? If so, why did he need his two undercover agents at the bar?

Beebe took her cell phone out of her purse. Tim figured she was going to get an interview whether or not anyone wanted to give one. Elias turned and, surprised, recoiled as if avoiding the small group.

"Well, well. News travels fast. We have nothing for you on the school shooter at this time, Miss Knoll. I'm assuming you have a police scanner. So, you know two deputies stopped to investigate what they assumed was an abandoned rental car. A white male began firing on the deputies, and he was ultimately subdued and arrested. His identity is unconfirmed at this time. He is currently en route to St. Mary's Hospital, where he will undergo surgery for a gunshot wound." Elias glanced at Tim, and a small smile flicked across his lips.

"Is he connected to the school shooting?" Beebe asked the obvious.

"As I just said . . . we have nothing for you on the school shooting." Elias handed her one of his cordial but insincere grins.

"But, I was wondering if *you* think he's connected—"

Tim stepped forward. "No comment. That's our official position." He scowled at Beebe in a way that finally made her back down. After a few moments, Beebe and the congressman turned to leave.

"We'll be in the bar if anything breaks," Beebe said, narrowing her eyes at Tim over her shoulder. "You owe me, and don't forget it."

Tim looked over Beebe's head. Discreetly keeping an eye on Berkstad's undercovers, he noticed that Lover Girl had left the bar and had taken a seat in one of the wingback chairs closer to the elevator. Just as expected, moments later Lumber Jack sauntered from the bar and casually window-shopped the hotel's men's store. Tim whipped his gaze to Berkstad's face. When the man looked away, he had his answer. They were looking for Roxie. *Why* wasn't clear in Tim's mind. What else did Roxie know about Bounds that made her such a target?

"Will you excuse me?" Tim couldn't let the agents get to Dani. He had to see where they were going and what their assignment was, even though he was pretty sure he knew. "I'll be right back."

"We'll wait," Elias said.

Lover Girl stood and made her way to the elevator. Lumber Jack inched his way there too, picking up his pace when she pushed the call button. Tim quickly assessed each of his adversaries. The woman had a pistol concealed under her jacket. She was a right-handed shooter. The man's weapon was stuffed in the waistband of his jeans—mid-back and covered by a loose fold in his shirt. Tim lengthen his stride, breaking into a jog as the elevator bell chimed. He nodded at each of them as the doors began to slide open.

"I'm dying for Mexican food." Dani's voice took him by surprise. She and Shannon stepped off the elevator. When she saw him she said,"-Tim! I thought you were out—working." She teased him and slipped her arm through his.

The two undercover agents stepped inside the open car.

"Are you going up?" Lumber Jack asked.

"No. He's going to dinner with us," Dani said, laughter in her voice. She encouraged him to turn toward the main door. Tim's first instinct was to ask about Miguel and Roxie. When he started to speak, Dani quickly shook her head no. He took hold of her hand and shifted his fingers to feel the pulse at her wrist. Elevated. She was stressed. As they walked through the lobby, he kept struggling to read her. Was Roxie already safe? Dani's behavior was way out of her norms. When Berkstad approached them, he had no choice but to let this little drama play out.

"Who are these lovely ladies?" Berkstad asked, acknowledging Shannon but devouring Dani with his stare.

Tim pulled Dani close to his side. At least this would dispel any idea Berkstad had that Tim had a romantic interest in Roxie. "This is my wife, Dani, and her friend, Shannon. This is David Berkstad. You remember Elias Cain."

"Nice to meet you, David. Hi, Elias." Dani graciously included everyone in her greeting.

"What are you ladies up to?" Berkstad asked.

"We're going for Mexican food. Oh, we should go. Shannon's husband just pulled up out front." Dani said. Tim guessed Berkstad rattled her calm.

Tim looked out to the drive under the portico. Mitch pulled a silver SUV to a stop.

"We'll join you," Berkstad said, glancing over at Elias for approval.

"Sure. We can. Our suspect won't be available for questions for hours. Sheriff LaCrosse just advised me he's in surgery now," Elias reported.

"Oh, no. I promised I would never interfere with Tim's work." Dani's voice had a barely perceptible tremor to it. Two plus two just came together in Tim's mind. Roxie was in that SUV.

In the background, Tim heard the ding of the elevator. Berkstad looked past him, and Tim followed his gaze. Lover Girl disembarked from the elevator and shook her head once. Berkstad just got confirmation that Roxie wasn't in her hotel room. It wouldn't be long before he connected the dots. Tim had to do something.

"I don't know about you, but I want to be there when our suspect comes out of recovery. We can all go to dinner, another time, when we get this guy behind bars. You go on ahead, Dani." Tim knew this was weak. Elias called BS with his scowl.

"That's a great idea. Then we won't have to rush." Dani smiled sweetly. She was better at the game than Tim expected. "We should go, Shannon." She rolled up on her toes and kissed Tim's cheek. "Another time?" Dani waited for a second for Berkstad's answer. When he nodded, she grabbed Shannon's hand, and they dashed for the car. Dani went around the car to take her seat behind Shannon in the back passenger's side. Tim noticed, but did Berkstad? Dani made sure he didn't have the chance to see who else might be hunkered down in the back seat.

Mitch drove away, but the direction of his turn at the exit point was wrong. Tim's thoughts raced. He could swear the man in the camo baseball cap who just walked out of the hotel gift shop and turned left down the corridor to a back door was Miguel.

"Good. I'm not in the mood for Mexican food," Elias said. "Let's eat here while we wait for Bounds to come out of surgery."

Tim returned his attention to Elias. "Okay," he agreed with a smile.

They made their way to the reception desk in the hotel dining room. While waiting for the hostess, Tim took several menus and passed them out.

"I'm ready for a big, juicy steak," Elias said.

Berkstad looked up. His smile suddenly faded. "Son of a bitch! Roxie was in that SUV!"

CHAPTER TWENTY-TWO

When the Cessna 340 started its take-off roll, Dani felt like she could finally relax. Never expecting to be caught up in anything like this again, she leaned back into the cream-colored seat and breathed in the scent of leather. Her hands trembled like they did when she had one too many cups of coffee.

"I don't think we were followed," she said, looking across to Miguel and Roxie in the forward-facing seats in the grouping. "We will be in DC in twenty minutes." She heard the landing gear begin its retraction into the belly of the beast. The steady thrum of the propeller-driven engines relaxed her even further.

Miguel opened the plastic bag from the hotel gift shop and handed out the pre-paid phones. Dani's heart had furiously pounded when he'd dashed in to get them. At that moment, she'd starred in her best role yet. Berkstad's failure—he was a slut. She'd easily distracted him with subtle flirtations. At first, Tim had been confused, but she reassured him by squeezing his hand.

She knew Miguel had planted Roxie's and his FBI cell phones back in their hotel rooms. It was part of their scheme. Berkstad could trace Dani's movements by tower pings, but not theirs. She worried about the

Cessna's flight plan, but proving Roxie and Miguel were on the plane with her would be tricky. No one had seen them board.

"I can't go home," Roxie said, sitting forward to the edge of her seat and repeatedly smoothing her hands down the pant legs at the thighs.

"We have options," Dani answered. "If worse comes to worst, Mitch can fly you to Walla Walla tomorrow. My sister, Rachel, lives at our vineyards there. We can put you in one of the bed-and-breakfast suites. You can heal up and have a quiet vacation."

Miguel straightened in his seat. Dani realized as she watched him look down to the carpet and slowly back up to her eyes, she'd suggested the wrong thing. Not for Roxie, but for Miguel. He still loved Rachel, and after all these years, it still pained him to think of her. Dani briefly closed her eyes in empathy. Rachel had mishandled the break-up. She would've saved them both so much heartbreak if she'd just told the truth. Dani adored her father, but he had been a tyrant while alive. He forced Rachel to end the affair with Miguel and bought her a more *suitable* husband. Still, Miguel worshipped Dani's father. His love was misplaced.

"I'm not going to Walla Walla. I can go to my parents' house in Connecticut."

"Rox, that's the first place Berkstad's going to look," Miguel retorted.

"If he's already sent agents, then he'll know I'm not there."

"He'll set up a stakeout. Don't be silly," Miguel argued.

Dani looked back and forth between their faces. "Is Berkstad connected to the school shooting? I'm so confused."

"I wish I knew." Roxie nervously twisted a lock of her dark brown hair around her index finger. She stared out the window. "I connect David and Bounds. When I'd meet David for lunch or whatever, I often saw Bounds leaving his office. I'm the one who saw him in the FBI hallway."

"Miguel?" Dani asked, wanting to know his thoughts.

He briefly flicked his wrists, turning his palms up. "Roxie is an eyewitness to some sort of relationship between the two men. If this turns out to be an assassin-for-hire deal, David Berkstad will need to answer some serious questions."

"Until the forensics come back from the lab, we're stuck." Roxie returned her gaze to the window.

"Are you expecting Berkstad to be implicated by the forensics?" Dani asked.

"Wouldn't be surprised." Roxie's bitterness flashed from her eyes.

"Okay, let's stick to our original plan, get Roxie settled somewhere safe for tonight." Miguel's brow pinched with worry.

"I've arranged for one of my household staff members to take you in. My ranch manager and his wife arrived this afternoon to help me set up the new house tomorrow," Dani said. "Mark Settle and his wife, Winona, will meet you at the airport and take you to the hotel in DC. You will stay with them in their suite and then go with them to the farm. I'll meet you there in the morning. By then, Tim and Miguel will have figured out our next move."

"If I survive, you mean."

"Rox, we are assuming Berkstad means you harm. What if he wants to offer protection instead? All we need to do is keep you safe until we figure out his intentions," Miguel reasoned.

"I need you to stay with me, Miguel," Roxie pleaded.

"We have got to stick with the plan. Berkstad saw Dani, Shannon, and Mitch leave for dinner. Dani, Shannon, and Mitch have to come back from dinner."

"He didn't see you, Miguel. Please stay," Roxie countered. Dani understood. If she were in trouble, she'd want Miguel to be there to protect her. That is, of course, if she couldn't have Tim.

Dani felt the Cessna bank left. Mitch had entered the downwind leg of the landing pattern. They had chosen this small general aviation airport on the outskirts of DC because it had no tower. Air traffic was light, and handing Roxie off to Settle's care would be less likely to be witnessed.

Dani felt a rush of adrenaline squeeze at her stomach as the landing gear lowered. Its vibration and rumble filled the cabin. Mitch turned base leg. In minutes they would be on the ground. Dani had arranged to meet Mark Settle next to the hangars now in view off the left wing. Out of her window, Dani saw the headlights of Settle's car flash twice, wait for a beat and flash again. Mitch turned into the wind on the final approach. Smooth as satin, Mitch touched down, wheels rolling on the tarmac without even a bounce.

Miguel immediately unbuckled his seatbelt and studied the hangar parking and taxiway as they passed by. When the 340 slowed to ramp speed and turned a one-eighty, traveling back toward the hangars, Miguel shifted to the other side of the cabin. Dani thought the little airport seemed eerily dark and abandoned. A fuel truck was parked at the northernmost end of the dimly lit terminal building, but the cab was empty. She imagined specters in every shadow.

Miguel flicked the strap on his holster and drew his Glock as the Cessna came to a stop in the transient parking. From between two hangars to the airplane's right, a black SUV with tinted windows inched forward. Dani unbuckled and went to the front of the cabin and released the retractable stairs. She opened the door. The cool, damp, evening air whooshed in, filling the fuselage. Dani stepped back. Miguel motioned for Roxie to come ahead.

The SUV pulled up close to the stairs. Miguel disembarked. Pistol drawn, and at the ready, he swept in both directions. Roxie trailed him down the steps. Once on the asphalt, she quickly slid through the SUV's open door. Miguel hesitated and looked up at Dani as if deciding what to do. Dani shrugged. The only person that could determine what was best for Roxie was Roxie.

The choice made, he jumped into the SUV. They sped away.

Dani leaned against the bulkhead, her whole body trembling. She felt like a character in a spy movie, and a nervous laugh tickled her throat. She closed the cabin door and pressed the button for the stairs to neatly fold into their compartment. Once the light confirming the stairs were stowed and the door locked turned green, Dani took her seat.

———

As he and Berkstad walked through the hospital, Tim studied the corridor. The facilities were spotless and modern. Though the walls were painted the typical institutional green, each patient room had a window and sliding door facing the common hallway. They stopped outside Bounds's room and looked through the glass. On the opposite side of the room, a plate glass window revealed a view of the forest-covered hills abutting the town's edge. Tim and Berkstad stayed outside the room and watched the doctor and Elias discussing Bounds's prognosis through the vertical blinds. Though Tim couldn't hear the conversation, he could guess what was being said. They weren't going to get any information from him tonight.

Sheriff LaCrosse walked up to Tim and looked Berkstad over skeptically. "Where were you, Tim? You missed all the fun. The bathroom window was too small, and our suspect got his . . . bum stuck. SWAT had to pull him through." She laughed.

"Leanne, meet FBI Section Chief David Berkstad, and David, this is Sheriff LaCrosse." Tim grinned at her. "Stuck. Gee, that's too bad."

"Kinda ruined his escape plans," she said. A lovely smile broke like a wave across her full red lips. She leaned forward and offered her right hand to Berkstad. "Call me Leanne."

She turned to Tim. "How's the patient?"

"Still out cold," Tim answered, disappointed.

"I've assigned Deputies Greenwood and Sparks to guard duty," she reported.

"I'll send an agent from my team to help," Berkstad said. Both Leanne and Tim stared at each other. The sheriff had invited the FBI in as profilers. Berkstad had no authority here. *Since when did Counterintelligence get involved in local domestic cases?* Tim thought. *Is terrorism involved?*

"That's okay. We've got this." Leanne squared her stance and lifted her chin slightly in defiance. Tim agreed. *Just who did Berkstad think he was?*

The sliding door opened, and Elias followed the doctor out into the hallway. He sighed. "Might as well go back to the hotel and get some sleep. We won't be able to interview Bounds until morning."

Tim followed Elias's glare. "Are you still here, David? Were you unable to connect with Roxie?"

Berkstad shook his head.

Elias took the clipboard the doctor held out to him, quickly read it, and signed the bottom. Apparently, the FBI was paying the hospital bill.

Tim couldn't resist. The questions in his mind had overpowered all other thoughts. "Do you suspect the school shooting was a terrorist attack?"

Elias stopped, dropped his hand, clipboard and all, to his side, and faced Berkstad. "Do you?"

"We have to explore every possibility," the man answered. There was a flash of resentment in his eyes. He didn't like Tim asking that question. Suddenly, Tim felt relieved he'd ask Dani to get out of town.

"Oh, crap. Don't say anything to the press until we can confirm," Sheriff LaCrosse said, adjusting her ball cap on her head, twisting and pulling the spiral curls through the opening in the back, making a ponytail.

"Nothing in Bounds's background check suggests he's a terrorist." Tim watched Elias. The boss believed Berkstad was lying.

"Would you like to go for a drink and discuss it, Sheriff LaCrosse? Leanne?" Berkstad ogled the pretty sheriff, top to bottom. Tim rolled his eyes and scrubbed a hand over his hair.

She looked over to Elias in desperation.

Elias handed the clipboard back to the doctor and cleared his throat. "Sheriff LaCrosse is going to ride back to the hotel with me."

CHAPTER TWENTY-THREE

T im's body was exhausted, but his mind wouldn't quiet down. He closed the door to the suite, peeled off his sweatshirt jacket, and removed his shoulder holster, slinging it over the back of one of the kitchen island chairs.

On the counter next to the sink, an empty shot glass sat next to one of the bottles of Maker's Mark Reserve he'd ordered from the concierge a couple of days ago. He walked over and inspected it. The bottle's red wax seal was broken, but bottle seemed full. With Berkstad's undercovers wandering the hotel, he wasn't about to take any chances. He dialed in the combination on the lock on the minibar and retrieved the second bottle. He took down a fresh glass and poured himself a healthy shot, and pounded it in one swallow.

Tim stretched, picked up the bottle and glass, and set them in front of one of the stools. He sat. *Damn Roxie!* He was worried and knew he shouldn't have involved Dani in this. Anxiety rolled with the whiskey in his stomach. Until he had a clear understanding of Berkstad's motives, he knew it was best that she disappear. She'd volunteered to help, but even though she thought she understood the danger, she didn't. Hell, neither did he. If he didn't hear from her in the next few minutes, he was going to call her.

The alcohol was affecting his thoughts. He'd quickly fallen back into the routine of holding Dani at night. He loved it and the warmth and softness of her skin against his and didn't want to be without her tonight. He sighed and belted back another shot of whiskey. It wouldn't be long before his mind would numb, and the sleep he longed for would come. Until then . . . .

He reached for his jacket and fished his phone out of the pocket. He stared at the blank screen. If he called Dani and Berkstad listened in, he'd give their location away. The need to know she was safe ate at him relentlessly. It was an ache that even two shots of whiskey didn't dampen. He scrolled over to the notes he'd taken on the case. If she didn't phone him in fifteen minutes, he was going to call her, no matter the consequences.

Tim tried to read through his case notes. He was too tired to think about the case, too wired not to. He massaged the bridge of his nose between his index finger and thumb.

"You should come to bed."

Surprised, Tim looked up, and Dani stood in the doorway to their bedroom.

"What are you doing here? We agreed you should go to DC." A wave of relief flushed through his veins. She was here, safe. He hadn't even thought to check the bedroom when he arrived in the suite. Though it added a new set of problems to his plate, he was glad. He wanted her here.

"I know. You're going to tell me I never do what you ask me to." Dani coyly bit at her bottom lip.

He nodded, chuckling to himself. She was right, but he admired her independence.

"I was so scared. But now, I hate to admit it, but it was fun. Like being in a spy movie." She hugged herself, satisfied.

"Yeah? It was dangerous. I never should've let this happen," he admonished himself. Dani laughed. He recognized early on in their relationship he was as likely to change her as she was him. So, he'd taken his dad and older brothers' sage advice; he let himself just love her. She walked to him, and he twisted on his stool to face her.

She wore one of his t-shirts—too big for her, but just small enough to look incredibly sexy. Her honey-brown curls spilled over her shoulders and down her back. One look at her long, shapely legs, and he was instantly aroused. Her smile and eyes in concert beckoned him to make love to her. That was an invitation he couldn't resist.

"Are you mad at me?"

"I'm never mad at you." He was often amazed, however, when he should be mad at her, how quickly she turned him to mush. He pulled her close and enveloped her in his arms. They kissed, and the scent of her perfume teased his nostrils with notes of roses and jasmine like a warm summer night. She did more to quiet his thoughts than shots of whiskey ever could.

"Come to bed," she whispered against his cheek, her soft lips lighting up every nerve ending in his body with the promise of pleasure. She stepped back from him and took his hands in hers, urging him toward the doorway.

He slipped off the stool but grabbed his shoulder holster as he passed. When they were next to the bed, he hung his Glock within reach on his side.

"I expected you to stay in DC. What made you come back?" he asked. As she untucked his shirt, he enjoyed the rush of excitement. He closed his eyes and relished her touches like savoring the first tart and sugary bite of a ripened peach.

"You. I didn't want to be away from you." Between kisses, she said, "Miguel thought since Berkstad saw Shannon, Mitch, and I leave, the three of us should come back so he'd assume Roxie was never with us."

Tim lifted his arms so she could remove his t-shirt. He kicked off his shoes. "He's pretty sure Roxie was with you. He said so. Mitch and Shannon are here?"

"In their room." Dani gestured toward the other side of the suite. "Then, by the three of us coming back together, acting all innocent, did we throw him off?"

"Probably not." He drew her close. She pressed her palms on his chest and pushed him back into the bed pillows.

"Not even a little?" She unbuckled his belt. When she slipped her fingers under his waistband to unfasten his jeans, a pang of desire swamped him, and he had to catch his breath.

"Probably not," he repeated. "I never should've allowed Roxie to suck Miguel and me into her drama."

Dani stopped and sat down beside him on the bed. "Do you think Berkstad is going to try to hurt Roxie?"

At that moment, he really didn't care. All he could think about was Dani, touching her, kissing her, loving her, and her loving him. He grabbed her and pulled her down on top of him. She giggled.

"Tim!" She scolded him, but it was playful. She wanted him, too. He understood she needed an answer to her question. She was afraid for Roxie. But he had to admit he wasn't sure of Berkstad's motives.

"I don't know. Roxie can connect our suspected shooter and Berkstad. If Berkstad is involved, she is a real inconvenient ex-girlfriend and a big problem." He reached up and touched one of the curls that had fallen across her cheek. Dani was everything to him; home, family, love. Just as they were about to get their home settled, he'd jeopardized it all by buying into Roxie's unproven fear.

"Ummmm." She straddled him and once again started to undo his jeans. Another wave of longing rocketed through him. He untangled from her, sat on the edge of the bed, and stripped away the rest of his clothes.

Dani watched. "You're so handsome, so perfect." She reached for him. Gently, he lifted the t-shirt over her head. Free of the fabric, she tossed her hair, and long satiny brown curls spilled over her shoulders. The incandescent light from a bedside lamp painted her smooth flesh in pink tones, like a sunrise.

"Do you think Roxie will be okay?"

"Dani, I don't want to talk about Roxie." With a light touch, he eased her back into the pillows and trapped her beneath his body. She purred with excitement, and he immersed himself in loving her.

CHAPTER TWENTY-FOUR

Where was *he* going in the middle of the night? Beebe Knoll glanced at the bedside clock; its illuminated green numbers read 11:36 p.m. She pretended to be asleep while Congressman Patterson quietly dressed in the dark. He was sneaking. She knew it because he seemed to pause to listen to her breathing. Beebe would be damned if she was going to let this little weasel cheat on her before she met her goal.

Once, just once, she wanted a faithful boyfriend. The fact that she didn't love Patterson was a minor, fleeting thought. When she got her promotion to the White House Press Corps, she'd hand him off to the next woman in line without looking back.

When she heard the hotel room door close, she popped out of bed, turned on the light, and threw on her jeans and a sweatshirt. She crammed her feet into her slip-on Sketchers, fixing the smashed-down heels as she headed for the door. She hung her purse across her body and snatched her phone from the dresser. For a second, she paused before opening the entrance to the hall. She grabbed the black leather case with the camera and the high-powered lens and slung it over her shoulder, too.

She huffed out a breath and slowly opened the door. *Crap! Hotels should oil their damn hinges!* She crept into the hallway. When she heard the elevator chime and the doors roll open, she knew that Patterson wasn't on to her.

On tiptoes, she dashed down to the turn in the hallway and braced herself against the wall that shielded her from Patterson's view. Sliding with her back against the wall, she reached the corner and peeked. Patterson stepped into the elevator, but not before looking guiltily around him. *What a twit! He is cheating for sure!*

She would lose him if she waited for the lift to come back up, so she decided to run for the opposite end of the corridor and take the emergency stairs. The lobby was only two flights down.

She ripped the door open and leaped down the stairs two at a time. She pushed through the lobby door just as Patterson reached the concierge desk at the north end of the hotel's main entrance area. Beebe ducked back when he looked behind him, seeming to shake off that *I'm-being-followed* feeling. Whatever he was doing, clearly, he didn't want to be caught.

Interesting! The concierge handed him a set of keys. He'd arranged for a rental car and wasn't engaging his usual car and driver. *Ooh! The sneaky dickweed was definitely cheating and making sure no one would witness it!* Anger was beginning to seethe inside her brain.

After Patterson was through the door to the outside, she strolled nonchalantly into the lobby, stopping and pretending to admire the new floral arrangement. She never really let him out of her sight.

Patterson slid into the driver's side of the silver Chevy Malibu and drove away. Beebe ran for her Honda parked in the lot in front of the hotel. She threw her bags across the console onto the passenger seat, slammed the door, and started the engine. Hurrying to catch up, she remembered he'd turned right out of the hotel driveway onto the main street.

She'd been too hasty. Now, she had to hang back for a few seconds, so he wouldn't notice her in his rearview mirror. At this time of night, in this little burgh, they'd rolled up the sidewalks hours ago. She and Patterson were the only ones on the road.

Beebe was taken by surprise when Patterson turned into the hospital driveway. A sense of shame suddenly swept through her like an ocean squall. Was Patterson sick and embarrassed to tell her, or out of kindness, letting her sleep? Why did her mind always jump to the worst possible conclusion? Maybe the man wasn't cheating after all.

She stopped for a moment to reason. He didn't seem sick. He didn't have a fever, or she would've noticed. She pulled into a parking space, took out the camera, and attached the telephoto lens. Sinking low in her seat, she braced the long lens against the dash and watched. He got out of his car, looked around him, and strolled to the backside of the three-story building. Beebe quickly hung the camera around her neck and followed. She was a top investigative reporter, after all. Patterson was nuts if he thought she wouldn't investigate him. She rounded the corner just as he slipped through a side entry.

Guessing the door would lock automatically, she sprinted to reach it before it shut. She grabbed the handle just as the latch mechanism started to retract at the strike plate. Leaning forward and catching her breath, she pulled the door slightly ajar, opening it enough to have a look-see.

Patterson stood about halfway down a dimly lit corridor in front of a closed door. He began to pace. When he glanced in her direction, she twisted out of sight with her back to the door yet still holding the handle. He didn't seem to notice. She gave it a second, then snuck a quick look.

"About time." She heard him growl.

A male voice, gravelly and just above a whisper, answered. "Sorry."

As Patterson followed him into the room, the rest of the conversation faded.

She slipped inside into the hallway. There were two rooms on each side, and obviously, these weren't patient rooms. A sign on the first door read BILLING AND ADMINISTRATION. She continued and stopped in front of the door Patterson had entered. PHARMACY EMPLOYEES ONLY was emblazoned in red together with DO NOT ENTER on the sign on this door. She tried to listen through the wood but could hear nothing.

Was Patterson a prescription drug addict? She'd never seen him use anything except alcohol. Not even aspirin. In relationships, though, you never knew what you didn't know.

Beebe heard the door handle rattle. *Oh! Shit!* She scrambled, looking around for a place to hide. Across the hall, only a few feet away, a medicine cart would provide cover. She bolted for it and ducked behind it just as the door opened. Patterson and another man, a doctor, or a nurse, maybe the pharmacist, stepped through.

Squeezing her eyes shut, holding her breath, trying not to make a sound, Beebe tucked into a tight fetal ball behind the cart. Her heart pounded a million miles a minute. She heard footsteps; both men were moving away, down the hall toward the door to outside. She dared to look. She lifted the camera and positioned the lens between the shelves in the cart. Patterson held the door open with his foot. The forced-air heater started up noisily, and she had her chance. She pressed the button and snapped pictures at sixteen frames per second. He reached inside his jacket pocket, retrieved an envelope, and handed it to the other man.

Another envelope? Her need to know kicked her investigative-reporter gear into high. The package was the same size and shape as the one he'd given Shadowman through the hotel room door Saturday morning. *What is in those envelopes? Money? And why is Patterson passing them out?* OMG! Patterson is buying drugs. Now, that's a breaking news story.

Beebe sat back on the floor and waited until the second man re-entered the pharmacy. Deep in thought, she stood and walked to the exit. When she rounded the corner to the parking lot, she watched Patterson back out of his space and drive out to the main street.

Suddenly, she gasped. How was she ever going to get back to the hotel and their room before he did? She ran to her car, started the engine, and called up her navigation system. She had to find a back street to the hotel, and fast.

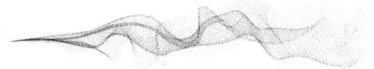

CHAPTER TWENTY-FIVE

Dani adjusted the pillows the way she did every night so she could cuddle against Tim's side and sleep on his shoulder. He loved their routine. It was comforting, and the one thing in his chaotic world of crime and punishment he could count on to bring peace. Lingering in love's sapphire and moonlight afterglow, he closed his eyes. Completely relaxed, satisfied, and ready to drift away. Dani took too long to settle in against him. He opened his eyes. With her legs tucked up under her, Dani sat up next to him, studying him.

The soft light from the bedside lamp painted her skin with an incandescent warmth. She was so beautiful; he couldn't help thinking how lucky he was, even if her eyebrows were drawn together with worry.

"Okay. What's bothering you, baby?" he asked, reaching to encourage her down and against him. She resisted, but not as if she was angry.

"What makes you think...?"

He laughed. "Because I'd be holding you, and we'd be half asleep by now if everything was *all good.*"

A small you-caught-me pout teased her lips for a second, and she toyed with her fingernails.

Tim lifted his arms and linked his fingers behind his head. His eyes explored her face. Whatever was bothering her couldn't be that serious. But whatever it was, he could tell she wasn't sure she wanted to talk about it.

Dani stretched out and settled her body against his chest as she did whenever they were about to have a weighty discussion. He enjoyed her little game. Even if she scolded him about something she thought he'd done wrong, she'd blend in enough caressing and kissing to make an argument a pleasant experience. He treasured the warmth and softness of her skin against his.

He was at a disadvantage in the first place. Tim had been raised in a family of all boys. His father adored his mother and insisted he and his older brothers treat her like a goddess. Women had always held a mystique that kept him a little off-balance. Dani especially did so. Everything about her was so loveable. Everything.

"Is there something wrong at home? With the girls?" He took a handful of her hair and let the silky strands slide through his fingers. The planned hospital interrogation of Bounds had ruined his chances to talk to his daughters by Skype before bedtime. They were fast asleep by the time he got to the hotel room. He missed hearing their little-girl voices and cheerful stories of school and play.

"No. They're fine. I talked to them on the flight home. They miss you."

"That's good. You told them I miss them, too. Didn't you? So, what's up?"

Dani took in a deep breath. "Did you know Roxie in Seattle?"

"I knew her in Seattle. Are you that worried about her? I'm not. She's a big girl—a well-armed big girl, and besides, Miguel is with her."

"How did you meet?" she asked, drawing an imaginary line down his arm with her index finger.

With Dani's history of a cheating ex-husband, Tim realized she might misconstrue this nothing-burger as a betrayal. "I'd been with the DA's office for about three months when Goddard assigned me as the liaison between law enforcement and the DA's office on the Fynn Creek Serial Killer Task Force. Roxie was with the FBI's Seattle Field

Office. That's where I met Elias, too. My first experience with a real FBI profiler. Elias was amazing. I remember sitting with him, poring through the crime scene photos and notes. He described Lee Roy Moran down to the make, model, and color of the vehicle he would drive." Tim paused. "I thought I told you this." He brushed a strand of hair away from her cheek with the back of his fingers, revealing her big, blue eyes.

"You told me about Elias. You—you never mentioned Roxie." Dani snuggled up and kissed his throat.

"I guess I didn't think it was important. I haven't mentioned most of the people on the task force. When you kiss me like this, it's because you want to talk about something you think I won't want to."

A big grin crossed her lips. "I do not!" Which was a confession that she did precisely that. She began to shower tender kisses on his shoulder, throat, chest. Her soft lips made his skin tingle with excitement. But he needed to sleep.

"Where are you going with this?" He licked his lips and laughed. "You'd better ask what you want because, in a few minutes, it's lights-out for me." He closed his eyes.

"Were you and Roxie lovers?"

Tim groaned. "No." He shook his head. "No. Where is this coming from? I didn't tell you about Roxie, because I didn't think of her. She was one of the investigators and on the task force arrest team, that's all."

"It's just—the way she looks at you."

"Dani, that's just the way she looks."

"All dewy-eyed and hanging on your every word?" Dani mimicked Roxie and Tim snickered.

"She doesn't do that. She actually trashes me every chance she gets. If she looks at me that way, I haven't noticed. Besides, you are the only one I want all dewy-eyed and hanging on my every word. You're my only one." He chuckled, making her laugh with him. He pulled her close and kissed her. She settled down, cozying up to his side.

Tim was on the edge, just at the moment wakefulness surrendered completely to sleep. The familiar sound of his cell phone ring disappointed him. It couldn't be morning already. He untangled himself from Dani and grabbed the phone, and swiped across the answer button.

"McAndrews," he answered, trying to clear the grog from his mind. He put the call on speaker and flopped back into the pillows, holding the iPhone in his right hand. He glanced at the screen. Unknown Caller was the message in the ID box.

"Tim, meet me in the bar. Right now." A desperate woman's voice panted into the phone.

"Who's this?" Tim looked over at Dani. She was resting on an elbow, an eyebrow lifted in question. He shrugged.

"It's Beebe," the voice said. "Listen, I have some information for you for your investigation."

"How did you get this number?"

"You gave Congressman Patterson your card, remember. Meet me in the bar."

"At 1:15 in the morning? Can't this wait?"

"No. Hotel bar. Five minutes. I mean it, Tim."

Tim paused and sucked a breath through his teeth. "Beebe, if this is one of your crazy schemes…"

"Don't be such a jackass. Just meet me before the bar closes. You're the damn cops! Do your job."

"Your sweet-talk really makes me want to jump right to it." Tim laughed.

"Tim, please."

He looked over at Dani and breathed out a heavy sigh. "All right, five minutes."

"Thanks."

They both disengaged.

"You heard?" Tim asked.

Dani nodded. "Do you believe her?"

Tim swiped his hand across his chin. "I don't know."

"Are you going?"

"Not without Elias." He tossed back the covers and started to dress.

—

Tim took a seat in a booth in the back corner of the empty bar. There were no patrons left at this hour, though he studied the room. Elias had bowed out of coming to the bar. He told Tim those facts of the case he could safely share and ask him to record his conversation with Beebe. If she had additional evidence, they could follow up in the morning and ask her to sign an affidavit under oath.

She might've heard they had arrested Bounds. But the sheriff had changed their police band to a secure channel during pursuit and arrest. The FBI's reports on the footprint and ballistic evidence they'd gathered so far would be back tomorrow. Until those results were in, they couldn't charge Bounds with the school shooting, only with attempting to murder police officers. Whatever Beebe had, or thought she had, better be good.

Tim rubbed his hand across his forehead and tired eyes. When he looked up, Beebe was headed for the booth. He took his phone from his pocket, set it in front of him on the table, and pressed record.

"Thanks for coming. You are saving my bacon, if you know what I mean," she said in her most cheery voice. "Now, here's what I want you to say when—"

"Want me to say? You said you had information for me about the school-shooting case." He scowled at her.

"No. See. Aaron—Congressman Patterson snuck out of our hotel room, and I thought he was cheating on me."

"You woke me up for this? The FBI doesn't investigate boyfriends for cheating." Tim slid to the edge of the booth and started to stand.

"Wait. I followed him. He's not cheating."

Tim rolled his eyes at her but didn't go any further. "And ...?" He motioned for her to explain.

"I think he's a prescription drug addict. He went to the hospital pharmacy, in the middle of the night, with envelopes full of money." She crossed her arms over her chest as if saying *so there.*

Tim squinted at her and slid back into the booth. "You should've called the DEA, not me. Have you ever seen him use drugs?"

"No. But that doesn't mean anything. I wasn't looking for it."

"You saw him buy drugs?"

"Well, um, not really. I just saw him give a fat envelope to the pharmacy guy. So, he's on his way back from the hospital now, and I need you to give me cover. I knew I couldn't make it back to the room before he did. So, I told him you called with an update on the shooter."

"I called you with an update on the shooter at one in the morning? Are you nuts? Never mind, you are stone-cold crazy," Tim complained. Once again, he was caught up in one of Beebe's goofy schemes.

"It was the only thing I could think of, so Aaron wouldn't know I was checking up on him." She grimaced as if hoping he wouldn't yell at her.

"You are telling me you watched Patterson buy drugs you didn't see with money you didn't see? You got me out of bed for this?" Tim groaned in frustration. "What update on the shooter were you expecting? I don't have an update on the shooter."

"I have pictures of Aaron passing the money. Here, take the SD card with you, return it later." She wrestled the card from its compartment in the camera and passed it across the table to Tim while guiltily sinking low into her seat.

Tim should've walked away. He wasn't sure why he didn't. For some strange reason, this new information folded into the school shooting case and hatched a whole myriad of possibilities that were now racing through his mind. Was Patterson somehow involved?

Susan Bower had claimed there was a second man that joined in the sexual assaults of the honor students. The autopsies showed that the murdered teens had Rohypnol in their systems. If Patterson was buying drugs, could *he* be the second man? The legitimate medical uses for Rohypnol were as a pre-surgical tranquilizer and a post-operative sleep aid. A hospital pharmacy would have it on hand.

Their own FBI profile indicated that the unsub would try to participate in the investigation. Patterson meddled daily.

Underaged Aiysha's pregnancy would give him motive. What congressman wants to be caught up in a scandal like this? Would he kill, or hire a killer, to make it all go away? It wouldn't be the first time. Suspicion piled up in Tim's mind like accumulations of winter snow.

Oh, hell! He was tired and slumped down in the booth. Beebe had him thinking all kinds of insane things. His jaw tightened as he looked across the table at her.

Tim sat up when he saw the congressman crossing the distance from the barroom door to their table. He slid the SD card off the table and stuffed it into the pocket of his hoodie. Before the congressman reached the table, he said, "Find the drug he bought and tell me what it is at the morning briefing at the sheriff's office."

Beebe nodded.

"Tim," Patterson reached across the table to shake hands, a big politician's grin swept across his face. "Beebe said you have some information on the case for us." He rubbed his hands together like a Simon Legree villain from a cartoon. "Tell me what you have."

CHAPTER TWENTY-SIX

Tim arrived at the sheriff's office early. The main floor bustled with uniformed deputies as the 7 a.m. to 3 p.m. shift took over for graveyard. The alcove LaCrosse had loaned to the FBI was a dark hole until he flipped on the light. At least he would be alone for an hour before the rest of the team showed up. He needed time to clear away the clutter and think.

Once again, he'd be spending the night here in Culpeper unless they could nail Bounds with the school shooting. Tim was afraid Dani would soon resent flying back and forth because of his job. She hadn't complained, but he knew the time she spent in the air could be better spent setting up their new house and her new wine shop.

He peeled off his camel-colored overcoat and tossed it across one of the workspace's wooden chairs. He set his hot coffee on the desk and cued up the computer. He opened his email and searched for the promised reports from the FBI's crime lab.

He found the first email and read it. Bounds's shoes were an exact match for those that had walked blood all over the school hallway. They were memorialized in mud on the rental car mats, and left prints in the dust at the hunter's cave. The sole of the shoe, down to the wear pattern, a split in one of the treads, and most impressive of all, a small rock that had lodged in between two of the waffle squares in the heel, made it as compelling evidence as a fingerprint.

The next report was also good news. The shell casings and the bullets and fragments recovered at the school matched the M16 rifle they'd found in the hunter's cave with Bounds's fingerprints and touch DNA all over it.

The black Darth Vader-like helmet and black clothing they'd found in the rental car matched witness descriptions of the shooter. DNA swabs from inside the helmet and gloves matched Bounds with a one in four billion certainty.

"Got you!" Tim said out loud to no one, smiling with satisfaction. He couldn't wait to interrogate Bounds. A confession, though unnecessary at this point, would be like a big scoop of homemade vanilla ice cream on top of a piece of fresh-baked cherry pie. For a moment, he leaned back in the chair and relished it.

His thoughts drifted to the parents of the murdered teens. They could never get their children back, but at least Bounds would be going to prison. Tim would see to that.

Tim sat forward and opened the next report. The exquisite feeling of victory vanished quickly. Susan Bower's version of the assault of the honor students was getting traction. The DNA recovered from Marty's body belonged to the principal, Edmond Crenshaw. Crenshaw could alibi his way out of the school shooting, *for now*. Tim couldn't wait to see him try to alibi his way out of the DNA.

If the school shooting was cover for the assaults, Aiysha's pregnancy had likely turned the perpetrators' world upside down. Did Aiysha know who the father was, and on her own, threaten to expose or blackmail him?

Tim sat back deep into the wooden chair. He could feel the turned spindles pressing against his back. He'd read somewhere about the phenomenon that now overwhelmed him. First, empathy for the victims flooded his emotions. Anguish over the needless loss of life rushed in. He breathed out, waiting for the dark shadow of grief to pass over. Tim wiped his hand across his lips and down his chin.

Disgust and anger started a slow boil in his core. With the serpent's guile, Crenshaw lured these children into a trap. Bounds ruthlessly shot them to cover their despicable crimes. At this moment, Tim wanted nothing more than to expose these shitbags and see justice done. They needed to pay.

He opened the last report. He blinked after the first read-through and reread it. *I'll be damned!* Aiysha's unborn baby's DNA did not match anyone's they had swabbed or collected. Not Crenshaw. Not Bounds. Not Aiysha's boyfriend. None of her friends at school. In fact, it matched no one in the CODIS database.

Tim's theory of the crime and very first field profile was right. A money shot. A bingo. Bounds was a paid assassin. Tim knew he should be pleased and proud of himself, and maybe he was, but for some reason, it didn't feel good. The unknown second man was probably the father of Aiysha's baby. He would have a strong motive for murder. *Who are you, second man?*

Slowly Tim stood and collected two copies of the reports off the printer. He placed one on the desk to be inserted in the main file. The other, he attached with a push pin to the corkboard they used to help the team visualize the crime and the evidence they had so far. He stood back, studying it.

Tim dialed Elias.

"Hey, Tim. Good morning," Elias said. "How'd it go with Miss Knoll last night?"

"We should go into that when you get here. I'm in the sheriff's office. Right now, I think you need to look at the lab reports. I just sent them to your email. It's time for arrest warrants."

"I'm on my way," Elias said. "See you in a few."

"Good. I'll be here." He disengaged.

Tim stood at the corkboard, poring over the evidence when the rest of his team members began filing in, ready to get to work. Melissa sat behind the desk and began to read the lab reports. Kandar dumped the stale coffee and started a new pot. The scent of the fresh brew filled Tim's nostrils.

Miguel quickly crossed the main office floor, entered the alcove, and stopped when he stood beside Tim in front of the case board. He looked refreshed and rested in his dark suit, crisp white shirt, and tie. Tim was amazed at how much the two of them looked like typical G-men.

"Don't worry, Roxie is safe. And don't ask. Just trust me," he said in a hushed voice. "What have we got?"

Tim glared at him for a moment and then recounted the evidence from the reports. Miguel listened while reading the board. "Well, that's it then. We've got our school shooter." A satisfied grin crept over his face.

"We have the shooter and the principal. But Aiysha's baby's DNA confirms Susan Bower's story about a second man," Tim said. "I wonder if Crenshaw paid Bounds to shoot up the school?"

"When we bring Crenshaw in, he'll give up the second man." He's a weasel and a coward. Bounds will be harder to crack, but in the long run, he'll make a deal with the prosecutor for the identity of the guy who paid him." Miguel was confident. "Let's see if we can find a money trail. We follow the money, and we catch them all."

"Guys like Bounds have figured out how to hide money," Tim said.

"They always make a mistake. Always." Miguel patted Tim on the shoulder, turned, and headed for the coffee.

Tim focused his attention back to the corkboard as if some evidence he hadn't seen on the twentieth read-through would suddenly pop out to him on the twenty-first. Miguel returned and handed him a mug of coffee.

"Thanks," he said, glancing toward the alcove's open archway. Beebe and Congressman Patterson had entered the deputies' floor and waited for the sheriff's morning briefing. Tim hadn't seen the sheriff yet. Elias and Berkstad arrived together. There was a quick flurry of morning greetings between the parties he watched but couldn't hear.

"Elias said that our unsub would try to insert himself into our investigation. Notice any two guys out there that have inserted themselves into our investigation?" Tim chuckled, glancing in the direction of Berkstad and Patterson.

Miguel swallowed his sip of coffee, stared out through the archway, and pinched his bottom lip. "Wait. You don't think?" He grinned.

"Naw, I'm just annoyed at their constant interference," Tim said. But underneath it all, he did wonder.

Miguel looked Tim square in the eyes. "Just for fun, we ought to . . . ." Miguel flicked his eyebrows upward, and a big, mischievous smile broke open across his face.

"We don't have time for fun." Tim laughed. He sobered when Beebe broke from the foursome and headed in his direction. He stepped out of the alcove to greet her, protecting the corkboard from the media's prying eyes. Beebe sidestepped up to him and touched her arm to his. He immediately frowned at her and moved away. They weren't friends now and never would be.

"I didn't find any drugs," she whispered.

Tim didn't think she would.

"While he was in the shower, I looked through his shaving kit, all his pockets. I didn't get to his suitcase, but I will," she muttered under her breath, making Miguel lean in to hear their conversation. "So, what do you think the envelopes of money were for?"

"Maybe it wasn't money. Maybe it was something else," Tim offered.

"No, it was money. The packet he gave out Saturday morning was definitely money. The bills were still in the bank wrapper," Beebe said.

"Saturday morning? Last night, you didn't mention any money exchange, other than at the hospital." Tim looked over at Miguel and then back to Beebe.

She twisted her lips to one side and mouthed, "Oops." After a brief pause she said, "So, I forgot. Saturday morning, around five or so, a man came to the door. Patterson gave him an envelope of money."

"Just for clarity, that was at the hotel?" What a coincidence! Just after five, Tim first encountered Bounds in the elevator.

"Yes. Jackass. Where else?" Beebe scowled.

Tim shook his head. "There you go again with the sweet-talk."

"Did you see the guy? Could you identify him?" Miguel asked.

"No. I just heard voices. Patterson's and a male voice I didn't recognize." Beebe started to speak, but her mouth shut like the slamming of a trap door. Was she connecting the dots? Tim was.

Elias walked through the alcove's archway and stared at her with disapproval. Beebe closed up like a sea anemone when touched by an inquisitive diver.

"Miss Knoll, will you excuse us? We have work to do." Elias issued his dismissal.

"Yes, I should get going. The sheriff's press conference is about to start. Later, guys." Beebe strolled out and joined Patterson. Tim watched as the congressman took his last sip of coffee and dropped his paper cup into the trash bin at one of the deputy's desks. Patterson took Beebe's hand, and they headed for the area set up for the press conference.

"What did Beebe want?" Elias asked.

"News." Tim waited for a moment. "Kandar, do you have an evidence bag?"

Kandar stood from behind the computer and retrieved one from his jacket hanging on the back of his chair. Tim took it and grabbed several tissues from the box on the corner of the desk.

"What are you doing?" Elias demanded.

Tim told him to wait by lifting an index finger. He strolled out to the deputy's desk, sat in the empty chair. He glanced around. The room was nearly empty. When he was sure no one was looking, he reached into the trash can and took the coffee cup Patterson had deposited there. He slipped it into the evidence bag and sealed it. He knew he had to explain his actions to Elias and his colleagues. Suspicion had gotten the better of him. Over his four years in law enforcement and the criminal justice system, he'd learned when it came to crime, there were no coincidences. A quick DNA analysis compared to Aiysha's baby would eliminate or confirm Patterson as the second man. They could get his permission or a warrant for a second sample that would be admissible in court later.

Tim walked back to the alcove. The hair on the back of his neck stood as if he'd been touched by a ghost's icy fingers. He turned to look behind him. On the other side of the room, with his arms crossed over his chest, Berkstad stood watching him, a dangerous smile curving his lips like a scimitar.

CHAPTER TWENTY-SEVEN

Tim shot a bring-it-I- dare-you stare of his own to Berkstad. When the man blinked, Tim turned and proceeded through the alcove's archway.

"What are you doing?" Elias asked. Before answering, Tim motioned for Elias to step to a corner of the room so they could talk privately.

"You said that you believed our unsub would try to insert himself into our investigation," he reminded Elias. "I thought I'd eliminate the guys who've done just that." He told Elias about the two suspected cash transfers Beebe had witnessed.

"Do you think she's telling the truth?" Elias asked.

"No idea. Beebe's crazy. But, we know a second man participated in the assaults on the kids. When Kandar researched the road trips that were supposed to be a reward for good grades, they were always overnights in DC." Tim's chest heaved with a deep breath. "After my talk with Beebe last night, I researched Patterson's committee assignments in Congress. I needed to link him to Crenshaw and Bounds."

"Did you?"

"Loosely. But it's there. Patterson is on The House Committee for Education and Labor, and Crenshaw often gave talks at those meetings. Patterson is also on The House Select Committee for Intelligence, where he might've run into Bounds. It's circumstantial. If there's a DNA match, the party changes."

Elias glared out to the main floor where Patterson glad-handed other members of the press that had arrived for the briefing.

"I have pictures of the congressman handing off something, maybe money, on an SD card. For what—that's the question." Tim reached in his pocket and dropped the small blue square into Elias's hand. "They're damning."

"That's big." Elias's lips curved in a smile. His disdain for politicians, especially Congressman Patterson, was legendary. No doubt he'd love to catch him doing something illegal. "Let's get that coffee cup to the lab."

Tim handed over the evidence bag just as Berkstad passed through the entryway to the alcove.

"McAndrews," Berkstad approached him and Elias. "I saw you take a coffee cup out of the trash. What have you got?" The man grinned, and changed up his unspoken threat to friendliness.

"Just eliminating people from the suspect pool," Tim said. For a moment, he hoped Roxie's opinion of Berkstad hadn't colored his thoughts. Still, there was something insincere and deceitful about the guy that Tim didn't like. If he had to work with him, he needed to trust him. He didn't.

"I thought we had our suspect in custody. Isn't Bounds our guy?"

"One of them, anyway." Elias pitched in.

Berkstad raised both eyebrows in surprise. He'd been hanging around, but hadn't bothered to read the case file to learn about the evidence. Tim guessed he was used to being briefed.

"Tim, I want you and Miguel to head over to the hospital to interview Bounds. I'll get a statement from Crenshaw once the sheriff's deputies bring him in," Elias said.

"Would you mind if I tag along with Tim and Miguel?" Berkstad asked.

"Fine with me. You boys good with it?" Elias picked up the case file from the desk and began thumbing through the pages.

What were they going to say? *Find your own ride* to the section chief of Counterintelligence? Tim looked over at Miguel, who swiped his hand up his brow and over his short black hair.

"Let's get going," Tim said.

Once outside, the men headed toward the FBI's SUVs. Tim clicked the keyfob's unlock button to determine which rig was theirs.

"I'm driving," he said, letting Miguel and Berkstad work out their seating arrangements. The section chief made a diplomatic move and chose the rear seat.

As they buckled up, Berkstad said, "I know you don't know me. Perhaps you might feel like I'm not on your side."

Tim didn't want to get into this now, but that choice was no longer on the table.

"I'm guessing Roxie told you about me," Berkstad continued. "I admit I behaved badly. But I still care for her. Very much. I'm leaving my wife for her."

His confession was cringeworthy. Tim gave Miguel a quick glance. "Sir, that's none of our business. That's between you and Roxie," he said. Sooner or later, Roxie was going to have to face her differences with Berkstad. Tim and Miguel couldn't do it for her.

"You made it your business, though, when you helped her go into hiding. She's not at her condo in the city or her parents' home in Connecticut. I know you know where she is. I assure you, I just want to talk to her."

Tim stopped himself before he said anything more. He wasn't about to admit he knew where she was. He looked into the rearview mirror and caught Berkstad's reflection. Either the man was a great actor, or he was truthful. No flames of malice danced from his eyes.

"You have it all wrong. We don't know where she is," Miguel stated as if it were fact. It wasn't exactly a lie—at this very moment, they didn't know her precise location. When he was a SEAL, Miguel trained to protect his team members, even under torture. Roxie was his team member. The threat of losing his job didn't faze him. Tim was impressed. He'd figured losing a job was probably the least of their worries. Counterintelligence guys were scary.

There were always two sides to every story. Four years ago, Tim had watched Roxie lead a whole group of task force members on a romantic chase. She was smart, sexy, and enjoyed the game. Berkstad could easily be the victim here.

What bothered Tim, though, when he'd searched last night to find connections between Patterson and Bounds, Berkstad came up front and center. The man admitted that Bounds was one of his former assets and ruthless enough to be an assassin for hire. The Congressional Select Committee on Intelligence was the link. Did Patterson find his killer through Berkstad? Tim hadn't shared his suspicions with Elias or the rest of the team. Not yet, anyway.

Any belief that powerful men wouldn't engage in sexually abusing underage teens had dissolved with Tim's naivety long ago. But, would a man who claimed he was in love with Roxie have the mindset to abuse drugged and unconscious children? Maybe not. But would a man planning to leave his wife and family, facing the financial hardship that brings, arrange a meeting with a killer for hire? Would he then choose to look the other way rather than investigate for envelopes of cash? *You betcha!* And according to Beebe, Patterson was passing those envelopes out right and left.

Tim decided he needed to put his uncertainties to rest once and for all. He had to get a DNA sample. He had to get that sample without Berkstad's realizing it. The man had all the resources of the Counterintelligence Division at his disposal. Once again, he studied the chief's face reflected in the rearview mirror.

"This is our turn, isn't it?" Miguel brought him back to reality.

"It is." Tim flicked on the signal and turned into the hospital parking lot. He drove up to the building's portico. "I'll let you off here. I'll park and catch up."

After Miguel and Berkstad exited the vehicle, Tim pulled into a parking space. He grabbed his iPhone and dialed. "Kandar, can you do something for me?"

"What do you need?"

"Can you get bank records for someone?"

"You know I can. Let me get the program up. Okay, whose records do we need?"

"Congressman Aaron Patterson and David Berkstad." He heard the gasp on the other end of the call.

"Holy SHIT! Really?"

"Can you do it?"

"I can, but should I?"

"Will you do it?"

"Shouldn't we talk to Elias?"

"Probably. But we aren't going to." Tim scrubbed his hand through his hair. He wouldn't blame Kandar if he told him to pound sand.

Complete silence filled the air for a moment, like waiting for the thunderclap after seeing a distant lightning strike. Tim heard deep breathing and a sigh.

"What am I looking for?" Kandar asked finally.

"Big deposits and big withdrawals of cash," Tim said.

"And if they're stuffing it in a mattress instead?"

"I guess we'll cross that bridge—you know the drill."

"This may take a few days."

"You're the best." Tim disengaged. He stuffed his cell back into his pocket, got out of the car, and strolled to the hospital.

Miguel and Berkstad waited for him at the elevator. They rode up to Recovery and ICU on the second floor. The doors rolled opened to utter chaos.

Code alarms sounded at the empty nurses' station. The air, full of antiseptic, stung his nostrils. One of the deputies on duty in front of Bounds's room escorted a sobbing nurse away.

Tim heard loud commands in a male voice. "Again, one-half milliliter epinephrine, stat! Twenty-five milligrams diphenhydramine IV!"

"Excuse me, out of the way!" Tim jumped aside as a technician rolled past him at a run with a crash cart.

A second deputy stood just outside the doorway to the recovery room, his mouth hanging open in shock.

"Whose room is this?" Miguel asked.

"The prisoner, Hamish Bounds."

"What happened?" Tim asked, lifting the FBI Lanyard that hung around his neck so the deputy could see.

"The nurse gave out this morning's meds less than a minute ago, and I heard a crash. I opened the door, and Bounds looked like some kinda fish outta water, trying to breathe," the deputy said. Tim read the man's name tag: Deputy Harrison. "She gave him the wrong meds."

"Is he going to live?" Miguel demanded, barging past the deputy into the room. "Is he going to live?"

Tim heard. "Get him out of here." And watched as a big orderly blocked Miguel and forced him to walk backward, even though he was showing him his FBI credentials. When he was out of the room, someone pulled the sliding glass door closed.

Stepping back and out of the way, Tim knew there was nothing he could do. He'd leave it to the professionals. Miguel paced a short line in front of the hospital room. Berkstad found a chair and slowly sank into it.

Minutes passed. Grim-faced nurses and orderlies filed out of the room, the jarring scent of ozone from the defibrillator lingering in their clothes. Tim's attention alerted. He wanted to talk to the doctor and stood in the middle of the hallway to wait. A young man, no older than Tim's twenty-eight years, handed a chart to a nurse before exiting Bounds's room. He looked Tim up and down.

"Are you the police?" he asked.

"FBI. Mr. Bounds?" Tim asked.

"Sorry, he didn't make it." He reached out as if to comfort Tim, then withdrew his hand. The shooter, key witness, and link to the congressman was dead. Tim looked over at Berkstad's nearly unreadable face and saw a strange smile flash briefly across his lips, almost as if he was relieved.

"Cause of death?"

"Anaphylaxis. I've never seen a case so severe. We couldn't revive him." The doctor sighed.

"Accident or homicide?" Tim asked.

"Autopsy will have to determine that." The young doctor bit his bottom lip. "Do you mind if I ask—why was Mr. Bounds under police guard. What did he do?"

No need to protect anyone's rights now. Tim took a deep breath. "We believe he was the school shooter."

Surprised, the doctor stood blinking at him. "Glad I didn't know. I might not have tried so hard to save him." He narrowed his eyes for a moment. "Will you excuse me?"

Tim nodded and stepped out of his way, watching the man walk down the hall.

Envelopes of cash, an ambitious congressman, a meddlesome section chief, and anaphylaxis? Coincidence? Not a chance, Tim thought.

CHAPTER TWENTY-EIGHT

The school shooter was dead. Quickly, Tim dialed Elias to tell him the news. Miguel and Deputy Harrison secured the crime scene by putting up yellow police tape. CSI was on the way.

Tim contacted the hospital administrator. She'd informed him that on every shift, two nurses worked the medicine carts together. The hospital hoped they would back each other up and prevent any medication errors.

He asked for a list of names and addresses for the overnight pharmacy staff and a copy of the surveillance video for last night and this morning. While the administrator pulled that together, Tim and Miguel would interview the nurses who'd administered this morning's meds, now waiting in the employees' break room with Deputy March.

Adrenaline raced through Tim's bloodstream, supercharging his thoughts. No wonder his best friend from Seattle, Detective Scott Renton, liked police work so much. Scott had told him about this reaction as the puzzle pieces came together when Tim was a King County Assistant District Attorney. At the time Tim had pretended to understand it, but feeling the rush personally was a whole new experience. He expected chemical rushes like this when standing at the top of a black diamond ski run, waiting to launch down a steep, snow-covered mountainside, but not while chasing down criminals.

The stakes couldn't be higher, and that was part of the thrill. As he and Miguel started down the institutional green hall, he realized that Berkstad trailed behind them like the nerdy kid in school, watching every move and ready to rat them out to the principal each time they took a wrong breath. Good guy? Bad guy? Tim couldn't pigeonhole Berkstad. He was still determined to get the man's DNA.

Tim hoped he wouldn't try to intimidate the nurses into silence. Berkstad had a harsh and sullen way about him. Tim wanted and needed the truth. Let the evidence lead them where it would.

As he opened the breakroom door, Tim was immediately greeted by with the aroma of freshly brewed coffee. The cheery yellow walls sported a gallery of framed crayon drawings that looked like contributions from the hospital's pediatric patients. As intended, it made him feel warm inside. In the center of the room, a long table surrounded by chairs took up most of the space. Both of the nurses who'd handled the medical cart sat at the far end with Deputy March.

For a moment, Tim studied the nurses and smiled, hoping to relieve some of their trepidation. No one wanted to be interrogated by the FBI. The younger woman's brown eyes were swollen and red, and a worried frown curved the corners of her mouth. She'd twisted her brown hair into a tight knot at the nape of her neck. Tim guessed she was barely twenty. He'd heard another nurse say this was the very first day of her first nursing job. What a crappy way to start, he thought.

The older woman radiated confidence. Her posture was straight, shoulders square, and no tears stained her cheeks. Without looking away from his face, she smoothed a hand over her graying blonde hair. She had done nothing wrong, and her bright blue eyes dared him to accuse her. Tim knew she hadn't. His money was squarely on the pharmacist.

Tim read the nurses' nametags: Angela Ramerez, Certified Nursing Assistant, was the younger of the two. Eve Comstock, Registered Nurse, was older and wiser, and viewed them skepically.

"Hi, Ms. Ramerez, Ms. Comstock, I'm Special Agent Tim McAndrews." He walked forward into the room. "We need to ask you a few questions."

Ms. Ramerez placed a trembling hand over her mouth, and tears filled her eyes and spilled down her cheeks. "I just gave him what he was prescribed," she blurted out. Her defense was far more plausible than she knew. The fact she'd voiced it before he even sat down also put a checkmark in the innocent column.

"This is Special Agent Miguel Gonzales and—"

"Special Agent David Berkstad." Berkstad interrupted and reached out his hand to the women one at a time. Tim wondered why the man wouldn't give his real title. Tim watched for a reaction between them. There was none. Neither woman recognized Berkstad, nor did he remember them. Once Berkstad took a seat next to Tim and opposite the women, Tim asked if it would be okay to record the interview. They nodded their agreement, and Tim set his iPhone in the center of the table and pressed the record button.

After gathering the necessary witness backstory—names, ages, addresses, and phone numbers—Tim dove into the interview.

"For the record, Angela, how are morning medications normally distributed?" he asked.

"About a half hour after our shift begins, we pick up our medication cart from the pharmacy," she answered, sniffling.

"You and Ms. Comstock?"

"Yes, sir. This morning it was Nurse Comstock and me. She's the supervisory RN on our floor for the shift. We both check over the medications, confirming each with the patient and their medical chart and prescription orders from the doctor." She looked over at Nurse Comstock as if for approval. The blonde woman gave her a quick nod.

"How is the cart organized?" Miguel asked, leaning forward.

"Every floor has its own cart. It is divided into compartments for each room. Ours is easy because we only have one patient per room. We start at the elevator and go from room ICU-1 around in a circle finishing with RR-12, or Recovery Room 12." Nurse Comstock explained as if teaching a nursing student. Tim didn't mind.

"When you get to a room, what do you do?" He knew there were federal guidelines each hospital complied with, but each hospital had its own variations.

"We confirm the patient's name and birthdate. We look at the patient's hospital wrist band and then confirm what we have on the cart to the medication the doctor prescribed by reading the chart. If everything is right, we give the medication." Eve's blue eyes sparkled. No deception, no combativeness he would ordinarily get from a guilty party.

"Am I going to lose my job? I need this job," Angela said, her face desperate.

Her question took him by surprise and was not one Tim could answer.

"I'm sure if you followed hospital procedures, you don't have to worry, ma'am," Berkstad chimed in.

Tim watched the tension in her shoulders relax. She believed she'd done everything right.

"Let's get to Mr. Bounds. What did you do when you got to his room?" Miguel asked.

"He was awake and said he was in pain. I changed his IV antibiotic drip and administered a shot of Dilaudid, 2 milligrams IM—Intermuscular for pain," Angela said.

"You're sure about the dosage?" Tim asked, making notes even though he was recording the conversation.

"Yes. Our prescriptions come in single-dose packages." Eve looked up from the table and locked her stare onto Tim's eyes, annoyed. It didn't matter. He had to get answers to his questions. If for no other reason than to eliminate the women as suspects. According to the deputies on guard, the allergic reaction occurred after the morning medications, and no one else had been in Bounds's room.

"Does that mean the injection syringe was prefilled and on the cart?" Tim asked. That would make it so easy to tamper with. The pharmacist could load the syringe with a lethal concentration of a drug, the wrong medication, or poison, and voila.

"No. The syringe is empty, and we draw the medication from a single-dose vial." Angela nervously rubbed her hands together. "I looked at the bottle and confirmed it was his prescription and the right dosage."

"Mr. Bounds's chart listed no allergies. He wasn't wearing a MedicAlert bracelet," Eve added. "I checked the medication before we gave it, too. I would've noticed if the metal seal had been removed or if there was a needle puncture in the rubber cap. Everything was brand-new. Mr. Bounds was given two prior doses of Dilaudid last night with no reaction."

"Tell me about the IV antibiotics. How does that work?" Tim asked.

"The antibiotics are in a separate bag hung next to the saline drip and attached to the central IV line. He received 500 mg of Cephalosporin with 5mg of Gentamicin administered over thirty minutes," Angela reported, proud of her memory.

"You made sure that the antibiotics were the ones prescribed, and you checked the chart for allergies?" Berkstad glared at her, his eyes cold and dark.

"I did. Of course, I did." She desperately looked back and forth between the interrogators' faces. CSI had already collected the IV equipment and the vial and syringe used for the pain killer shot. They would match Bounds's toxicology to the contents of the medical devices. Tim felt a small electric charge of anger buzz through his system. Berkstad had no reason to challenge and frighten the young woman. But then, Tim realized, it was possible Berkstad didn't know about Patterson's midnight hospital visit. At this point, Tim wasn't going to be the one to tell him, either. He still didn't trust the man.

Tim's theory of the crime was fleshing out, and it was ugly. What if Congressman Aaron Patterson was the second man? What if he'd paid the hospital pharmacist to brew up a concoction to kill Bounds? Once Patterson's DNA was back and a match for Aiysha's baby, he'd know for sure and have enough probable cause for an arrest warrant. Tim stared ahead, not focusing on anyone or anything as his thoughts whirled in his head. It was one thing to know the answer; he had to prove it.

"Angela, would you be able to show me your medical cart?" Tim asked, breaking the strained silence that permeated the room like a thick tule fog.

"Yes. It's out in the hall." The young woman was eager to please.

Tim followed her and took pictures of the medicine cart with his phone. He caught the attention of one of the CSI team members and handed it off for a thorough analysis.

"Am I free to go?" Angela asked, hopeful.

He nodded. "If we need to talk to you again, we'll call you. Don't leave town." Tim wanted to laugh. He sounded like a TV cop, not like the real deal. They always warned witnesses not to leave town.

She smiled at him, and he watched her walk away.

When the administrator's list of the pharmacy employees came through, Tim planned a photo line-up for Beebe. Her pictures had caught Patterson handing off a big fat packet of something but failed to capture the recipient's face. She'd inadvertently put herself in the awkward and untenable position of being the only witness. Theirs had always been an adversarial relationship. But he'd make sure she got to safety if things turned rough. With Beebe in the suspect's camp, though, he could use her to get information. Did he feel guilty in the slightest? Nope.

"You let her go?" Berkstad's voice was accusatory, gravelly.

Tim whirled to face him. "Did you want to arrest her? For what? I thought we'd at least wait for the autopsy and toxicology." Tim saw two hardworking nurses doing their job. Not criminals.

"Good idea," Miguel said. His eyes glittered with laughter. "Did you forget? Here in the United States, there are laws about the presumption of innocence."

Miguel intentionally shot the barb at Berkstad's Counterintelligence career. Overseas, in different countries, there were different rules, different laws. Like Miguel, Tim was troubled when the Spy Guys pulled their shenanigans here in the States.

"Oh, Mr. McAndrews." Tim turned when he heard his name. "These are the names, addresses, and phone numbers of the pharmacy employees and a copy of the video you asked for." The hospital administrator hurried up to him and handed over a piece of paper. and the thumb drive that contained the surveillance camera information. She smiled, and her reading glasses slipped further down toward the tip of her nose. Tim looked around making certain Berkstad didn't see. He wasn't ready to show his hand just yet. Especially, since he wasn't sure where the man fit in. Berkstad was down the hall, conversing with one of the deputies. Tim quickly put the small thumb drive in his pocket.

"Thank you." Tim scanned the page. The overnight pharmacist, Philip Dockery, had the only male-sounding name on the list. In Beebe's pictures, Patterson handed off the envelope to a man. Tim would still confirm with a photo line-up. He walked back down the hall and faced Miguel. "Let's head back to the office. Elias is going to interview Crenshaw, and I want to hear what he has to say."

CHAPTER TWENTY-NINE

Tim didn't fight Miguel for the privilege of driving back to the sheriff's office. He tossed him the keys and took his place in the front passenger seat. Berkstad was excess baggage, and Tim would be happy to leave him behind, even though he knew he couldn't. With the section chief in tow, he and Miguel couldn't bounce their ideas off each other. Tim knew Miguel agreed with him that the man could be involved somehow. Miguel waited impatiently, tapping his palm on the steering wheel, for Berkstad to seat-belt in before starting the engine.

As they turned out of the hospital parking lot, Tim retrieved his iPhone from his suit coat breast pocket and examined his notes. He missed the quiet office he'd had when working with the King County DA.

Police work came at you fast. He hadn't given it the appreciation it deserved back then. As an Assistant District Attorney, he'd had the luxury of taking hours to sift carefully through the evidence the police had painstakingly gathered. He'd had time to construct his theory of the crime for court. Now, everything was jumbled together, like the pieces of a new jigsaw puzzle dumped out on a table. The big difference—they didn't have the benefit of the completed picture on the box cover.

On his iPhone, Tim started a list of the facts he had connecting Patterson to Bounds. The prepaid Visa card and the burner phone in

Bounds's possession were purchased at Walmart in Hayward, California, smack in the middle of Patterson's congressional district.

Thoughts of Beebe's story about an envelope of cash paid in secret at 5 a.m. reminded Tim he needed to collect the video he'd ordered from hotel security. The hallway camera would've caught that transaction and thus confirm Beebe's account. He wanted to see what the videos would reveal, but couldn't do it with Berkstad hanging around.

Patterson's obnoxious intrusion into their investigation and demands to be kept informed fulfilled Elias's profile of the perpetrator. His midnight hospital visit and Bounds's mysterious sudden death this morning put another big, black check-mark in Patterson's "guilty" column.

"Who wants a coffee? There's a drive-through just ahead," Berkstad suddenly said.

Tim glanced back at him. He thought of a to-go coffee. The lid would be the perfect place for Berkstad to leave his DNA. Now, Tim would have to make sure he collected it without the Counterintelligence section chief knowing it.

"That sounds good." He hoped his big grin wasn't a giveaway.

"I'm getting hungry, too," Miguel said, flipping the blinker for a right turn into the drive-through.

"I need to swing by the hotel on our way to the sheriff's office," Tim commented. Miguel wrinkled his nose at him. "What? I ordered something, and I want to see if it's there." He couldn't wait to view the surveillance videos.

He also looked forward to seeing how Crenshaw reacted to Berkstad and Patterson. He'd be watching for some sort of a tell when they walked him through the sheriff's office to the interview room. He assumed Crenshaw was going to be the weakest link. Patterson was a politician; lying was part and parcel of his business. Disguise and deception were Berkstad's tradecraft. But a school principal probably had none of those skills.

If Crenshaw recognized either man or both, it would only be a matter of time before the principal flipped on his partner, the second man.

Miguel pulled up to the Starbucks order window. Tim felt his stomach rumble. He was hungry, too, but hadn't recognized it until now. They ordered coffees and breakfast sandwiches. When they pulled forward to collect their food and beverages, Tim noted the grande mocha boxes checked on Berkstad's coffee as he passed it to him. He needed to make sure when the time came, he grabbed the right cup. He also kept the bag the sandwiches were delivered in. Under the ruse of cleaning up the SUV at the sheriff's office, he'd collect Berkstad's cup, That was his plan, anyway. He knew he needed to be flexible. Not everything went according to plan.

"What did you think of the nurses' version of events?" Berkstad asked, in between bites of sandwich.

"Truthful," Miguel answered. "I saw no obvious signs of deception."

"What do you think is going on here?" Berkstad stuffed another bite in his mouth.

When Miguel glanced his way, Tim gave two quick shakes of his head in a nearly imperceptible way. He hoped Miguel caught his drift. Tim still hadn't decided whether Berkstad was good or bad. Any information they gave him could be used to warn the other players.

"Until we get the toxicology and autopsy results, I don't know what to say." Miguel briefly smiled at Tim as he pulled to the front of the hotel.

"I'll just be a sec," Tim said as he unhooked his seatbelt and jumped out, even before the vehicle had come to a complete stop.

He dashed into the hotel and waited for the receptionist to greet him. She was the hotel owner's seventeen-year-old daughter, and Dani had engaged her in conversations each time their schedules matched up. Dani believed it helped make the girl feel good about herself, and friendliness wouldn't hurt when they needed service. When she finally finished with her customer, she asked, "How may I help you, Mr. McAndrews?

"I'm expecting a package."

"Yes. I have that for you." The young woman set the sealed manilla envelope on the reception desk between them. She gifted him with a big, broad smile, as if expecting a kudo for doing her job.

"Thank you."

"Oh, Mr. McAndrews, I also have a message for you. A Miss Stauffer stopped by and wanted me to let you know she's in town." She handed him a pink message page from the suite's letterbox.

"Miss Stauffer?" Tim took a moment to get his head around it. What was Roxie doing back after all the pains they'd gone to, to secret her out of here? He nodded, slightly bewildered. "Is she in the hotel?"

"No. She said she'd call you." The young woman narrowed her eyes suspiciously at him.

"Okay. Thank you." He pulled the package toward him the rest of the way across the counter.

"Will Mrs. McAndrews be back this evening?" The receptionist's question and tone wasn't the first time someone dropped a thinly veiled question of infidelity his way. He wasn't sure if she meant to or if he was being overly defensive. It would be easy for a teenage girl to think another woman leaving him messages was a bad thing. Thanks in part to Beebe Knoll and her tabloid column, Dani's wealth gave her notoriety and fans.

"Yes. She will." He tapped the manila envelope softly on the counter. "Thanks again for this." His smile was as fraudulent as a dead man's vote. He turned and jogged back out to the SUV. Jerking the door open, Tim knew around seventy percent of men cheated on their wives. He wasn't one of them and shook off the unspoken insinuation.

"Let's go," he said. For seconds he sat in the passenger seat drumming his fingers on the envelope. Roxie was probably waiting for them at the sheriff's office. And, as Miguel would say, she had some 'splaining to do. A collision with Berkstad was imminent. But Roxie was a big girl, and she had to suspect he was still here. The confrontation between the two would send the behind-the-scenes office gossip and melodrama to new heights. He caught himself thinking they might need to break out the popcorn. He laughed to himself.

As Miguel pulled into a parking space, Tim remembered his other goal. "Anybody have any trash to contribute?" He held out the bag that had earlier held their sandwiches. Miguel tossed his wrapper and empty cup into the sack. Berkstad opened his door, poured out the remainder of his coffee on the ground, and added his cup to the mix of trash. *Oh! Sweet!*

Tim waited for Berkstad to turn his back, took out one of the latex gloves from his pocket, and wrapped the coffee cup lid and its precious DNA in the glove by turning it inside out. He stuffed the prize in his pocket.

When he caught up to Miguel and Berkstad, Tim crinkled up the bag. He dropped it in the trash can outside the sheriff's department's door. Berkstad looked at him with a question in his eyes. Tim let a confident grin curve his lips. If Berkstad knew Tim had his DNA, he didn't challenge him.

The sheriff's office was awash with activity. Leanne stood with two of her detectives, directing their next moves. Elias emerged from the alcove with Melissa.

"I'll interview Crenshaw in Interrogation Room 2. Set that up for me." Elias directed Melissa. He spotted Tim and Miguel. At first, he looked relieved, but his expression turned dour when he saw Berkstad still with them.

Tim suddenly realized why. Roxie passed through the archway, and when she spotted Berkstad, lightning bolts of anger flashed from her brown eyes. Amazingly, when Berkstad glimpsed Roxie, the arrogant, brash, intimidating man melted into a puddle of contrition. *Well, no doubt who had all the power in that relationship.* To think he and Miguel had been worried about Roxie.

Elias gestured for Tim and Miguel to approach. Tim was glad to leave Roxie and Berkstad to their own devices. If they weren't here in among all the agents and police, he might not have been so willing.

As Tim wove past her, she whispered, "We have to talk."

He nodded and grumbled, "Oh, yeah. We need to talk."

CHAPTER THIRTY

Tim lifted a hand to stop Roxie from speaking.

"Later," he snarled, glaring at her. Roxie backed away from him.

Oh, he wanted to hear her excuses for the drama, all right. He especially wanted to know why she thought it was okay to put Dani in danger, and to cause the expense of flying her out of harm's way, when apparently there was no big crisis. Not enough, anyway, to keep her from showing back up at work this morning.

More important than Roxie's excuses, the thumb drives in his pocket needed to be reviewed. He wanted to confirm the suspicions that kept circling in his mind like a whirlpool.

Now, he questioned whether or not he needed to get Berkstad's DNA to the lab. If this was nothing more than a lovers' tiff, he didn't want anything to do with it. It was stupid to waste the lab's time on useless pursuits. The moment had come to sit down and talk to Elias.

"What the hell happened? I thought Bounds was under guard," Elias started right in, a perplexed frown creasing his brow.

"The ER doc believes it was anaphylaxis. He was allergic to something the hospital gave him. But, about that . . . ." Tim sucked in a deep breath.

Elias tipped his head to the side, intrigued. "What about that?"

Tim glanced around. He got a bead on Berkstad. The man was trying to convince Roxie to talk to him. Hopefully, she'd keep him distracted long enough for Tim to show Elias the video evidence. "Can we talk privately somewhere?"

"One of the interrogation rooms is free," Elias said, curiosity arching one of his eyebrows.

"That will work. We need Kandar and a laptop," Tim announced.

"Okay." Elias motioned to their teammate.

Kandar rose from behind the desk.

"Grab the laptop and follow me," Elias said. When everyone settled down inside Interrogation Room 3, he asked, "Okay, Tim, what's this all about?"

Tim walked the concrete block room's perimeter, ensuring all cameras, intercoms, and recording devices were off. He could see the confusion on Elias's face.

"I collected video from the hotel corridor from the morning I first noticed Bounds, his shoes, and the M16. I also have the tape from the hotel last night when Beebe called me downstairs to tell me about the pharmacist's package. I had the hospital administrator get me their surveillance video from last night and this morning." He retrieved the thumb drives from his pocket and set them in order beside the computer. "Which do you want to see first?"

"Start at the beginning. I'm listening." Elias toyed with an ink pen he'd brought with him, clicking the ballpoint in and out. He did this sometimes when he was interested but skeptical.

"I believe Congressman Patterson is the second man, Crenshaw's partner. I believe he paid the pharmacist to mess with Bounds's drugs and kill him," Tim said.

Elias did not show any signs of surprise. Kandar's eyes, on the other hand, bugged out.

"I'm getting another cup of coffee," Elias said. "When I get back, show me what you have." He left the room.

When the door eased closed, Kandar asked under his breath as if Elias could still hear him. "Are you going to tell him about the bank accounts?"

"Do you have that back?" Tim hoped he did.

"Came in about ten minutes ago, but I haven't had a chance to look at it." With two fingers, Kandar adjusted his shirt collar as if it had suddenly become too tight.

"Yes, let's see what we have."

"But, we didn't ask Elias…"

"You didn't ask Elias what?" the boss asked as he came back through the doorway.

"Earlier, I asked Kandar to get some bank records."

"Whose bank records?" Elias asked, narrowing his eyes as if he'd already guessed.

"Patterson's and Berkstad's," Tim answered. He stood tall, all the while cringing inside as if expecting a dressing-down.

Elias wiped his hand over his lips. "Do you really think Berkstad is involved?" That he didn't mention Patterson confirmed he agreed with that part of Tim's theory, anyway.

"I could be wrong, but—yes, it's possible." Tim had to confirm or discount his hypothesis once and for all. He reached inside his suitcoat pocket and touched the nitrile glove encompassing the coffee cup lid. He still had reservations about Berkstad. The two men, Patterson and Berkstad, were connected through the Congressional Select Committee on Intelligence. That was a perfectly legal connection—until it wasn't.

Tim took in a deep breath and blew it out. The image of his and Dani's two adopted daughters filled his mind, and with it, overwhelming emotion driving him to protect them against predation of any kind. The honor students didn't deserve their unconscionable treatment. They deserved justice. He was going to see to it they got that.

Tim pulled the cup lid wrapped in the glove from his pocket and plunked it down on the table next to Elias. They locked stares.

"What's this?" Elias asked, not even blinking while waiting for Tim to answer.

"Berkstad's DNA."

"You are fearless. I don't know if I would've gone that far." Elias grinned.

"He fits your profile."

"That he does," Elias agreed. "Kandar, get Melissa to drive this over to the FBI lab. Tell them to rush it. Then get right back here."

They watched as Kandar hustled out to the alcove.

"You know, Berkstad and Roxie were having an affair. You don't think he's here to win her back, instead?" Elias asked.

"You know about that?"

"I know pretty much everything that happens with my team." Elias smiled. "I figured Berkstad is jealous. When he saw the composite picture and recognized Bounds, he used it as an excuse to see Roxie."

"But, you're okay with the DNA and bank records search?" Tim sank into the chair next to Elias, turning it to face him. Kandar returned to the room and took his seat in front of the computer.

"We're investigators. That's what we do—investigate. Either way this goes, guilty or cleared, we're doing our job," Elias said. "Now, let's look at that surveillance video."

"Where would you like to start?" Tim asked.

"Start with the hotel. Let's see it in chronological order." Elias leaned in to view the computer screen.

Kandar inserted the first drive.

The video was crisp, clear, and in full color. The hotel's hallway was empty and illuminated by soft light from ornate brass sconces. After a few seconds, a man entered frame from the direction of the elevators.

"That's Bounds," Tim narrated. The man in the trench coat stopped at a doorway around the middle of the corridor. He lifted his hand and knocked. It took a few seconds, but the door opened. It was Patterson's room. The number was clearly visible on the door. They could see a silhouette, a shadow, but nothing more.

"Come on, step into the light! Come on," Elias said, fully engaged.

A hand reached out from inside the room, and Bounds took the package, looking in both directions, making sure he was alone, as he slipped it into an inside pocket in the trench coat.

"Whatever is in that package is illegal. Could this guy act any more guilty?" Elias commented.

"Damn it! Step into the light!" Kandar said, and just as he did, the room's occupant stepped forward. They couldn't see his face. But as Bounds turned to walk away, the man in the shadows rotated ever so slightly. For only a second, maybe only a fraction of a second, he turned full-face to the camera.

Tim blew out a breath. "It's Patterson, just as Beebe said."

Elias grinned ear to ear. "What's next?"

"Last night. Beebe claims Patterson gave one of those envelopes to the pharmacist." Tim could barely contain the excitement he felt fluttering in his stomach like the sudden flight of a thousand migrating butterflies.

Kandar inserted the next drive. Elias moved directly behind Kandar so he could get a better view of the computer screen.

"This is the time frame where Beebe says she saw Patterson hand off the envelope." Tim said.

They watched. The pale green hospital corridor was quiet. Two nurses appeared at the end, chatting and laughing happily. As they walked down the hall and while still in the camera's range—poof! They disappeared like magic.

"Wow. What was that?" Kandar sat back in his chair so hard it scooted backward on the floor. Elias scrambled to get out of his way. Now, only an empty hallway occupied the screen.

Kandar pressed the arrow at the bottom of the video and moved the tape back to the spot where the two nurses first came into view. He replayed the video. When they arrived mid-corridor, they vanished. "Did they get beamed up by aliens? This video has been altered and not very professionally."

Tim enjoyed Kandar's fantasy approach to everything. The shooter dressed like Darth Vader and aliens beamed up the nurses. "Can you prove it's been altered?"

"Of course," Kandar answered. He scrolled the tape back and started to play it forward in slow motion. "We mark it here—see the flash? This is where the insert begins and here—where it ends."

He rolled the digital recording back and played it forward. "See, right there."

Tim did see it. At 11:37 p.m., there was a small flicker of light you wouldn't notice if you weren't looking for it. At 12:32 a.m., approximately fifty-five minutes later, another flash of light caught Tim's eye. Anyone watching the video would suspect nothing more than computer glitches—except law enforcement.

"Is there a chance you could restore it to the original?" Elias asked.

"If I can have that computer. Nothing is ever completely deleted from a hard drive."

"All right, you'll have it. Let's look at the rest." Elias glanced over at Tim, and a big smile crossed his lips.

Tim narrated as Kandar inserted the next thumb drive. "This is back at the hotel around 1:15 a.m., hotel lobby. That's me, coming from the elevator," Tim said. "I go into the bar. Beebe comes in from the rear entrance to the lobby. She's already called me from her car to ask me to meet her. My guess—she doesn't know if Patterson is back or not."

As the video rolled, Beebe entered the lobby, looked around purposefully nonchalant, and entered the bar. Minutes passed with only small activity from the concierge and hotel clerk.

Two minutes ticked by with everything quiet. Then Patterson entered the lobby from the front door, dropped off the keys to the rental car at the concierge desk, and made his way to the bar.

"Well, this proves he went somewhere," Elias commented. "What else have you got?"

"The last tape shows the nurses picking up their morning medicine cart in the hospital hallway. I wanted to see if we could catch them tampering with Bounds's meds," Tim explained as they watched. To Tim, it looked like two nurses preparing for the morning medication distribution, nothing more. "Without the toxicology from the medical examiner, I don't even know what to look for," Tim said.

"All right. Tim, get Leanne to put together a photo line-up for Miss Knoll. If she confirms the pharmacist is the guy who took the package from Bounds, we'll get a team to go pick him up. Oh, and pull her away from Patterson any way you can without alerting him. We need the element of surprise. Because of his connections to the intelligence community, Patterson may have help with a cover-up. Very dangerous help."

He continued to bark out orders. "Kandar, you study the bank statements and see if you find anything out of the ordinary. No one says anything to anyone about what we are doing until we can narrow down our suspects. I'll interview Crenshaw when he gets here, and Tim, you'll join me after Miss Knoll's photo line-up.

"Let's see if there are any cameras along Main Street that catch Patterson on the road between here and the hospital. I'll get Miguel and Roxie started on that," he concluded.

"Is Roxie going to be okay to go?" Tim asked.

"She begged me to let her come back to work. She's the only one who knows if she's ready or not."

CHAPTER THIRTY-ONE

T im walked briskly past the walnut-framed two-way mirror toward Interrogation Room 2, but stopped short as he
approached Room 1. Through the interior window there,
he could see Roxie and Berkstad standing on opposite sides of the
interview table like two combatants in a face-off. Roxie's arms were
across her chest, and she wore a cold, angry, and closed-off expression.
Berkstad appeared to be pleading his case, but it looked like he was
getting nowhere fast.

Those years ago, back in Seattle, Tim had intuitively known Roxie
would be a tough customer as a girlfriend. It was one of the reasons,
among many, he'd avoided the entanglement. Dating co-workers was
a bad idea. He imagined Berkstad could easily attest to that right now.

He continued down the hallway until he reached Sheriff Leanne's
office. She sat behind her big oak desk, shuffling papers, so he rapped
on the doorframe before entering.

"Tim, come in. I have that photo line-up you asked for," she said,
looking as if she'd been up all night. Already this morning, she'd held
the AM briefing with her deputies and staff, facilitated a press update,
and dispatched a CSI team to handle forensics on Bounds's death.
"Deputies are on their way to pick up Crenshaw for Elias's interview.

I'll be so happy to get this wrapped up." She sighed. "Crenshaw sure had me snookered. He abused those kids right under my da—darned nose."

"That's usually the way it works. Nice guy in public, especially in front of law enforcement and parents; total scumbag when out of sight." Tim approached her desk to retrieve the line-up photos.

"He doesn't know we know. He thinks he's coming in to help in our investigation. Scumbag is right." Leanne shook her head in disbelief. "Probably thinks I'll buy him lunch after we talk. I guess I *will* be buying lunch in a sense. The jail serves lunch." She snickered.

"I don't think Crenshaw knows we plan to arrest him today." Tim took the color photo pages from her hand. "Elias will use that to get him to turn on Patterson if he's involved."

"How are you going to get Miss Knoll away from Patterson? They're attached at the hip," she said. "I could always drop one of those chocolate-flavored laxatives in his coffee."

"Now, there's a tactic I hadn't thought of." Tim grinned at her. He liked Leanne. She had a great sense of humor when she warmed up to you. He'd never asked about family and looked around her office quickly for any pictures to learn something about her life. Framed awards, including several for heroism and marksmanship, decorated the wall behind her desk. In the center spot, one image stood out to him. In a beautiful blue formal gown, Leanne stood next to a handsome man in Marine dress uniform. "Your boyfriend?" Tim asked.

"My husband. We've been married for ten years," she answered, an affectionate smile played on her lips at the thought of him. "Ben is Elias's nephew."

"Really?" Tim nodded. Now, he understood why Elias had been so protective when Berkstad flirted with Leanne the other day. Tim made a mental note to make sure Miguel knew. His partner was attracted to the pretty sheriff.

"Kids?"

"Not yet. We're considering it." Leanne's smile indicated she wasn't sure she was ready for that step. "You?"

"Dani and I have two girls, Lettie is five and Chloe, four." Tim's thoughts drifted to the happiness they'd brought. Especially to Dani. "They are precious."

"Pictures?"

"I do have some." He pulled out his iPhone and scrolled to a video he'd taken of them skiing at Schweitzer Mountain. She looked and smiled in surprise.

"Elias told me about you. You are the agent who adopted kids from the ones rescued at Christmas by The Exploited and Missing Children Unit, aren't you?" She playfully wagged an index finger at him.

Tim felt the warmth from a blush race up into his cheeks. "Blame my wife for that." He laughed. "I just went along to keep the peace."

"Liar. That's not what I heard," Leanne joked. Her eyes sparkled as she handed his phone back to him.

He shrugged. "You don't expect me to admit I like children, do you? Gotta keep that big, tough, guy image going."

"You can be both, you know. They aren't mutually exclusive." Leanne held his gaze and then returned her interest to some papers on her desk. Their conversation had strayed beyond her comfort zone.

"Thanks for this, Leanne." Tim stepped out into the hallway between her office, the interrogation rooms, and the primary deputy and detective's floor. Before he left on his mission to get Beebe to identify who at the hospital Patterson had given the secret envelope to, Leanne gave him one of her warm smiles. Tim knew they'd be good working partners in the future. In law enforcement, you had to know who would have your back.

Now, he had to come up with an excuse to have Beebe look at the line-up without alerting Patterson. The longer it took for the congressman to realize he was under suspicion, the better.

Tim searched the open space where the deputies and detectives did their day-to-day work. Looking over the heads and computer monitors of busy officers and general clutter, he found Beebe sitting at a desk close to the FBI's temporary facility in the alcove. She caught his stare, held it for a moment, and then returned to typing furiously on her laptop, probably writing a story for the evening news. Patterson was nowhere in sight.

"Tim," Elias said. Tim turned to see him approach from Interrogation Room 3.

"Sir?"

"Leanne just called. Crenshaw will be here in five minutes."

That was his cue. He had to find Patterson and force a confrontation. They wanted to see the men's reactions to each other.

"He's not with Beebe. I haven't seen him," Tim said.

"He's coming this way. Keep him here however you can," Elias said under his breath and then nodded a greeting to the congressman.

Tim folded the photo line-up in half and quickly slipped it into his suitcoat's inside pocket. He wheeled to face the congressman, just as the man took his last stride to join them.

"Good morning," Tim said. "You remember Elias Cain?"

"Yes. Of course." Patterson reached out to shake Elias's hand and immediately turned to Tim. "What's going on around here this morning?" Patterson was anxious. He jangled some loose change in his left pants pocket, and his gaze darted to and fro, as if he looked for a boogeyman in every shadow.

Tim decided. He'd try to catch him off guard and gauge his reaction. "Our school shooter, Bounds, died this morning."

Patterson rocked back on his heels, but only for a moment. His face morphed from relief quickly back to a pretend shock. "I thought he was under guard. How did that happen?"

"We'll know for sure once the tox screen is back, but the doctor on duty believes it was an allergic reaction to one of his medications," Tim answered, watching for a micro-expression from Patterson. He saw one. The congressman's pupils tightened, and he took in a deep breath and let it out as if he'd just run a red light and narrowly escaped a crash.

Elias glanced over at Tim and smiled with satisfaction, like he did when he tricked a criminal into inadvertently admitting his crime.

The second part of this exercise now headed their way. Two sheriff's deputies escorted Edmond Crenshaw toward Interrogation Room 2. They would need to pass right by each other. Intrigued, Tim concentrated on their exchange. He could hear each step as Crenshaw's leather-soled wingtips softly scuffed along the tile floor. Crenshaw did a double-take when he noticed Patterson in his path.

In what seemed like a slow-motion film, Crenshaw recoiled and looked away. Fear flashed from his downcast gaze. But he quickly recovered and corrected his response, a sheepish grin teased at the corners of his mouth.

"Aaron? Is that you?" He asked.

"Edmond? Edmond Crenshaw?" Patterson said. A hint of surprise colored his voice, followed by an awkward shuffle.

The guilty tell was precisely what Tim was looking for. The men knew each other well enough to be on a first-name basis. Patterson didn't offer to shake hands. It was clear, Patterson held all the power.

"What brings you here to Culpeper?" Principal Crenshaw asked.

"This school shooting is the very reason we need gun control. I came down here to make sure the police caught the shooter and to confront Sheriff LaCrosse. I want to hear what she has to say to her constituents about her pro-gun stance, now." Patterson huffed. "I'm introducing my gun bill to the committee tomorrow. What are you doing here?"

"I came to see if I could help," Crenshaw answered, an almost imperceptible shudder running along the top of his shoulders.

"Haven't you heard? Didn't you tell him?" Patterson directed his question to Tim. His mouth contorted with outrage.

"What didn't I hear?" Crenshaw studied Tim's face and then looked over his shoulder as if trying to get an answer from the two deputies.

"We arrested the shooter yesterday evening, and he died in the hospital this morning," Elias said matter-of-factly.

"You caught him? Oh. My. God. That's good news. Do you still need me?"

"We have a few loose ends we need to tie up for the victims' parents. You know how it is." Elias locked stares with Tim. Intentionally, Tim kept his expression blank, unreadable. "Shall we get started?" Elias gestured for Crenshaw to enter Interrogation Room 2. Tim had never seen a person so happy to be walking into a police interrogation room.

Before Crenshaw turned toward the doorway, Patterson's smile clouded over and went to the dark side. Like the crooked black fingers from a bottle of spilled ink, an unspoken threat spread throughout the corridor. Crenshaw rounded his shoulders and hunched his back as he walked by, as if trying to avoid a blow.

When Elias closed the door with Crenshaw inside, Patterson's whole demeanor changed. The glad-handed servant of the people returned, a counterfeit smile sliding across his lips. Tim automatically took a step back.

Patterson looked at his watch. "Well, I must get going. There's a vote on immigration reform today. I have just enough time to get back to DC." He studied Tim's face and added, "You don't suppose Miss St. Clair would let me join her on her private plane?"

"*Mrs. McAndrews* left early this morning, sorry." Tim returned a smile as phony as Patterson's, only with an added dash of poison. After their marriage, Dani had willingly taken Tim's name. She chose not to use even a hyphenated version. Patterson insisted on throwing out her maiden name to provoke and belittle him. Tim wouldn't take the bait. He was actually amused by the congressman's attempt to demean him.

"Maybe next time," Patterson said, dismissing Tim, looking him up and down, turning on his heel, and walking briskly to the main door. *Jerk!* Tim thought. Taking down this insufferable blowhard was going to be fun.

Patterson left Beebe sitting in front of her laptop at the desk by the alcove. *That's not going to sit well*, Tim thought. Being left behind when a highly controversial vote was going down on the floor of the House might make her head explode.

For Tim, though, the Fates had just handed him a golden opportunity to show her the photo line-up. He grinned to himself as he started toward her. As he passed by Interrogation Room 1, he noticed the open doorway. His first thought—Berkstad and Roxie had resolved their differences. Maybe she'd accompanied Miguel to find surveillance video along Main Street. He saw Berkstad standing alone in the doorway, hands planted firmly on his hips.

Tim realized they'd had the same FBI training. The Counterintelligence section chief might've seen the exchange between the congressman and the principal and developed his own theory about the crime. A strange smirk curved Berkstad's lips.

"So, McAndrews. I think it's time we had a little talk."

CHAPTER THIRTY-TWO

"Tim!"

At the sound of Kandar's voice, Tim turned away from Berkstad.

"You've got to see this!" Kandar shouted from the alcove door.

"Excuse me, sir," Tim said to Berkstad. There was no way on Planet Earth Tim wanted to get embroiled in a Berkstad vs. Roxie fight, which was what he suspected Berkstad intended to talk about. He took this moment to escape. "I've got to see this, whatever *this* is." He jogged through the main floor to the door of the FBI area.

At the desk closest to the alcove, Beebe suddenly stood in his path; no way she wanted to miss the fun. Berkstad, undeterred by the interruption, trailed behind.

Tim stopped at the entryway to the alcove as Beebe tried to muscle past him. He blocked her by putting one hand on each side of the doorframe.

"Sorry, you're not authorized to go beyond this point."

"Tim, please."

He didn't say anything—he stared her down. She knew not authorized meant NO.

"Oh, you jackass!" She sulked.

Tim laughed. He wasn't exactly ready for her name-calling when he lifted his arm and let Berkstad through.

"You let him in!"

"He's FBI. He *is* authorized." Tim grinned at her.

Furious, she pressed her glossy lips tightly together and paced in a circle in front of the doorway. "You make me so mad!"

Tim reached inside his suitcoat and produced the photo line-up sheet. "That's why you love me. Now, get over it. I have something I need you to do."

Still pouting, she squinted her eyes at him and angrily tapped her fingers on the sides of her pant legs. Intrigued, she asked, "All right. What do you need me to do?"

Tim shot a look of apology to Kandar. "Hold on a minute. I'll be right there." With a hand on Beebe's back, he guided her to the desk where she'd been working on her laptop. He set the six-picture line-up in front of her.

"Beebe, can you tell me if any of these men is the one that took the package from Patterson at the hospital?"

She glared at him. Patiently, Tim waited until she sank into the chair and looked at the photographs. Recognition immediately crossed her face like a flash from a camera. She opened her mouth to speak, but hesitated. Was she unsure now that she should provide him with the information?

"You called me. You gave me the SD card from your camera, remember? Help me now. Even if you think I'm a jackass." Tim set his hand along the back of her chair and leaned forward, encouraging her to look again. "Is any one of these men the one Patterson gave the envelope to?"

"I know. I need to do the right thing. So what if it means I won't get the White House Press Corps promotion?" She returned her stare to the pictures.

"The shooter died in the hospital this morning," Tim said. There was no sense keeping that information from her. For all he knew, Patterson would assemble a press conference to announce it. The man was a media whore.

Beebe gasped and spun in her chair to see Tim's face. "You think Aaron paid the guy at the hospital to kill the shooter?"

"I need more data to speculate about that. We will pursue every lead."

"Why? Why would he do that?" Beebe's look implored him to tell her. He couldn't. If she ran with his theory and it proved not to be true, he'd be up the proverbial creek without a paddle.

"That's why we want to talk to the guy at the hospital. For all I know, Patterson could've given him ballgame tickets or—say—grocery coupons," Tim commented. "Do you recognize anyone or not?"

"At midnight? Grocery coupons?" Beebe rolled her eyes. "You really are nuts, McAndrews."

"I follow the evidence."

"Well, there's no evidence Aaron Patterson ever clipped grocery coupons. At least not when he's with me. This man is the one." She pointed to the driver's license image of Philip Dockery. Tim matched it to the list of pharmacy employees he'd received from the hospital administrator. Dockery was the pharmacist on overnight duty. Was Dockery supplying the Rohypnol, too? Tim guessed he'd soon find out.

Beebe didn't know it yet, but she was in danger. If Patterson paid to have innocent kids murdered, then to have Bounds killed, he'd do the same to Beebe without missing a beat.

The fact that Tim had to deal with her as she gathered stories for her evening news segment, *Crime Beat,* exasperated him to no end. Even though she was the most annoying woman Tim had ever met, he didn't want her tipping off Patterson. But even more, he didn't want her dead.

"Beebe, for your safety, I want you to leave town. Tell Patterson SBC News called you back to Seattle." It was a shot in the dark. Beebe would resist, of course. But with Patterson's shadowy connection to Berkstad and Counterintelligence, this could go really bad for her, really fast.

"Don't be silly."

"Why? Because you think he doesn't know you ratted him out to the FBI? What happens when he does know it? If he did pay to have Bounds killed, what do you think your chances of seeing your next birthday are?"

"I think he was buying drugs. I don't think he paid to—Wait. You're scaring me."

"I mean to. Go back to Seattle, get away for a few days, or I could put you in protective custody, your choice."

"You wouldn't dare!" Color raced into her cheeks. "You can't. I have a job to do."

"Try me." He motioned to one of the deputies on the main floor.

Beebe stood, her hands raised and fingers curled into claws as if she wanted to scratch his eyes out like a cornered feral cat. Then logic must've hit her, because her eyes widened and she lowered her hands. "You're right. What if? I'll lay low for a few days if you give me the exclusive story, otherwise—screw you. You can't tell me what to do."

Tim had to admit that, as vexing as Beebe was, she was a good writer—one of the best. He remembered the times she'd come to his office in Seattle to taunt him about an article she was about to publish on one of his court cases, giving him the 'first read.' She'd be the perfect investigative journalist to reveal Patterson's bad deeds. Win-win.

"Okay. The exclusive is yours," Tim said. He didn't have that authority, but as long as she thought he did, he'd use it.

When the deputy joined them, Tim asked, "Would you take this to Sheriff LaCrosse for me?" He handed the photo line-up to him. "Thanks. Oh, and would you mind escorting Miss Knoll to the press area?"

"What press area?" The deputy asked, confused.

"Anywhere outside the sheriff's office," Tim said, barely keeping a smile from breaking through.

Beebe slammed her laptop shut and slid it into its protective case, glaring at him the whole time.

Tim felt more comfortable after she left. Though he knew Beebe would do whatever she wanted without regard to peril, it would take time to set up protective custody. Time, he didn't have. She took him seriously, he was sure.

He turned his attention to Kandar inside the alcove. Now that he'd diverted Beebe's attention and confirmed the money hand off was to the pharmacist, he couldn't wait to see the new evidence he'd received. Kandar sat at the desk in front of the computer, flanked by Berkstad and Melissa. They studied the screen over his shoulders.

"Tim, we received the video footage from Walmart," Kandar said.

Tim took his place beside Berkstad behind Kandar. "What have we got?"

"We can see who purchased Bounds's burner phone and the prepaid Visa card. It ain't Bounds." Kandar reversed the thumb drive to the beginning and started it forward again.

From the camera's-eye view, they looked down on the check-out line. A shapely blonde woman set two burner phones and a prepaid Visa card on the conveyor belt. She walked forward as the cashier processed her order, coming into full view of the camera.

"Wow. Not Bounds. Who's this?" Tim asked, watching as she paid, peeling off bills from a stack of cash.

"You don't know?" Berkstad asked, one eyebrow arched in mockery, and a smile like triumph curled his lips. He knew they didn't know, and Tim was instantly annoyed.

"Do you?" *This isn't a contest.*

"That's Samantha Wordsworth, Congressman Aaron Patterson's chief of staff."

Tim straightened and stepped back a stride. He never expected it to be this easy. If only the DNA were back from the lab. He wanted to ask Kandar to check on it and would've—if Berkstad wasn't lurking around like a great white shark. "We need to find Samantha Wordsworth."

"I'm on it," Kandar said, leaning forward and typing her name in a search bar on the computer screen.

"I'm going to see if Elias needs help with Mr. Crenshaw. Let me know when you find her." Tim hurried to their case board and studied it for a second. After he checked on Elias, he was determined to sit down, alone, and do a timeline with paper and pencil, as he'd done on his court cases in the DA's office.

As he turned toward the interrogation rooms, he realized Berkstad was at his side. "Are you my shadow again today?" Tim stared at the man.

"I need to talk to you and Elias. You're driving this investigation in a dangerous direction. You have your shooter. Close it down." Berkstad frowned, and the furrows along his mouth deepened, giving him the appearance of a much older man than his actual years.

Tim realized Berkstad had not been read in on the assaults on the honor students and Aiysha's pregnancy—the very motive he believed to be responsible for the school shooting in the first place.

"Yeah, well, you see Elias about that," Tim said. "He had me skip the 'Run From Danger and Don't Solve Crime' classes at Quantico." So much for Fidelity, Bravery, and Integrity. Tim no longer sat the fence concerning Berkstad. The man just tipped the scale all the way over to shitbag.

Tim turned on his heel and continued to the two-way mirror outside of the interrogation room where Elias interviewed Crenshaw. He knew Berkstad could and should fire him. But his quick wit had often won cases for him in King County. It certainly would give Berkstad pause.

He looked behind him to see if Berkstad still followed. Instead, the section chief, with his cell phone to his ear, walked along the wall of windows that separated the main floor from the corridor and interrogation rooms. He was probably ordering up Tim's dismissal papers. Or worse yet, calling Patterson to let him know he was a person of interest.

Oh, boy! Guilt came rushing in. What if he lost his job? Because of his career choice, Dani'd bought the new house, the furniture, and the wine-tasting shop, and was about to move the whole family here to be with him. Tim rubbed his hand back and forth across his forehead. Dani was about to learn what an incredible jerk she'd married. Tim knew he'd have to make amends with Berkstad and fast. He turned around just as Berkstad returned to his side.

Tim cleared his throat."Sir, I want to apologize for my remark. I was disrespectful and out of line."

Berkstad raised an eyebrow. "Is that so? Your apology is accepted."

Momentarily stunned, Tim continued, "I should never—"

Berkstad lifted a palm to stop him.

"Well, I needed to hear it. There are no classes at Quantico that teach cowardice and fear. After riding a desk for five years, I've lost my vision. Agents like you and Roxie are bringing it back to me." He breathed in deeply. "I am going to be in the alcove. When Elias gets free, I want to be fully briefed on your investigation. I have information that you need to hear."

And just like that, the needle swung back to the positive side of the shitbag scale. Not quite all the way, though.

CHAPTER THIRTY-THREE

Beebe sat in the front seat of her blue Honda and pressed her forehead against the steering wheel. This wasn't the first time that Jackass McAndrews had unceremoniously tossed her out of his place of employment. Nor would it be the last. There was an unspoken conflict between law enforcement and the media. Cops tried to keep their cases tight to the vest, releasing only small bits of information. The press needed dramatic headlines so the public would tune in. The two goals were opposed to each other; what the cops wanted kept quiet, journalists wanted out in the open.

Beebe didn't really give a rat's behind about the TV audience as long as they watched her segment. High Nielsen ratings and a chance to be a top-named journalist, on the other hand, had her full attention. One thing she had learned about being around the cop shops and Tim, though, was that she'd better listen when they warned her about something.

She pressed the ignition. Why would Patterson kill the school shooter? Something was missing from her understanding of the crime. Getting that piece from McAndrews was about as likely as winning the Nobel Peace Prize.

Instead of going to Seattle as Tim had suggested, Beebe decided to go to her apartment in DC and lay low for a day or two. She put the car in reverse and headed back to the hotel room she shared with

Patterson. Patterson had a vote this morning and wouldn't be back until late afternoon, and she could pack without distraction.

If Tim kept his promise, she could turn the exclusive into a comprehensive piece. Getting too close to the action wasn't all that much fun, anyway. She remembered the last time she was "in the action." At Christmas, running for her life, child-trafficking bad guys pursuing and shooting at her. That kind of fun she could do without. She'd barely escaped with her life. A shudder ran in little mouse steps across the top of her shoulders. Tim was right. She needed to get out of here. If she wanted to be terrified, she could watch a horror movie.

At the hotel, Beebe parked and walked through the lobby to the elevator bank. *Wait a minute! Wait a doggone minute!* She had a job to do. Journalism was her career. She'd spent six years in college to land this job. Because of her critical thinking skills, boldness, and craft, she'd risen to the top of her field. Well, that's what she wanted to believe, anyway. She remembered when she'd interviewed for the job. She'd walked into a hallway, sparse resume in hand, and stood for hours for her turn. When she studied the other women auditioning for the job, she felt she was at an open casting call for blonde bimbos.

Ultimately, she realized that instead of an interview process, SBC News held a beauty contest, with the winner's "talent" being good oral reading skills. When she landed the job, her feelings were a mixed bag. She wasn't just a newsreader—she was a news personality. In the years that followed, she'd worked hard to move up the ladder, even secretly writing articles under the pseudonym "Alice Carroll" for a gossip rag, the *National Globe,* on the side. She'd be damned if she was going to let some FBI jackass run her off a story. Now, it was her job to figure out what that story actually was. Just how was she going to do that?

Was Aaron Patterson, congressman from California, doing prescription drugs? Why would the FBI believe he'd paid to have a school shooter killed? Did he not believe in the justice system and decide to take things into his own hands?

Distracted, she finally pushed the second-floor button on the open elevator. The doors closed, just as a man dressed in a flannel plaid shirt, like lumberjacks wear, tried to get on. She'd been so deep in thought she didn't even think to push the door open button to help him out.

When she stepped out of the elevator onto the second floor, she noticed a woman in a pink business suit walking down the corridor toward her from the direction of Patterson's room. The woman's stylish, attractive suit caught Beebe's eye. Nodding a greeting as she passed by, she once again felt a tingle along the top of her shoulders. Had she seen that face before? She whirled around to see the woman hurry away.

Tim's warning reverberated in her mind. Overwhelmed by a sudden panic, Beebe quickly reached in her jacket pocket and retrieved her key. She inserted the card into the reader, and as soon as she heard the click, she raced inside. Instead of waiting for the door to close on its own, she shoved her weight into it, feeling resistance from the air shock hinge.

"Damn you, Jackass! You have me scared of my own shadow!" she said out loud, as if Tim could hear her. She needed to get packed and out.

Flipping on the light, she studied the walnut tables and pale green walls of the room. Everything looked normal. She wasn't sure she would notice if it weren't anyway. She slammed open the mirrored closet slider and pulled out her suitcase, tossed it on the bed, and unzipped it. Without care, she shoved all her clothes from the hotel dresser into the case. If she didn't slow down, she'd never be able to get it closed.

She flopped back onto the bed, trying to quiet her mind and lower her heart rate. As her thoughts calmed, she realized she'd seen the woman in the pink suit several times before in the hotel. She was probably just another hotel guest, just like Beebe herself.

Sitting up, she caught her reflection in the mirrored closet doors. She fussed with a few blonde curls crushed by the bed pillow. Then, she saw Patterson's suitcase. A corner of navy blue caught enough light to trigger a devious impulse. It wasn't as if she hadn't snooped through boyfriends' stuff before. She had. Just not Patterson's. Vacillating between *should*

I or shouldn't I, Beebe scooted to the edge of the bed. *I should* won the toss. This was all Tim's fault, she rationalized. He was the one who'd planted the seed of suspicion.

"Why would Aaron Patterson kill the school shooter?" she asked herself out loud.

Glancing at her watch, she made sure there was enough time to sneak through his things. Currently, he was at the Capitol for the vote, and had suggested he'd be back late.

She decided to look through the suitcase while it remained in the closet. That way, if he came back early, she could close it up quickly, and no one would be the wiser. She knelt in front of the case, rubbed her palms together, and unzipped the main compartment.

Taking in a deep breath, Beebe vibrated with an adrenaline rush. Tim had once told her she would never make a spy—ha! If only he could see her now. She threw back the top flap and looked inside.

What a fricking letdown! What? Was she expecting to find some dramatic answer in neon lights? There was a neatly stacked row of various pale-colored shirts, all starched and pressed, with the dry cleaner's little cardboard collar thingies still in place. In the space next to the dress shirts, a row of white t-shirts and tighty whities, then multicolored socks and ties to match whatever outfit he decided to wear that day. *Well, whoop-de-doo!* This sure was spy work at its finest. Beebe rolled her eyes. Why on earth did she listen to Tim in the first place?

She sat back, and as she did, the overhead light gleamed on a small metal latch she hadn't seen before. She lifted the clothes, and there she found a secure compartment under the top one with a battery-operated digital locking device. When she knocked on it, it resonated with a metallic sound. It was safe-like. Defeated, she slumped down. It required a four-digit code to open. What would a narcissistic, self-absorbed man like Patterson use as a passcode? His birthday? She tried it. Wrong. His birthday backward? Not it, again. *This was going to take all day!* Then she thought, what was the day that had changed his life? The day they met? No. He wasn't that romantic. The day he was elected to Congress? She entered that date, and instead of the expected red error light, a green one flashed on. Who would've thought? She'd guessed right.

Carefully, she turned the toggle so it would fit through the hole made for it. She lifted the lid. Two shirts, caught by gravity, slipped out of the case and onto the floor. Crap! She knew that was going to happen. She turned her wrist slightly so she could see the face of her watch again. She had time. Cautiously, she unpacked the top layer, setting the clothes in order so she could put them back the way she'd found them. Again, she lifted the black divider.

Payday! Patterson, or whoever had packed the case, laid five envelopes out, one touching the other in a neat row. For all his blabber about gun control and gun violence, secured by a cut-out foam insert was a black, scary-looking semi-automatic pistol, a silencer, and one fully loaded extra magazine. *A gun for me, but not for thee? Hypocrite!* There was also a phone. Not an expensive iPhone or comparable brand, but an old-fashioned, cheap flip phone, and his passport. No drugs. No answer, either, as to why Tim thought Patterson paid for a murder-for-hire scheme.

She picked up one of the envelopes. By weight, she guessed it contained a stack of bills, denomination unknown. As she explored the outside with her fingers, she thought she felt a paper money band wrapped around the stack, as if the banknotes inside were brand-new. She held the package up to the light. Of course, Patterson had used security envelopes to prevent seeing inside. She had no choice. She flipped the pack over and carefully slipped a fingernail under the center of the glued flap. It opened easily at first, but firmly held at the end of each side. Slowly, carefully, she worked her finger along the glue-line, tearing a tiny part away at a time, keeping it mostly intact so that she could reseal it.

This envelope contained four straps of 100-dollar bills. With 100 bills in each strap, times four—*Holy cow!* That was forty thousand dollars! If the other four envelopes contained the same amount, Patterson had at least 200,000 dollars stashed in the bottom of his suitcase. *Didn't he believe in banks?* But then again, if what he was doing with the money was illegal, such as payoffs for blackmail . . . .

She grabbed her iPhone and took pictures of everything, including the packets of money and the call logs on his cheapo phone. On her way back to DC, she'd drop the photos off to Tim at the sheriff's department. For a moment, she sat completely still. Here she was, once more, doing things to help and impress Tim. She couldn't think about that right now. She closed the secret safe, and waited for it to lock. She had to get out of here.

Suddenly, she heard the click sound the door made when someone inserted a keycard. She couldn't remember if she'd latched the security bar. A maid would've knocked. Besides, the bed was made, and fresh towels were left in the bathroom. How could she possibly explain what she was doing if Patterson was at the door?

"Beebe? Are you in there?" A muffled voice came through the door.

It was Patterson. Her heart began to race. At least she'd locked the bar. Now what?

"Let me in."

She got up and crept closer to the door. "Aaron, I'm indisposed. I'll be there in a second," she shouted through the door.

"Hurry up. I feel like a fool out here."

"Just a second," she answered and then bolted back to the closet. She threw his shirts back in the case, then the t-shirts, the underwear, the socks, the ties. She studied it for a moment, making sure it looked undisturbed. *Screw it!* She'd be long gone before he noticed. She closed the flap and zipped it up.

She made her way to the door, feeling almost dizzy with the surge of fight-or-flight hormones racing through her bloodstream. At the last second, she remembered she'd used the toilet as her excuse. She dashed into the bathroom and flushed, then she opened the door.

"Thank God. I felt like a jerk standing outside the room." Patterson tossed Beebe a wicked glance as he peeled his overcoat off and threw it on the chair.

"I'm not going to apologize—when you gotta go, you gotta go. Besides, I thought you said you'd be back in the late afternoon," Beebe retorted, not one to back down.

Patterson looked at her suitcase lying open on the bed. "Going somewhere?" He slowly turned to face her. His eyes narrowed into small dark slits.

"SBC News has called me back to Seattle for a couple of days. I know you turn off your phone while working. I left you a message." She regurgitated the excuse Tim told her to use. Frightened now, she could barely think. She knew she had to play along. Patterson, her former lover, had become a brooding monster and maybe a murderer. Nervously, she continued to pack.

"I don't want you to go."

She could feel the warmth of his body as he moved behind her wrapping his arms around her waist. He kissed the back of her neck, stopped, and sat down next to her suitcase on the bed.

"I know, darling. But it's work," she cooed. "It's only for two days." After the final blouse was folded and packed, she zipped up her case and lowered it from the bed to the floor. She pulled up the handle and hung her laptop case and purse over it.

"Do I get a kiss before you go?"

Beebe wanted to run; she could feel her legs twitching in anticipation. Barely containing her fear, she walked over and kissed him. By the passion in his caress, she knew he wanted to linger there, to make love. She could barely hold back her gag reflex and swallowed.

"Sweetie, I'll miss my flight."

"Catch the next one."

"They're expecting me. Besides, the sooner I get there, the quicker I can finish my piece and get back," she whispered against his cheek.

"All right. I don't want you to go, but if you must . . . ." He released her from his embrace. He didn't ask her the question she dreaded: could he join her?

"See you in two days," Beebe chimed. Her heart beat so fast; she felt weak in the knees.

Slowly, she walked out of the room, her luggage in tow. As soon as she hit the hallway, she sprinted for the elevator, and her luggage arrangement became unbalanced and almost tipped over. Once inside the elevator, she started straightening things. She removed her purse and slung it over her shoulder. Before the door closed, the woman in the pink suit joined her. A curious fleeting smile passed between them.

After the doors closed, the woman moved near her side. Beebe felt something hard pressed into her ribs. Instinctively, she knew it was the barrel of a gun. She felt her knees begin to buckle. She almost fainted, but held on.

"Don't say anything. Don't scream. Don't run. I will shoot you," the woman growled.

Beebe could only nod that she understood. Dread overwhelmed her.

Did Patterson watch her rummage through his suitcase with some hidden camera and send this goon to take her out? How was she going to get out of this? She tried to think of a way, but her mind wouldn't focus.

As the elevator doors opened, her first impulse was to run. But to be shot in the back didn't really work for her. She was averse to pain, any pain.

Just then, the man in the logger's plaid grabbed her luggage from her and slipped his arm under her suit jacket at her back. Now there were guns on each side of her. Her abductors escorted her through the lobby and out of the building without a single protest from Beebe. She wanted to scream, she even opened her mouth to scream, but nothing came out.

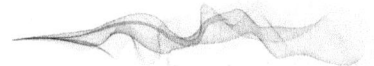

CHAPTER THIRTY-FOUR

Tim stood next to Elias in front of the two-way mirror, watching Edmond Crenshaw tap his fingers impatiently on the wooden interview table.

"You ready for this?" Elias asked, performing a last-minute check through the folder he carried with him. Because of his size, Elias's routine was to come on like a gentle giant, a big teddy bear.

Tim nodded.

"If I hit a roadblock, I'll signal by asking if he'd like a cup of coffee. That'll be your cue to show up with three cups and join us. Put the coffee in ceramic mugs rather than paper to make him feel like we give him the utmost respect," Elias continued.

"I understand," Tim said.

"Well, here we go." He stepped forward into the interrogation room and introduced himself and Detective Greenway from the sheriff's department. Then he pushed the start button on the table's side, and both audio and video recording began. In the viewing area, Tim could hear everything through speakers flush-mounted in the walls. The light on the camera turned green.

Leanne walked up and handed Tim a cup of coffee.

"Thanks," he said.

"Have you ever watched Uncle Elias do an interview?" she asked, and took a sip.

"He's formidable," Tim said, smiling at the memory of several he'd seen.

They watched a master at work through the two-way mirror. An Elias Cain interrogation wasn't just stellar police work—it was art. He'd already put Crenshaw at ease with questions about school protocols and procedures during a shooting, rewarding him with kudos on how well they'd done under the circumstances. Now, he led the principal down the path to talk about the special reward program he'd established for the honor students. He laid out the students' pictures on the table and asked Crenshaw to acknowledge they were the members of his group, *The Scholastic Honor Society*, he'd called it. Their research had established that it was a 501(c)(3) non-profit. Donations to the group would be tax deductible.

"Describe a typical outing you'd take with the kids." Elias's voice was mellow, soothing, musical, like Motown-style soft rock.

Tim could see Crenshaw relax in his seat, his hands neatly folded, one on top of the other on the table before him. He was as calm as if he and Cain were old friends at coffee.

"We would leave Friday at noon, drive to DC for cultural enrichment. We would go to dinner at a nice restaurant, then to a ballet, a symphony performance, a play, the museum, things like that. After the event, the students were welcome to voluntarily come to my suite and discuss what they'd experienced. They were always so keyed-up and excited, it was hard to get them to settle down. Then everyone dispersed to their rooms. The next morning, we would meet up for breakfast, and we'd return home by Saturday afternoon." Crenshaw's smile was confident, and if Tim hadn't known the truth, he too might have been persuaded. "As far as I know, we were the only high school around with such an honor program." Crenshaw lifted his chin in a snobbish display of pride.

"Your last trip was on Thursday night before the shooting. Why was that?"

"This month's trip was originally scheduled for this weekend, but Friday was the last day before spring break, and many families had plans. Knowing that most of my teachers typically scheduled a light day, we voted to go on Thursday. The kids returned to school on Friday, and I headed for my education meeting on Capitol Hill." Crenshaw's grin was almost more than Tim could swallow.

He felt Leanne stiffen beside him. She seemed to throw off the anger by rolling her shoulders—Tim's stomach knotted instead. Knowing the truth made it hard to listen to the BS. The intercom crackled to life.

"The activities you planned sound expensive. Nice restaurants, a fancy hotel near the Capitol, plays, museums, and symphonies—those all cost money, more than many families could afford. How did you get that past the school board?" Elias asked.

"It didn't cost the families, or the board, a dime. We procured private donations to fund it. Important investors that have a stake in our community," Crenshaw boasted.

Tim swiped his hand over his mouth and down his jaw, trying to contain the revulsion brewing up inside like lava. Pedophile rings were like the mythical Hydra. Cut off one head, and two spring up in its place.

"Wow. Big investors like—say—Aaron Patterson? Was he one of your investors? I saw you talking with him in the hall." Elias continued.

"Why, yes. He's one of our most generous contributors."

Tim and Leanne locked eyes for a moment. Tim pulled his iPhone out of his pocket and called Kandar. "It's Tim. Check on the DNA results on Patterson's sample. Put a rush on it if they aren't ready," he whispered into the phone and hung up.

"Do you have a list of your contributors?" Elias asked.

"Of course. My secretary, Janet Doyle, can fix you up with that. They contribute annually."

Elias motioned for the deputy, and he quickly exited the room on his mission to collect the information.

"So, how many years did you do these field trips?" Elias asked.

"I believe this is our tenth year." Crenshaw smiled, and Elias shuffled through his file.

When Tim glanced over at Leanne, her hands were balled into fists at her side, and her lips tightened in a grim line. She said, "I was an honor student at that high school, five years before Crenshaw came to town. That man pulled this off right under my damned nose."

"I don't think we expect people to be as bad as they are. I'm constantly surprised. But of course, that's why they used Rohypnol. The kids pass out and wake up in their own bed in the hotel room in the morning, maybe confused, hurt in ways they don't understand, and a little sick, but they have few memories. What memory they do have seems like a dream. They are afraid and tell no one." Tim breathed out his sadness. He couldn't relate to the disrespect, the utter lack of empathy, the psychopathic selfishness it would take to commit an act like this.

Elias's voice through the speakers drew their attention back to the interview. "Umm, looks like you obtained parental permission for these outings, is that right?" Elias asked. Tim recognized the barely perceptible tone change in his voice. *Crenshaw, the piece of crap, is just about to be flushed.* A feeling of satisfaction flooded his system.

"Oh, yes. Every field trip, every time." Crenshaw sat up all proud and then cocked his head slightly to the side. "Did someone say we didn't?"

"No. No. Not at all. Is this the permission slip you used?" Elias slid a piece of paper across the table.

"Yes. I have signed ones in my office for everyone and every trip."

"Do you know Susan Bower?" Elias threw it out there. Tim knew if Crenshaw acknowledged her, it made her accusation more plausible. Elias set her picture in front of Crenshaw.

"Susan, why, yes. She's one of our honor students. Lovely girl. Is Susan saying she didn't have permission to go? I always get parental consent in writing. I have the original in my office." Defensive now, Crenshaw squirmed in his chair.

Tim knew Elias intended to increase Crenshaw's anxiety by a long pause before speaking. They wanted the man to start worrying about what the police knew.

"I don't see anywhere in this permission slip an authorization to administer Rohypnol. You know Rohypnol, the date rape drug?" Elias pulled the toxicology screen from the autopsies out of his file and set it in front of Crenshaw. He stood to his full height and loomed over the table toward the sputtering man. The big teddy bear just became a grizzly.

"I don't—I didn't—I don't know what you're talking about."

"We established earlier, Mr. Crenshaw, that Thursday night's trip to DC was a special occasion. At autopsy, we found traces of the date rape drug Rohypnol in all three of the students who died in the shooting Friday morning."

Crenshaw's relaxed demeanor had morphed to full-blown panic. Beads of sweat formed along his hairline and glistened under the florescent lights as they trickled down his cheeks.

"I had nothing to do with that. I don't know what you're talking about. They must've taken that drug when on their own," Crenshaw replied, his voice cracking. He pulled a cloth handkerchief from his pocket and wiped away the nervous sweat.

"Could've, you're right." Elias pulled out another sheet of paper and dropped it in front of the man. "But then tell me, Mr. Crenshaw, why is your DNA all over Marty Schultz's body?"

Crenshaw stared across the table incredulous, his mouth forming words of protest he couldn't vocalize.

"You know what I think, Mr. Crenshaw? I think you took these children on outings, and then you drugged them with Rohypnol so that you and your fellow 'contributors' could abuse them and rape them without having to worry about consent. You knew the kids would have no memory of it. That's what I think. You and your boys were having a grand old time until Aiysha Conrow turned up pregnant. How'd you find out? Did Aiysha come to you for advice? The school nurse make a wild guess?"

Crenshaw set his elbows on the table, dropped his head into his hands, and began to cry. "I never touched her. Never."

"But you touched Marty, didn't you?"

"I want my lawyer," he whimpered.

They didn't need him to say anymore.

"You'll need him. You have one phone call, Mr. Crenshaw. You are under arrest for the drugging, rape, and sexual abuse of a minor, just for starters." The deputy in the room cuffed Crenshaw and began to lead him away.

"I didn't kill those children! I didn't. I'm not the school shooter! I had nothing to do with it!" Crenshaw screamed.

"We'll just have to wait and see about that, Mr. Crenshaw," Elias said coldly.

Tim turned and noticed the whole team—Roxie, Miguel, Kandar, and Melissa—were crowded in the doorway between the interrogation rooms and the sheriff's deputies' work area, watching Leanne and her detective take Crenshaw on a perp-walk to a jail cell to await his transport to FBI headquarters. He assumed Berkstad had rounded them up and was herding them like cattle to Interrogation Room 2, where Elias had just finished up with Crenshaw.

Tim watched confusion cross Elias's face as he stepped out of the interrogation room door.

"If you all came to congratulate me, don't. We have a lot of work to do yet." He scowled at the team. Tim knew Elias wasn't one to accept praise for what he considered his job. "You can congratulate me when I go above and beyond."

Berkstad stepped forward, and the rest of the team crowded in the doorway, parted like pigeons in a New York park.

"Elias, I need a few minutes to brief you and your team," he announced. "In private."

Both of Elias's eyebrows shot up, and he tipped his chin slightly. Tim shared his curiosity. He was open to hearing what Berkstad had to say. Elias stepped aside, and with a sweeping gesture of his hand, he encouraged the team to go into the interrogation room.

As Kandar passed by, he tapped Tim's hand with several pieces of paper he'd rolled into a cylinder. Tim took hold of the pages like a baton passed off between relay runners. The team members slow-walked into the room. Tim let them pass so that he could be last. Quickly, he unrolled the pages and glanced at the first one.

It was the toxicology report from Bounds's autopsy. The pathologist had found the metabolites succinic acid and choline in Bounds's bloodstream sufficient to assume succinylcholine to be the cause of death. The lab report found traces of succinylcholine in both the vial labeled Dilaudid on the nurse's cart and the syringe used on Bounds in the patient's medical waste disposal bin.

Tim learned about succinylcholine, also known as "sux," early in his career as a prosecutor. A favorite drug of medical murderers, it used to be thought of as the perfect weapon since it was quickly metabolized in the body. But these days, the by-products could be found after death by Gas Chromatography and Mass Spectrometry (GC-MS) tests.

Sux's medical use is for the short-term paralysis of the muscles to ease surgical intubation. Its effects start within about a minute after administering the drug and last for about ten minutes. Since the body's demand for oxygen must be met in less than ten minutes, death is a sure thing without intubation.

Jesus! Tim thought. What a way to go. The man knew he was dying. Even trying to force his lungs to breath by concentrated thought didn't work. Completely paralyzed, there was nothing he could do about it.

No wonder the doctor couldn't resuscitate Bounds. There is no known antidote. By the time they would've suspected 'sux' as the culprit, the victim would be dead by asphyxia.

Tim dropped his hand to his side, still clutching the report, after reading the next page Kandar had given him. He scrubbed his other hand over his hair. Crenshaw's contributors were the who's who of the political world. Three congressmen, including Patterson and one senator, were on the list, along with several high-ranking members of the intelligence community. His stomach dropped like when cresting a hill on a Nebraska backroad. He looked at it again, expecting to see Berkstad's name on it. It wasn't. But now Tim understood why he'd suggested that his theory of the crime was a dangerous path to pursue. Too many powerful men where involved.

Only one piece to this jigsaw puzzle remained outstanding. Tim still needed the DNA match to Aiysha's unborn baby. Everything else was circumstantial.

CHAPTER THIRTY-FIVE

"**A**re you coming?" Elias asked.

Tim, still holding the papers, dropped his hand to his side and nodded. Slowly, he followed Elias into the interview room. He took a seat in chair beside his boss and slid the reports to him. Elias stared, his eyes wide with a hint of curiosity. Tim tightened his lips.

As Elias browsed the reports, Tim watched Berkstad walk the perimeter of the gray concrete block room, making sure all recording devices were turned off.

"I want all of you to power off your cell phones and put them in the center of the table," Berkstad said as he took up a position at one end. "No one, no police, no sheriff, no press, no friends, no one—and I mean no one—can know what I am about to tell you."

Surprise and trepidation mixed like heavy humid particles in the air. No one was ready for Berkstad's seriousness. As he looked from one face to the next of his team members, Tim suspected they all knew what he knew. While he'd watched the Crenshaw interview, the reports had most likely circulated from one team member to the other in the alcove. Berkstad was probably excluded—they didn't trust him. Reluctantly, they turned off their phones and placed them side by side in the center of the table. One good sign: Berkstad had not asked them to surrender their firearms.

Berkstad retrieved his own iPhone, turned it off, and placed it with the others on the table. Clearly, it was a maneuver to bolster confidence. Tim would wait and see how that panned out.

"First, I'm sure you want to know why I'm here," Berkstad started. Tim studied him for micro-expressions. Everything about his demeanor confirmed openness and honesty. But then again, unlike Tim, he'd been trained to mask his emotions just in case he was captured in a foreign land. "When I found your composite drawing circulating FBI headquarters, I recognized Bounds. He used to be one of my civilian assets. Counterintelligence seldom gets involved in domestic crime unless there is a terrorist element to it." Berkstad paused to take a sip of coffee. Every team member gave him their rapt attention.

"When I saw the news reports and heard Patterson gushing his usual talking points, I researched which BAU team was assigned to the shooting. When I found it was your team—Elias's team—I knew it wouldn't be long before you discovered the unsub was not a typical disgruntled student. The way he dressed, the disabled security cameras at the school, the military-grade weapon, the clean getaway would tell you he was older—experienced. He didn't want to be seen or have his grievances heard like the usual shooter." Berkstad momentarily paused as if to catch his breath.

"My decision to come here was cemented when I heard Roxie sustained a gunshot injury. I felt somehow responsible. Something stopped her from firing her weapon when Bounds tried to escape. I realized she'd seen him before at the bureau, likely leaving my office. She didn't want to fire on a fellow agent. She didn't realize Bounds wouldn't feel the same way. Luckily, she wore a vest."

Tim remembered she hadn't wanted to. He glanced across the table at her, and she shrugged her shoulders ever so slightly. Was she glad he'd made her? She wasn't going to thank him. She didn't have to.

"Six months ago, I terminated the FBI's relationship with Bounds as we finished a project we were working on. He had displayed behavior, brutality, and cruelty beyond the pale. I remembered, though, that I'd introduced Bounds to Congressman Patterson long before—at a casual meeting in a bar in DC, after a committee hearing. I never expected Patterson to contact him.

"Next, you need to understand your number-one person of interest. Congressman Patterson's appetites and hunger for power are equal to his overinflated ego. He believes he's the smartest man alive and that the law does not apply to him.

"He married his current wife after cheating with her on his first. He is presently involved 'romantically' with two women outside his marriage—one, Beebe Knoll, with SBC News, and the other, his chief of staff, Samantha Wordsworth."

Tim hoped Beebe had heeded his warning and had taken the earliest plane back to Seattle. If Patterson suspected she'd betrayed him, he'd have her eliminated without a backward glance. They needed to connect with Ms. Wordsworth. Tim made a mental note.

Berkstad appeared to wait for the team members' murmurs to settle down before continuing. "We have evidence Patterson has used and is using campaign contributions to pay family members' salaries, which is questionable in the first place. No family member should profit off a government official's position. An audit of his campaign bank account shows he received a kick-back of a third of their salaries for himself, personally. He is also under investigation with two other members of Congress in a foreign aid pay-to-play scheme. They sponsor what seems to be charitable payments of foreign aid to impoverished countries. In exchange, we know they receive millions in kickbacks from that country when the aid package arrives. It's laundered through a labyrinth of shell companies, investment accounts, and offshore accounts where the bank has no duty to disclose account information to the U.S. Government and the like." Berkstad took a moment as if to collect his thoughts.

Tim's muscles tightened in the back of his neck, and he rolled his head side to side to relieve the tension. He'd always wondered how people in Congress became wealthy on a government salary, besides voting themselves raises, of course. He was thoroughly disgusted. Long ago, he'd realized the so-called public servants and representatives of the people thought they were entitled to taxpayer money rather than stewards of it.

Berkstad continued. "Three years ago, we informed Patterson that he'd chased his 'appetites' right into what we call 'a honeypot' with the Russian spy, Katristka Nicholova. He said he dropped all communication with her, and we immediately deported her. However, through monitoring family members' social media accounts, we have learned of a different outcome. His brother and parents have not stopped corresponding with her. We suspect she still supplies dark money to Patterson's campaign war chest. Not only is that illegal, but now that he's been appointed to the Select Committee on Intelligence, it's become a national security threat."

"Arrest him!" Roxie blurted out.

A slow smile traveled across Berkstad's lips. "That's exactly what we were planning to do. We've had Patterson under surveillance for three years. The only missing piece—we haven't figured out the exact route of the laundered money. Once we have that, we plan to move in. Then, all of a sudden, your team plows up this theory he's somehow connected to the school shooting."

How inconvenient for you. Tim thought, and licked his lips. He caught Elias's gaze, and their eyes locked for a moment. Elias skimmed their file folder along the table's surface toward Berkstad. Startled, he slammed his palm down on the table to catch it as it slid his way.

"You have some reading to do," Elias said. "We started looking at Patterson because he inserted himself into the investigation. At first, we suspected it was for publicity. When we concluded the shooting might be part of a cover-up for an unplanned pregnancy, we realized whoever ordered the job would want to keep tabs on what we knew."

In silence, Berkstad thumbed through the pages in the report. He looked up and asked. "He *consented* to a DNA test? I see you ordered one."

"No. He had coffee in a paper cup this morning and threw it in the trash. It became discarded property and in the public domain. I collected it and sent it to the lab," Tim said, wanting to assure Berkstad he'd followed the legal protocol. "You saw me do it."

Berkstad widened his eyes as if remembering, and then narrowed them as if warning Tim to keep that information to himself. *Too late,* Tim thought.

Elias grinned and said, "You are right. When Roxie, Miguel, and Tim went to the crime scene the day of the shooting, they concluded the shooter was not a disturbed or bullied teen. They thought it closely resembled a professional hit. Next, we had to zero in on who ordered the hit and why anyone would want to kill honor students."

"That's when little Miss Susan Bower and her mother came to the station to tell their story of the druggings, rapes, Aiysha's pregnancy, and a second man. You'll find that in the file," Roxie said, leveling her gaze at Berkstad. Almost as if she dared him to refute her. Tim studied Berkstad for his reaction. He took a sip of coffee, never dropping his gaze from Roxie's face. Had Berkstad already known about the rapes? He had to, if they'd been surveilling Patterson for three years. Tim glared at him.

"The profile we delivered to the sheriff was that of a male of undetermined race, thirty-five to forty-five, fit and active, possibly military or police services. He used an automatic rifle with a select-fire feature that included a single shot, three-round burst, and fully automatic capabilities. This kind of rifle is not available to the general public. Witnesses described the shooter as wearing all-black, including a solid black dirt bike or motocross helmet with an orange or gold reflective faceplate," Miguel added.

"The shooter left us footprints in blood. He wore men's size twelve, Nike SFB Gen2 tactical boots. We found most of these items the next day in a rental car. Bounds had parked it on a farm road up behind the school. The lab matched his boots to the prints on the school's floor and matched the blood on the boots to several of the shooting victims. What we didn't find in the car, we found in a hunter's cave," Roxie reported and watched the smiles break out on the team members' faces.

"You found evidence implicating *Patterson?*" Berkstad asked, his face pinched with skepticism. Tim first looked at Elias. He wasn't sure he wanted to tell Berkstad what they had. Elias nodded the go-ahead.

"Some circumstantial evidence. First, our profile indicated the mastermind would try to learn everything he could about our investigation," Tim said.

"Pffttt. That could just as easily include me," Berkstad grumbled.

Tim bit off what he wanted to say before he spilled it, cleared his throat, and continued. "We found a prepaid Visa card and a prepaid phone in Bounds's possession at arrest. You saw the video we received from Walmart and the items purchased in cash by Samantha Wordsworth. We found video of Patterson giving Bounds an envelope around 5 a.m. on Saturday morning at the hotel. The field office in DC is searching his apartment as we speak. We are in the process of obtaining a warrant for his bank accounts and safety deposit boxes."

"You'll never find the money. Bounds is trained to secret away money," Berkstad said.

Tim continued, "Beebe Knoll thought Patterson was cheating on her with another woman. She followed him Sunday night, where he passed an envelope to Philip Dockery, the hospital's overnight pharmacist. Beebe contacted me because she believed Patterson might be involved in trafficking prescription drugs. Then Bounds mysteriously died this morning. Patterson could've been paying for Bounds's murder, instead. We know it was a homicide. Succinylcholine is a horrible way to die. The body becomes paralyzed, and yet the brain is fully functioning until the oxygen runs out." Tim sat back deep into his chair.

"Beebe Knoll? Is she working with you?" Berkstad asked, clearly upset. "We bugged Patterson's room. This afternoon, we observed Miss

Knoll going through Patterson's belongings at the hotel. We took her into custody and to a safe house on the outskirts of town."

Tim laughed quietly to himself. Beebe would think he was the jackass responsible for that. He'd suggested protective custody; now he'd be blamed for it no matter the truth. "Did you kidnap her?"

"We didn't throw a black sack over her head, if that's what you mean," Berkstad sniped. "We just wanted to interrogate her."

Tim frowned at Berkstad, "Did she have her suitcase? Her laptop? Purse? Car keys?"

"Yes, why?"

Tim rubbed his fingers back and forth over his brow. "Did it even cross your mind she might be leaving on her own?"

Berkstad didn't answer; he just stared.

"She agreed to lay low, not talk to Patterson for a few days until we sorted this out. In exchange, I promised her an exclusive story." Tim looked daggers at him. His interference was a colossal fuck-up.

What was Berkstad afraid she'd found? Once again, Tim jumped back up on the fence of indecision; was Berkstad incompetent or just plain bad news? Would he hurt her? Beebe was an aggravating pain-in-the-rear, but Tim didn't want her mistreated. Kidnapping and rendition were illegal in the United States. Berkstad was right. He had lost his way.

"You're holding her in a secret safe house. Why didn't you bring her here?" Tim asked.

"We didn't want her to confront Patterson. We need him in the dark. He has contacts, powerful ones. That's why we've always proceeded with caution," Berkstad explained.

"Powerful contacts? Proceed with caution? Is that why you didn't report the rapes of the honor students? How could you—-how could you let that continue?" Tim groaned his complaint.

Berkstad looked up from his coffee cup, shocked. "I wasn't briefed on the rapes."

"Who was assigned to surveil Patterson? Bounds?" Tim demanded.

Berkstad recoiled. That defensive gesture told Tim all he needed to know. Some how Patterson had made Bounds and they made a deal. Bounds didn't report the rapes to his superior. Tim knew it. He had to prove it.

Tim noticed Roxie set both arms on the table and slowly tap her folded reading glasses against one wrist. What was she cooking up in her hyperactive brain now? They had to do something and fast. If Beebe thought the kidnapping was Tim's idea, it would be just like Beebe to blow up their case. No telling what Berkstad's agents might do to her. Roxie stared back at Tim, and a devious little smile curled the right side of her mouth.

Roxie announced her plan. "We pull off a fake rescue . . . we make Beebe believe her abduction was Patterson's doing! We put a big wedge between her and Patterson and retain protective custody, without her even realizing it."

It could go wrong, but it wasn't bad, Tim thought. His confidence in Roxie, shaken when she didn't shoot Bounds, rallied.

"Our target is Patterson. You're losing focus," Berkstad warned.

"The best way to keep Patterson in the dark is to let Beebe do her job. Business as usual. If Patterson thinks she's in custody, he's going to think she's betrayed him," Roxie said.

"We should have our missing piece on the money laundering in a few days," Berkstad argued.

"What do you care which way Patterson goes down?" Elias asked, leaning forward and resting his forearms on the table. "It's hard to get convictions on foreign campaign contributions. There's usually a juggernaut of shell companies, investments with money managers, and shady banks. Influence-peddling is normal for politicians on all sides—unethical, but normal. The party leaders just circle the wagons, and the press buries the story. But, the voting public won't tolerate the drugging and rape of children. Powerful connections or not. If Patterson's DNA implicates him, and we have enough to connect him to a murder-for-hire scheme, he's in prison for the rest of his life. You won't have to worry about him selling national security secrets."

"I didn't think of it that way," Berkstad said. Adding to Tim's skepticism, Berkstad's frown evidenced he wasn't thrilled about Elias's logic. Why were FBI Divisions arguing about what crimes and when to arrest Patterson? Wasn't it their job to get these sick fucks off the street?

"You can even have the collar, if you want it. Our BAU team identified the bad guys. We can step back and take a lesser role. I'll even bet Tim can talk Miss Knoll into giving you glowing headlines and a sensational story that sets you up for a promotion to the seventh floor," Elias commented.

Tim's mouth dropped open. He wanted to protest. He knew where this was headed. He'd been handed the short straw and was stuck rescuing Beebe Knoll.

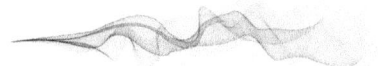

CHAPTER THIRTY-SIX

T im strolled out to the front steps of the sheriff's department and realized he hadn't been outside since morning. The evening air was fresh and cool. Sunset pinks merged softly into darkening hues of blue. One by one, stars and galaxies concealed by day in the sun's brilliance sparkled to life.

A slight breeze carried the scent of charbroiled hamburgers and greasy French fries, reminding him he hadn't eaten anything since morning.

"What time did Berkstad say his agents would leave the safe house?" he asked, turning to catch a reply from Roxie. They'd agreed to Roxie's rescue plan and to transport Beebe to another safe house the FBI controlled closer to DC. Tim, not completely trusting Berkstad, made modifications. Rather than drive the seventy miles to DC, he asked Mitch to wait for him with the Cessna 340 at the small airport outside of town. It was his plan "B," in case plan "A" didn't feel right. He liked having options.

"Six thirty-ish," she replied. Tim glanced at his watch. They had an hour.

Roxie took the steps slowly. Tim imagined even the slightest jarring would hurt. He'd never had a broken rib, but he'd heard from friends it was painful. "You're driving," she said. Tim caught the keys she tossed to him.

He slowed his pace to match hers. "What are you even doing here? Elias said you could take off as long as you needed." As they walked, he slipped his arms through his bulletproof vest and adjusted the Velcro closures.

"Take off, and then what? Watch TV? I'd be bored to tears."

"Bored to tears, but healed." Miguel caught up and carefully slipped his arm over her shoulders, a big grin on his face. "I'm starving. Let's grab a burger before we mount up on our trusty steeds and rescue the helpless damsel in distress."

Roxie rolled her eyes. "Beebe Knoll—a damsel in distress? Any *distress* she's in, she brought on herself."

"Berkstad—you don't think he'd hurt her, do you?" For the last half hour, a nagging worry about Beebe lingered at the edge of Tim's thoughts. This whole mess made him uneasy. Roxie stopped and stood completely still, glaring at him.

Counterintelligence was a different animal, with different rules for the kind of criminal that hated everything about America and Americans. "You know him better than we do. Would he allow his agents to . . . ."

"Torture her?" Roxie said slowly. "Don't be silly. He'd only do that if he was involved and she had information he needed. You don't actually believe he's involved, do you?" The dismissal in her tone of voice receded like the sunset's colors before him. "Oh, crap!"

Tim sprinted to the car, pushing the button on the keyfob that unlocked the doors. He could hear Miguel's and Roxie's footsteps behind him on the pavement. Roxie jumped in the front seat, and Miguel took his place in the passenger's behind Tim.

"Go. GO!" she screamed.

Tim started the engine and whipped the SUV out of the parking space. "Call Elias. Let him know."

"He's interviewing the pharmacist," Miguel said.

"Call Leanne. Get back-up." Tim navigated to the main road. "Lights and siren?"

"No, wait. Just wait." Roxie waved her hands in the air as if frustrated. "Berkstad called his agents. I saw him. We're just panicking."

"You saw him, but did you hear what he said?" Tim glanced her way, then immediately returned his attention to the road.

"No. But Tim, do you really think he'd do something to her, knowing we know? That would be stupid," Roxie complained. "What is it with you and that girl?"

"Don't even start! There's nothing *with* Beebe and me. She's a pesky reporter and a major thorn in my backside. Still, I don't want her to get hurt." Anger started to brew. But Roxie was a relentless teaser, so he simmered down.

"Street is coming up on the right," Miguel said.

Tim felt a brush on his shoulder and weight drop into his lap. He flinched and immediately corrected to stay in his lane. "Damn!"

"Sorry. Night vision scope," Miguel explained .

Glancing in the rearview mirror, Tim nodded. Miguel passed a bulletproof vest over the seat to Roxie. "Put it on."

Tim clicked off the headlights and turned right onto the residential street. There were no street lamps, no moonlight. He reduced his speed to a crawl. The tires crunched on the asphalt. As they crept away from the main road and its ambient light and got closer to the safe house, darkness oozed around them in ever-increasing tones of black on black. He turned off the engine and let the car roll to a stop behind a giant maple tree in the neighbor's yard, about fifty feet from the safe house's driveway.

"Wait. Let's watch for a minute," Tim said, his voice subdued. The house was dark, and a sense of foreboding rose into his throat. This was Roxie's idea. He didn't appreciate being put in charge of rescuing Beebe when it was first proposed. He liked it even less now.

"Did you see that?" Roxie asked, just above a whisper. She seemed to melt lower into her seat. "Movement. There, against the hedge at the east side of the driveway."

Tim lifted the night vision scope to his eyes and focused the lens. He gave himself a few seconds to adjust to the street's new look, everything bathed in varying shades of green.

"We're not alone. Do you see him?" Roxie asked.

An enhanced olive-green image snuck along the hedge marking the property's eastern border. Tim flipped the switch on the scope to infrared, and the image glowed bright yellow where the face and hands were bare to the night air, and a rainbow of orange, red, purple, and blue outlined the body from warm to cool, measured by the density of his clothes.

"I see two. Dressed in camo. Hoodies. Balaclavas. I think I see handguns," Miguel said in a low voice.

Roxie moaned, "This isn't the way Berkstad said this was to go down. That sneaky bastard. Something isn't right." Her breath rate increased. "Do you think they've seen us?"

Miguel said quietly, "Your boyfriend wasn't on board with your plan after all, Rox."

"They're on the move." Roxie's voice turned into a raspy whisper.

"I don't think they've seen us. If they had, they would've adjusted their track by now. Unless there are more of them than we know." Tim couldn't chance any light giving away their position when they opened the doors. He reached up and pressed the button that turned off the SUV's dome lights. Who were these guys? Patterson's? Berkstad's? Why were they here?

Slowly, Tim scanned the terrain all around them, both in night vision and infrared modes. Then he returned his view to the front. The unknown men crept toward the house like cats stalking unsuspecting prey. They were so focused on the house, he didn't think they'd noticed his team, or their SUV, shielded by the maple tree.

Tim, Miguel, and Roxie put on their communication gear, wireless microphones, and earpieces to kept them in constant contact with each other.

"Do we have a way to contact Berkstad's agents inside? Let them know what's coming their way?" Miguel asked.

"No. Berkstad's agents are supposed to be gone," Tim said. He hung the night vision scope around his neck. "I have a bad feeling about this. We better get Beebe out of there."

"We arrived to the party early." Roxie chuckled quietly. "Maybe we should wait." The unknowns crept along the side of the house. Tim wondered what their role was in this unfolding drama.

He opened his door, stepped onto the pavement, and silently pressed the door closed. "Miguel, you want the front or the back?"

"Back."

"What about me?" Roxie asked.

"You wait for the deputies. Keep them quiet," Tim said. Roxie pouted, but he warned her with a stare. Her injuries made it impossible for her to go in. Pain would slow her reaction time. She shouldn't even be on this mission and could be injured all over again. Tim couldn't let that happen. But once they were on the move, he knew he couldn't control her. He pressed his earpiece deeper into his ear.

He chambered a round in his Glock, lowered his profile, and dashed across the neighbor's lawn, taking cover in the darkest shadows. When he reached the corner of the safe house, he waited and listened. A small puff of wind rustled through the treetops. Miguel caught up to him and leaned back against the wall. Tim quickly rounded the corner and dropped to a crouch behind a boxwood. He lifted the scope and flipped to infrared to determine if the unknowns were still at the side of the house. No one was there. He returned to stand against the wall with Miguel.

The crack and tinkle of breaking glass startled them both. Miguel motioned with his index finger and headed around to the back. Tim headed toward the sound. Quietly, he scaled the railing surrounding the front porch, dropping silently to the covered deck's wood floor. He braced himself against the exterior wall. To his right, a large plate glass window looked out to the front lawn below. The draperies were shut. Just as he started to pass in front of the window, someone inside lifted the draperies' far edge. Tim flattened himself against the wall.

For a moment, he could only hear his breath racing in and out of his lungs, his heart pounding in his chest. Then the draperies flowed back into place.

A chain rattled, and the door lock released. Tim slipped down behind a white wicker love seat and waited to see who would emerge. After a few minutes passed, he realized whoever was inside had unlocked the door for him.

"Miguel—it's an ambush," he whispered into his wireless microphone.

"Copy that. My kind of party."

Tim felt every hair on his body stand on end. Suppressed gunshots thumped in the air. "Shots fired! Shots fired!" he called out.

He listened for return fire. None. Dread seeped from every pore.

"Miguel? Report." No answer. "Miguel?" Tim darted to the front door and kicked it open, lunging to the side in case the shooter decided to take him next.

He turned on his tac-light, aimed his pistol in front of him, and proceeded cautiously into the main room. He heard a groan and wheeled to face the noise. In the brilliant glare of his flashlight, he saw one of the unknown assailants standing across the room, pistol drawn, but like Tim, unwilling to shoot.

"FBI! Drop your weapon," Tim demanded.

The man ignored him and turned as if to flee. Behind the man, Tim saw blurred motion. Miguel delivered a blow to the man's elbow, causing his arm and the pistol to fly up toward the ceiling. He lost his grip, and the gun dropped to the floor. He attempted to defend himself, but Miguel kicked the side of the man's knee. When he tried to rebalance, his leg failed, and he screamed in pain. Miguel sidestepped, keeping in position behind his adversary, and as the man fell forward, Miguel slipped him into a forearm chokehold. Though Camo-man struggled at first, within seconds, he passed out and crumpled like a rag doll the rest of the way to the floor. Miguel booted the pistol out of reach, and it clattered across the wood floor. Tim raced over to help.

"And that's two!" Miguel said, wrenching the unconscious man's arms behind his back and tightening the flex cuffs. Tim covered the man's mouth and shackled his feet together with the duct tape he'd found next to the overturned coffee table. The guy never saw it coming, and as he slowly regained consciousness, he wriggled helplessly against his bonds.

"Wow," Tim said, looking Miguel in the eyes. "Just, wow!"

"The three D's—disarm, disable, detain." Miguel chuckled. "The other guy is by the back door."

"Dead?" Tim asked. "I heard gunshots."

"No. The rounds went into the ceiling. But he's not going anywhere, and he's very unhappy." Miguel laughed. "Go find Beebe. I'll collect their weapons and get them ready to turn over to Elias and the sheriff."

Cautiously, Tim proceeded down the hallway. He opened the first doorway and flipped on the lights. Side by side, duct-taped to dining room chairs, sat Lovergirl and the Logger, Berkstad's agents he'd seen in the hotel bar. His first impulse was to help them, but he hesitated. This wasn't right. It was not what they'd planned. Had Berkstad betrayed them and sent Tim's team into a trap? He didn't know who to trust. He decided to find Beebe first.

He re-entered the hallway and opened the final door. He paused to listen. Nothing. No sound. After clearing the master bathroom, he went to the walk-in closet where she was alleged to be. Shoving the hanging clothes aside, he stared at the back wall. He holstered his Glock. Expecting to locate the compartment Berkstad said was there, he pressed each panel one by one. The last section clicked open toward him when he pushed it. A tiny light bulb, no bigger than an oven light, flicked on.

Inside the tiny space, Beebe lie on her back, her knees uncomfortably pressed into her chest. Her arms were wrenched behind her, and her ankles bound together. A measure of silver tape stretched across her mouth. She tensed, hunched her shoulders and squeezed her eyes shut as if expecting a blow.

"Beebe, it's Tim. I've come to get you," he said softly.

Her eyes popped open, and her whole body went limp as if her bones had turned to Jello. She tried to talk, but all Tim could hear was muffled jibberish.

Tim knelt beside her and took hold of her by the arms under her shoulders. He wrenched her forward into the closet. Carefully, he removed the tape from her mouth.

"I knew you'd come. I knew it. Untie me. Oh, God. Tim, I knew you'd come for me," she repeated breathlessly. For a second, Tim wanted to smooth the tape back over her mouth. Beebe would make this into something it absolutely wasn't. He frowned at her. Taking in a deep breath, he pulled out the pocket knife from his vest and sliced through the tape at her wrists and ankles.

"Are you all right? Can you stand?" he asked. He let her stretch out and restore circulation.

"I think so."

Tim stood first and then helped her to her feet. She limped her first step toward him, then slumped forward against his chest. She hugged him. Gratitude was one thing; this was way too much. He grabbed both of her shoulders and pushed her back.

"Enough! We have to get out of here!"

"You saved me. I knew you'd save me."

Tim rolled his eyes and shook his head. He walked in front of her, still unsure if they were out of danger. As they came to the closet opening, he drew his pistol. He observed the right side of the room, repositioned, and viewed the left.

As he stepped into the room, Roxie was there. Hands on her hips and shaking her head, she snickered at him. Beebe rushed out of the closet and began clinging to him as if he were her life-raft.

"Here, Roxie, take Miss Knoll to the SUV," Tim said, encouraging Beebe to let go, move forward, and out of the room.

"Right. Are you okay, Miss Knoll?" Roxie asked. Beebe nodded. He watched them go. Tim's thoughts hadn't had a chance to coalesce.

Something was very wrong, and he needed time to think so he could figure out what made him feel that way.

Miguel entered the doorway. "Deputies are here. Let's go."

"What's our situation?" Tim asked.

"From what I can gather, Berkstad assigned the two in the spare bedroom to babysit Miss Knoll," Miguel explained. "They were surprised by the camo-boys, roughed up, but injuries are minor. They'd already secured Ms. Knoll in the closet where you found her. The deputies and Berkstad's agents think it was a home invasion gone wrong."

"Oh, sure. I'm buying that," Tim answered. "What do you think?"

"Camo-boys have already started to scream for lawyers. When I searched their backpacks, I found Berkstad's agent's guns, cash and credit cards, cell phones, and Beebe's purse, computer, and phone."

"A home invasion, just when we were supposed to arrive. Now, there's a coincidence," Tim said. He didn't believe in coincidences.

"But then I found these." Miguel held up the IDs he'd collected.

"Blackmark Security?" Tim asked. "Didn't Bounds work for Blackmark Security?"

"Yep." Miguel chuckled. "And isn't Blackmark the company Patterson uses to provide his bodyguards?"

Tim drew in a deep breath. "Berkstad sent us into an ambush."

"Let's exfil for now. Before anyone can send reinforcements." Miguel thumbed like a hitchhiker in the direction of the SUV. "Our mission is to get Miss Knoll to safety. Let's do that." A half-smile curved his lips. "Take this chance to walk away—live to fight another day."

CHAPTER THIRTY-SEVEN

The safe house buzzed with activity. As he passed by the bedroom, Tim saw Leanne's deputies releasing Berkstad's agents from their bonds. A deputy forced one of the camo guys to his feet while medics helped the other onto a gurney.

Tim opened the front door to bedlam. The police's red and blue bar lights splashed color over lawns and houses and up into the trees. At least five sheriff's vehicles and Elias's black SUV held back the curious neighbors swarming into the street. What started as a covert pretend rescue on a dark, sleepy lane turned into a full-blown block party. Every light in every house along the way was on.

In the medic unit's headlights stood Roxie, her face only inches from Berkstad's. Tim could hear her yell even at this distance.

"You complete idiot! You stinking liar! You put my life in danger! You put my team in danger!" She shoved his shoulder.

Elias's deep voice boomed. "Roxie, stop!"

Tim and Miguel looked at each other.

"Do you think Roxie's pissed at Berkstad?" Tim mused, knowing it was an understatement.

"I wouldn't confront Berkstad like that, he's a jerk, but he's still her boss. I get where she's coming from," Miguel commented.

Tim could hear Berkstad reply in soft, soothing tones, but couldn't make out the words, as he tried to calm Roxie's ire. Whatever he said seemed to work. Tim suspected he repudiated knowing how this happened or who the men were, and laid the blame squarely at Patterson's feet. Had it not been for Miguel's SEAL Team training, this could've had a very different outcome.

Tim stepped aside, allowing two deputies to escort one of the men in camo, the one who could still walk, to a cruiser. The other man, on a gurney, was slated to go to the hospital. He gave Miguel a threatening glare as they passed by.

Berkstad's freed agents lingered behind Elias's SUV, out of Beebe's line of sight. Beebe sat quietly in the back seat of the other SUV, head bowed.

Elias approached Tim and Miguel from the street. He motioned for them to join him away from the crowd of deputies. "What the hell happened?" he asked.

"When we pulled up to get Beebe, we had company," Tim said. Miguel handed Elias the two Blackmark Security IDs he'd collected. "It wasn't anywhere near what we'd planned."

"Well, well," A wry smile curved Elias's lips. "I know no one from *my* team leaked to anyone on the outside. Leanne and her deputies weren't in the loop. That leaves . . . ."

"Berkstad." Tim filled in the blank. "His agents were supposed to leave. We were supposed to walk in, retrieve Miss Knoll, and move her to the new safe house."

Elias twisted the ends of his mustache, deep in thought. "He claims not to know anything about this mess."

"Do you believe him?" Tim asked.

"At first, yes. It's hard not to trust a colleague. You want to believe them. Our Director is a political appointee; he didn't come up through the ranks. The seventh floor could be protecting Patterson," Elias said.

"That wouldn't be a first. Historians claim our very own J. Edgar was utterly corrupt," Tim answered.

"You know what they say about power. I called in a favor from a friend in the DC field office. I put a tail on Berkstad. So far, he's doing what he's supposed to," Elias reported. "Ever since Bounds was poisoned, we've had Patterson followed. *He's* been doing what he's supposed to do, also."

"Are we chasing the wrong rabbit?" Tim asked, realizing they were in a very precarious position. Worst case, Tim and his team members were considered expendible.

Elias shook his head. "I don't think so. I'll call Kandar and get him to research Blackmark Security. Maybe we can get a client list. Berkstad warned us to proceed with caution," Elias said. "Here's what we're going to do. We're going to keep quiet. We support Berkstad's theory that this was a home invasion robbery, wrong place, wrong time—while we search for evidence to prove otherwise." Elias leveled his stare at Tim and Miguel as if requiring their unspoken agreement. Tim nodded. "Now, you and Miguel take Miss Knoll to the safe house."

"Any safe house in Berkstad's control may not be safe," Tim commented.

Elias twisted the ends of his mustache. "Then—there's that. All right, Roxie stays with Miss Knoll. Berkstad is unlikely to do anything to Beebe when his girlfriend is in the picture."

"I'm not telling Roxie." Miguel laughed.

"I'll tell her," Elias grumbled. "Now get going."

Tim walked briskly to the SUV. When he opened the door, he thought: *This is a first.* The combative, ever curious, and boisterous Beebe Knoll sat perfectly still, almost reflective, not like Beebe at all. He guessed Berkstad had given her a good scare. A top investigative reporter would need to suck it up and get over it if she wanted to continue in her career. These days it was a tough job. He remembered how CBS foreign correspondent Lara Logan had been violently assaulted in the middle of a crowd. Still, he felt empathy for Beebe.

"Are you okay?" he asked, leaning into the car before climbing into the driver's seat next to Roxie.

Beebe looked up at him, her eyes soft. "Thank you, Tim. You saved me."

Tim felt a twinge of guilt. Did he? Would Beebe still paint him a hero if she knew his team was only trying to cover up Berkstad's over-zealous blunder with a rescue? He rubbed his tongue along the inside of his cheek.

Miguel slid into the back seat beside her and started to take hold of her hand. "What's this?" he asked.

"My cell phone. Roxie grabbed it, my laptop, and my purse as we left the house." She sighed softly. "Do you know who kidnapped me? Was it Aaron—Congressman Patterson?"

Tim knew he'd fumble his answer. He wasn't a good liar, so he waited, hoping Roxie or Miguel would explain.

"I know you're dating him . . . ." Roxie started, hesitation in her voice.

"Don't worry about that. Dating Patterson had nothing to do with feelings or love," Beebe interrupted. "I was working him for a promotion."

That was Beebe, unashamedly ruthless. Shaking his head with amusement, Tim slid behind the steering wheel and started the engine.

"Well, we're not sure," Roxie said. When Tim looked over at her, Roxie cringed a little. "We are taking you to a safe house and putting you under protective custody, just in case."

Tim made a U-turn and headed up the road toward Main Street. As he passed the second house from the corner on his left, he saw a dark gray sedan edge forward in the driveway, lights off. Wariness seeped into his consciousness, and his thoughts began to cycle through a bunch of what-ifs. Before letting the hunch take hold, he glanced in his side mirror, just as the car slowly rolled onto the street. No headlights. Without question, it was a tail. Tim stopped at the sign and quickly assessed the map on the GPS display. Quickly, he turned right onto Main Street. The car turned right seconds later, and the headlights came on.

Tim made a left turn onto West Edmondson Street, and within the first block, by glancing into his rearview mirror, Tim confirmed the gray vehicle completed a left turn and trailed at least three car lengths behind him. He veered right onto North West Street and increased his speed. The gray sedan followed his move. His pursuers hadn't bothered to be discreet. Was this headed for gunplay?

"We have company," Tim said as the car closed the distance between them to one car length. "Gray Chevy Caprice. Two men." Tim whipped the car right onto West Piedmont.

Roxie flipped around in her seat. "Crap on crap! Did you see that? He missed the road and is backing up into traffic! He's coming after us, and fast!"

Tim had to take a chance. He slowed to look and then blasted through the stop sign at Main Street, timing it so the car approaching his driver's side would block the gray car's crossing by several seconds. He heard the horns sounding and brakes squealing as he traversed to the other side of Main, but no crunching metal. No collision.

Roxie called it in. Tim could hear the words, "Gray Chevy Caprice, Virginia plate number Alpha. Zebra. Tango. Five. Seven. Nine."

Tim turned right onto West East Street. From the GPS map, he remembered that Precious Blood Catholic Church had a driveway that went behind the building, then curved back up to East Street. He bore right into the driveway, gunned the engine, so they quickly made the loop. He killed the headlights and rolled to a stop, sheltered by the tall red-brick spires facing out to the darkened street.

He heard the gray sedan before he saw it. Whoever they were, he guessed they'd seen him turn right, but by the roar of their engine, they lost him when he drove into the church's parking lane. They were speeding to catch up with the SUV they could no longer see. The gray car flew by.

Roxie repeated the radio transmission. "Deputies are in position at the corner of Edmondson and East." Tim turned on his headlights and entered East Street, just as deputies pulled out in front of the gray vehicle. Tim slid the SUV at an angle behind it, blocking it in. He slammed the SUV into park.

"Down on the floor, Beebe," he demanded.

Tim, Roxie, and Miguel were out of their seatbelts, behind the protection of their open car doors, with pistols drawn before the drivers in the gray car knew what hit them.

The driver and passenger of the gray sedan chose the better part of valor and within seconds complied with the deputies' commands, and both sat handcuffed on the curb.

Deputy Sam Watkins strolled over and handed the men's IDs to Tim. He read them, took a step back, and delivered both to Miguel.

"Well, well, Blackmark Security." Miguel read out loud.

Beebe finally emerged from the floorboards of the SUV and walked up beside Tim. He watched her, evaluating her every move through narrowed eyes. "What have you done that put the bug up Patterson's keester?" he asked.

"This. I was going to give it to you, but he kidnapped me. At gunpoint." She pulled her iPhone out of her jacket pocket and made sure he watched. Slowly, she scrolled through the data and pictures she'd stored on her phone. The photos were all about the contents in the secret compartment in Patterson's suitcase. Confirmed. They weren't chasing the wrong rabbit.

—

Tim stood in front of the two-way mirror in the viewing area just off the cold concrete block walls of Interrogation Room 1. The driver of the gray car fidgeted nervously, lighting a new cigarette off the one he'd nearly finished. Like the other Blackmark Security agents they had encountered at the safe house, he wore forest camo.

During the traffic stop, they'd found a cache of weapons, including some questionable gadgets: metal wrist bands on lengths of chain, dental pliers, and car batteries with toggle switches that Tim associated immediately with torture. So, Blackmark Security wasn't a run-of-the-mill, garden-variety bodyguard shop. Tim recounted what he knew so far. Bounds was an assassin—a brutal one. So cold-blooded, in fact, he'd shoot unarmed fifteen-year-old students.

Tim wondered what his fate would've been had the men in the gray car found an out-of-the-way place to ambush them. Usually, law enforcement officers, including FBI special agents, were expendable. It was Beebe's phone they were after. The pictures on her phone needed to be destroyed, and it looked like they were prepared to do whatever it took to get them.

Tim speculated Patterson had let the rush of power overtake his caution and reason. He dabbled in things offered to powerful men that he should've turned away from. The first crack in his above-the-law glass house came when he was outed for his affair with the Russian spy. That, in turn, made the FBI look closer at his other dealings. They scrutinized his campaign finances; they studied his trips abroad; they unearthed the pay-to-play. Patterson probably bribed people along the way to stay quiet and felt safe for a little while.

But then, Aiysha turned up pregnant. Only a few years back, this would've been no threat, but today, DNA technology could find him out. This was Patterson's Cain-slew-Abel moment. Aiysha's baby's blood cried up to God from the ground. Desperate men take desperate measures.

It took Tim only seconds to realize the objects that Beebe had filmed were not for purchasing or selling illicit drugs, but an escape kit. Patterson was in a battle for his life, and he was prepared to run, taking whatever he could with him as bargaining chips for asylum. Maybe even state secrets?

Tim turned when he heard footsteps behind him. Kandar's face was grim. His brow pinched together as if every worry of the world had just landed on his narrow shoulders.

"What is it?" Tim asked.

"Which do you want first, the bad news or the worse news?"

Tim shook his head and chuckled. "Hit me with it."

Kandar sucked in a deep breath. "We have a DNA match. Patterson is the father of Aiysha's child." He paused to swallow.

"And the worse news is?" Tim asked.

"Blackmark Security is a non-government organization. But it only has one client. That client is the CIA."

CHAPTER THIRTY-EIGHT

T im let out a low whistle. He wiped his hand over his mouth and jaw and took in a deep breath. "Does Elias know?"

"Told him before you," Kandar sighed. "Now what?"

Tim turned his gaze downward. It was the first time he'd noticed the worn traffic spots in the concrete floor. How many detectives had paced outside of Interrogation Room 1, waiting for statements or confessions from the accused interviewed between the gray block walls? It was his way of distracting his mind from traveling through a gruesome list of consequences for being on the wrong side of his country's clandestine agencies.

"Remember that speech the senate minority leader gave when the last president started his term in the White House?" Kandar asked. "Didn't he say don't mess with the covert services—they have a hundred ways to Sunday to take you down?"

Tim could see terror in Kandar's eyes, and his pupils narrowed as if trying to focus on everything and everyone around him. "Something like that," he answered gently. Even if he felt a twinge of fear, he wouldn't feed Kandar's. He tightened his jaw.

The evidence suggested Patterson had participated in the drugging and rape of children, and when Aiysha turned up pregnant, he paid to have those precious ones murdered. Twenty-three other students from the school were recovering from gunshot wounds, not to mention emotional scars that may never heal.

"Does Berkstad know?" Tim asked, still unsure if the man could be trusted. Tim's internal *truth-o-meter* kept sending him mixed results.

"Not from me," Kandar said, squaring his stance.

"I need some fresh air," Tim said, his heart pulsing with sorrow. He thought of his daughters. Would they ever be safe? He and Dani had rescued them from child traffickers, and now this? When had it become okay to use children for selfish pleasures without caring for their futures, happiness, and lives? Had it always been this way, and he just didn't know it? His sadness morphed quickly into a wave of slow-burning anger.

What if Elias asked him to stand down, to close his eyes, and to walk away? From his study of history, he recalled Edmund Burke's words: *The only thing necessary for the triumph of evil is for good men to do nothing.*

"If Elias comes looking for me, tell him I've gone for a walk to clear my head."

"Are you coming back?" Kandar asked. Tim reached out and set his hand on his companion's shoulder.

"Of course."

He strolled briskly away from the sheriff's office and crossed Main Street at the light. He continued east until he arrived at the corner where they'd taken the gray car's driver and passenger into custody for questioning. For a moment, he stood looking at the church where he'd hidden behind the red-brick spires waiting to turn the tables on his pursuers. He continued until he stood in front of the concrete steps that led to the sanctuary's arched wooden doorway.

It had been years since he'd been inside a church. But he felt compelled now. He needed to offer a sinner's prayer for the children's souls, whose lives were cut short by one man's lust for power.

If he wasn't struck by lightning when he passed through the door, he guessed maybe God would listen to his prayers. He laughed to himself and pulled the door open.

The sanctuary was empty, but bathed in soft, honey-colored light. Rows of wooden pews lined either side of a center aisleway that ended at a beautifully appointed altar. A stained-glass window depicting an empty cross and several doves soaring to heaven served as a backdrop. An unspoken but clear invitation permeated the air: sit for a while, be at peace. Tim slipped into the last pew, and head bowed, he whispered a prayer for the dead and injured.

He took in a deep breath and felt emotion pressing hard behind his eyes. Since he'd become a grown man, he hadn't been one for tears. The images of the teens cut down before they had a chance to live crushed him with grief. He quickly wiped away the droplet that tried to trickle down his cheek. He imagined this was how the students' parents felt—helpless, broken-hearted. He wasn't helpless. This was the very kind of evil he'd taken an oath to pursue.

He stood and went to the small alcove off the vestibule, where an ornate iron rack held votive prayer candles. He lit five, one for each of those who died in the shooting.

"This one is for Julie, this one for Aiysha, for her unborn baby, for Sam Gruman, and this—for Marty," he said aloud. He lit one more. "This one is for me." He wanted the strength to stand strong and do the right thing.

When he walked outside in the cool evening air, the sky was crystal clear, and his gaze followed the cross-topped steeples skyward. A billion stars glittered like precious jewels on black velvet. His burden of grief lifted, and resolve replaced it. Patterson was going to get justice, even if Tim had to serve it up cold and alone.

"There you are." Elias stood at the bottom of church's stairs. "I didn't know you were a religious man."

"I don't think we ever discussed faith." Tim smiled and descended the steps.

"Do you mind if I walk with you?" Elias asked.

"No. I appreciate the company."

"Berkstad wants a meeting in an hour. Are you hungry? I keep getting whiffs of that burger joint up by the station, and I'm starving." Elias smiled, his dark eyes full of kindness and wisdom. Like a proper mentor, he would offer Tim some sage advice. Tim had to make his position clear.

"Just so you know, if you ask me to drop Patterson as a suspect, you'll need to fire me." Tim surprised himself with the conviction in his voice.

Elias tipped his head and laughed. "Do you think I would let Patterson get away with this? Son, my children are junior-class honor students. They are never going on another field trip unless *I'm* the chaperon." Elias snorted. Tim laughed with him. They walked in silence for a while. "Southern Baptist," Elias suddenly said, pointing to his chest. "You know, Hallelujah Brother! Amen! and Praise the Lord! You?"

"Irish Catholic. But not a very good one," Tim answered.

"Here's the thing; none of us are," Elias said. They circled the block in silence until they were in sight of the sheriff's department across the street.

"I've already sent my report and recommendations to the director with copies going to the Attorney General. If they want to hold off on Patterson's arrest, they risk the story finding its way to the New York Times. I've never been able to figure out how that happens." Elias screwed up his brow, but still maintained a smile. "Then watch the cockroaches scramble from the light. Patterson's allies will abandon him and turn into the biggest backstabbers of all time. DC politics."

Tim stared at Elias's face. "Blackmark Security is CIA. Won't they want a say?"

"They will. But the director, Bud Masterson, is a smart cookie. Patterson crossed the line. Whatever special favors and protection Patterson was getting from the CIA will vanish. Patterson is expendable."

"Is my family? Am I? Are we? Expendable?" Tim asked. It worried him when Elias didn't answer. He took it as a solid yes. Suddenly, he had an overwhelming urge to be with Dani to make sure she was safe. How would he protect the ones he loved from the clutches of corrupt and powerful men?

"The next few days are going to be crucial," Elias said matter-of-factly. "Ah, Berkstad is pulling up to the sheriff's office now. Shall we?" He gestured to the building across the street.

As they walked across the street, Tim looked at his watch. It was already ten p.m. He called Dani and reminded her to keep all the gates and doors locked and arm the security system. With great disappointment, he told her he wouldn't be able to make it to their new home tonight. He called Mitch and informed him he wouldn't be needed, after all. He rolled his shoulders, preparing his body for another night in the uncomfortable hotel bed, alone. Tim jogged to catch up with Elias on the other side of the street.

"Ready?" Elias asked.

"Ready, I guess. But remember, if you ask me to stand down, you'll have to fire me."

A big grin cracked Elias's face wide open. Did he understand? Tim hoped so.

—

Eventhough the players at Berkstad's the late night meeting were upset at having to attend, Tim had seldom been in a more productive meeting. Berkstad had shown exceptional candor and bolstered Elias's team's assessment of the criminal charges that were justified against Patterson. The CIA Director, Bud Masterson, seemed genuinely surprised by the situation. When he vowed to get to the bottom of it, Tim believed him. If he was truthful, the head of Blackmark Security might lose their one and only customer.

The U.S. Attorneys for Virginia's Western District and the District of Columbia agreed they needed to impanel a grand jury for each of their districts. The drugging and rapes happened in DC, and the murders occurred in the Western District. Though Tim argued that Patterson might flee, even after showing Beebe's pictures of the escape kit, he was overruled. An arrest warrant would be issued upon indictment, and only then.

After the meeting, Tim leaned against the battered desk in the alcove and stared at their investigation board across the room. They had more than sufficient probable cause to arrest Patterson now. And that's precisely what he wanted to do. The grand jury would take time. Time might lead to leaks, and leaks to defensive moves they hadn't even imagined. Tim knew Patterson was capable of murder.

Why were the U.S. Attorneys so unwilling to tug on the thread? Were they afraid it would unravel their careers instead of bringing Patterson to justice? It wouldn't be the first time. Just how deep did Patterson's connections go? Did they think if they stalled long enough, the whole mess would just melt away? The parents of the murdered teens weren't going to drop this. He remembered the words of Pastor Dietrich Bonhoeffer, who'd famously lost his life for standing firm against Nazi tyranny: *Silence in the face of evil is itself evil: God will not hold us guiltless. Not to speak is to speak. Not to act is to act.*

Miguel approached. "I received this email while we were in the meeting," He leaned against the desk, next to Tim.

"I'm listening."

"CSI found Dockery's fingerprints on a bottle of succinylcholine and a syringe in his medical waste bin. They empty the bins at the end of every shift. Hospital records show that no doctor on duty Saturday night or early Sunday morning ordered a dose. CSI believes he injected the sux into Bounds's Dilaudid vial. When they put the cap under a microscope, they found a small puncture mark in the rubber cap under one of the prongs holding it onto the bottle. The duty nurses wouldn't see it because they look for tampering in the center circle where they draw their shot, not under the rim. I can't wait to hear his explanation." Miguel arched both eyebrows, and a satisfied grin parted his lips.

"Leanne said her deputies found an envelope containing $47,000 in cash, matching the envelopes Beebe photographed, and a deposit receipt for $3,000 in Dockery's home office. He can explain that, too.

My guess—he was planning to spread the money out between banks or deposit a little at a time to keep us from finding it." Tim shook his head. Criminals always assumed the police were stupid and they'd get away with their deeds. They didn't realize the resources and the lengths to which law enforcement would go to get them off the street.

"Why do criminals think we won't find this stuff?" Miguel asked.

"Maybe they don't watch *The FBI Files* on TV?"

"I guess!"

"What are you two still doing here?" Elias asked as he walked into the alcove. "Get out of here and get some rest. I need some innovative stories for the press tomorrow morning, without cluing in Patterson."

"Where are Roxie and Miss Knoll?" Miguel asked.

"Leanne has given them one of the holding cells. We figured no one is going to want to break into jail." Elias chuckled. "Why?"

Tim took in a deep breath, as if on a doctor's examination table. "What if Berkstad is one of the good guys? What if Roxie planted bias because of her fear, not reality?"

Both Elias and Miguel glared at him like he was crazy.

"I'm not saying I believe it, but let's just try it on for size for a second," Tim suggested. "What if he did stumble on the composite of Bounds, and because of his—*affair* with Roxie, and knowing what he did about Bounds, he rushed here to help with our investigation?"

"Patterson orchestrated the raid on the safe house. We already know that," Miguel said, rubbing his right palm with his left thumb.

"We assumed Patterson did it because Berkstad told him where Beebe was," Elias added.

Tim shifted his weight and raked his teeth across his bottom lip. He needed to settle his mind, but it kept circling back to that hamburger joint across the street. His stomach rumbled incessantly. He wished he and Elias had stopped for that burger after all.

Then it hit him. "Of course! I know how Patterson found Beebe. He put a tracker on her phone. There's an app for that. People download the app and track where their friends and family members are," Tim said, launching himself from the desk.

"Oh, boy! He knows she's here and not in Seattle. He knows we're lying to him," Elias said.

"Kandar, can you defeat it?" Tim asked, still walking briskly toward the holding cells. "We've got to get her out of here."

"I need the phone, but probably." Kandar stood from behind the desk.

"I'll get it. Wait here."

Tim and Miguel entered the hallway to the holding cells at a sprint. Tim had no idea which of the holding cells the girls were in, and he paused briefly to check each one. Miguel stopped to roust one of the guards to unlock the door.

When Tim reached them, the women were both sitting on the edge of their bunks, as if awakened by the commotion.

"Get up, get dressed. We have to go," Tim commanded. Roxie sent him a questioning look, and Beebe began to protest. Roxie did not. She shoved Beebe's sweater and shoes at her instead.

"Hopefully, you can arrange better accommodations?" Roxie grumbled as the guard unlocked the cell door.

"Hopefully," Tim repeated sarcastically. "I need your phone and laptop, Beebe."

"Oh, no, you don't, Jackass. I have tomorrow's news story on that." She hugged her laptop to her chest as she slipped her feet into her shoes.

"Patterson put a tracker on your phone and computer." Tim held out his hand. Reluctantly she handed the computer case to him. He knew he was harsh, but he had to get them out of harm's way and quickly. "Patterson knows you didn't go to Seattle. He also knows you're here."

"But I thought you said this was the safest place to be," she argued.

Miguel stepped forward and helped Beebe into her sweater. "We're not sure how far Patterson's reach might be. We need to disable your phone and move you. Right now."

Tim was glad Beebe listened to Miguel. She usually resisted anything Tim suggested. He was surprised she thanked him for the rescue and didn't give him grief earlier. He hustled her out of the cell and down the hallway.

Elias and Leanne met them in front of her office. "Because we think they might've installed tracking devices on our SUVs, Leanne wants you to take hers." Elias stretched out his hand and delivered the keys to Tim.

"Let us know where you are when you get settled. I'll have a deputy drive me to pick up the cruiser. Now, go," Leanne said.

Tim handed Beebe's computer case to Elias. "If Patterson shows up—her phone and computer were seized in the botched robbery." It was all he could think of but went along with the theory they were giving out to the press.

"Good. Now go."

Tim dashed out to Leanne's SUV, jumped into the front seat, and started the engine. As he pulled forward, headlights flooded the front windshield.

"Get down!" Tim watched as the limousine pulled forward until the passenger window was level with his. Patterson rolled down the window. Tim glanced in his rearview mirror to find Roxie and Beebe had disappeared from view. They were on the floor between the seats. He didn't open his window. Returning Patterson's glower, he smiled as the man rolled past to the front of the station.

Tim called Mitch. "Where are you?"

"At the hotel. What's up?"

"Meet me at the airport."

The pause was brief. Tim assumed Mitch was processing the request. "I'll be there in five."

"Good. Five minutes."

Tim made a snap decision he was pretty sure he'd regret.

CHAPTER THIRTY-NINE

Tim turned onto Main Street and started for the small, uncontrolled airport seven miles out of town. He looked in his rearview mirror and watched for a second as Roxie and Beebe retook their seats and buckled in.

He decided to follow protocol and made a series of right turns, looping back to Main Street to ensure they weren't followed. Once they left town and Main Street merged into Highway 15 East, he'd take off-ramps with re-entries to confirm they were still alone.

"Miguel, do you still have those burner phones you bought for Roxie?" Tim asked.

"They're stashed in the Cessna," he answered.

"All right, let's power down our phones. Let's eliminate that tracking option, at least."

Tim could hear rustling as Roxie and Miguel complied. He tried to think of all the other ways they could be traced.

Patterson knew about Dani's plane. He probably knew the N-number on the tail. Tim could only hope he would assume that the Cessna was with her, since she'd left Culpeper early this morning, and not waiting on the taxiway for him, now.

Tim monitored the traffic around him. There were several cars ahead and behind him moving briskly along at a consistent freeway speed. From the crest of the small hill behind him, a pair of headlights appeared in his rearview mirror, distant now but approaching fast. Tim read the lighted green sign informing that Exit 75B was two miles ahead.

Miguel turned to look out the rear window. "Are we being followed?"

"Don't know," Tim answered, making a quick assessment of the rapidly approaching car behind him and the distance between them and the exit.

"If they are, they won't be messing around this time," Miguel warned. Both he and Roxie almost simultaneously removed their Glocks from their shoulder holsters. Tim heard the click-snap as they pulled back the slides, and rounds moved up from the magazine to the firing chamber. Any ambush was going to be met with a well-armed resistance.

Anxiety squeezed his stomach into a tight ball. The fast-moving black car changed into the left lane as if to pass and slowed. As it came alongside him, the driver suddenly veered right. Fuck! He was trying to ram them. Tim swerved, avoiding the collision, and sped off the highway onto the off-ramp. He braked at the top of the overpass, sliding in the loose gravel scattered on the asphalt.

"I can see his taillights! He stomped on the slammers!" Miguel said excitedly, leaning forward to watch the suspect vehicle as it passed beneath the highway bridge. "But there's too much traffic—he can't back up. He'll have to take the next exit. After yesterday's rain, I don't think he'll try to cut through the center divider."

The GPS began to insist that Tim return to the route. But after a second, it recalculated. A back road to the airport quickly displayed on the screen. By the time their pursuers retraced their steps, they'd be way ahead, but not necessarily out of the woods. Tim quickly turned left, crossed the overpass, and whipped the SUV onto the narrow street. Miguel handed Tim back his cell phone.

"Thanks." Tim nodded and called Mitch, engaging the car's speaker.

Without introducing himself, he asked. "Where are you?"

"Airport by our usual tie-down," Mitch answered.

"We are on Gaithersburg Road and coming in hot. We have a shadow."

"Shit! All right. I'll taxi to the east end of the airport near the closest hangar to the road. How much time do we have?"

"Minutes maybe, if that."

"I'll be there in thirty seconds. Stop at the first hangar you see. The gate isn't locked. Pull down on the padlock, and it will open. When you pass through, lock it behind you." Mitch took a breather. "I'll be there with the stairs down."

Tim disengaged and punched the accelerator, driving the remaining three miles at dangerous speeds. Miguel kept watching behind them. When they reached the first hangar, Tim slid the SUV sideways into a parking space beside the building, like a stunt driver. It wasn't his intention. He could hear seatbelts release, doors open. Miguel helped Roxie and Beebe out of the vehicle. Tim stashed the keys under the floormat and locked the door as Leanne had asked. He'd advise her where to find her vehicle in the morning.

Tim jogged to catch up to his group, and just as Mitch had explained, the gate was not secure. He pulled down, and the padlock released. He could hear the rumble of the 340's twin engines echoing off the hangar's walls. The unique smell of Avgas combustion teased the air.

"Run!" Miguel commanded, and the women did. Tim locked the gate behind him and dashed for the cabin door. Once on board, he retracted the stairs, and as the Cessna started to roll, he pulled the hatch closed and pushed down the lock lever.

Just as they made it to the active runway, Tim saw headlights turning onto the frontage road behind the hangars through one of the airplane's portholes. The car raced along, matching the twin engine's speed.

"They found us. Take cover!" He fully expected gunplay. Knocked off-balance by the plane's take-off acceleration, he tried to keep track of the enemy as best he could by looking through each of the fuselage's windows as he made his way down the aisle. When the pursuers located the driveway to the taxiways and runways, they blasted through the guardhouse gate's striped restraining arm. Shattered wood, red-and-white fragments and splinters, flew forward onto the tarmac. The vehicle burst onto the taxiway parallel to the runway as the 340 raced ahead.

Tim stumbled into the remaining seat and felt the transition both in sound and vibration as the airplane rotated from the pavement to flight. He held his breath as he watched out the window. Both the black car's front doors slammed open, and the dome lights exposed men stepping out on either side. Tim saw firearms, but no muzzle flash. The men gestured wildly and pounded the car's roof with clenched fists as the Cessna ascended into the sky. As the aircraft banked left, Tim realized why the men from the black car hadn't fired. They were saved by a small Piper Cub that gracefully descended from final approach onto the parallel runway.

For a moment, Tim sank deep into the leather seat and let relief wash over his skin. With the back of his hand, he wiped away the beads of sweat that had formed on his upper lip. As he regained his composure, he knew their pursuer wasn't Elias or any of his team members. Who was it? Who else knew they were taking Beebe to safety? *Blackmark Security? The CIA? A foreign government protecting Patterson? A criminal enterprise? Was Beebe right? Was Patterson involved with trafficking prescription drugs?* At this point, nothing would surprise him.

When he turned his gaze toward his fellow passengers, he realized the chase had rattled them, too. Miguel, across the narrow aisle from him, linked his fingers above his head and took in a deep breath, letting it out through his mouth. Beebe, in the seat facing Miguel, was pale as if all her blood rushed to her toes. Roxie, opposite Tim, sank into her seat cushions, peeking at him with one eye closed as if by closing them, she could disappear.

"That was—fun." She nervously giggled as she disarmed her pistol and returned it to the holster.

"Your idea of fun sucks!" Beebe retorted. Tim could see her hands trembling. She quickly tucked them under her legs.

"Hey, there is always an *at least*. At least they didn't fire on us," Miguel said.

Tim felt the Cessna level off. He sat forward and let go of the seatbelt he had failed to buckle. "Change of plan," he announced.

"Great news. Since I didn't know our first plan." Roxie huffed out a breath. "What is the plan?"

"I need to talk to Mitch. I'll be right back." Tim stood, ducked because of the cabin's height, and made his way toward the cockpit.

"Mitch is making the decisions now?" Tim heard Roxie's complaint.

"He's driving." Miguel chuckled at her.

Tim knocked and opened the cockpit door. He slid into the right seat next to Mitch.

"Those guys—friends of yours?" Mitch asked.

"I think I stepped in it, and I can't seem to wash it off."

"Bad?"

"Yeah. I need you to fly Dani and some people out of DC." Tim sighed.

"To where?"

"Somewhere, far away. Don't tell me. I don't want to know. If I don't know, can't spill it."

Mitch whipped his gaze to Tim's face. "Those men—they'd hurt Dani?"

"They've painted themselves into a corner. I suspect they'll come out fighting. Take the jet," Tim suggested. When Mitch scowled at him, he continued. "You know all those conspiracy theories about FBI agents suddenly committing suicide for no apparent reason when investigating the powerful elite?"

The pause was potent.

"Does Dani know?" Mitch's jaw tightened.

Tim shook his head no. "I don't want her to."

"Do you know who they are?

"We believe *they* work for a man with big money connections. The less you know, the safer you'll be. Other than by cell phone, can you reach Dani?"

"Yes. We have radio communication with the farm." Mitch banked the airplane slightly left.

"Can it be monitored by anyone on the outside?"

"They'd need to know the frequency."

"We'll have to chance it," Tim said.

"Leesburg's Executive Airport is a relief site for Dulles. I'll have to talk to the tower to land. If they are monitoring communications, they'll find us before we hit the ground."

Tim had no answer. He stared at Mitch's profile.

Mitch suddenly scrolled through the airport map on the screen in the center of the Cessna's instrument panel. "Wait, there's an uncontrolled VFR—visual flight rules strip fifteen miles north of the farm." He pointed to the map. "I need to talk to DC Center for traffic advisories, but I can land there. When we're closer, I'll turn off the transponder and limit the ADSB—sorry—the Automatic Digital Surveillance Broadcast to input only. I will be able to see traffic, but they won't be able to see us."

Tim could only agree with a nod.

"It's far enough out that it'll take your buddies a while to find us. If we radio Dani to meet us, we could land just about the time she arrives to pick us up."

"Let's do it." Tim put on the headset Mitch handed him from a compartment in the center console. He paused while Mitch dialed in the home radio channel.

—

Mitch landed the Cessna seamlessly with only the slightest stutter as the wheels touched the ground. Tim made his way to the cabin door, preparing to deplane when they stopped in the transient parking area. Once there, he opened the door and lowered the stairs.

In the distance, he watched as a Delight Valley Winery van approached and pulled up to the plane. He scanned the horizon all around. There were no other airport personnel or patrons in sight. Everything was eerily quiet. So, his danger radar automatically turned on high.

Dani rushed from the van's passenger door and met Tim at the bottom stair, flinging her arms around his neck. He lifted her off the ground, hugging her to him. Slowly, he lowered her, drifting for a moment in the delicious sensations rushing through his body from her kisses.

He removed her arms from around his neck, but kept hold of her right hand in his left. Needing to speak to her privately, he tugged her to follow him away from the stairs. The other passengers waited on board for the trip to Leesburg Executive Airport and Dani's Gulfstream. He tipped up her chin so she would have to look into his eyes.

"What made you land here? Leesburg Executive is closer. Was it full?" Her eyes were clear and bright, her smile beautiful and engaging. But her naivety and innocence about the dirty world of politics left him feeling sick inside. He couldn't tell her. Until the grand jury did its job, Patterson was a threat. And if higher ups decided to protect him, Tim's life wasn't worth two cents.

"I need you to take Beebe, Roxie, Shannon, and your female employees with you on the jet and get away from here."

"Just the women?" she teased. "Is this a women-and-children-first thing?"

The women in his life were quite capable, but no one could deny he was taller, bigger, and stronger. He never claimed to be smarter. Even though their relationship was adversarial, Beebe was a solid investigative journalist. Roxie was as good a partner as any of the guys on the team. Dani's success as a rancher, vintner, and businesswoman was without question and very real. But Dani had always occupied the ethereal realm, delicate and almost magical, in his thoughts. No woman in his life had ever affected him as she did. Contrary to the current popular theory, Tim believed women, especially his wife, were precious. As unreasonable as they might think it was, protecting them wasn't optional; for Tim, it was a need.

"No. Not just the women. You," he said softly, brushing the skin of her cheek with the back of his fingers. "I don't feel guilty for loving you. I don't want anything bad to happen to you."

At first, he thought his words moved her. She rolled up on her toes and kissed him tenderly on the mouth.

After the kiss, though, she squinted her eyes and curled her lips in a half-smile. He wasn't capable of hiding anything from her. "What's happened, Tim?"

"Things aren't going the way they should in the school shooter case. There are developments—Baby, I need you somewhere safe."

"What do you mean? The news reports said you caught the suspect, and he died in a shoot-out with the sheriff. Isn't that true?"

"Partly."

"Which part? Oh, ugh!" She raked her hands through her brown curls. "You can't tell me, can you?"

He took both her hands in his. "No. I can't."

"How long?" She let out a breath and dropped her shoulders.

"Just for a few days." He tried to reassure her but was pretty sure he failed. Completing their move, reuniting with his daughters, becoming a whole family again had to be put on hold. Dani wasn't thrilled. Disappointment flowed like an incoming wave from her eyes.

"When do you want me—us—to go?"

"Tonight. You need to leave tonight—as soon as you can. Mitch will fly you straight to the jet from here. Mark's picking up the others and will meet you."

Her mouth dropped open, and she moved closer and slumped against his shoulder. "Where will you be?"

"Miguel and I will take the van and grab hotel rooms in DC. Mostly, we'll be at FBI headquarters."

Dani stood back from him. A hopeful smile played on her lips. "The Leesburg farm is like a fortress. Come on, you'll see. We'll be safe there." She squeezed both of his hands and encouraged him toward the Delight Valley Van. He resisted.

Was she right? Was it possible to be safe at the farm? There were definite pluses. With Mitch's tactical experience added to the team, the three men made up a formidable defense squad.

Anyone who'd been around Tim for more than five seconds, though, knew he'd never intentionally put Dani in harm's way. That he adored her was blatantly obvious to even less observant bystanders—bystanders that had nothing to lose. Patterson had everything to lose: his freedom, his power, his fortune, his family, not that Tim believed he cared one iota about family.

In this dance between right and wrong, the lines had been drawn. Tim's and Patterson's futures teetered precariously in the hands of an uncertain and unpredictable grand jury. If they didn't indict, Patterson would be a fool to let him live. At the very least, he could leverage Dani and his daughters' safety for Tim's silence. Letting Patterson walk was a compromise he didn't think he could make. Tim chose to take his family out of the equation like a magician removing all the aces from a deck of trick cards. It was his only option.

Tim looked down into Dani's blue eyes. How easy it would be to give in to her. Instead of being alone tonight, he could sleep in the warmth and comfort of her love. He shook his head and smiled at her. "This is an argument I can't let you win. I need you to go somewhere far away from DC—somewhere safe. I need you to do it now."

CHAPTER FORTY

Tim and Miguel rode the elevator down to the BAU offices in the lower level at the FBI Training Facility at Quantico. Dani and the ladies had landed earlier somewhere in the West. She checked in when they settled into their hiding place, lifting the weight of worry from Tim's shoulders. It might've been his imagination, but he thought he heard the cheerful little-girl giggles of his daughters in the background. It was reassuring that, for now, they were safe.

Tim sipped from the venti latte he'd grabbed from the hotel's coffee shop on the way. He needed the triple-shot coffee to slap him fully awake. Last night, he'd spent his three hours of fitful sleep tossing and turning at every creak and sound. Dark, puffy circles ringed Miguel's eyes, and Tim realized he wasn't the only one.

Miguel glanced at his watch. "Is it really only 7 a.m.?"

Tim guessed the question was rhetorical and didn't answer. Elias wanted them here to go over the evidence should they be asked to give testimony to the grand jury. Since he was a former prosecutor, Tim figured he'd be tapped for the role. He took another gulp of coffee, hoping it would clear the fog.

As the elevator door opened, Tim saw Elias waiting for them. He grinned at them, but it wasn't really a greeting, more nervous. They didn't have to say it out loud to each other; they all knew the stakes. Last night, when Tim reported they'd been attacked, Elias had fumed. Tim guessed he'd called Masterson at CIA and told him to make Blackmark Security back the fuck off, in more diplomatic terms, of course. He just wasn't sure Blackmark Security was the culprit. He had heard of inter-agency disputes, but the CIA's protection of Patterson was more than problematic. The alphabet agencies were supposed to work for the interests of the American people, not politicians. And yet, everything these days had become so divisive and political. Tim wondered if America would survive it. For his daughters' sakes, he hoped so.

"It's going to be a long day," Elias said. He ushered Tim and Miguel toward his office.

"What did Masterson have to say?" Miguel asked.

"He agreed to stop surveilling us." Elias flipped on the overhead lights and motioned for Tim and Miguel to sit at the round cherrywood conference table that occupied the left side of his office.

"So, he acknowledged CIA knew what Blackmark Security was doing?" Tim pulled out one of the teal upholstered chairs.

"Not directly. He just said, 'Consider it stopped.'"

Tim sat and glanced around the room. The matching cherry credenza along the wall was stacked with case files five or six deep. It reminded him that Elias not only participated in their active investigations, but also completed all the mounds of paperwork that accompanied his title of supervisory special agent.

"The first grand jury is convening at nine a.m. Watson Hardwick, U.S. Attorney for Virginia's Western District, has asked for you, Tim. He read your bio and knows you were a prosecutor," Elias said. "He'll meet you at eight a.m. in Room 144 to go over the evidence. Hardwick figured you might understand the process." Elias slid a 24-by-24-inch file box across the table to Tim.

Tim had seen this assignment coming. The thought of getting back in the courtroom fueled a surge of excitement. He always loved court, especially when the evidence was so intriguing. He savored another swallow of coffee and dumped the paper cup in the trash. He wrote the room number in pen on the box's top.

"The helicopter will take you to the federal courthouse in Charlottesville. You should leave now," Elias said, pointing to the roof.

"Good." Tim was ready.

—

The grand jury foreman asked his last question.

"You have DNA evidence. What conclusion did you come to from that report?"

"Congressman Aaron Patterson is the father of high-school student Aiysha Conrow's unborn baby. We believe he hired Hamish Bounds to shoot up the school and murder Aiysha to keep from being exposed for the other crimes we've presented here today," Tim said without hesitation and as clearly as he could. He heard a collective gasp from the jury members. One of the women in the second row even wiped away tears.

"Thank you, Special Agent McAndrews. You may step down."

Tim stood in the blond wood witness box and took the two steps down to the courtroom floor. He discreetly studied the twenty-three jurors. They had enough evidence to indict and authorize the arrest of Patterson and his cohorts. Tim was sure he'd convinced them. But he didn't like what he read on their faces as he passed by. He'd presented to grand juries before and had seen a variety of emotions. Fear had never been one of them—until now.

Tim boarded the helicopter that waited for him in the parking area behind the Federal Courthouse. He donned the headphones and listened to the pilot's chatter with air traffic control. They lifted off.

In the last few days, cherry and dogwood trees had exploded with delicate pink and white blossoms. Meadows awash with yellow daffodils made a patchwork with the lush spring green pastures and dark forests below. To the west, clouds billowed up in fluffy white towers reaching well into the atmosphere. From this height, the world looked at peace. But later this afternoon, the clouds would turn dark, flash, thunder, and rain, mirroring the real world, churning with human turmoil.

Could he have done better? He sat forward in his seat, looking down once again at the pastoral scene below. The occasional farmhouses and barns dotting the landscape transitioned to smaller and smaller parcels. The closer they came to the Beltway, suburban-style subdivisions replaced the rural setting.

Tim was unable to dismiss the looks on the jurors' faces from his mind. Patterson was a powerful man. But by law, the identities of the grand jurors were secret. Didn't they believe that the promise of law would be kept? Were they afraid of consequences if Patterson found out they'd voted to indict?

Tim fidgeted in his seat. He tried contemplating the city below to distract himself, but it didn't work. What would he do if the grand jury failed to deliver? It was all part of the criminal justice world. Win some—lose some. His imagination spun through scenarios of what he'd *like* to do to Patterson if they lost—but wouldn't. He believed in law and order. He reminded himself that vigilantism wasn't his style.

He hated waiting. Waiting for evidence from the crime lab, waiting for a judge to sign off on a warrant, waiting for a jury to render its verdict—it was never easy.

The helicopter landed on the pad on top of the main FBI building at Quantico. Tim disembarked and ducked under the spinning blades. He couldn't stop second-guessing himself. Was there more he could've, should've done? He just didn't know.

He took the elevator to the basement. As the doors opened, he could see his team members busily tapping away at their computer keyboards, but they weren't talking. *Odd.* They were encouraged to bounce ideas off each other, and usually, their station was in a constant hubbub.

Kandar half stood from behind his desk, shaking his head no. He lifted his right hand and shielded his left index finger while he pointed at Elias's office. Tim glanced over as the door opened. Congressman Patterson emerged from inside, his chin lifted in victory. Elias followed, but stopped only two steps outside his office.

"Ahhh, Special Agent McAndrews, nice to see you again," the congressman said with a smirk on his lips. He crossed the distance and extended his hand. Tim pumped it once and withdrew. Inside, his spirit recoiled away from the evil.

"Congressman." Tim looked to Elias for any indication of where they stood. Elias's face was a blank canvas. Tim steeled himself for a healthy dose of reality.

"I understand you were giving evidence in court." Patterson dismissively looked at his watch as if speaking to Tim was taking too much of his valuable time. "How did that go?"

Tim tightened his jaw and involuntarily ground his teeth together. *Crap!* Patterson had just played the power card. Smugness wafted from him like the stink from a skunk. Did power best murder? Tim guessed he was about to find out. He swallowed down his disgust.

"I think it's not going as well as I'd hoped," Tim said, biting back anger and disappointment.

"Yes, well, better luck next time." Patterson's lowered brows threw a shadow over his eyes, making him look dark and threatening. It was the wrong message; it only fueled Tim's need to see the congressman face justice.

Tim acknowledged him by letting a weak smile tick across his lips. He watched Patterson board the elevator to the upper floors. He stared at the closed doors for several seconds and heard the electric motor hum.

"That man is insufferable," Elias growled.

Confused, Tim asked, "Did the grand jury refuse to indict?"

"No word yet," Elias said, motioning for him to come into his office. Tim joined the rest of the team as they headed for the conference table.

"Did the seventh floor hand Patterson a get-out-of-jail-free card?" Tim asked.

"No. Patterson came looking for you. Demanded an update on our case. I told him what we told the press. Bounds was the school shooter and died in an armed confrontation with the police. I told him you were testifying on a court case. He doesn't know which one." Elias grinned and closed the door.

"He has to suspect something. Why else would he come here?" Tim asked.

"Sure, he suspects something. He knows we interviewed that sorry excuse for a principal, Crenshaw. He's worried his buddy will give him up. He doesn't know his girlfriend, and his very own DNA, already have." Elias twisted the ends of his mustache. "Leanne's deputies found Bounds's envelope of money. He wasn't as adept at hiding it as Berkstad thought."

"Speaking of being incompetent, where is Berkstad?" Miguel voiced Tim's question before he could.

"He's on his way back from DC. The seventh floor." Elias looked concerned.

"Do you think the director will intercede for Patterson?" Tim asked.

"The director has teenage kids. No self-respecting father could," Elias said. "Assuming the grand jury rules in our favor, we need to plan our arrest." Elias clicked on the computer mouse, and a map appeared on the screen on the west wall. "My thought is, we stop him after he leaves the congressional chamber and is en route to his apartment." He drew the route with a laser pointer.

"No fuss, no muss?" Miguel laughed. "We could have the Capitol police do a traffic stop and then swoop in."

"What about you, Tim?" Elias asked.

Tim looked away from the map and smiled. "I think we have two objectives here."

Elias tipped his chin to one side and said, "Elaborate."

"Our first objective is to get Patterson off the street. He needs to be locked away for the rest of his life and forgotten. Second, we need to broadcast the message that being a congressman does not set you above the law. I say we send in SWAT—full gear—to arrest him right there on the floor of the House," Tim announced. "Let all of them know if they drug and rape children, if they commit murder, we're coming for them."

"Ooh, boy!" Kandar said excitedly.

"I can't tell you how much I want to do that," Melissa agreed.

"But, aren't congressman and senators immune from arrest while the House and Senate are in session?" Miguel asked.

"For misdemeanors, sure. But not for treason, felony, and breach of the peace, Article 1, Section 6, Clause 1 of the Constitution." Tim recited the passage. "Is there a more egregious felony than first-degree murder? It hasn't been tested before the Supreme Court, but I'd like to see him try to pull that off."

"Yeah, he'd have to argue, 'Yes, your honors, I drugged, raped, and hired a hitman to murder my victims, but you can't arrest me on the floor of the House.'" Miguel laughed.

Elias set his elbows on the table and steepled his fingers. He touched his tongue to the bottom edge of his top teeth as a big grin split his face.

The intercom on the phone in the center of the conference table buzzed. "Line three is for you, sir," a female voice rang out. "Watson Hardwick."

Elias looked at each face around the table one at a time, rubbed his hands together, palm to palm. "Here goes nothing." He picked up the receiver. "Elias Cain."

Tim and everyone at the table held their breath.

"Yes. Yes. Would you repeat that?" Elias said, pushing down the button engaging the speaker function on the phone.

"The decision is unanimous. All twenty-three jurors voted to indict on all charges," Hardwick said. "I'm sending the indictments now, and your warrants will be ready within the hour."

CHAPTER FORTY-ONE

Tim cut the headlights and engine and allowed the SUV to roll quietly into the parking space. They'd chosen this small office building lot as a staging area because of its strategic proximity to Patterson's DC home.

The director put the kibosh on Tim's idea of arresting Patterson on the floor of the House of Representatives. He was right, of course. Why test the law when they had other viable options? At least, the director had conceded to a 4 a.m. 'no-knock' surprise.

Unwilling to give up entirely on seeing Patterson become notorious, Elias had an "anonymous FBI source" deliver a tip to SBC News. That move fulfilled two promises: first, to see Patterson's name flashed in the media non-stop, exposing him as a pure evil low-life. Second, honoring Tim's pledge to Beebe Knoll, she'd get an exclusive in exchange for her help. Tim heard she was flying in on a red-eye from Seattle and would arrive with her crew just about the time the arrest went down.

Tim stepped out of the SUV and made note of the surroundings. The three-story office building blocked Patterson's line of sight to the staging area. Elias had obtained the owner's consent to use the roof for sniper positions. Kandar and Melissa met with the owner, and he gave them a key card to enter the building.

Tim cautiously strolled to the edge of the lot, staying behind a tall, six-foot hedge, and took out his night vision scope. He studied the darkened, tree-lined street. Miguel stood beside him.

The FBI had kept Patterson under surveillance for days. Actually, since Beebe delivered Tim the SD card containing the pictures of the money handoff to the pharmacist. Tim hoped this was going to be his only early-morning stake-out on this case. Anticipation filled the air like a stadium full of fans just before the Rose Bowl.

Tim turned when he heard footsteps crunching on the gravel in the parking lot. As Melissa walked over, her breath condensed into small clouds and then dissipated in the cool early-morning air.

"Have you got something for us?" Tim asked. He knew Kandar and Melissa had been here since midnight.

"Patterson's armed."

"Wait. Patterson is anti-gun. He doesn't believe anyone should own guns, remember?" Tim joked.

"Maybe he's not holding a gun, but his two bodyguards are," she breathed. "There are at least two on his roof garden over the garage."

"Does SWAT know?" Tim asked.

"You didn't? The field agents we relieved said they called it in," Melissa said, perplexed.

"Nope. No one . . . ." Tim had a sudden attack of roller-coaster stomach. Whether a screw-up or intentional, either way, it was bad news.

"Kandar had me run down and tell you. He said he had a bad feeling," Melissa added.

CIA had pledged to get Blackmark Security to back off. Who then pulled the strings? Was a foreign government involved? Berkstad said Patterson was Mata Hari-ed by a Russian operative. Did she flip him? All of a sudden, the dynamics of the all-for-show arrest just shifted to high stakes—maybe even to life and death.

"But that's not all. There are women with him in the house," Melissa said.

Tim groaned.

"That's what I don't understand." Melissa shook her head. "He was supposed to be alone."

"*¡Hijo de puta! ¡Hijo de la chingada!*" Miguel gestured angrily. His words didn't make sense until Tim realized Miguel swore in Spanish.

"Now what?" Melissa asked.

Tim rocked back away from her. He didn't relish the idea of a SWAT raid with women, innocent or otherwise, in the house. Too much could go wrong. They had to come up with a plan B, and fast.

"SWAT boys are here," Miguel said, dipping his head in the direction of the driveway and licking his lips in anticipation, like a wolf at the thought of his next meal. Tim dreaded the raid, while Miguel savored it.

Two black FBI Mine-Resistant Ambush Protected (MRAP) vehicles pulled to a stop, side by side. A six-man team quickly deployed from the back of each. To Tim's surprise, Elias jumped down from the right front seat of one in full gear. He had to admit the fifty-five-year-old Elias looked as fit and battle-ready as the youngest of the rest of the SWAT team members.

Melissa, Miguel, and Tim joined Elias. "This is Jesse Stampton, our SWAT Commander. We need a SITREP," Elias explained.

Melissa began her report. "There are two armed bodyguards on the roof garden that runs for the entire length of the garage along the north side of the house. One is stationed toward the front, the other to the back. There may be more inside that we didn't see." Though she tried to be calm, her voice held a slight tremor. Tim placed a comforting hand on her shoulder for a second. The SWAT Commander pulled up a map and house plans on his iPad. "Also, there are two women in the house," she added.

Elias loomed up to his full six-foot-six-inch height. It was evident to Tim that no one, whether it was called in or not, had passed that information to Elias or SWAT.

"Where's Kandar?"

"He's up the street. He stayed in the SUV to keep watch on the house," Melissa said.

Commander Stampton paused for only a second and then barked orders at his team. "Deploy the UAV, full infrared. Let's see where the bodies are."

Tim remembered some of the tech the FBI guys brought with them last time he'd worked with a SWAT team at Schweitzer Mountain. This UAV wasn't a typical fifty-dollar toy-store variety. It was equipped with the latest noise suppression and digital optics technology. Quickly, noiselessly, two squad members launched the UAV. As the drone reached altitude, infrared images appeared on a drop-down digital screen in the back of the SWAT vehicle. The drone's infrared could easily see through the wood-framed walls.

Each of the crew members had a view of the house's interior, the location of obstacles that would block their progress, and most importantly, where the people were. Two white-hot images glowed on the roof, while three presented themselves in a room in the back of the house. Tim assumed it was Patterson and his lady friends.

"We have to neutralize the bodyguards on the roof," Stampton said.

"Hit them with ketamine darts. They only have on chest body armor," Miguel said. "At this distance, a sniper could easily make that shot." He turned to look the SWAT Commander square in the eyes. "Hell, I could make that shot."

"That will give us enough time to get in, disarm the bodyguards, arrest Patterson and be out before the neighbors are out of bed," Elias argued.

"'They can watch it on TV with their morning coffee," Miguel said.

Tim knew once the darts impacted, they would fully inject the drug before the guards knew what hit them. Within two or three minutes, it would be lights-out for about ten to twelve hours. Ketamine wasn't without side effects, their darts were tempered with benzodiazepine to mitigate those. But bullets were lethal.

Stampton stared at Miguel. "It's not authorized," he said.

"Someone always had to be a stick-in-the-mud." Miguel's SEAL training made him want to use down and dirty, fast and easy. Tim thought Miguel was right. "Yeah, but I lost sympathy for Patterson's guys when they tried to run us off the road and shoot us out of the sky. Unethical? A K-nap is better than dead," Miguel laughed. Both he and Tim started to put on their vests and communication gear.

"I'm giving you authorization to use ketamine," Elias commanded. "Can you do it?"

Stampton hesitated but then repeated, "A K-nap is better than dead." He sent his snipers to the roof.

"Are we ready?" Stampton spoke into his throat microphone and nodded as he received the reply. "Fire at will."

Tim walked closer to the display screen and monitored the feed from the overhead drone. He heard the *whap-whap* as two nearly simultaneous suppressed shots echoed off the side of the building. The guards in the rooftop garden hopped in circles as they tried to knock the darts away. They looked all around as if trying to determine the assault's origin. By now, the ketamine would already be picked up in the capillaries and well on its way to the brain. One of the men already started to stumble. He dropped his rifle off his shoulder, slumped down to his knees, and toppled face-first to the floor of the roof garden. The second man raced toward him, but the drug hit him, too. He sat on the edge of a lounge chair, released his weapon, and crashed forward, upending the chaise as he toppled to the deck.

Without waiting for their commander to say a word, both six-man groups jogged forward to Patterson's house. One unit split off to cover the back, the other to breach the front door. Miguel joined the rear-entry team, leaving Tim to go with the main squad.

Tim thought how little a castle breach had changed throughout history when one of the SWAT members dashed forward with a small battering ram. Two hits, and the front door splintered off its hinges.

"FBI with a warrant!" and "Clear!" shattered the silence. Flashlight beams danced on the walls and up the main staircase as they turned their attention to the second story. The drone circling overhead sent real-time images, and the team received constant feedback from command. The prone figures in the last bedroom remained still—unmoving, asleep, or drugged—Tim didn't know which. His six-man group headed steadily down the hall, clearing all other rooms along the way.

The point man kicked the bedroom door open. He announced, "FBI with a warrant!"

The six-man squad rushed in, rifles ready. Patterson sat up, pulling the bed covers up to his neck. Tim quickly assessed the situation.

"I need medics, upstairs, last room." The two females in Patterson's bed looked as if they couldn't have been more than fifteen-years-old. The smaller of the two looked twelve. Horrified, he holstered his Glock.

The girls didn't move, even when two officers yanked Patterson out of bed and threw him facedown on the floor. "Aaron Patterson, you are under arrest for murder, conspiracy to commit murder, solicitation of murder, for starters." The point officer read the charges and dropped the warrant on a bedside table. He recited the Miranda warnings. They flipped him over and tossed his clothes at him.

In the commotion, the girls hadn't even stirred. Tim rushed bedside and felt each girl for a pulse. They each had one, faint but steady. Neither girl responded to his touch. There was no doubt in Tim's mind were under the influence of drugs.

As he was cuffed, Patterson's outburst began. His face contorted into a grimace of pure evil. "Do you know who I am? I'm a United States congressman! You're bringing hell down on yourselves. I'll have your badges!" He wrestled slightly against the officer until he saw Tim. "McAndrews! Tell them who I am!" There was a pause as the SWAT members turned to look at him.

Tim walked over, leaned down to where Patterson sat on the floor. He locked a cold stare into Patterson's eyes. "They know who you are.

I don't think they care. I know I don't." Tim straightened and turned away to watch for the EMTs.

Patterson's voice choked with rage. "I'll make sure you pay for this! You'll never get another job! Not ever! Do you know who my friends are? You'll be sorry!" The one thing Patterson forgot to demand in his long list of complaints and threats was his lawyer. *Oh, well.* Tim shrugged.

He tuned out Patterson's tirade and guided the EMTs to the two girls. Neither woke up, not even to the EMTs' urgings. The smallest and likely the youngest groggily moaned but slipped back into the drug-induced sleep. Tim grabbed a blanket for each and wrapped it around their shoulders. He choked back thoughts of his own daughters. If these were his….This wasn't the time and place for this. He shut down those emotions.

"Send Melissa up," Tim called over his throat microphone. He was sure he knew what had happened here, and he fought back revulsion.

The EMTs were listening to vitals, determining the girls' condition, and he stepped back to get out of their way.

The SWAT point man approached. "What do you want to do with *Congressman* Patterson?" He asked dismissively.

What did Tim *want* to do with Patterson? He was pretty sure it had something to do with a rusty knife. Tim balled his hands into fists but kept them tight to his sides. *Innocent until proven guilty*, he repeated over and over in his mind to drive away his more primitive urges.

"Who are the girls, Patterson?" Loathing filled every word Tim hissed through his teeth.

For a moment, Patterson must've realized he was in deep trouble. Fear flashed from his eyes. But then he became defiant and wouldn't answer.

"Take him to FBI headquarters. We'll process him there."

"You'll get yours, McAndrews!" Patterson resumed his threats. Tim glared but forced himself not to snap back.

"I'll get the girls taken care of," he said to his crew as if Patterson wasn't there. He glanced around the room for a purse or something that would identify the victims as they led Patterson away. He had to learn who the girls were, how old they were, and find their parents. Suddenly, he hoped they weren't runaways, trafficked girls, lost girls. He desperately wanted someone to be there to care.

"Do you know what drugs they've taken?" one of the EMTs asked.

Tim shook his head no. "Patterson has used Rohypnol in the past."

"Rohypnol? These girls are so young." The EMT's lips tightened with anger. It replaced her initial shock. "There's no reversing agent. We have to transport them to the hospital."

Tim nodded. At least the girls would wake up with little or no memory of what had happened to them.

Melissa dashed through the bedroom door. Tim took her aside. "Go with the victims in the medic unit. Make sure you get rape kits and have them include a tox screen for Rohypnol or GHB metabolites. We'll send their personal effects along when we recover them."

Tim watched as the girls were taken away on stretchers.

The room finally cleared. Quiet settled in around him like a thick fog. It was the brief space of calm between arrest and the onslaught of crime scene techs swarming the place to gather evidence. All of a sudden, Tim was exhausted. The adrenaline had run out. He was operating on three hours of sleep, no food, and too much emotion.

Slowly, he walked down the stairs and out the front of the house. He sank to the porch steps and sat resting his elbows on his knees. Transfixed for a moment, he watched Miguel finish packing the two bodyguards into ambulances. For the next twelve hours, they would be monitored at the hospital, cuffed to their beds.

Elias sat beside him and stretched out his long limbs. "You okay?"

"Yeah. Tired. But no one said this was going to be easy." Tim smiled.

Miguel joined them, leaning up against a support column for the porch roof. "Roxie is going to be furious that she missed out on this!" He laughed.

"Ahhh!" Elias waved his hand in a dismissive gesture. "There'll be plenty more."

"So, what's the plan?" Miguel asked.

"I'm going to get breakfast. Then I'm going to watch Patterson stew in the interrogation room for an hour or so until I decide to interview him," Elias said.

"I thought I'd go see how Melissa is coming along with the victims." Tim wanted to make sure they were reunited with relatives and cared for.

"Want some company?" Miguel asked.

Tim nodded.

Elias looked at his watch. "Okay. Interrogation begins at 10 a.m. Get some food, clean up, and meet me downtown then. It's going to be a long day."

Tim and Elias stood. When they started to their cars, suddenly their path was flooded, and they were blinded by TV news-camera lights. Tim lifted his hand to shield his eyes. Beebe Knoll stood in front of them, microphone in hand.

CHAPTER FORTY-TWO

"Wow! Guys! This is so great. I got the whole thing on tape." Beebe was beaming. Her smile was as dazzling as the bright camera lights. "Now, give me the whole story."

On that note, Tim decided to defer to Elias. Tim looked Elias's way and saw *uh-oh* drawn all over his face. Elias had used him so many times for a "no comment" response, Tim prepared himself to do it again. Beebe wasn't going to like it.

"You know I can't comment on an open investigation." He put on the most convincing smile he could muster.

"Oh, no, you don't. Don't you dare! We had a deal!" Beebe's sunshine had turned into thunderstorms, violent ones. "McAndrews!"

"Miss Knoll, nice to see you made it for the arrest. I hope you got some good footage," Elias said, slipping his arm over her shoulders and turning her away. He'd just given Miguel and Tim the cue and the time to go. "Now, why don't you meet me down at the FBI headquarters, downtown, and I'll get you up to speed."

Beebe seemed placated, but turned to cast a glance over her shoulder at Tim. She lifted her hand and pointed at him with a perfectly manicured index finger and mouthed the words. "You promised me an exclusive, Jackass!"

Tim never thought of himself as an expert lip reader, but he got her message loud and clear. He could only grin at her.

—

At the hospital, Tim found Melissa in the emergency room waiting area. When she saw Tim and Miguel, she jumped from her seat.

"How are they?" Tim asked.

"Very drugged. The doctor says they won't be fully awake until afternoon," she said. "I've called local police, child protective services and scheduled some victim's assistance counselors. Oh, there—there's the doctor now." She pointed him out. He acknowledged her, lifted his hand indicating he'd be a minute, and continued inputting information on an electronic chart.

"Did you find out who the girls are?" Tim asked.

"Working on it. But not yet," Melissa answered. "We may have to wait until they come around."

Tim looked at his watch. It was already 7 a.m. He wanted to know who the girls were before interviewing Patterson. The more details they had, the easier it would be to get a confession.

"Kandar said CSI found the girls' phones. They are working on unlocking them."

The doctor walked over. Tim and Miguel both identified themselves and showed FBI credentials. Melissa introduced him as Doctor Palmer.

"How can I help you?" The young doctor asked. His dark eyes were full of genuine concern. Tim guessed Palmer was around his age, a new resident, serving out his first months in the emergency department.

"We believe the two girls are victims of a crime." Miguel started.

"Indeed, they are. Luckily, they will both survive. In my medical opinion, both girls have been drugged and sexually assaulted. There are abrasions consistent…"

Tim lifted his palms to stop the doctor. "At this point, sir, I'd like a copy of their charts. We have a suspect in custody. We need to confront him with your initial findings." Tim knew it was a defense mechanism but couldn't change it. He couldn't stand to hear the extent of the girls' injuries spoken out loud. He stood in the small opening in the curtain surrounding the youngest girl's treatment room. Tim watched the digital monitors memorialize her every heartbeat and record each breath as she slept.

Once the charts were printed, they became written reports—just black letters on white paper. The description of their injuries would be surrendered to Latin medical terms. That alone made it easier to detach, push his emotion and anger aside, and build a case for the U.S. Attorney with logic and reason.

At least the drug Patterson had given them would erase their memories of being victimized. However, he didn't know what the unconscious mind would hold on to. Would there be long-term consequences? He hoped not.

"As soon as they are available, I'd like to see the toxicology reports as well." Tim handed the doctor his business card with phone numbers and an FBI email address.

"Will you notify me once you find their relatives?" Dr. Palmer asked.

"Yes. Of course. Special Agent Grant will have them call you immediately," Tim continued. He and the doctor shook hands. It was time to get back to headquarters. He tapped Miguel on the shoulder and tipped his head in the direction of the exit. Miguel crossed himself before he turned away from the girls, as if he, too, whispered a prayer.

While Tim waited for Miguel to load into the SUV, he checked in with Dani. When he'd called after they took Patterson into custody, she'd decided to come back to Leesburg.

He wanted to see her. It was good to know she'd landed safely. Even the thought of her left him breathless, his heart opened like a rose. When the world around him got too crazy, too dark, she grounded him, reminded him goodness and decency still existed. They became each other's sanctuary, each other's safe place. She was his and he was hers.

As they seat-belted in, Miguel said, "You know, maybe I'm an out-of-touch Neanderthal, but I prefer women over twenty-one."

Tim laughed. "Well, yeah. I'm a one-woman guy. And I want her in love with me, conscious, and actively participating in the whole thing." Tim shook his head, dismayed. "Patterson is one sick dude."

Miguel snickered. "He would've done better to buy himself one of those plastic life-sized sex dolls. Now, he gets to go to jail."

They pulled into the FBI headquarters parking area and headed for the interview rooms to meet Elias. The goal was to get a confession. In his days as a prosecutor, Tim seldom had as much evidence as they had on Patterson. Under normal circumstances, they didn't need a confession. But the congressman had clout, so Elias's team would try to get one and use it against him.

"Glad you're here," Elias said, smiling as Miguel and Tim approached from down the hall. He took them aside into his office. His office here, at main headquarters was a smaller room than his office at Quantico, but just as nicely appointed. He gestured for them to sit at a small round conference table.

"Patterson is stressed, but he hasn't asked for an attorney."

Tim smiled. "That would be my first request."

"He's arrogant. It's almost as if he believes this won't go anywhere," Elias continued. "Before we go in, let me get you up to speed. Crenshaw has made a plea deal. He's agreed to testify against Patterson if we take conspiracy off the table. He admits to the drugging and abuse of the students, but says he had nothing to do with the school shooting. Apparently, it went down like this: Aiysha went to the school nurse when she started to get morning sickness. The nurse confirmed the pregnancy and went to Crenshaw. They aren't required to inform the parents anymore. They called for a social worker, and she advised Aiysha to have an abortion."

Tim leaned back in his chair, surprised. "Let me guess: Aiysha refused, didn't she?"

Elias rolled his tongue along the inside of his cheek and nodded yes. "Crenshaw went to his buddy Patterson because they feared Aiysha would get a paternity test. The results would blow up their whole scheme. They had everything to lose."

"So, Patterson came up with the school-shooting idea, then?" Miguel asked.

"He made the bet no one would do an autopsy. Why bother when the cause of death was a gunshot wound?" Elias added. "He was so sure, he didn't even bother to modify his behavior."

Miguel laughed. "That's not going to work out."

"Dockery, the pharmacist, confessed to supplying the Rohypnol and mixing succinylcholine into Bounds's meds. He has agreed to testify against Patterson if we take the death penalty off the table," Elias said.

"Patterson underestimated our team." Tim grinned.

"They always do," Elias said. "Yessir, they always do." Elias rose from his chair and picked up the case file. "I think we've kept Congressman Patterson waiting long enough. Tim, you and Miguel come with me."

As they walked toward the interview rooms, Elias resumed his instructions. "He's going to want you in the room, Tim. He thinks you two have a connection because Beebe introduced you. I'll go in first with Leanne. We will make nice. I'll give it a few minutes, and maybe Kandar will be able to come up with the little girls' names. If not, we will go with what we have. It's plenty. If you get the identity info, come right in. Otherwise, I'll signal you by asking for more coffee. You bring that and the case file. Now, when you come in, you aren't his friend. We aren't going to give him that comfort zone. It will throw him off-balance. You are the 'bad cop.' When he lies, you confront him with the hard evidence. One of two things will happen: he'll confess, or he'll scream for a lawyer." Elias pressed the case file into Tim's hands. "You ready?"

All his courtroom experience would serve Tim now. He felt that tingle of excitement, like when the defense held tight on a fumble and offense took over the field on the twenty-yard line. Elias called a screen pass play, and a touchdown was in his sights; Tim could taste it.

"I'm ready."

"Miguel, keep an eye out for Kandar's identity report. We checked Missing Persons and there's nothing that matches, yet. I want to know who those two young girls are," Elias said.

When Tim glanced over at Miguel, his friend's eyes had taken on a luster. Sheriff Leanne strolled toward them down the hallway. She looked as lovely as ever, and Miguel was clearly smitten. They all nodded greetings, keeping it on a very formal and professional level. Elias and Leanne entered the small interrogation room. Tim and Miguel stood in the viewing area just beyond the two-way mirror.

"She's married, you know," Tim said quietly. He didn't look Miguel in the eyes. Crushes were personal, and he wasn't sure his partner knew he knew.

"I know. I asked her out, and she told me." Miguel sighed. "The good ones always are. I can still admire perfection from afar, though, can't I?"

Tim chuckled to himself. "Can't argue with that. You can."

"Wait? You didn't . . . ?"

"No. I already have perfection at home. I saw his picture in her office."

"She says he's a real good guy. A Marine." Miguel looked to Tim as if for confirmation. Tim reassured him anyway with a quick nod and a smile.

"Looks like they are ready to get started."

It was going to be a long morning, but Tim enjoyed watching Elias work. He was the best interrogator in the business. He'd already made Patterson feel like a guest. They'd served him a cup of coffee, chatted about the spring weather and how this was probably all just a big misunderstanding. Elias promised they'd have it all cleared up in just a few minutes.

"Kandar found out who the girls are!" Melissa's voice broke through. Tim and Miguel both turned as she burst into the room, waiving a print-out. "Brianna and Barbara Patterson. I've called the parents. They are out of town but will get here as fast as they can. CSI also found a bubble pack of Rohypnol tablets in the bathroom, and three six-ounce glasses that tested positive for roofies and alcohol."

"Patterson? Did you say, Patterson?" Miguel screwed up his brow. "That's an odd coincidence."

Tim swallowed and grabbed at his shirt collar. He loosened his tie and undid the top button of his shirt as if he needed more air. "Oh, no. Aghh, No. Are they related?"

"Oh, sick!" Melissa squeezed her eyes shut and covered her mouth with both hands as she shuddered with a silent scream.

Tim dialed Kandar. "Does Patterson have a brother?" He asked without a greeting. "He does...Samuel, older brother...two years older. Does Samuel have any kids? He does...Daughters. Brianna, fourteen, and Barbara, twelve. Thanks, Buddy." Tim took in a deep breath, he wanted to speak, but words just wouldn't come.

"I get it! Brother Samuel left the girls with good ol' Uncle Aaron for the weekend. He volunteers to watch them all the time. He's a little strange, but hey, they're sure he's completely harmless," Miguel said sarcastically. "He's probably been abusing his nieces for years."

Tim rubbed his hand along the bottom of his chin. "You know, I think being the bad cop is going to be a whole heck of a lot more fun than I first imagined." He snatched the print-out from Melissa's hand and then rapped twice on the interrogation-room door and opened it.

"Ah, Tim. Come in. You remember Congressman Patterson, don't you?" Elias's smile was big, broad, and welcoming. "Well, now that Tim's here, I think we can get this all cleared up."

Tim dropped the case file down on the table and took a seat.

"You don't mind if we record this. It's standard operating procedure," Elias said with a wink. "We like to have a clean record, so there is no mistake about what was said." He tinkered with the equipment and kept the reassuring smiles going. "Sorry about this, but we have to do it. Bureaucratic BS, paperwork, and all that. Tim, do you have some questions?"

Tim opened the file in front of him and shuffled the papers around. "Now, when the SWAT boys brought you in earlier this morning, they gave you a Miranda warning, advising you had the right to have counsel present during questioning. Is that right?"

"Yes. Of course. Why is that relevant?" Patterson asked, glaring at Elias.

"We've got to make sure they followed procedure," Elias reassured him. "Quality control."

"They did. Let's get on with this. I have things to do."

"As Elias said, we have a few things to clear up. So, let's start at the beginning. Can you give me a timeline of your activities on the evening of Thursday, March twenty-fourth?"

"March twenty-fourth? After Congress adjourned for the day, I went to dinner with Congressman Jenkins, my chief of staff can get his information for you. Then I went back to my apartment."

"You're sure? Thursday, March twenty-fourth?" Tim gave Patterson a chance. One.

Annoyed, he answered. "I'm sure."

Tim took out a still from the case file and slid it across the table. "We have video of you in the hallway of the Marriott Hotel DC. See there, that's you. Right? The timestamp on the photo is March twenty-fourth at 9:54 p.m." Tim waited until he got an acknowledgment from Patterson, then took out a second sheet. "This one has you leaving at midnight." *Caught in lie number one.* Patterson should remember from his prosecutor days; the FBI doesn't ask questions without first having the answer.

"Wait, you said March twenty-fourth right? I had a Department of Education meeting with Edmond Crenshaw. I forgot."

Tim set his elbow on the table and rested his chin on his hand. He studied Patterson, waiting until the man squirmed in his seat.

"Right. Okay." Tim smiled and sat up, and Patterson relaxed. "Was Aiysha Conrow at this Department of Education meeting?"

"Aiysha? Who? I don't know any Aiysha Conrow." He tisked at Tim as if he should know better than to ask and leaned back in his chair.

"You're sure?" Elias steepled his fingers under his chin.

"Of course, I'm sure! What is this about?"

Tim pulled the DNA report from the file and set it in the space on the desk between them. Patterson started to reach for it, but withdrew his hand.

"What's that?" he asked. He couldn't keep his gaze from darting around the room as if looking for the way out. *No way out*, Tim thought.

"Aiysha Conrow was one of the kids killed in the school shooting on Friday. She was pregnant. Around eight weeks." Tim felt his blood pressure pulsing in his temples. He took in a deep breath to quiet the anger he felt brewing in his stomach.

"What has that got to do with me?" Patterson blurted out.

"Everything. How can you not know Aiysha and contribute half of her unborn baby's DNA? That DNA report says *you* are the father," Tim said, his eyes narrowed, hostility in his voice.

"You're crazy!" Patterson stood. "I'm not putting up with this."

"Sit down! I'm not done," Tim warned.

"Don't you dare talk to me like that! I'm a congressman."

"Sit your ass down, Con-grass-man," Elias said, his bass voice reverberating off the walls. "We're the FBI, and you are under indictment by a grand jury for first-degree murder."

Patterson's mouth dropped open, and he sank into his chair. Tim waited until a measure of calm returned.

"Tell me if I have this right. You and your buddy Crenshaw drugged and sexually assaulted high-school honor students. And, you were having a good old time doing it until Aiysha Conrow ended up pregnant. Then you had to do something about it. So, you hired Hamish Bounds to help you out. Am I right so far?" Tim asked.

"Lawyer. I want my lawyer," Patterson mumbled just slightly above a whisper. "I want my lawyer." It was a demand now.

"Yeah. I'll bet you do. You're going to need him." Tim collected the pictures and DNA report from the table and put them back into the file. He stood. Elias and Leanne joined him and headed for the door.

"An agent will be here in a few minutes to help you get in touch with that lawyer." Before he left, Tim turned back. "Oh, one more thing, I almost forgot. You've had a phone call from your brother and his wife. They said something about wanting to talk to you—now what was that? Oh, yeah. They want to talk to you about why their daughters are in the hospital." Tim leveled his glare and locked eyes with Patterson. The once defiant congressman sheepishly dropped his head in his hands. Tim closed the door behind him.

CHAPTER FORTY-THREE

At two in the afternoon, Patterson's counsel emerged from the private conference room they had given him to confer with his client, and stood in the doorway. He glanced around the room as if trying to find U.S. Attorney Watson Hardwick.

Tim had expected one of the 'big guns' from Whitsal, Warren, and Williamson. After all, it was Con-grass-man Patterson, as Elias had put it, they represented. Instead, they'd sent this guy? He looked like he'd just graduated from law school, wearing a suit he'd bought off the rack at the Salvation Army, and not at all like one of the slick and polished associates from Whitsal. Tim knew looks could deceive, never judge a book and all that, but the small, dark-haired, rather unkempt man looked truly in over his head. Maybe that was part of the defense's strategy. Perhaps they thought the U.S. Attorney would feel sorry for the newbie lawyer and go easy on him.

Hardwick stood from the desk beside Tim's. "Here we go. Let the negotiations begin." He grinned and made his way to the conference room.

Tim missed this part of being a prosecutor. But as Elias had said, their part was over. Though they would be asked to help prepare the government's case and give testimony at trial, it was time to hand off the baton to the U.S. Attorney's office.

"Twenty bucks says he pleads not guilty." Roxie sauntered over and sat on the edge of Tim's desk, looking at the closed conference room door. She slapped a twenty-dollar bill down in front of him.

"Don't you know how to take a vacation when you get the chance?" Tim scolded her. He noticed Berkstad standing against the wall, straining to see and hear as if he wanted to join in their game.

"Vacations are too boring. Besides, you bums barely pulled this off without me. Pure luck," Roxie teased.

"Your friend is here. Want him to join us?" Tim asked.

"I do—and I don't."

"That's your problem. You have to choose one or the other, or you're stuck, and nothing gets resolved."

She wrinkled her nose at him.

"Hey, David, we're taking bets on Patterson's plea. You want in?" Tim asked. He wanted to be wrong about the man. Any guy who loved Roxie as much as Berkstad deserved a chance. He couldn't be all bad.

"I'm in. I bet he pleads not guilty." Miguel joined them, folded his twenty lengthways, and dropped it on top of Roxie's. Berkstad walked over. Tim could tell he liked being included, even if he wasn't on their team.

"You in?" She arched both eyebrows at Tim.

"I'm thinking." Tim had the impression that Patterson's party leaders had abandoned him to his own devices. With even the slightest hint of impropriety, Patterson would lose the support of his mega-donors. Child sexual abuse, criminal conspiracy, solicitation of murder, first-degree murder were as improper as it came. With the evidence they had, and factoring in the unpredictability of juries, Tim was sure he'd be convicted.

"Yep. I'm in. Patterson's arrogant enough to think a jury would acquit him. I bet he thinks his name alone will do the trick," Tim said.

"What would you suggest, I mean, if you were his defense lawyer?" Berkstad asked.

"First of all, I wouldn't take his case. I have kids, and the minute I saw the evidence about the roofies and rape, I would decline him on principle." Tim noticed Berkstad evaluated his answer as if there was a scoring system. He was trying to be nice, but again, Berkstad left him cold.

"Hypothetically, what would you advise?" Berkstad asked. Tim wondered if he was testing him, and if so, why?

"I've always been on the prosecutor's side of things in court, but hypothetically, I'd tell him to proffer a *nolo contendere* or an Alford plea. He should not step a foot in front of a jury. Unless he can intimidate or bribe them all, he's completely unsympathetic. Hell, he had Bounds killed 'just in case.' What would stop him from arranging to take out a juror or two? How does he even justify himself? He can't," Tim reasoned. "Yeah, he's just arrogant enough to plead not guilty." He retrieved his wallet, pulled out a twenty, and added it to the pile.

"Who's going to take guilty?" Roxie asked. "You take guilty Tim, you're rich."

Tim rolled his eyes at her.

"If no one takes guilty, we have a pizza lunch on Monday," Miguel said.

Elias came out from his office and motioned for them to join him. The whole team gathered at his small conference table, but Berkstad hung back by the door, his arms folded defensively across his chest.

"Tomorrow at 9:00 a.m., Patterson will be arraigned." Elias brushed each side of his mustache away from his lips. "Hardwick has accepted his Alford plea. The judge may not."

Roxie looked up at Tim, and a big smile split her face. Berkstad wrinkled his brow and seemed to scrutinize him. Was he surprised Tim knew the law? He shouldn't be.

"He's going to contend he's innocent but stipulate we have enough evidence to convince a jury or judge he's guilty beyond a reasonable doubt. He's asked to forego a jury trial to keep his public exposure to a minimum," Elias continued. "In exchange for the Alford, the death penalty is off the table, but he's relinquished any chance of parole. If the judge doesn't accept the Alford plea, we're back to square one. In that instance, he must plead guilty or not guilty. We assume he will go with not guilty. Then, we proceed to trial.

"After the arraignment, Hardwick and I will hold a press conference," Elias said. "As for all of you, you have earned a three-day weekend. Fantastic effort. I am proud of you."

—

The drive from DC to the farm in Leesburg was relaxing. The busy city streets gradually thinned, and soft rolling hills and bright green pastures with borders of pristine white split-rail fences replaced the suburban sprawl. Just minutes before sunset, light filtering through the cherry and dogwood blossoms tinted the whole landscape with a pinkish glow.

Tim spent the time deep in thought. There was just one thing unresolved that bothered him about this case—Berkstad. Again, he crept around and lingered in corners like an eavesdropping spy. Oh, right! He *was* an eavesdropping spy. Tim failed to mention his concerns to Elias since they were in the thick of the interrogation and plea bargain.

He reasoned that if Berkstad honestly had Patterson under counter-intel surveillance for the Russian spy caper, he would've known about everything—all of it. Berkstad's contention that he wasn't briefed was strangely unsettling. It wasn't his place, against protocol, but Tim was going to suggest the US Attorney send his investigators to dig into Berkstad's files.

He passed a road sign promising only two more miles to Leesburg. He packed the investigation into its compartment and thought of Dani. Just knowing she waited for him warmed him to the core.

Tim turned right and pulled in front of the ornate wrought-iron gate blocking the driveway to his new home. He punched in the code and watched as the two sides parted. He pulled through and made sure it closed behind him. The dark pavement glistened like a black ribbon under the rising moon. He wound around a knoll, and the house came into view. It looked so much smaller in the pictures. He stopped the SUV, shifted to park, and stared at the mansion. The house was constructed of sand-colored stone, reminding him of the country palaces of the French aristocracy. The main structure was surrounded by covered decks so that the views could be enjoyed in any weather. The drive circled in front but split under a covered breezeway between the main house and what looked like a converted carriage house.

He never expected to have this life. Simply a middle-class guy, he felt completely unworthy and incredibly lucky, all mixed up in the same cocktail. Though he was intimidated, he wouldn't change a thing. Dani and the girls were everything to him.

He shifted into gear and proceeded the rest of the way to the house.

He entered his code, and when he opened the front door, the cavernous entryway made him take a step back. Squares of polished white marble with veins of tan and taupe made up the floor. Twenty-five, maybe thirty-foot ceilings arched up to the sky, and a wide staircase curved to a mezzanine above. The alarm beep reminded him he needed to reset it, and he did on the keypad near the front door. As he turned back, Dani came down the stairs toward him. She was perfect in this place. Though in blue jeans and one of his oversized t-shirts, she still looked like a princess.

"You're home! I wasn't sure you would be." She put her arms around his neck, pulling him down toward her for a kiss. Tim dropped his go-bag and fully engaged, pressing his mouth against hers. He loved the way her lips felt.

She stepped back and took both his hands in hers. "Are you hungry? I can have Winona whip you up something."

"Maybe. I haven't thought about it." He gazed up the staircase. "I'd like to get cleaned up."

"Come on, then. I'll show you our room." Dani bubbled over with excitement and energy. While he was off chasing bad guys this week, she'd completely furnished and decorated this giant house, even though, more than once, he'd interrupted her progress by asking for her help. He followed her up the stairs. She was an amazing woman.

"When you feel refreshed, I'll get you fed," she announced as she opened the double doors to their bedroom suit. Tim knew the room was fabulously decorated. How could it not be? But his attention focused on the king-sized bed across the room. In the last forty-eight hours, he'd only had three fitful hours of sleep, and the sheets seemed to be inviting him loud and clear.

When he emerged from his shower, Dani had turned down the bed for him. A clean pair of his most comfortable sweats were carefully draped across the chair next to the bed. He stripped off his bathrobe and sat on the edge of the bed. His whole body relaxed, every muscle longed for sleep. He lounged back against the pillows, closed his eyes, and let himself drift for a minute or two.

When he opened his eyes, the light in the room had changed slightly. Dani had covered him and reclined next to him, propped up on her elbow.

"Whatcha doing?" he asked, softly.

"Watching you sleep." She smiled, and hers was the smile he most wanted to see.

"That's a thrill a minute, I'll bet." He stretched and locked his fingers above his head, then encouraged her to come closer.

"For me, it is." She snuggled up against his side, her head resting on his shoulder. He savored the feeling of her warm, smooth skin against his. It was deliciously comforting and so arousing all at the same time.

"What time is it? I didn't mean to doze off."

"Seven o'clock."

"Oh, is it too late for Winona to fix me something? I'm hungry, after all."

Dani laughed. "She'd be happy to."

"Okay, I'm missing something. What?" He cast her a sideways glance, grinning at her.

"It's seven—seven in the morning, and breakfast will be ready in a few minutes."

He groaned and rubbed his right hand across his brow. "Wow. I crashed. What a crappy husband."

"Or a very tired one. You solved your case in seven days." She did it again—made an excuse for him. Living up to her expectations was so damned easy, so comfortable. He felt surrounded by unequivocal love. He was going to make it up to her and enjoy every second of doing it. He wasn't the least bit tired anymore.

—

David Berkstad took the elevator to the forty-fourth floor. The old man had the ten-thousand-square-foot penthouse overlooking the Potomac River. He was always surprised by the opulence. The space was decorated with priceless antiques, hand-loomed oriental rugs, paintings by the old masters worth millions, and some, Berkstad speculated, were stolen.

Rumor had it the old man was a remnant of the Stalin communist regime, though he'd only been seventeen at the end of the Second World War. No one knew where he'd amassed his vast fortune; they just knew it was there.

Forbes magazine listed his net worth at a hundred billion, but there were whispers—it was closer to three hundred billion, as much as the annual budget of a small country.

The butler took Berkstad's coat, hung it in the closet by the door, and guided him to the study. He could see the old man's silhouette against the city lights beyond the floor-to-ceiling glass window. He stood straight and tall for a man of 93.

This room always smelled of expensive cigars, leather-bound books, and fine whiskey.

"You wanted to see me?" Berkstad asked. The old man turned. His appearance always startled him. His face was a landscape of wrinkles and deep folds as if draped with old cheesecloth. The skin around his eyes was puffy and red, but the eyes were unexpected—bright blue, as if a young man was trapped in an ancient mummified body.

"Patterson has been indicted and arrested?" His voice was surprisingly strong for a man of that age.

"Yes," Berkstad answered.

"I told him long ago to temper his appetites. Patience, I suggested. But he let power go to his head." The smile on his craggy face seemed to hold on to a memory of pleasure for the moment. Pleasure, in which he could no longer participate. Berkstad felt his stomach clench in disgust. But he'd heard the rumors.

"Yes, sir."

"The new world is coming and can't be stopped. Patterson will talk, and we can't have that. Take care of him, will you?"

"Yes, sir." Berkstad knew what the old man asked. He could arrange a prison yard altercation. Patterson had lied, made campaign promises he couldn't, and never had any intention of, keeping. Everyone hated him. It would be easy. He wouldn't be missed.

"Tell me about Elias Cain's new boy, McAndrews. Can he be bought?"

"He's married to money, lots of it. Daniela St. Clair."

"Lucky man. She's lovely. But her wealth is nothing compared to mine."

"Sir, I don't think the usual enticements will work. Roxie says he's a real law-and-order, hurray-for-America kind of guy."

"Ah, Roxanne, speaking of incorruptible, how is my little vixen?"

Berkstad knew the old man had always found Roxie irresistible. He actually enjoyed their adversarial combat. He'd even let her win the battle when it suited him.

"She's fine."

"Fine? If I were a younger man . . . ." Again, the faraway look, the remembering of a past time. "Never mind. McAndrews—can he be turned?"

"He's just a profiler. He isn't important to our cause," Berkstad argued.

"Rich, intelligent, young, innovative. Sounds to me Mr. Baseball-and-Apple-Pie *is* important. He was the driving force that brought down Patterson. Even though it's not a loss, it is an inconvenience. And you know how I hate to be inconvenienced." The old man smiled, deepening the trenches radiating out from the corners of his eyes.

Berkstad should just walk and pull the lever on the old man. But now that he was in the middle of a divorce, he needed the money the man generously sent his way. To land Roxie, he'd need to prove he could pay child support, alimony, college educations, and provide for her, too. He'd never meant to fall in love with her. But now, living without her wasn't a possibility.

"My time is short. You have two options, David. You turn McAndrews to our side, or you eliminate him."

Sarah Vail spent forty years in private industry before retiring to write mystery-suspense fiction. In addition to a liberal arts degree, she has continued her education in Creative writing, Criminal Justice, Forensic Science, Criminology, Criminal Interrogation, Weapons Handling, and World History through the years. Ms. Vail is the author of the mystery-suspense novels *JAMES STREET* and *SNOW COUNTRY LANE*. She currently lives in Northern Idaho at the edge of the pristine Bitterroot Mountains.

Here's what readers are saying about Sarah Vail's books:

JAMES STREET:

"Vail is a master at crafting a story so rich in subplots and character development that the reader will find himself turning page after page, wondering who's doing the crime and how will that person get caught…when it comes to crime drama, this one truly sets the bar high!"

"A murder mystery love story…loved it from beginning to end and look forward to reading more of her books."

"Romance while a serial killer is on the loose? Amazingly it works…a good story with well-written characters and good twists and turns."

"…This story is a wonderful mix of a fear-fueled suspense and a heart-melting love story. I can't wait for the next book."

SNOW COUNTRY LANE:

"…this book satisfied all the senses for a mystery/thriller. It was fast paced, kept you guessing, and the characters were great!"

"Who says reading a thriller is not the same as watching an action movie? Sometimes it's even better! Reading Snow Country Lane made me feel like I'm right in the middle of the action. Fair warning, once you start the book you can't leave it, so keep food and water close!"

"Sarah Vail built a suspenseful and engaging story. You will end up being enamored of the characters, even the minor ones, and wishing for a happy ending…"

"This riveting action filled tale is filled with misdirection, plot twists and red herrings as well as well-developed characters…Very intense read!"

"There is a lot of action and well-developed characters in a beautifully depicted setting…"